MAG—MARJORIE
and
WON OVER

MAG—MARJORIE

and

WON OVER

TWO NOVELS

Charlotte Perkins Gilman

IRONWEED PRESS
NEW YORK

Introduction © 1999 Ironweed Press, Inc.
All rights reserved.

Ironweed Press, Inc.
P. O. Box 754208
Parkside Station
Forest Hills, NY 11375

Manufactured in the United States of America.
Ironweed American Classics books are printed on acid-free paper
and meet the guidelines for permanence and durability of
the Committee on Production Guidelines for Book Longevity
of the Council on Library Resources.

Cover painting "Summer" (1909) by Frank W. Benson,
courtesy of the Museum of Art, Rhode Island School of Design.
Bequest of Isaac C. Bates. Photography by Erik Gould.

Library of Congress Catalog Card Number: 99-71485

ISBN: 0-9655309-4-9

CONTENTS

INTRODUCTION

The story of Charlotte Perkins Gilman's life reads something like a novel. Despite her birthright as a descendant of the prominent New England Beechers (she was the great-niece of Harriet Beecher Stowe and Henry Ward Beecher), Charlotte Perkins Gilman was born into poverty in Hartford, Connecticut, in 1860. After her father had deserted the family, her mother "was forced to move nineteen times in eighteen years" in order to flee mounting debt. As a result, Gilman received just four years of formal education. When she was eighteen, she enrolled briefly at the Rhode Island School of Design, where she refined her already considerable artistic talent. The training enabled Gilman to earn a small income designing hand-painted greeting cards and teaching drawing and painting, but she dismissed these activities as mere "means of support" and set her sights on the loftier goal of promoting social reform. Gilman's commitment was such that she was prepared to forgo marriage and motherhood to devote her life to activism.

In 1882, however, at the age of twenty-one, Gilman met Rhode Island artist Charles Walter Stetson, a handsome and persistent suitor. Gilman explained to Stetson her reasons for declining marriage: "As much as I love you I love *work* better, and I cannot make the two compatible." But two years later, and despite grave reservations, she married Stetson. Just a few weeks after her wedding, Gilman discovered she was pregnant, and the depression to which she was already susceptible quickly deepened. Two years after the birth of daughter Katharine in 1885, Gilman became so despondent that she sought treatment at a Philadelphia sanitarium. After a month she returned home and subsequently suffered a nervous breakdown. In 1888 she separated from Stetson and fled west with Katharine to California, where she immersed herself in writing and lecturing to local organizations.

During her first three years in California, Gilman published thirty-three poems and fifteen stories, including her autobiographically inspired masterpiece, "The Yellow Wall-Paper" (1892), chronicling the mental collapse of a young mother. In 1893 she published a slim volume of poems, *In This Our World*. A year later Gilman divorced Stetson, relinquished custody of Katharine to him, and endured the painful public condemnation that followed. In 1895 she went on the national lecture circuit, speaking on such topics as physical culture, women writers, and the need for dress reform. At the age of thirty-eight, Gilman achieved international acclaim for the publication of *Women and Economics* (1898), a seminal work exploring the causal relationship between female oppression and economic dependence on men. The book was quickly translated into seven languages. In 1900, at the age of thirty-nine, Gilman married her first cousin George Houghton Gilman, a Wall Street attorney.

Over the next thirty-five years, Gilman wrote more than a dozen books and hundreds of stories and poems, many of which were published in the monthly magazine she founded, *The Forerunner*, in circulation from 1909 to 1916. In 1932 Gilman learned that she had inoperable breast cancer, and in 1935, a year after Houghton's sudden death from a cerebral hemorrhage, the seventy-five-year-old Gilman committed suicide. An advocate of euthanasia, Gilman wrote in her suicide note, "When all usefulness is over, when one is assured of unavoidable and imminent death, it is the simplest of human rights to choose a quick and easy death in place of a slow and horrible one. Believing this open choice to be of social service in promoting wiser views on this question, I have preferred chloroform to cancer."

Over the course of her long life, Gilman not only rose out of the poverty and obscurity into which she had been born, and emerged as an internationally recognized activist on behalf of women, but she also amassed an extraordinary body of work. Her oeuvre consists of three utopian romances, six novels, seven nonfiction books, some two hundred short stories, approximately five hundred poems, a handful of plays, hundreds of essays and articles, and an autobiography.

Regardless of the genre she employed, Gilman relied heavily on didacticism in advancing her world views, many of which were shaped by reading Edward Bellamy's socialist-utopian novel, *Looking Backward* (1888). Gilman was drawn to Bellamy's emphasis on political, social, and economic equality and quickly became a convert to Nationalism, the movement spawned by Bellamy's book. Based on the principles of reform Darwinism, Nationalism reflected a belief in environmental determinism and embraced the view that society would evolve peacefully and progressively. It promoted an end to capitalism and class distinctions and envisaged an egalitarian society organized along socialist lines. Attracted particularly by the novel's emphasis on women's rights, Gilman began actively advocating such social reforms as economic independence, social motherhood, and the restructuring of the home environment.

The primary purpose of Gilman's fiction was to advance a progressive agenda by illustrating the possibilities of a world reformed, where women would enjoy the same political and economic rights as those accorded men. Literary style was not her main concern: "As far as I had any method in mind," she remarked, "it was to express the idea with clearness and vivacity, so that it might be apprehended with ease and pleasure." Because Gilman used her fiction to demonstrate viable alternatives to the patriarchal society that forced women into subservient positions, her artistry was often subordinated to her message. As a result, much of her fiction has improbable elements that could occur only in the restructured, and undeniably idealistic, world that she envisioned. Her female protagonists typically face some type of crisis, but rather than collapsing under the strain or letting fate take its course, they devise a way not only to confront the dilemma effectively but to grow in the process. *Mag—Marjorie* (1912) and *Won Over* (1913), both originally serialized in *The Forerunner*, are prime examples of Gilman's "problem" fiction.

Mag—Marjorie begins as a tale of seduction and betrayal, not unlike Susanna Rowson's sentimental novel *Charlotte Temple* (1791), in which a fifteen-year-old English girl is led astray, impregnated, and ultimately abandoned by a British soldier. Unlike Rowson's novel, whose heroine pays for her sins by dying shortly after giving birth, Gilman provides an eventual happy ending for Mag Wentworth, a sixteen-year-old orphan, who falls in love with the much older Dr. Richard Armstrong and becomes pregnant with his child. After Armstrong deserts Mag, she is rescued by Miss Mary Yale, "a woman of wide and varied experience in mending broken lives." Relying on a familiar convention in her fiction, Gilman pairs the wiser, older woman with the distraught younger woman, and together the two effect a solution that not only saves the girl from utter ruin but enables her to lead a full and productive life. "He's not going to be ruined by this summer's sins," Miss Yale reminds Mag. "Why should you?"

In *Mag—Marjorie* Gilman underscores the importance of economic independence for women, a theme that is also prominent in

Won Over. Particularly noteworthy in *Mag—Marjorie* is the illustration of Gilman's concept of social motherhood, a system that allows for the "fullest development of the woman" so that "she may be better qualified" for her maternal duties. "A mother economically free, a world-servant instead of a house-servant," Gilman argued, "can be to her children far more than has ever been possible before." Mag's daughter Dolly is reared by a number of surrogate mothers during Mag's years in medical school, without any ill effect. On the contrary, Dolly emerges as a strikingly intelligent, happy, and well-adjusted child.

In *Won Over* Gilman explores the stunting effect that conventional family life has on women. Like many of Gilman's fictional characters, Stella Widfield suffers from an acute form of mental myopia that results from her self-imposed isolation within the domestic sphere. After fifteen years of marriage, she becomes shorn of her defining role as "mother" when her children leave home for boarding school, and, in response, reverts to being a "wife," lavishing all her attention on her husband, who finds her reliance on him suffocating. Then a young playwright to whom she is introduced awakens Stella to the world outside, and she begins "to feel again the impulse to write," a practice she had abandoned in her youth. Only when Stella begins working as a freelance writer does she realize how circumscribed her life had been when it was focused solely on her husband and children. "In all her earnest conscientious fulfillment of duty . . . she had never felt the peculiar personal satisfaction that now refreshed her tired nerves."

Despite their serious subject matter, both novels bear the imprint of Gilman's wry humor. Gilman is particularly adept at seeing the comic potential in the foibles of her characters, such as the social ambitions of Mrs. Briggs or the unrelenting defensiveness of the playwright. As in many of her fictional works, the names of the characters are often a play on words. Dr. "Armstrong" suggests his villainous nature as he attempts to strong-arm Mag since "Submission, to his mind, was the woman's part," whereas Dr. Newcome embodies the qualities of the progressive male, a relative "newcomer" to Gilman's era, who enthusiastically embraces gender equality. Ironically, in *Won Over* Stella's unwillingness to accompany her husband on a visit to the "Spateses" results in a spat between the two.

Gilman's propensity for writing reform fiction was born from her conviction that because masculine literature had dominated the marketplace for so long, the story of the self-reliant woman had not yet been adequately told. "In all the length and breadth of literature, you do not find one case in a thousand where the woman's real business is given its true place," she argued. "Literature is far too great a thing," she insisted, "to be held to the rigid canons of the androcentric past." Charlotte Perkins Gilman strove to break from that androcentric past by creating a new generation of women characters who, like Gilman herself, would find ways to surmount life's obstacles, take charge of their destinies, and emerge as strong, self-assured, and productive members of society.

Denise D. Knight
State University of New York at Cortland

MAG—MARJORIE

1. *Two Men and a Girl*

A lean, angular, freckled, red-haired woman in a stringy brown ging-ham dress and a brown sunbonnet rose to her feet from the clump of blueberry bushes she had been stripping, pushed back her sun-bonnet, and looked about her.

There was much to look at, both of beauty and grandeur—the cool blue background of far hills across the valley, and the warm foreground a vivid color, great moss-embroidered rocks, the loaded blueberry bushes, the balsam firs that shot up everywhere, the mul-ticolored carpet of moss and grass and all manner of small under-brush—but she seemed wholly dissatisfied with the prospect.

"Mag! Mag!" she called, raising a harsh thin voice that made the sharp monosyllable an offense to the ear. "Where *is* that girl?"

She shaded her eyes from the afternoon sun, and turned slowly, looking everywhere. From this rocky ridge she could see far and near, down on both sides over the steep berry patches and wooded slopes, up to the higher ranges of dark fir, to the distant village in the eastern valley, easily down upon her own small farm.

But she did not see through the sheltering low-hung boughs of the big balsam fir, to the fragrant hollow between its spreading roots, in which one could cuddle so comfortably out of sight, and yet see out across the warm wide valley to the fir-fringed hills beyond.

A girl slipped from the nest, down to the westward behind the tree, and presently reappeared up the ridge swinging her pail. She, too, was lean, angular, freckled and red-haired; she, too, wore a stringy gingham dress and sunbonnet, but blue, as were her ribbons, that strong discordant blue which seems to be the judgment of heaven upon red hair.

"Where under the sun've you been?" demanded her aunt. "Here 'tis supper time already! Have you got any berries?"

"Got some," said the girl, indifferently, swinging her pail forward.

"You are the laziest young one I ever saw!" was her aunt's com-ment. "I could pick more'n that in half an hour. You come down and help me get supper this minute." She did not speak angrily; it was her customary mode of speech.

"You don't have to get supper tonight," the girl answered. "They're all off for a picnic, don't you remember?"

"That's so," said the older woman, irresolutely, almost minded to sit down again, but thinking better of it. "There's enough chores to do, anyhow," she added sharply. "These berries'll do. You come along."

The girl swung her pail. "You go on," she said. "I've got a big bush back here—and I want to finish it. I'll come pretty soon."

"Well, see't you do!" said her aunt sharply. "I know you! You'll loaf around here till sunset 'n' after—and then claim you spilled 'em! I never saw a lazier girl in my life—if you are my own sister's child! You don't get it from the Binghams, that's sure. But your father never was any account."

The girl colored hotly under her freckles. She had never known her father, who died while she was yet a baby, but cherished a secret conviction that the Wentworths were far superior to the Binghams. It was a grief to her, a constant mortification, that she "took after" the Binghams in personal appearance, at least in coloring. Her features, the outline of her head, and some hint of further growth in her young spareness would have been counted on the Wentworth side by her father's people, if they had known her.

"I guess my father's folks are as good as any of yours, Aunt Joelba," she said sullenly.

"They ain't good enough to look after their poor relations, I notice," was the caustic response. "They was glad enough to drop your father when he didn't please them. And as to your father's orphan young one—they never picked you up, much less dropped you!" Regarding her niece critically, she nibbled a wintergreen leaf, her thin lips guiltless of berry stain. "And what's going to become of you I don't know—if you don't quit your laziness. You've certainly got to work for a livin'. You can't depend on your looks."

The girl flushed again. "They say I'm all Bingham as to looks," she replied, with some satisfaction. But her aunt accepted the rebuff coolly.

"Handsome is that handsome does," she retorted. "We're not good lookers, but we are good workers. You ain't either." She turned to go down, with two big pails of berries, adding in a kinder tone, "However—you're young yet, Mag—you'll do better by'n by, I don't doubt."

Her meager figure disappeared down the steep slope, and the girl stood watching her, calmly eating berries from her half-filled pail.

Aunt Joelba had been her domestic horizon from earliest childhood. She scarce remembered her mother, or the poor and transient homes in which she had lived before this somewhat grudging adoption.

From three years to twelve she had known only this New Hampshire farm, the rigors of the New England climate outside and the equal rigors of its chill dumb family life within. Even from affectionate parents there was little petting, little expression of love and cheer, and from an unaffectionate elderly aunt, "doing her duty" by a child whom nobody wanted, there was none at all.

Perhaps it was on the Wentworth side, possibly from a much discredited ancestress of European descent, that the child had inherited an appetite for petting, a fierce longing to be held close—close—and called tender names.

Only in storybooks had she known of any such behavior, reading of mothers who "drew the child to her side and kissed her tenderly" or who "clasped her to her heart in a passion of maternal love."

Little Mag was drawn to no one's side, never "kissed tenderly" in her life, and as to being clasped to anyone's heart—New Hampshire as she knew it did no clasping.

In her brief years of schooling she had made no satisfying attachment. Her sturdy mates, with hard tight braids of hair and faces already stern from the discipline they were brought up on, had no delusion about "Miss Bingham's sister's girl" whom they had heard coldly discussed by their parents.

The teachers were objects of her respectful admiration, but there had not come to that district one of those born child-lovers whose influence can lighten and change the lives of unhappy little ones. School had been mostly work to her; she had not been a brilliant scholar, not particularly interested in the studies forced upon her, much preferring to read, and always short of material.

She had been glad when her aunt let her go to Millville to work, that hard year when there was so little to meet the mortgage; and in three seasons of shop and factory life, her views of life had hardened rather than widened.

Her keen young intelligence, so ill-supplied with the blessed truths of life, had formulated a narrow and bitter creed, and at sixteen she looked out on the world with a bravely bitter cynicism, considering herself quite "grown up" and independent. It is true that her aunt had demanded her help this summer with the boarders, but she had earned her living—and meant to again next winter. She did not mean ever to come back to Aunt Joelba. But during this last summer, something had happened, something of which she was thinking now, rather than of picking berries.

She heard a step on the crisp gray moss, and turned, an eager light in her eyes, a light that faded as she met those of a tall young man carrying a large basket. He saw the change but smiled serenely upon her.

"Good evening, Miss Wentworth," he said. "Don't go,"—for she was turning away—"stay and share our picnic, won't you?"

"Good gracious!" she answered sharply. "You ain't goin' to have that picnic *here*, are you?" He sat back on his heels from where he was investigating the big basket, and regarded her with freshened interest.

"Why not, Miss Wentworth?"

"Why should you? It's way up on top of all creation—an awful climb for the ladies—and all these things to lug! I can show you a lot prettier place—where it's flat—and smooth—all pine needles, and real shady! Come on! I'll take you there right now—and then you can bring them to it."

"Sorry to disappoint your philanthropic intentions—but the ladies you refer to are very determined characters, at least two of them. Miss Yale, especially, gave me most explicit orders. I was to bring this; lay out the things, take back the basket, and ascend again with ice, rugs, a teakettle, and other objects."

He talked on cheerfully but did not fail to note that she was annoyed.

"I'm sorry you don't like it," he pursued, "but it lets you out of waiting on table for once—and you'll be very welcome to join us, Miss Wentworth."

"What do you call me 'Miss Wentworth' for?" she demanded sullenly.

"You are, aren't you?"

"No, I'm not Miss Anything—I'm just Mag."

"I like Miss Wentworth better," he said. "It's a fine old name. You ought to be proud of it."

The girl giggled a little. "I'd look well, wouldn't I," she jeered, "being proud of anything?"

He opened his basket and began to take things out. She stood so on the edge of flight that he urged need of assistance, hoping to keep her.

"Help me spread this out, won't you?" he said, and she came, with the feminine habit of service and took the cloth from him, remarking:

"Guess I can spread a tablecloth, without any help about it." They had some difficulty choosing a place for it, one at least relatively flat and free from stones.

"What on earth you folks want to lug all those things up here for *I* can't see," she protested, "when you might sit at the table and be waited on."

"Pure foolishness, Miss Wentworth," he admitted. "Suppose we put the sugar over there."

"Suppose you don't," she took him up. "Suppose you don't take out anything at all till you're ready to eat it. You'll have ants all over 'em if you do."

"You are right," he agreed. "Perfectly right. They won't be up for some time yet. I brought up this basket ahead—meaning to go back and get the other."

"Well—why don't you do it then," she inquired, saucily, but he leaned back against a big boulder with a most contented expression and replied, "Because I'd rather talk with you."

"I can't talk," she answered. She had taken off her blue sunbonnet and swung it by its limp string. Her red hair shone like a sunset. He regarded it admiringly. She saw him look, and put her bonnet on, flushing.

"Don't," he said, "please don't! You have beautiful hair, don't you know it?"

"I know better!" she said, "a lot better, and I won't be made fun of, either."

"I should never dream of making fun of you, Miss Wentworth," he said, sincerely. "I respect you too much. Look here—I wish you'd tell me why you are so bitter. Has your life been all unpleasant so far?"

She laughed, a hard, defiant little laugh. "Life!" she said, "I never had any!"

"Tell me about it," said he. "I know you lost your father——"

"Yes—he died when I was two—and Mother when I was three—and Aunt Joelba brought me up—because somebody had to! They didn't want me on the town, that's why!"

"You poor little kid!" He regarded her with honest sympathetic eyes. "And you've had to work for her all the time?"

"Oh, I've been to school some—before I was twelve. And I've worked three winters over to Millville, once in a store and twice in a mill. I can work all right—if I have to——"

"But you don't like to?"

"I'd like to do some things, of course; but—oh, what's the use of talking? I've got to get more berries before sunset."

"Sunset's a long time off," he said. "Please sit down. Here's a nice moss cushion and a fine rock back. You don't ever give me a chance to talk with you."

"I've no time for talking," she said, but seated herself nonetheless, not where he indicated, but on a rounded stone, still seeming ready for flight. Her eyes wandered down the long slope. She seemed to listen for something beyond his voice.

"I am most sincerely interested, Miss Wentworth. I am sure you have character and ability beyond what you think—and I want you to use it."

She looked at him mischievously, her bright brown eyes twinkling under their light lashes.

"Me!" she said. "I'm skinny and freckled and redheaded and ignorant and—lazy!"

"You are not lazy! And you need not be ignorant. You can have a beautiful life, Maggie—if you don't like Miss Wentworth. May I call you Maggie?"

She giggled appreciatively. "I should say you might. Ain't I the waitress and chambermaid? Don't everybody call me Maggie—or Mag?"

He regarded her seriously. He was an earnest young man, with grave eyes, and a mouth both humorous and determined.

"You don't mean to be a chambermaid always, do you?" he persisted. "You know that you can learn to do better work; can grow into a bigger life than this. I wish you'd let me help you."

She turned away her head. He could not see under the sunbonnet, and did not know how carefully she was scrutinizing the path in the pasture below, beyond his sight.

"I could get you books to read," he pursued, "interesting and helpful ones. I could get you a place in Boston—to work—where you'd have some time for study."

"What sort of a place?" she asked suspiciously.

"With a friend of mine," he replied; "a good woman, who likes to help girls work their way through school and college."

"Housework?" she demanded.

"Yes, helping her in her housework. She has nice girls with her— one Radcliffe student."

"Not any housework in mine!" the girl replied with decision. "No, siree! Shops are hard enough, and mills are harder; but housework I *won't* do."

"Why not? You'd earn more."

"Oh, yes—I'd earn more money. But I just won't do it, that's all."

"Well, I don't know that I blame you," he said thoughtfully, studying the hard, defiant expression already showing around her young mouth. "Call it a place in a store, then, and a good boarding place— you've heard about that big home where the girls have rooms to see their friends——"

She interrupted him scornfully.

"Courtin' parlors! No, sir! If I want any courtin' I don't propose to be watchin' the clock—with a waiting list outside!"

He laughed with her.

"I admire your independence, and your originality, Miss Wentworth. I don't believe you do justice to your own powers—honestly. Don't you want to have an education—to make a place for yourself— to be able by and by to marry, better than you could expect to from a factory in Millville?"

"I don't have to work in Millville always," she answered him. "I may have plans of my own, you see. What makes you so interested, anyhow?"

She glanced up at him, a childish innocence behind the premature worldly wisdom of which she was so proud.

He rose to his full height and looked down at her without speaking. His eyes were earnest and tender, and under their fixed gaze her own dropped again.

"I'd rather tell you that five years from now," was all he said.

She started to her feet, laughing. "Five years from now, we may all be dead. How about that other basket you were going to bring?"

His eyes followed hers down to the right. "Oh, I don't know. There's lots of time," he answered.

She seemed uneasy. "They'll all be up here before you know it," she insisted.

"All right," he agreed. "Let Dr. B. carry them, or young Battle-smith."

The girl fidgeted a little, swinging her pail.

"Guess they'll need you, too—to bring water and things," she urged.

But he was stubborn, suggesting, "It certainly looks as if you wanted to get rid of me."

"No need to wait for that," she tossed at him. "You can stay here till doomsday, for all I care!" And she flashed over the rocks to the westward and was out of sight in an instant.

He did not follow her. His eyes grew cold and his mouth set and hardened as he watched the ascent of a strongly built man in fishing costume, who was climbing up from the eastern valley. He knew him well enough—had known him from boyhood; they had been chums at school, roommates at college, classmates in their medical school, and were friends still, though the years had brought a wider divergence in character than either was aware. He watched him pressing lightly up the steep hillside, the broad shoulders looming large as he looked down at them.

Years of old association held them together, yet today, as Newcome stood gazing at that sturdy ascending figure, there was no warmth in his heart toward Dick Armstrong.

The latter stopped and looked toward the ridge, with a lilting whistle, but caught sight of Newcome's tall figure standing motionless there and seemed half minded not to come up. He hesitated a moment, half turned about, then shrugged his broad shoulders and came on apace.

Reaching the top, he saw the cloth and basket and stood still.

"Are those confounded old hens coming up here to gabble and gobble?" he asked sharply.

"Looks like it," said Newcome, "and I'm a packhorse, sent in advance."

Dr. Armstrong strolled about in evident discontentment, casually observing the surrounding country.

Dr. Newcome reseated himself in comfort, casually observing the stroller.

Armstrong viewed the basket with extreme disfavor.

"Why in thunder do they want to have a picnic on this ridge pole?" he demanded, snappishly.

"That is what Miss Wentworth said," observed Newcome, placidly. "At least, that was her state of mind. She did not express it in exactly those words."

The other stood still, regarding his friend from under lowering brows.

"She's been here, has she?" he remarked, resuming his dissatisfied walk.

"Yes, she was here a few moments ago, and seemed as displeased at the idea of a picnic on this particular spot, at this particular time, as you are. It's quite a coincidence."

Armstrong stopped short, with a gruff, "What are you driving at, Newcome?"

"At something that is only too obvious, I am afraid. I wish it wasn't."

He did not look at his friend, but punched careful holes in the moss with a dry stick.

"Look here, Newcome," said the other, after a few moments' silence, "I can stand a good deal from an old friend, but what are you butting into this for? I've never interfered with any of your little games."

Newcome said nothing for a little. There were several easy things to say; that he had never played that kind of a game, and never would; that this was too serious a matter to be so lightly described, and similar dispute-provoking suggestions; but he was too much in earnest to waste words, and merely answered:

"No, nor I in yours—before."

"Well, quit it," said Armstrong, and swung around, grinding his heel into the soft moss. He seemed uncertain whether to go or stay, glanced viciously at the basket and walked about again, kicking at small stones with apparent relish.

Newcome said nothing, but his silence seemed only to irritate his friend, who came back presently and stood angrily looking down at him, remarking: "You're no Galahad, that I know of."

Newcome rose quietly to his feet and met the other's eyes steadily. "Did I ever claim to be?" he asked.

"Well, let me alone, then! What business of yours is it anyhow?"

"Oh, come, Armstrong, you know you're a little ashamed of yourself. This isn't an even game. The girl's a mere child, ignorant and helpless, and you're a fetching devil. Let up on her, can't you, for once?"

The words were light enough, but the tone was earnest, as was the look.

Armstrong had more respect for his friend's opinion than he would have admitted. Possibly, too, he was in this particular instance a little ashamed of himself. But he squared his heavy shoulders and set his heavy jaw obstinately. Earlier in the summer he might have considered the matter, but not now.

"I believe that you're in love with her yourself," was his counter-charge.

Newcome met it imperturbably. "If you believe that, you'll believe anything. This is cradle-snatching, Armstrong, and you know it. It's unworthy of you. . . . Of course"—there was a slight stiffening in his manner—"if you mean to marry her, just say so, and I'll apologize at once."

Armstrong laughed, shortly. "You need not apologize on that score," he said. "I'm not in *that* deep. But I'm in, all right."

Newcome looked at him narrowly. He would have given a good deal to know how deep, but could not ask.

"I'll tell you one thing," pursued the other, "I'm off tomorrow. Then I'll be out of it." After a little, he added, "And I'll tell you another thing, if it will do you any good. I'm glad enough to get out of it. It's time."

Newcome seemed to find singularly little consolation in these concessions, but presently replied, "Thanks, I shall miss you—but I'm glad you're going."

"Well, then, can't you get this confounded picnic to go somewhere else?" queried Armstrong, laying violent hands on the basket.

"No use, old man. The ladies are starting this minute, you can see 'em; and they've set their hearts on this particular spot. I tell you what, you sit in—they're confidently expecting you, and they'll be off the minute the sun sets, if not sooner. The Mrs. Reverend cannot outgrow her early fears as to 'night air.'"

"I'll be hanged if I will," said Armstrong morosely.

"Might as well," pursued Dr. Newcome. "Nothing doing in the way of supper at the house, you see, and no one but the excellent Miss Bingham for company. Miss Wentworth," his back was turned to his friend at this moment, as he assiduously straightened the tablecloth, and began unpacking wooden plates and paper napkins, "is, I believe, hovering in the circumambient air. She'll appear when she gets ready. If you want to be useful, or at least to look as if you wanted to, you might start a fire by the rocks."

Dr. Armstrong surveyed the ascending party, cast rather a hopeless glance at the wild country about him, and began to build the fire.

2. *A Man and Two Women*

The speed of an army is that of the slowest man in it, or used to be when armies walked; and the speed of the little procession, winding upwards through the steep berry-patched pastures, was that of Mrs. Leicester-Briggs. Her husband, the Reverend Edward Briggs, or Leicester-Briggs, as she insisted on writing it, could not be called a brisk person, but the movements of his wife were so heavily influenced by dignity that she sometimes seemed scarce to move at all.

"Now, Edward," she announced at starting, "I will set the pace, else you will all go streaming up the hill, and I shall be left alone." So she placed her broad, well-gowned back at the head of the party and proceeded upward.

Mary Yale, her friend from childhood days in high-minded Boston kindergartens, a woman of spare and agile construction, refused to accept this order of exercises. "Not for me, Laura!" she stoutly proclaimed. "There is plenty of room in this pasture, and I should get the spring-halt if I followed you. I'll wait for you at decent intervals." So Miss Yale coursed ahead at a brisk gait, and then put in her time by gathering balsam fir till they caught up.

Daisy Briggs, vibrating between respect for her mother's wishes and a natural desire for freedom, divided her steps among them, now loitering by her parent's side, and again flitting up the path to rejoin Miss Yale.

"I should think you had balsam fir enough to stuff a mattress, Aunt Mary. What do you do with it all?"

"Make cushions, of course, child, and give them away. People like mine, because they are carefully prepared." She carried a denim bag, of large extent and careful construction. It hung around her neck by a broad strap, and when in use its mouth stood open, by a simple arrangement of stiff wire. Then, with both hands free and a pair of strong scissors, she snipped off the soft, green tips, twig by twig, leaving a little blue balsam tree to look, for some five feet from the ground, as if it had been attacked by a species of caterpillar of limited ambitions. "My pillows have no sticks in them, you see, Daisy. Also it is less work. I do not have to wait for the stuff to dry and then go all over it again, breaking it up."

"You *are* the most awe-inspiring person, Aunt Mary! I never saw anyone like you. Here they come. Oh, Papa, do let me carry some of those things!"

She tried to relieve him of a basket, but was prevented by the assiduous Mr. Battlesmith, who brought up in the rear, his rate of progress being limited, not by natural incapacity, but by the weight of his burdens.

"No, indeed, Miss Briggs," he protested, "not for a moment. Allow *me*, Mr. Briggs," and he hooked a finger around the added handle.

Mr. Battlesmith was a cousin of Mrs. Briggs, the kind of cousin that looks like a nephew, and was being "put through college" by her efforts, and those of other relatives. In summer he maintained himself by various gentlemanly occupations, this year acting as secretary to Mr. Briggs, while he labored on his book. This work, being of a strictly theological character, commanded no present interest from the other members of the family, and it is to be feared no future market; but Mr. Briggs seemed to enjoy writing it, and Mrs. Briggs spoke to her daughter of "your father's book" as if it was an indispensable concomitant of dignified paternity.

"It is a pity Dr. Armstrong has not returned, Mary," she said. "Do you know where he went, Gerald?"

Mr. Battlesmith replied that he did not, but that Miss Bingham had agreed to send him after them when he returned. He, himself, seemed little interested in that return, even if he did have to carry two men's baskets. When they finally reached the top, the missing one was discovered, lounging discontentedly, while Dr. Newcome tended the smoky little fire and added finishing touches to the table decorations, or rather the tablecloth decorations.

Mr. Briggs set down his load with a sigh of relief, as did Mr. Battlesmith, though less audibly. Daisy knelt by the baskets, laying out that superfluity of discordant food common to picnics, while Mrs. Briggs determined in her mind where everyone should sit, and used her best powers to compel them to sit there.

The arrangement, as consummated, involved a mossy seat with a boulder behind it for Mrs. Briggs, Daisy beside her on the left, and Dr. Armstrong beside Daisy. On the right Mr. Battlesmith, Miss Yale and Mr. Briggs. Dr. Newcome seemed a sort of fifth wheel, but was generally useful between the fire and the feast, and finally distinguished himself by producing a tin box of marshmallows, which he toasted to admiration.

"It was lovely of you to bring marshmallows!" cried Daisy, with enthusiasm. "How do you always hit on the right thing?" Miss Yale inquired, and Mr. Briggs, still munching serenely, found voice to answer, "It is his heart, dear lady. He has a good heart. A great gift."

Armstrong smiled rather maliciously. "He doesn't always hit it. For instance, when he brought *Jane Isabel* to Mrs. Briggs."

Mrs. Briggs at this moment scrambled, no, loomed, to her feet. "It is astonishing how hard a rock back becomes," she said. "I must really stand a while." She moved about for a little and reseated herself with dignity. "What have you got in the bag, Mary Yale, not more food, I hope?"

"Balsam fir, as you perfectly well know," her friend replied.

Dr. Armstrong smiled again. If he must endure this picnic, he would get some amusement out of it. "I believe you accumulate fir cushions in summer to save buying Christmas presents," he said.

Daisy joined in mischievously. "Yes, Aunt Mary always was penurious."

Miss Yale looked from one to the other. "Say much more, and I'll send you all one—and nothing else!"

Daisy forthwith capitulated. "Oh, Aunt Mary! I apologize! On my knees! Do forgive me! And please in the meantime lend me one of your forty-'leven handkerchiefs to cry in."

Among the useful peculiarities of Miss Mary Yale was the wearing of a costume of businesslike simplicity and possessing many pockets. Her coat had pockets above and below, without and within; her skirt had pockets, visible and inferred; her neat blouse had a pocket, and it was rumored among friends that she had pockets in her petticoat. In the list of contents, handkerchiefs bulked large. "The stupidity of women in the matter of handkerchiefs is inexplicable to me," she would protest. "They buy good-for-nothing scraps of diaphanous material with decorations that are worse than useless, and then lose them every few minutes, as if life were an everlasting game of 'drop the handkerchief.' I believe they only drop them to be picked up by men—like a spoiled baby with a rattle! I carry handkerchiefs enough for myself and other people too!"

It always pleased her to be asked for one, as Miss Daisy well knew.

"Speaking of handkerchiefs," said Dr. Armstrong, turning politely to Mrs. Briggs, "what was your objection to *Jane Isabel*?"

Mrs. Briggs cast a reproachful glance at him.

"One can't like every book, even if they are given one by kind friends." She smiled benignly at Dr. Newcome, continuing, "But where is that sunset you dragged me up this mountain to see, Mary Yale?"

Miss Yale sniffed. "If you call this little ridge a mountain you'd better live in Holland, Laura! I don't own the sunset!"

Mr. Briggs, still toying with small cakes, here took up his favorite role of peacemaker, with his usual overestimate of the necessity.

"We must not ask too much, my dear," he said to his wife. "I am told the sunset is usually very fine from this eminence. We cannot expect to control the weather, can we, Armstrong?"

Armstrong smiled amicably back at him, and turned to the head of the tablecloth.

"Speaking of sunsets, did you object to Jane Isabel's character, or conduct, Mrs. Briggs?"

"What a tease you are, Dr. Armstrong," said that lady. "To both, of course." Again she rose to her feet and stood, looking about through her lorgnette, remarking, "I think the sun will come out later, after all."

"But why?" pursued her tormentor. "Don't you think she was more sinned against than sinning?"

This time she quite ignored his question for the moment and spoke to her daughter.

"Daisy, dear, I think there are some fine blueberries over by that rock yonder. I wish you'd get me some."

"All right, Mama!" the girl agreed, glad of an excuse to get up, and taking the small pail Dr. Newcome offered her, she skipped off cheerfully.

Then Mrs. Briggs turned to reply.

"Excuse me, Dr. Armstrong, but I dislike to discuss a book of that sort before my daughter. She is only eighteen, you know, and quite a child yet."

"She'll never be anything else, Laura, if you keep her from knowing anything," Miss Yale remarked, but the Reverend Edward remonstrated, "O, my dear Miss Yale! Our Daisy is by no means ignorant! We do not wish her to know any evil, that is all!"

Dr. Newcome, who had begun to busy himself with collecting wooden plates and paper napkins, and the baskets full of fragments, which make every picnic a miracle, now spoke with cheerful apology.

"I'll do better next time, Mrs. Briggs. I hadn't read the book myself, but people were all talking about it, and I thought you'd be interested."

"I think it is an excellent book," Miss Yale assured him, but Mrs. Briggs took her up sharply.

"How can you say so, Mary? The book extenuates vice."

"O, come, Mrs. Briggs," Dr. Armstrong lazily objected, "surely that poor girl suffered enough to extenuate anything."

"I quite agree with Mrs. Briggs," said Dr. Newcome, magnanimously. "She probably refers to the hero."

"No," said the lady, with precision, "I do not refer to him. Of course his behavior was to be deprecated, but he is not an unnatural character by any means. But that girl! Actually to have such a creature rehabilitated!"

Her husband here recorded his approval: "You are right, my dear, as you always are! 'The wages of sin is death.'"

But she rather ignored him, and continued, graciously, "Of course, we all have a right to our opinions, Dr. Armstrong. Life must look differently to men and women. Would you oblige me by taking Daisy her jacket? It is liable to get chilly at this hour."

There was nothing in the August evening to suggest chilliness so far, but maternal solicitude is a beautiful thing, and Dr. Armstrong rose with no apparent reluctance and moved off with the jacket under his arm.

The reverend gentleman sat back against a stone, replete and urbane, snapping off crumbs from the horizontal creases of his garments; his wife, using the same boulder, wore an air of present contentment over an undercurrent of conscientious alertness.

Miss Yale helped Dr. Newcome as he repacked the baskets, and nodded approvingly when he poked the bundle of remnants deep into a crevice of the rocks and scattered the assembled fragments of food far down the slope.

"You show excellent judgment," she said. "The food will be eaten, and not draw ants—and the ridge is clean for the next party."

"Next year, I'm afraid, Miss Yale," said the clergyman, smiling, and rising to his feet with dignity, if not difficulty. "Suppose we have a cigar, Dr. Newcome, and stroll about a little."

As they departed, the older man picking his way cautiously downward, Dr. Newcome stopped suddenly by the big balsam fir and lifted something from beneath its wide, drooping boughs. Neither the ladies behind nor the gentleman in front observed him as he hastily crushed into his pocket a large, tumbled bow of blue ribbon and departed. Mr. Battlesmith, inspired by an ever-active sense of duty, followed them, bearing baskets.

Mrs. Briggs, disinclined for immediate movement, selected this quiet moment as suitable for conversation.

"Mary Yale," she began, "there's something I want to speak to you about. If you have any influence with that redheaded little scarecrow I advise you to use it."

"Well, you are severe, Laura. I think her rather pretty."

"Pretty! With those yellow eyes, and freckles, and atrocious blue ribbons! Why is it that redheaded girls will insist on wearing blue hair ribbons? She is carrying on disgracefully!"

"Is she?" Miss Yale was trimming off the tips of a small balsam with an absorbed expression.

"O, you are so oblivious, Mary. See here!"

Mrs. Briggs seized her friend's arm and drew her to the further side of the ridge. "Do you see the house down there? Well, our windows look this way, and almost every evening I can see figures up here—right here where we are! This is a regular trysting tree."

"What's the harm in that? People coming to see the sunset, I suppose."

"People! It's Maggie and a man!"

"Well, well, Laura, what of it? The girl's only a child. She's barely sixteen this summer. And she's a nice child, too. I take a real interest in her."

"You take an interest in every lame duck you come across, Mary! I should think your experience with that little Italian girl you adopted would have discouraged you. Or that rascally young Greek!"

Miss Yale smiled good-humoredly. "Yes, I've made some mistakes," she said. "I'm young yet."

Mrs. Briggs seemed to think this a poor excuse, replying tartly, "You're as old as I am."

"Yes," her friend admitted, "and don't you make some mistakes?"

"I don't adopt vagabond children by the dozen and waste my money on them!"

"You don't have to, Laura. You've got little Daisy there, and your good husband."

"If you had married when you might have, Mary Yale, you would have a family, too!"

"I'll have a bigger one if I keep on adopting."

"I sometimes wish you hadn't so much money, then you'd have to be more careful," said Mrs. Briggs, solemnly. She realized that the idea was well-nigh impious. "But seriously, Mary," she continued, "I do wish you'd speak to Maggie."

"How do you know it's Maggie?"

"I can see her red hair and her blue bows."

"You can, can you? You must have good opera glasses!"

"I have," she admitted promptly. "And I use them to advantage. I tell you that girl is flirting outrageously with Dr. Armstrong!"

Miss Yale murmured to herself, "I've been afraid of it," and the other added, "There'll be a scandal here as sure as fate! I wish you'd speak to that young fool!"

Her friend regarded her speculatively, and suggested, "Why don't you speak to the young scoundrel? You don't suppose that man's offering to marry her, do you? If there's any scandal, he's to blame, I take it."

"Men aren't to blame for being men, Mary. And a girl is always to blame who lets a man make a fool of her."

"Poor, headstrong, ignorant young one," murmured Miss Yale. "And you stand up for the man! You have, all summer. Look here, Laura," she remarked with sudden attack, "is it possible you are scheming to have him marry Daisy?"

"Nonsense, Mary Yale. I'm ashamed of you!"

"I hope it is nonsense. You know he has a reputation for this sort of thing."

"I know he is an extremely agreeable, well-mannered gentleman, and already stands high in his work. He's only twenty-six or -seven."

"And Daisy's only eighteen, I believe, and Maggie sixteen. The maternal instinct always was a puzzle to me, Laura. I declare I'll tell the girl about him!"

"Maggie?"

"Perhaps, but I meant Daisy."

"You shall not, indeed! I am her mother and I forbid it. The idea! You'll do no such thing, Mary Yale. If I hadn't been your friend for forty years we should quarrel. I'm positively ashamed of you!"

Mrs. Briggs arose, ponderously, and took her descending path toward home, having observed that Daisy had joined her father and was returning to the house, with or without blueberries.

Miss Yale let her go, and stood slowly shaking her head. She had for her friend that affection which is founded upon long usage, and which often exists without the aid of gratitude, sympathy or admiration.

There was as yet no sunset, in the spectacular sense; the supper was eaten and most of the baskets removed, but Miss Yale remained in possession of the ridge, moving from tree to tree, and trimming off tips with a fine regard to symmetry.

She did not desist when Dr. Armstrong reappeared and stood looking at her vertical back, with anything but approval.

"They're almost home, Miss Yale," he suggested. "Aren't you coming?"

"Not just yet." She continued her clipping, and then turned rather suddenly with a somewhat sharp "Dr. Armstrong!"

"That is my name," he replied, noting the menace of her tone. He had no intention of "taking any nonsense" from her, nor of being driven from the field. He stooped by the berry bushes and picked here and there among them.

"I'm old enough to be your mother," the lady remarked, looking down at him, "and I'm going to speak plainly to you. I want you to let Maggie alone."

He rose, flushed and angry, remarking rather weakly, "Well, I must say!"

"What can you say? She's a poor, unprotected little girl, and surely not pretty enough to be much of a temptation to a man like you."

He stared at her, displeased and astonished, striving to preserve what he held the proper manner to a lady, in spite of the lady's most improper manner to him, and replied, "I don't know what you're talking about, Miss Yale. And for the life of me I can't see——"

"What business it is of mine? Merely one woman trying to protect another. Is that so unusual?"

"It is, if you'll excuse me, deduced unusual."

He stood, his hands in his pockets, extremely irritated, and nonetheless so that a sound of pensive whistling was heard and his other undesired adviser reentered.

"Hello, Newcome," he observed dryly. "Here's Miss Yale still standing up for *Jane Isabel*."

"I'm quite with you, Miss Yale," said Dr. Newcome. She looked from one to the other and replied with decision, "I thought at first the lover was only an ordinary man. I begin to think he's a rascal!" With which pointed statement she closed her big bag with a snap and marched off.

Newcome took up the remaining baskets and followed her.

"Deliver me from meddlesome old maids," said Dr. Armstrong, gloomily watching him. He walked about, looking down over the pastures, and finally seated himself on the rounded boulder which had been recently graced by Mrs. Briggs's back, his elbows on his knees, his square chin looking squarer as its weight rested on his hands.

Up, over the ridge, behind him presently appeared Maggie's halo of red hair and sharp brown eyes. She watched him for a moment unobserved, repleating one of her bright braids which hung ribbonless. Then she stole silently forward in her rubber-soled "sneakers" and tickled his ear with a long grass stalk.

He started, looked around, and greeted her rather gloomily with "Hello, Kiddles!"

"Hello yourself," answered the girl, with spirit. "Aren't you cheerful, though!"

"You don't expect a fellow to be cheerful every minute, do you?" he said, still gloomily.

"Oh, just as you like. I can do that, too!" and she seated herself on another stone at some distance, her sharp elbows on her knees, her hard little chin in her hands and a most dismal expression.

He gazed at her for a moment, laughed shortly, moved over to her rock, and sat beside her. She turned away. He slipped an arm around her waist. She did not notice it. He drew her to him and tried to kiss her, but she eluded him with a little laugh, and skipped away, expecting him to follow her.

When he did not she tossed her head and stood sulkily at a distance.

"Come here, Maggie."

"Yes, Mr. Armstrong," she answered primly, and came.

"Don't act like that, little girl. See here. Come and sit down."

"In our place?" she suggested.

"Yes, in our place, if you like."

They both took possession of the hollow under the boughs of the big balsam, Maggie still silent and sulky. He played with her hair for a little and turned her face toward his.

"Oh, come, Maggie, you might as well give me a nice kiss, just for good-bye."

"Good-bye!" she said. "Have you got 'another engagement' this evening?"

"Only with you," he answered, with a kiss. "But tomorrow I'm going."

"Going? Going where?" she asked.

"Going away. Going back to the city. This is a p. p. c.—a particular parting call—Maggie. So you must be nice to me."

She had drawn back, and was staring at him, a slow horror rising up in her eyes.

"When'll I see you again?" she asked, temporizing with fate.

"It is painfully possible that you won't see me again, Kiddles. So let's be happy while we can."

His tone was light, but she could not meet it.

"Do you mean you've done with me?" she demanded.

"Oh, don't be cross, Maggie," he said, a caressing hand stealing around her. "Let's have a pleasant evening, seeing it's the last one."

She paid no attention to his words.

"I thought—you said——" She evidently found it difficult to go on. Then in a low voice, "I thought you were going to marry me."

"Oh, Maggie!" he protested, "now play fair! You know better than that! You and I have just been having a nice time together, and that was all there was to it. Come, haven't we had a good time?"

The girl looked at him bewildered, puckering her faint brows. "But, look here, you mean to say—you thought—I knew——" She could not say it.

"Why, of course you knew I was not meaning to marry you. I never said I would, never dreamed of it. Neither did you, Tiddlewinks. Cheer up, my dear, no harm's done. We've had a pleasant summer. Don't be cross now and spoil the end of it."

She sat quiet for a moment, staring at him, then suddenly burst into wild tears, silent, intense, and dropped down in a miserable little heap at his side, holding blindly to his coat. He stroked her hair and drew her to him, saying, "Too bad, little girl; too bad. Brace up, Kiddles, there's no harm done!"

"Oh, there is! There is!" she cried, passionately, holding to him. "You don't know! You won't leave me! You mustn't leave me!" She put her arms about his neck, drew his face down, and whispered something in his ear.

Armstrong was startled. He pushed her from him and stared into her face. The girl looked up at him, glad, afraid, loving, triumphant. The gray clouds along the western horizon lifted a little at this moment, and a huge red sun shone through. It lit the shimmering tips of the fir boughs and made of her loose hair an aureole of rosy gold.

All the faith and happiness and vague high hope of the summer rose in her heart. "You will marry me now, won't you?"

The man looked at her with real pity. "Oh, you poor youngster!" he said, rising and walking about, much disturbed. Then he turned on her sharply. "Look here! Are you *sure?*"

She nodded slowly, with pale decision.

"Well, you mustn't worry, little girl, I'll see you through, of course. I'll take care of you all right. See here!" He drew an envelope from his pocket and wrote on it, then took out a roll of bills and put several in the envelope.

"Look here, child," he said, going back to where she sat staring at him with incredulous eyes, "you see this address? That's my lawyer. By and by, when it's necessary, you write to him and he'll tell you what to do. Don't you worry a bit. It will be all right." He approached her, offering her the envelope. "Here's something for now, there's more where that came from."

The girl looked at him steadily, refusing to touch the money. "And you're not going to marry me?" she said.

"Why, no, Maggie, I can't do that."

She started to her feet with sudden fury. "Do you think I'll take your dirty money?" she cried, "and be—and be a——" She snatched his offered gift, threw it from her, and faced him, panting.

"Don't be a fool, Maggie! You'll need it. Of course I've got to see this thing through," he said, adding rather lamely, "Come, don't be a little fool. Kiss me good-bye."

"I'll never kiss you again," she burst out at him, "you—you—— Oh, how I *hate* you!" Her head was up now, her hands clenched.

He stood regarding her rather awkwardly. "Oh, *well*," he said, "I suppose it's only natural. I am sorry, my dear, I never meant it to turn out like this. Hang it all! Well, good-bye!" He made a futile effort to kiss her, but she stood like a post, giving him no sign of interest. With a gesture as of one washing his hands of the whole affair, he turned away, and tramped off down the hill.

She watched him go, her face slowly changing from fixed anger to a growing distress, made a step to follow, stretching out her arms toward him, then stopped, dropping her hands in impotent despair. She looked up at the blank gray of the sky, around her at the still blue firs and bluer distances. Then she threw herself down at the foot of the tree again, and sobbed wildly, beating the ground with her small red hands.

She did not hear the returning steps of Mary Yale, who came slowly up over the curving summit, saw the sobbing girl under the tree, and, looking farther, the disappearing back of Dr. Richard Armstrong. She nodded wisely, caught sight of the envelope and yellow-backed bills, and picked them up, reading the address, counting the bills, and nodding still more wisely. Then she looked carefully over her various handkerchiefs and selected a large clean one, remarking, "Have a handkerchief, Maggie?"

The girl stopped sobbing and sat up, red-eyed and disheveled, hastily trying to arrange her hair. "Thank you," she said stiffly, and took the friendly offering.

Miss Yale sat down by her, and raised a handful of the fragrant brown needles to her nose. "Nice, sweet-smelling carpet to cry on," she observed.

"I hate it!" said Maggie, with fierce intensity. "I shall hate it as long as I live!"

"I don't wonder, little girl, I don't wonder. Has he gone?" Maggie nodded, choking back her sobs. "I thought as much. And you're in a peck of trouble. Sit right still now, and tell me all about it. Maybe I can help."

The girl shook her head despairingly and turned away. "No, thank you, Miss Yale. You've been very kind to me. I'm going now."

"Going where, Maggie?"

Maggie, moving slowly off, turned her head over her shoulder and answered, "Going to the devil!"

"What for?" asked Miss Yale, calmly. "The devil's no godfather."

The girl stopped short, and turned a look of horrified amazement on Miss Yale, who smiled kindly.

"Come back, Maggie," she said, "and let's have a good talk. I know what's happened. No, it isn't witchcraft. It's what usually happens when a foolish child tries to play this game. You poor baby!" She held out her arms and Maggie sank down in a miserable little heap and cried, her head on the older woman's lap. Miss Yale petted her quietly, with a strangely motherly look on her strong face. Then she said, slowly and clearly, "You were a poor baby, now you are a rich woman!"

The unhappy girl lifted her head and looked at her in startled wonder.

"I'm forty-five, Maggie, and I never had one! Think of the happiness!"

"*Happiness!*" The girl's voice was that of one for whom life held nothing.

"Yes, Happiness, Joy and Pride!"

All the girl's New England upbringing revolted against this strange suggestion.

"Why, it's—Shame!" she answered, protestingly.

"Yes," said Miss Yale, slowly, "yes, more's the pity! But that can be lived down."

"And it's—Sin!" said the girl, in a dull, relentless voice.

"Yes, it's sin; you have done wrong. You've made an awful misplay, Maggie, and you'll have to suffer for it. But it is sin for two! You haven't sinned any more than he has—not as much, for he was play-ing this thing for his own pleasure and you took all the risks. He's not going to be ruined by this summer's sins—why should you?"

Maggie gazed down at her hands, lacing and interlacing the slen-der fingers.

"I can't talk like you do, Miss Yale. You're very kind, you always were; but it isn't any good—now!" Then she broke down in wild dis-tress again, sobbing, "Oh, I want to die! I want to die!"

Miss Yale watched her for a moment in sympathetic silence. Then she said, firmly, "I'm ashamed of you, Maggie!" The poor child stiff-ened at this and sullenly wiped her eyes. "For the way you're taking it," her friend went on. "The time is past for foolishness, my dear. You have been fooled into becoming a woman before you were hardly a girl—now you've got to live up to it. Let's talk sense." She rose and walked, hands in her coat pockets. "Here you *are*—and the thing's done. Off goes the gentleman responsible, and you are left with a big undertaking before you. It is lucky you are strong and brave."

Maggie's face was turned away, but she was listening. "This dying and going to the devil is all nonsense. You've *been* to the devil—now we'll go somewhere else."

"What do you want me to do?" asked Maggie, after a pause.

"I want you to live," said Miss Yale, slowly, "and work—and suc-ceed. You can study, take a profession, be a doctor, if you like, be a better one than he is! Get ahead of him in his own line, wouldn't you like that?" Maggie nodded slowly, her lips tightening. "Besides," her friend pursued, "I want you to be an example. You needn't look so in-credulous. I mean it—an example to all the others. Maggie, my dear, you are not the only poor girl who is left crying tonight. Come, show what a brave woman can do!"

A flicker of purpose rose in the girl's eyes, but it faded.

"It's no use talking," she said. "I've got no education."

"Plenty of time for that yet, you are only sixteen, you know. And you've got a good head. I'll see to the education, Maggie."

But Maggie Wentworth lifted her head proudly. "I won't be be-holden to anybody, Miss Yale."

"Oh, yes, you will. You have more than one to think of, remem-ber. And it's only a loan. I invest in you as I would in a prospective gold mine. You shall pay it all back in cold cash if you like—every cent of it. Listen, child. We'll step right out from under. I'll send someone for you, so that no one will know, to take you away from here. We'll arrange you shall go abroad with me. I'll give you my name. I'll take care of you—and yours! You shall start clear in another country—and make good!"

Maggie regarded her with wondering eyes, hopeful, fearing, uncertain.

"What makes you want to do—so much for me?" she asked.

"It's a hobby of mine, Maggie," Miss Yale replied. "I don't believe in this ruining. You've done wrong—and you'll have to suffer on the best of terms. But that's no reason you should be hanged, drawn and quartered!" She walked about, her hands behind her. "Make up your mind that you've got some fifty or sixty years to live—to work—to accomplish something—to prove that there's something more to a woman than this one performance!"

Then she stood still before the girl and held out her hand.

"Come—will you do it?"

Maggie took the offered hand, and answered solemnly, "I will!"

3. *A Designing Woman*

"It's a large order," said Mary Yale solemnly to her looking glass. "It's a very large order. It's the largest order I've ever undertaken."

She sat long that night with her chin on her palms, her elbows wide on the dressing table, seeming to derive all the comforts of conversation from the kind, strong face opposite her.

"The plotting and planning are easy enough," she continued slowly, "as easy as a dime novel—but there are the three 'ologies to consider. The physiology can be handled all right, and the sociology, I *think*; but the psychology of the case is the hard part. . . . I've got to refill that child's mind!"

As she said, the plotting and planning were not difficult. With genuine pleasure she devoted herself to this task, using her busy fountain pen in strange diagrammatic arrangements, and destroying each piece of discarded paper as carefully as if anyone but herself could imagine the meaning of those cabalistic figures.

She was a woman of wide and varied experience in mending broken lives, from the placing of hoary inebriates in asylums to the rescue of starved babies from incompetent parents; and besides experience, she had friends similarly interested in more than one country.

Carefully she arranged her plans with the ultimate purpose always clear in her mind, and before midnight she had come to certain definite conclusions.

She returned to her room next morning while Maggie, red-eyed and silent, was making the bed. Dr. Armstrong had gone by the nine o'clock stage, and she could not even say good-bye to him—if she had wished to. She told herself that she did not wish to; that she wished never to see him again.

"Did you sleep any, child?" asked Miss Yale softly. Maggie shook her head. Her face was blank and hopeless, but she cast piteous, trustful glances at her friend, like a dog with a hurt paw which you are trying to bandage.

"Can you go for berries again this afternoon, Maggie?"

"Yes, I guess so."

"Well, can you meet me about three o'clock on Breen's pasture—up there where there's a big oak all alone, you know?"

"And lots of blackberries just below in the holler?"

"Yes, I have ever so many things to talk to you about—you'll be surprised. And look here—did you ever read this?"

This was a story from some magazine, cut out and pinned together.

Maggie had not read it, and looked at the vivid pictures with a shade of interest. Miss Yale folded it up small. "I want you to read it if you will," she said. "There's something I want to ask you about—later."

"All right," said Maggie dully, rather suspecting a moral lesson.

When her bedroom work was done she ran to the end of the orchard and lay down a little breathless, under a grove of locust trees by the brook. She meant to cry, and reaching for her handkerchief, found the story. The pictures were interesting, anyway. She began to read suspiciously, looking for the moral, for some allusion to a misfortune like her own; but soon forgot that purpose in the gripping interest of the tale. It was funny, too, in one place, so that she gave a little chuckle in spite of herself. "Served him dead right," she thought, with decision, and in her emotional condition she found tears of sympathy and tears of joy at the ending.

"Mag! Mag! Wherever has that girl gone to?" Her aunt stood screaming for her at the barnyard gate, and she went back to end the noise. "You haven't even picked the corn yet—and here it's 'most dinnertime—and me with the bakin'. Do get busy now, for goodness sake."

So Mag got busy among the long rustling streamers of the sweet corn, the grief and terror in her mind lifted a little by a sense of hope, and stirred still more by curiosity as to what Miss Yale was going to do, while again and again, across her own real troubles, flashed the picture of that troubled tale, and the intense gratification she had felt in the result.

Miss Yale was sorting stories on her bed. She had not many with her, only this summer's extracts, but they were all good ones.

"Not love stories," she was saying to herself. "That cuts out a lot. And not baby stories, but children ones do no harm." She made little piles separately. "Adventure—funny ones—and, yes, I guess ghost stories; that's a different note, anyway. . . . And it's only for a day or two now." She selected three that pleased her, and put the rest away.

Maggie with her pails, and Miss Yale with her bag, met under the shade of the big oak that afternoon. It was a fine place for two conspirators, for the open pasture fell away on all sides, odorous of bayberry and sweet fern, and very bright in spots with that amazing fruit which is black, and yet red when it's green.

"Here I am," said Maggie, and sat herself down, her filled pail carefully established on a level space. Her manner was as of one with an incurable disorder, willing to be experimented upon, but utterly incredulous of help. She fingered the straps of Miss Yale's denim bag, and suddenly shrank from its odor as if stung.

"Too bad—I shouldn't have brought it"; and Miss Yale stood up and tossed her fragrant burden some way down the hill. "There—now we can talk. You see you are a grown person, and a free agent, and what I want to do requires your cooperation. I've got to tell you about my plans. I cannot do it unless you are willing to help."

"Yes, ma'am," said the girl.

"I'll lay the outlines before you—it's a big game, and a long one. And will take some playing. There are several important points that we must be sure of. In the first place—no one here dreams of this, do they?"

Maggie shook her head. "I didn't myself, till now," she said. "And I wasn't likely to tell Aunt Joelba."

Miss Yale smiled appreciatively.

"Well, hardly," she agreed, thinking that Maggie's sense of humor would be a great help to her. "Our first play is to get you out of here without anyone's knowing it. Let them think what they please. You are to disappear."

A spark of interest stirred in the girl's eye.

"The next thing is to get you adopted without anyone's knowing it's you—ever. That is harder, but I've arranged it. The next thing is to keep you in health and peace of mind until the baby comes."

Maggie winced and flushed.

"Don't feel that way, my dear. You know we have to face this thing——"

"And live it down," murmured the girl.

"And live up to it! It isn't anything to be afraid of, not at all. Then—where are we? The fourth thing is to educate you. Let me see—you're just sixteen, aren't you?"

"Sixteen last June."

"Well, you'll only be about seventeen then. Seventeen—and with a good mind of your own—not overfilled. After that it is education—growth—building."

"It'll take forever, won't it? Beginning so late?"

"Not a bit of it, child. You don't have to go through all the motions. You're going to be really educated. And you'll enjoy it."

"And what—what'll become of—It?"

"I'll adopt it, too—temporarily. I think that would be best—at first. Then you will stand clear till you have chosen your work, made your place in the world. When you are ready to claim her, she is yours."

Maggie's face was turned away. She was looking further into the future, more definitely into the future, than she ever had before.

"Perhaps," she said, and paused, the warm pink rising to the warmer red of her hair; "perhaps—it'll be a boy."

"Perhaps. A son. Son or daughter, Maggie, it's coming. It has only you to look to—it is all yours. You will have to be very brave and strong and patient and hardworking—to make a place in the world for your child.

"Have you any place in your room where you can hide things?" she suddenly asked.

The girl's eyes came back from that far prospect, and turned on Miss Yale with a puzzled expression.

"Why, yes," she said. "I've a trunk that locks. Had it when I was to Millville."

"All right," was Miss Yale's reply.

"What am I going to hide?" asked Maggie, with natural interest.

"They haven't come yet. The important things. All I have for you now are these stories. How fast do you read?"

"I don't know—I read that other one in about an hour, I guess. It was real interesting. What was you goin' to ask me about it?"

"That comes later," said Miss Yale. "Do you think you could read all these tonight—before you go to sleep?"

"I guess so."

"Of course, if you get real sleepy, you needn't, but if you can, read them all in this order. I've marked them, you see—one, two and three."

"Do I have to take notice of anything?"

"No, not particularly. Just read them easily. One thing I want to know is this." Miss Yale looked very solemn, and added slowly, "I want to know which one interests you the most."

"All right. I'll read 'em—and tell you. But Aunt Joelba'll see my light, and if she don't do that, she'll see the lamp's empty."

Miss Yale smiled broadly.

"I thought of that, too." Then from the hidden depths of her garments, she produced an electric pocket lamp. "That's newly charged," she said. "It'll last you, I think. I always have one in the country—they don't smell. So you can read in bed and screen the light altogether."

From another pocket came a small box, tightly covered with pink paper.

"This is part of the prescription," she added seriously. "You are to divide these in three equal parts, and eat them with each story. Don't open it till you begin."

Maggie had some difficulty in concealing all these objects about her angular young frame; but though her aunt sharply demanded to know "what made her walk that way?" she got safely to her little room and after that had no more to carry than a trunk key on a string. The box puzzled her more than the stories; it persisted in popping into her mind across the dark curtain of her grief, even before the lifted curtain of wide, new hope. When she did get to bed, with her small, clear light well-hidden, the mystery was revealed. It proved to be nothing more than caramels—caramels superior to any that Maggie had ever tasted.

"Isn't she just lovely!" thought the poor child, and religiously devoted herself to the task of spending a very pleasant evening, going to sleep at last, with her mind swinging widely about between the concerns of several sets of most interesting persons as well as her own. Even if she wakened to loneliness and grief, these new ideas persisted in sharing her attention.

Her aunt kept her so busy next day that she had small time to think of anything beyond brooms and dust cloths; and since Miss Yale had taken Daisy Briggs and Mr. Battlesmith on an automobile trip, and Dr. Newcome, deprived of his usual companionship, had lured Mr. Briggs from his book to a morning's fishing, Mrs. Briggs found opportunity to oversee the cleaning of her room and at the same time bestow good advice upon the cleaner.

"How old are you, Maggie?" she began, in a voice at once friendly and firm.

"Sixteen, ma'am, goin' on seventeen."

"You should be at school yet, or learning a trade. Here—don't raise such a dust! Have you no tea leaves?"

"Tea leaves, ma'am? What for?"

"To lay the dust, of course. You should save your tea leaves and scatter them on the carpet, then sweep lightly, with a short stroke—here, let me show you."

Mrs. Briggs always maintained that a lady should know how to do whatever she required done for her, and then she would be well served. This applied, of course, only to the work of the household. She did not insist on a lady's knowing how to run locomotives, ships or shoe factories, or even that a gentleman should understand these arts. But then one cannot think of everything. She gave Maggie a lesson in sweeping that was really of value, yet the obstinate girl fulfilled her directions under protest, inwardly vowing that she never would sweep that way—never.

Added to these instructions the good lady gave advice as to the proper conduct of young girls in regard to gentlemen.

"You are only a child," she said, "but you are quite old enough to get yourself talked about. It does not look well for a young girl in your position to be seen about with gentlemen."

To these remarks Maggie made no reply whatever. Her mouth was shut tight, and the muscles of the jaw made a firm angle in her soft cheek. She flushed, too, more from anger than mortification, and was half minded to "answer back" in such wise that Mrs. Briggs would remember it; but the thought of that large new future before her gave her sufficient strength to finish her task and leave the room with no more reply than a most decided closing of the door.

"Impertinent child!" thought Mrs. Briggs. "They never do know enough to appreciate their friends."

Miss Yale had gone to the largest town within easy reach, and there promptly disposed of her young companions, leaving them at the mercy of one of those beguiling establishments, something between a shop and an arbor, planned to satisfy the summer boarder's thirst for buying things.

Then did Miss Daisy's youthful enthusiasm strive against her better judgment in the matter of various preferred confections; and Mr. Battlesmith's better judgment also strove with his youthful enthusiasm in the matter of pleasing Cousin Daisy. But when two youthful enthusiasms unite upon the same box of candy, it would take a dozen better judgments to prevent them from buying it.

Miss Yale, meanwhile, went to the best bookstore, such as it was, to the jeweler's and the dry goods establishment, and spent some time in the telegraph office. She also purchased the best New Hampshire road maps to be found, and added judiciously to her own store of sweetmeats, none of which purchases was revealed to her young friends.

Early that evening, while the others rocked and chatted on the moonlit porch, she summoned Maggie to bring fresh water to her room.

"Shut the door, Maggie," she said. "Never mind if it is hot. Come and sit over here, not so near the window." She spoke softly, and the girl felt a pleasant excitement in this atmosphere of conspiracy. "We mustn't talk long," pursued Miss Yale, quite as if she knew that detectives were all about the house. "But I have to arrange all the preliminaries tonight, for tomorrow I leave. I'm going to New York."

Maggie's face fell. "Going?" she said; "I thought——"

"Why, I can't take you with me, child. It's got to be all covered up, you know. I go off tomorrow, bag and baggage; then when you go, no one will associate it with me. This is very important. You must attend carefully, and do just exactly as I say. I'll tell you enough to think about for a week. You see the moon is full just now. By next Thursday it will be dark early in the evening. You are to go out of the house, somehow—you might even get off in the afternoon and not come back to supper. What would your aunt do?"

"Nothing but scold. I do stay out, sometimes."

"Then do that. Go off in the afternoon, and be seen if you can, over by Black Pond."

The girl's sad eyes brightened. "So they'll think I'm drowned," she agreed almost eagerly. "Shall I leave my hat there?"

Miss Yale smiled. "No, I guess not. We mustn't be too melodramatic; but be sure nobody does see you later. You know that turn of the road, where the woods are so thick, over beyond Haskins' and the big white rock, right on the edge of the road?"

"Yes——"

"You must hide in the woods up there, and when it's quite dark, slip down softly near that rock. At ten o'clock precisely, an auto will stop there, just stop, not blow its horn, or anything, and you get in."

"And you'll be in it?"

"No. I can't be in it; you know you and I are to meet as strangers, later. But a friend of mine will be in it."

"How will I know it's the right one?"

"I don't believe many cars will be going through Haskins' woods and stopping by that rock at night. You hop in and you'll find a friend. Here's a watch for you to wear, so you'll be there in time, and not be discouraged with waiting. And here's another little electric light. Don't use it up. This one won't last long, but you can hide it in your hand and look at the watch, this way."

The girl took the watch, and turned it over with admiration, yet reluctance.

"I hate to have you getting all these things for me. I just hate it."

"That can't be helped, Maggie. Hate it or not, you've got to put up with it, now. But I solemnly promise you that you can pay it all back when you are earning your living by and by—if you want to. You can earn more, then, if you let me take care of you now, lots more. Be a good child and take your medicine. Of course you have to have a watch; better keep it in your trunk till then, or your aunt may hear it."

The girl nodded. "Do I bring anything with me?"

"Not a thing. Not one thing. That lends color to the drowning idea, you see. You'll find what you need. I've brought this jersey, veil and raincoat; they'll cover you for the ride."

"Can I know where I'm going?"

"Yes, of course, I'm going to tell you all about it. We must be quick, too. My idea is this. I am going abroad this fall with friends. I'm going to find you in France, as an orphan, and adopt you over there."

"In France? I'm an orphan all right, but how'll I pass for a French one?"

"That's what I've arranged. This friend of mine who is going to take you is French. You and she are going straight up to Canada. You are to spend a few days in Montreal, and buy what things you need, and then you sail from there. She takes you to this French town. And while you're with her, you'll learn a good deal of the language. But you see you were a Canadian orphan, half English. You're not supposed to have a Parisian accent. Then I'm sorry to say, she deserts you, and I find you there."

"I won't lie," said Maggie, stoutly.

Miss Yale was pleased. "You needn't, my dear. You needn't say a thing that is not true."

"Am I left alone over there?"

"Only for a few days, and in a nice boarding house. I know the woman who keeps it. That will be all right. Now have you got all that straight?"

Maggie solemnly repeated her instructions with evident understanding.

"Yes, that's right. Oh—and here are some books to last you till Thursday. Better take those and lose them somewhere—before you start. But I want you to read them if you can, for a special purpose. Now good-bye, child, for the present. I shan't see you again for a month and more. But you will like Miss St. Clair. You can tell her anything you please. She's safe. When I see you again, you'll be six weeks older, nearly, and talking French."

She laughed, and gave the bewildered girl a friendly kiss. Then Maggie took her books and the seven little boxes which accompanied them, and stole away to her room, unobserved. Her heart was so full of mystery and excitement that she forgot her gratitude. She almost forgot, for the moment, her heavy, hopeless grief.

In spite of Mrs. Briggs's fervent protests that it was all nonsense, that she might just as well wait another week and go when they did, Miss Yale departed next day, and betook herself forthwith to New York, and to the Martha Washington. Here she was met next morning by a short dark woman in the dress of a nurse.

"I'm so thankful you can do it, Genevieve," said Miss Yale. "There's nobody who could meet this situation as well as you can," and she explained at length.

Genevieve St. Clair was full of interest in the plan. "It is for me to be thankful," she said. "An adorable journey in the machine and also an ocean voyage—how beautiful! And to see my country again! But then you are always doing such things! Tell me more about the girl."

Miss Yale smiled a little shamefacedly. "I don't really know much about her myself," she said. "She comes of good stock, and has a sense of independence—doesn't want to be 'beholden' to anyone. I had to pull every string I knew to make her accept my proposition. Also she had spunk enough to be furiously angry at the man, instead of merely being brokenhearted. He offered her money, you see."

Miss St. Clair's eyes glittered. "The villain," she said, bitterly.

"Oh, no, he's not a villain," Miss Yale corrected, dryly. "He's only a young medico, enjoying himself. I think he really felt badly when it turned out this way. And Maggie's no village lambkin, understand. She's a sharp little thing. Thought she knew it all and could take care of herself. I tried my best to warn her, but bless me! what does a girl know, ever?"

The other nodded, darkly. "And she is beautiful?"

Miss Yale laughed again, "Why, no, Miss St. Clair. I'm afraid you'll be disappointed in the romance. She's a scrawny little piece, red-haired and freckled. But of course, any young girl has a certain attractiveness."

"She will become beautiful when she is older," Miss St. Clair stoutly protested. "I have seen them like that."

"Well, have it your own way. I hope she will. But she's a mighty interesting child, has a good deal of spirit, and what I care for, you know, is the principle of the thing. Here's one summer's foolishness, and her whole life gone to ruin—unless we can stop it."

"We can," said the other. "You have planned it beautifully, you always do. I will do my part."

Henry Newcome stayed at Miss Bingham's, finding much to occupy his thoughts. He studied Maggie, as far as opportunity allowed, and was puzzled. At the table he had no speech with her; she kicked the swing door open with her little rubber-soled shoe, set down the dishes with no regard for symmetry, and whisked out again. Also Mrs. Leicester-Briggs's eye was upon her, disapprovingly. "That girl never will learn to wait on table," she said.

Here and there he tried to snatch a word with the unhappy child, but she had little to say, and always hurried away from him.

"I cannot make her out," he thought, studying over the affair. "She doesn't look real heartbroken, and yet I'm sure she cared for him. She has a kind of waked-up look. It's peculiar. Maybe he writes to her."

He thought about it a good deal, trying in vain to get a chance at further talk, but Maggie avoided him easily enough; she was either working in the house or the garden near it, in plain sight, or she disappeared completely, going far afield after berries, which Miss Bingham was putting up for the winter. He deliberately lay in wait for her one afternoon, watching her with his field glass from the ridge, to see which way she went berrying.

He saw the blue ginghamed little figure slip down behind the house, through the orchard, and off across the valley. She carried a big pail, carried it as if it was heavy, he noticed. If he was to catch her he must hurry.

He noted her direction, judged she was headed for the pastures over the western ridge, and started directly across toward the top of it. Reaching a commanding position there he raised his glass again and scanned the farther slopes. Yes, there was the moving bit of blue. She must have run to get so far in that time. She had left the road again, and was making a short cut down the open hillside.

"She's passed the best berry patches, already; I wonder where she's bound," he asked himself, following her quick steps with the glass. Then there swept across that limited field of vision a blank gleaming space—Black Pond.

The shadowy depths lay for the most part between steep banks, well-wooded. But at this end, a shallower bay ran out into the pasture. He saw her pushing through the bushes toward the deeper part. Suddenly a panic struck him, and he ran, leaping fences and stone walls, straight down the rugged hillside toward her. "Maggie," he shouted, "Maggie," long before he was near enough to be heard. At last he reached the place where he had seen her, and followed the shore, still calling. There was no answer, but beyond him, out of sight, he heard a heavy splash. He rushed forward, tearing through the underbrush. There was no Maggie anywhere in sight, but the smooth water was broken by concentric ripples, widening rapidly. He marked the center of their spreading, threw off coat and shoes and dived. The water was cold, and very deep, but he was a good swimmer, and again and again he went down, paddling about slowly underwater with open eyes, looking, looking. At last he saw something blue, darted to it and rose spluttering, with a bundle in his arms. For a time he sat on the bank, getting his breath, and trying to arrange his ideas. One of Maggie's blue aprons, being undone, disclosed a number of wet novels, loose sheets of magazines and small tin boxes. He went home slowly under the strong impression that he had made a fool of himself.

But Maggie had heard the anxiety in his voice as he shouted behind her. She had seen his instant pursuit into the dark water, seen him rise to breathe, and dive again and again. She saw him puzzle over the books, and finally tie them up as before and throw them in once more. It gave her something further to think about in the long hours of her hiding. She still thought about it, even after she was speeding through the dark toward Canada.

4. *The Building Years*

That midnight ride brought no peace to Maggie's mind, so suddenly overcome by grief and shame, so torn with fierce anger, so confused by the sudden flood of hopes and interests supplied by her new friend.

She had been a sturdy, self-contained child, with very definite economic ambitions, and less definite aspirations for better things. In her lonely, loveless life with her aunt, and the bare hardness of that hilly township, she had developed self-reliance, and added to it in her time as a mill and shop worker. These experiences had taught her a poor cynicism, learned of the girls who said, "Cheer up, you'll soon be dead!" or "The worst is yet to come!" and a premature acquaintance with life's worst, as known by working girls. She had seen more than one girl whose feet had slipped from the steep, narrow path of self-support, under the pressure of bitter necessity, or the attraction of pleasure, pleasure that was to their starved young hearts as water in the desert.

Maggie had felt herself quite wise and strong, aware of danger, yet competent to frisk along its edge in safety.

This danger, which she thought she knew so well, consisted mainly of cheap bribes or more costly ones, with presumptuous awkward liberties, and her New England temperament was easily able to refuse them. But the danger she had not learned to estimate lay in fun and kindness, in easy, lazy, friendly ways; in gentle approaches of small, safe tenderness; in sudden kisses that left her angry—yet not displeased. She knew nothing whatever of the ally within, which so traitorously helps the enemy without.

But Richard Armstrong knew. He knew the mechanism of the human body and its imperious laws; he knew from small successes of his college days and the more serious adventures of later years, the best lines of approach—when to stop, when to advance, when to withdraw.

He had found much to attract him in little Mag. She was not beautiful, but she was young, fresh and innocent, for all her absurd airs of worldly wisdom. It was fun to tease her, fun to frighten her a little, fun to allay her fears, flatter her conceit, let her believe that they both "knew life" and could "take care of themselves."

He had even grown rather fond of her after a while, but not enough to spoil his summer's amusement. Possibly, he too had overestimated his own knowledge, for he had by no means intended what seemed to him so inconvenient a calamity. For all his experiences and his claim to "knowing women" he knew only one side to their natures; and the real character of this girl was quite beyond his researches. She had hardly known it herself.

So far life had demanded of her but few qualities, and those not the best. Suppressed and neglected, lonely and ill-nourished in mind, she had slipped down this easy path and met her catastrophe so suddenly that even now she could hardly believe it was a fact. He was gone; Miss Yale had loomed up in the foreground of life like a fairy godmother, and the sudden diet of fascinating stories left her actually confused between her own adventures and those she had been reading about.

*   *   *

Miss St. Clair, sturdy and silent, ran the car herself, and they made as much speed as mountain roads allowed, the fierce acetylene light flaming white before them. The girl sat huddled in the tonneau, holding on in unnecessary alarm as they plunged down the hills, feeling as if all life was flying by her with the shadowy, streaming trees. She was cold and stiff when they stopped for breakfast in a small town over the border. That night they spent in St. John, and slept long and late, reaching Montreal comfortably on the following day.

They were fairly acquainted now, and Maggie had become reconciled to her new name—for her companion registered her in the hotel as Miss La Salle.

"It is legal," she said. "I have learned about that. Any person can take any name at pleasure. What would you have? You must be called something until you are adopted, and why not my cousin, Marguerite La Salle?"

"All right," said Maggie, but she felt like one walking in a dream.

The purchases for the voyage would have pleased her, but for the dreadful fact that it was all "charity."

"I'll pay her back!" she assured herself. "I'll pay back every cent!" She tried to keep the wardrobe as cheap as possible; but Miss St. Clair had her orders, and the girl was outfitted with pretty and suitable clothes.

They took quiet lodgings, and in the fortnight before they sailed the French lessons were well under way, in the easy and impressive methods of the illustrative school. There were well selected, easy books besides, and all the way across the ocean, after a few days of blank resting, the two read and talked together in easy French. The girl had nothing else to do, and gave herself to the new study with keen delight, both on the steamer and in the quiet pension in Marseilles.

Presently Miss St. Clair departed, explaining to the sympathetic lady of the house that she would leave her cousin there for the present, and paying her board for two weeks in advance. Then Maggie, left alone, found use both for the French she knew and the French she did not know, in parrying the too solicitous inquiries of the amiable Madame.

She was bitterly lonely now, and afraid, miserably afraid that something might keep Miss Yale from coming to her. The French reading was still too difficult to distract her easily, and in the strangeness and double solitude of a foreign language and a foreign land, the danger and shame of her position would dominate her mind. Beneath its deep resentment, her girlish heart mourned for the tenderness she had lost, but she hated herself for this.

With a sense of passionate relief she at last heard Miss Yale's clear voice in the hall below, and was halfway down the stairs to meet her before she bethought herself, checked her mad rush, and slowly returned to her room.

But the voluble hostess was not surprised to see her come.

"Ah, the poor child!" she said to Miss Yale, as she ushered her to her room. "She thought you were her cousin! It is a little orphan from Canada—and she is left on my hands, I fear. You are so benevolent! You will be interested." Miss Yale was interested, and when a few days passed and Madame Charbonnier continued to complain, she offered to take charge of the girl temporarily.

"I will leave you my address," she said. "If the cousin comes back you can refer her to me at once."

"And if she does not come back—ah, Mademoiselle Yale—I sympathize, but my hands are full."

"If she suits me, I may be able to find a home for her, Madame. Of course, at worst, you could turn her over to the authorities here. But she looks to be a nice child."

Then the worthy dame extolled the benevolence and discretion of Mademoiselle to the heavens, and called down a number of Catholic blessings on her Protestant head. She was assured that Mademoiselle would find the girl charming—so docile—so affectionate—so quiet.

Miss Yale did not underrate the difficulties of the work she had laid out for herself. Never in her life had she planned more carefully, or for more years ahead. Before they left Marseilles Miss Yale had her plan well in mind.

"I'll educate her in France and Germany—the best—if she'll take it. I hope she'll choose the medical profession. We need women there. She can't see much of the child—except on vacations—we'll try to fix that.

"No—the child is the spur—a splendid one. Maybe it won't live. Perhaps that would be as well—but never mind *that* possibility.

"Now for the hard part—the mind building. I need help here. . . . This year especially. . . . This year must be health, and peace of mind, and—just foundations. Then she must work.

"Dear me—suppose she shouldn't be equal to it!"

But doubts of that kind never troubled Miss Yale long.

She had fixed her determined mind on the difficulties confronting this misguided child as a type of world-old injustice, an injustice which she was sure could be remedied. If any of her friends had known of this particular undertaking they would have branded it as the most quixotic yet, but it was no part of her plan to have it known or criticized.

She wrote to this friend and that of her next two or three months of easy travel, and if any of them chanced to meet her or to hear of her having a young companion, she made no secret of "the La Salle child" or of finding her in Marseilles. The absent cousin was quite generally distrusted; and some thought Miss Yale was being victimized; a few even said "as usual," but twenty years of benevolent eccentricity, based on perfect independence and a comfortable fortune, allows one considerable freedom of conduct.

"She always has some lame duck in tow," they said.

In these three months, besides enjoying, as she usually did, seeing new places or revisiting old favorites, her most constant exploration was in the rapidly opening mind of the girl beside her.

It was not difficult, with a few good maps and well-selected books, to mark out the foundation of later studies, even to lay the cornerstones of historic knowledge. In the language work, Maggie made rapid progress, and the mere process of seeing a strange country, its people and customs, had an effect at once stimulating and soothing.

Miss Yale was increasingly happy. To the satisfaction of her benevolent impulses, she now added the growing hope of establishing a principle, and in this stage of the process she found not only the pleasure of giving instruction and experience to an eager mind, but, somewhat to her surprise, a growing affection for the girl herself.

Little Mag, in New Hampshire, had been raw and rude and willful, self-confident, a little vulgar. Marguerite, in Europe, began to show agreeable changes. Her self-esteem was for the present quite in abeyance. No ruder proof could have been given her of her real ignorance and deficiencies. In the new land and language there appeared, from unused depths within her, new characteristics far more pleasant than the old ones. She showed a patience, a perseverance and courage in meeting difficulties, and a quiet gentleness which was beyond her friend's immediate hopes.

She had feared recurrent trouble as to "obligation," but the girl seemed to have quite settled that question. She brought the matter up once, very early in their travels, when they had a compartment to themselves.

"Miss Yale!" she suddenly demanded—in the one hour a day that English was allowed, "can you tell me how long it will take—and—how much it will cost?"

"It" was not difficult to define.

"If you choose a profession," the other answered, "and I very much hope you will, it will be ten years I should think before you'll be absolutely on your feet. Twenty-seven is young enough to be a lawyer or a doctor. If you do as well as I think you can, you'll know enough by the time you're twenty to take up your special studies. Then there will be the apprenticeship years—clerk or intern, and all the harder because you are a woman."

The girl's eyes were far away, across the flying landscape.

Miss Yale went on calmly, "Ten years—yes—she will be ten years old before you can give her a home. As to how much—I will show you the estimate I have made."

Maggie was appalled.

"Could I *ever* earn that much?"

"Bless you, yes—easily."

"In how long, do you think?" The girl's voice was very low.

"In another ten years' time, at the outside—in half that if you are very successful."

"Twenty years!" said Maggie. "Twenty years! I shall be thirty-seven!" She said it as if it meant centuries.

Miss Yale faced the fact cheerfully.

"Yes, you'll be thirty-seven by that time. You'll have a daughter of twenty—or a son. You'll have an honorable and paying position in the world. You'll be useful, respected, beloved. You'll be able to save life—that is, if you choose medicine—to heal the sick, to help women and children—men, too. You'll have a home of your own."

"Twenty years!" murmured Maggie again. Then, eagerly, "Couldn't I do something less—expensive?"

"I've thought of that, too," explained Miss Yale. "You could, as a matter of fact, go to work as soon as you can leave the baby. But you could not have her with you that way, any more than this way, and you could not afford to give her the kind of education and the kind of home you'd like to. Besides—though you would not owe so much, it would take you just as long to save it out of your small wages."

Maggie counted the poplars as they rushed into sight and out again, across their darkening window. Her fingers twisted and untwisted themselves in her lap. Large, slow tears rose, swelled and dropped on the slender fingers.

Miss Yale leaned forward and took the girl's hands, holding them in a strong and tender clasp. "Now my dear child," she said, "don't be appalled by this. Remember the mischief is done and cannot be helped. We won't give a thought to that. Remember that, though this road I'm trying to start you on is hard and long, it is the best that opens. You can't get out from under as if it had never happened. In any case you have to pay, pay heavily. But in this case you get something worth paying for!"

The girl turned grateful eyes to the kind face opposite but found no words.

"And *always* remember this, my dear, when everything else fails— your own ambition is a good deal, your mother love will be more; you may even want to prove my experiment a success; but the big thing to remember is—the other women! The principle of the thing, Maggie! You are working to establish a principle."

The shadows grew outside, the small dim button of light glimmered overhead. When at last the girl spoke, she delighted her friend by remarking slowly, "*Oui, mademoiselle; je comprends. Je ferai cela*" in quite passable French.

Toward Christmastime they made a visit with a family in a remote Alpine valley, old and beloved friends of Mary Yale.

Gerard Hauptman was a real teacher, of German birth and training, a man of large ideas and very small income. His wife was French, also a teacher by profession before her marriage and a social theorist, in eager agreement with her husband. Their home was quite outside the town, a place of wide, far views and bracing air, and their only family a young widowed daughter, Julie by name, who had returned with her baby to her father's house.

To her particularly Miss Yale talked of Maggie, of her orphanhood, of her misfortune and her good fortune, of the brave future she was facing; and the young mother's heart warmed to the lonely girl, so soon to be a mother, too. When their old friend asked of the family in conclave assembled if they would take her protégée as a pupil and boarder, teach her and befriend her for the next year at least, father, mother and daughter were all willing.

It was hard indeed for Maggie when Miss Yale left her, but by this time she felt at home with these good people, and really fond of Julie.

There she stayed in peace and quiet for nearly two years, growing in health and strength and peace of mind, helping Madame about the house and in the wide blossoming garden, walking and climbing with Julie as long as she was able, spending peaceful hours alone with the lake, the mountain and the sky for friends, and studying under the wisest care.

The talk at that family table was an education in itself, the books they read and discussed, the atmosphere of easy acquaintance with things worth knowing; and the lessons given her were not the year-consuming drills and examinations of the schools, but such selections and combinations as best and soonest gave the foundation knowledge she most needed.

Her baby came with the May blossoms; and if the neighbors criticized the American woman's protégée they quite appreciated that it was some object to the Hauptmans to have this boarding pupil, even if she was under a cloud.

In the summer, Miss Yale came again, making a long visit, sitting by the hour to watch Marguerite's quiet happiness with her little one.

They called her Dorothea, and her girl mother found her wholly charming.

"I don't have to leave her now, do I?" she pleaded.

"Not for another year—if you do as well as you've been doing. You couldn't have better care for body or mind. It's going to be like pulling teeth when you do go, I know, but that's part of the price, sister. I think they will keep little Dolly here for you. I believe they would even for nothing—and I know they need the money. We'll call her Yale from the first. I'm to adopt her for the present, as you know. If you should die—and I'm sure I hope you won't, for I've grown very fond of you, my dear—I'll stand by Dolly as I would have by you. But you don't look much like dying!"

She did not. This peaceful, pleasant home, the high sweet air and noble prospect, the society of people who thought far and clearly and talked out their thoughts together, and the comforting affection of Julie, made a most congenial environment for the long-starved girl.

Dorothea was born to a mother strong, calm and cheerful, safe in the present and confident of the future; and if the mother's heart was wrung as she saw the father in that small pink face, she had power to put that pain aside.

The child's orphanage would be not so hard to bear as her own had been.

"She has a mother, anyway!" she said, and her heart seemed to grow like a giant as she faced now not only her own future, but the child's.

Miss Yale had watched eagerly for just that dawn of future power. She had expected it, counted on it theoretically, and was not disappointed.

Maggie turned her eyes upon her wise friend.

"I begin—just begin—to see what you have done for me," she said, "and what you are going to do! When I think of what sort of a mother this child would have had—without you—— O, Miss Yale! You can trust me! I won't fail! I'll do just as you want me to. I'll be a doctor. I'll be a good one!"

Miss Yale patted her hand, and kissed the baby.

"That's all right, Marguerite. I knew I should be proud of you, and I never had such a satisfactory baby before. I'm really much obliged to you, my dear."

Then they planned for the coming years, planned more freely and in detail than had been possible before. The young mother now growing strong again, plumper and rosier than Miss Yale had yet seen her, listened eagerly, and appreciated the careful outline of her coming work far better than she had the year before.

"You see, you have certain advantages now, as well as disadvantages. My friends have lost track of you altogether. When any of them asked me what I'd done with 'that La Salle child' I said I'd placed her with a good family in the country—and this little place is entirely out of the way. From here I want you to go, a year from this fall, to a good school I know—in Germany. You'll be just a girl there, a girl of eighteen—as far as they know. I think you are quite wise enough now to carry it through."

"I have to leave Dorothea—altogether?"

"Yes, for a while. For her sake as well as your own. You see you're staying long enough to see her through the second summer—and not long enough for her to miss you. These dear friends will keep her and teach her for the present. She couldn't be better off. But—she must not know you are her mother until you are ready to claim her. I shall be 'Aunt Mary.' I shall come to get her in the summer, and if I happen to bring her to a place where I have another protégée with me—a brilliant young scholar I am interested in—it is nobody's business!"

"After this year, I only see her on vacations?"

"Yes, until she is ten years old. I'll see that you pass your summers together."

"And what will she call me?"

"Sister. I'm sorry, Margaret. It is going to hurt. But think it out for yourself. You will be able to make a better record without her—the world being as it is. When you are able you shall claim her openly if you wish to. Anyway you can be with her—as a sister."

The young mother held her baby close, close, and hid her tears in the white little garments.

"Anyway she won't call anybody else 'Mother'!" she said.

*　　　　*　　　　*

Margaret Yale, in her special course year in that exacting school, made a record that astonished her teachers. They did not know what coiled springs of repressed emotion urged her on. She was friendly and pleasant with her classmates, and many were much attached to her, but they seemed somewhat young and light-minded to the girl who was no older in years, but who had lived so much more.

She herself was astonished, as well as her instructors, not at her progress, for she had put her shoulder to the wheel with the highest determination, but at the amount of pleasure she found in her work. Having no experience of any other educational processes, she had no means of appreciating the kind of training which had given her French, German and Latin in three years' time, had opened the world of science as a field of boundless fascination, had taught her how to study and how to avoid unnecessary labor.

Herr Hauptman was an enthusiast in natural science. In her eighteen months in that scholastic household she had acquired with pleasure an amount of knowledge which would have meant painful years of ordinary schooling. Both the good man and his wife had given her a special interest in biology and physiology; and the books, so cautiously selected and liberally supplied by Miss Yale, had filled her eager mind with a consistent background of general information.

Her mental strength had not been exhausted in forced study; she knew what was necessary for her to know, did not know much that was unnecessary, and realized the need of such elimination and concentration in the study of science. Her mind was easy about the child, though her heart ached steadily. She knew that "Aunt Julie" was as good to little Dorothea as to her own boy, only a year older; that both children had the loving care of wise grandparents; that the place was ideal for happy and healthy childhood—yet her heart ached for her own baby in her arms.

Then she learned, out of her own keen intelligence, what no books could have taught her, how to hold down her grief, and use it as a spur. She rigidly closed her mind to thoughts of her child during the hours of work, and the hours of play. She allowed, however, one period of tender retrospect, before sleeping, letting her mind dwell on that small rosy sweetness her arms so hungered to hold; and then she checked her tears and restocked her armory of patience by the thought that if she really loved her child and wished to serve her, she must simply work.

And she did work.

Wise teaching, the excellent rules of the school, and her own vivid intelligent perception of its advantages made health an immediate necessity, special strength and endurance for the long years of effort. "For her sake," she said to herself—meaning sometimes Dorothea, and sometimes Miss Yale; and she applied her mind to physical development as well as mental. Her hope was high and steady, and set far ahead.

For immediate joy she had the growing delight of feeding and exercising a healthy brain, and the recurrent happiness of summer vacations. In one and another sweet wild place, by the seashore or in the wooded hills, she met Julie, now dear as a sister, and Julie's two babies. Sometimes, Miss Yale was with them, sometimes not; but the two friends rested and read together and the two babies loved them both.

No part of Miss Yale's program showed more wisdom and resulted more effectively than her choice of friends in placing the girl. Her own life of travel and wide interest in human improvement had put her in touch with all manner of progressive doers and thinkers, and among them were always some who from either necessity or goodwill to Miss Yale, or both, were willing to take an earnest girl student to board.

In Heidelberg, she was particularly fortunate, finding a home with a widow of limited means, but unlimited ideals, a lady in whose parlors Marguerite met men and women who thought and taught and wrote to help the world. She was always quiet, listening much and talking little, but she opened like a flower in this stimulating atmosphere. She grew from year to year in more ways than one, more than she could possibly realize.

When Miss Yale, after an unexpectedly long absence, arranged to spend a winter in Paris, and to have Marguerite with her there for the year's studies, she found a young woman of twenty-three who had even added to her stature since she had seen her.

"Why, child, I do believe you're growing!"

Marguerite laughed. "Yes, I'm almost an inch taller than when I was sixteen. And haven't stopped, either."

"You're looking splendidly. How do you do it—with all your work?"

"I work to do it," said the girl, "or at least play. Julie and I learned a lot that summer you took your family to Sweden. You haven't been over since—but you remember she has taken it up as a regular business, this physical culture work. She teaches in two schools already. In my school we had good training, too. When there is no gymnasium I walk—and run—and row, and play tennis."

"And what will you do in Paris?"

"Fence!" cried Marguerite, "I've always had a secret ambition to fence, but no chance for more than the rudiments. Now, if you're willing, dear friend, I'll add that to my accomplishments."

"You will please me through and through, child. Go ahead and fence. We'll beat them at their own game."

The following years were full of satisfaction for Miss Yale. It was quite true that a large majority of her human investments had been total or partial failures, some worse than failures; but now she felt sufficiently pleased to make up for many losses.

Up in that little Swiss valley was a strong and happy child, here was a vigorous young woman, full of health and promise, already crowned with honors in her studies and developing steadily. What she undertook she mastered, whether it was in her chosen work or in the sports she deliberately selected from year to year, and in addition to her rising affection for the girl, Miss Yale now developed a pride that was almost maternal.

Miss St. Clair's prophecy that her whilom "Cousin Marguerite" would develop beauty was well fulfilled.

With years of nourishment and exercise the spare young frame had filled and rounded, not only with the softness of womanhood, but with the smooth interplay of strong muscles under a satin skin. There were no freckles, now, but a warm tan in the long, light summers, and the steady glow of health at all times.

Her hair had steadily deepened in color, its raw red turning to a coppery brown, dark in the heavy shadows, fiery gold in the curling lights. It crowned her shapely head like a coiled flame. Her very eyes were darker, or looked darker, beneath their darkening brows and lashes.

Yet the men who were drawn by the light of this vivid beauty were painfully disappointed by its lack of warmth. She turned on them a clear disheartening steady glance, that seemed to understand, but not to feel, and the red mouth had a hardness of determination wholly incongruous with her years.

"It is the cruel study!" they said. "It unsexes a woman! How terrible—that a beautiful young creature like that should be so cold!"

She had lovers of various nationalities, of various age and station, some most passionately sincere, but to none was given any ground for hope.

"I have my profession to live for," she said, if any insisted on forcing the question.

They cursed the profession, the unnatural unfeminine profession which stood between her and "love." They did not know what set her whole nature in such a stern revulsion against their advances, that between them stood the grave of love itself, love premature, ill-born, most cruelly killed and shamed; neither did they know that the heart they sought to win for themselves was already wholly given—to a little child.

5. *In a Doctor's Office*

The first floor of a city boardinghouse ever seeks to adorn itself with a doctor's eminently respectable small sign. The house of Mrs. Murray, conveniently placed not far from Boston's beloved Trinity Square, had attained its desire in this respect, and was otherwise comfortably filled. Nevertheless, she continuously trembled on the verge of disaster, and confided her fears to her boarders for lack of other family, notably to her "star boarder" on the first floor.

He had three rooms: a bedroom in the back, whose high windows opened upon a naked little balcony and a view of the usual civic flora, fauna and rearward architecture; the middle chamber, of an unavoidable dimness, yet antiseptically clean and smelling like it, used as a waiting room; and in front, the office.

Early one hot morning in mid-July there sat in this front room, in a high-backed wooden office chair—a chair that swung almost automatically toward the one placed beside the desk for patients, or tipped back with a resigned squeak when the occupant was thinking—a tall, lean, dark-skinned man, reading *Le Journal de Médecine.* The strong, tanned face wore an expression of quiet pleasure as he slowly reread the columns devoted to incidents of recent progress, and the clear, deep-set, iron-gray eyes smiled as well as the mouth. The broad desk was piled high with current literature of his profession, and the book-lined walls resembled those of a library of a medical college. One case, however, was filled with volumes attractive to the lay mind, if it was a well-trained one. In the waiting room was a more miscellaneous array, warranted to please visitors of any age, class, sex, or nationality, with a large proportion of alluring children's books among them.

The doctor laid down the paper he was reading, glanced at his watch, opened a drawer and took out a number of similar papers carefully marked with red ink, covering a period of several years. He arranged them in sequence, and read the marked places evidently not for the first time. As evidently he enjoyed what he read, taking up one paper after another, sometimes going back to one he had laid down. He put them all together again and carefully returned them to the drawer, sitting back in his chair for a while, with gray eyes looking far away, and tilting slowly back and forth, regardless of the squeak.

He rose presently and paced thoughtfully up and down the room, glanced at the various diplomas which set forth so solemnly how Henry T. Newcome was entitled to the degree of Doctor of Medicine, and to other impressive initials following his name, and stood for a long time before two photographs upon the mantel. One was of an elderly woman, whose grave, kind eyes and square brow were very like his own; the other, younger, prettier, in a bride's veil.

Dr. Newcome's practice was large, his income tolerable, though much reduced by the great proportion of patients who paid him only in polyglot blessings, and his position well established. Among the younger men of Boston he stood highest in his chosen field of pediatrics; some placed him above old Dr. Goldhill, of national fame; but that sweet-faced mother, only last year dead, and that little sister, only this year married, had kept him poor. Neither of them had ever imagined it. If they criticized his locality, he told them a doctor could not afford to change—his patients knew where to find him. If they pitied him for living in a boardinghouse, he praised the handiwork of Mrs. Murray's last cook, and extolled the tender mercies of that good woman herself.

"Why don't you marry, dear?" his mother had urged. "I should be so much happier about you—when I go."

"Don't go till I do, then, Mother dear," he would reply, and promise that he would marry as soon as he found a woman his mother would think good enough.

She had gone, unexpectedly soon. Alice was in good hands now—and Dr. Newcome turned with a little sigh and sought the basement dining room.

He was, as usual, the earliest down, and as usual, Mrs. Murray was on hand, partly to wait on him and more especially to confide to him her various perplexities and troubles.

Mrs. Murray was one of those women who cause one to speculate on the ruthlessness of fate. One feels at first as if the inefficiency, the heavy, ill-borne load of responsibility of these struggling women who cannot keep house successfully as a business, was a well-chosen penalty meted out to them for previous inefficiency as private housekeepers when they did not have to pay the bills. Continued observation shakes this theory. It can hardly be that all these good ladies, so numerous, so industrious, so pathetic in their visible and audible incapacity, are thus singled out for punishment. They seem in no way to differ from other ladies of their age and station less unfortunate. Then rises the horrid thought—"Suppose these are merely average women, robbed of 'the shelter of a home' and forced to expose their housekeeping abilities to the glaring light of business competition!"

Then do their abilities seem as disabilities. Then does it appear that the ripe wisdom Miss Ida Tarbell supposes to accrue from the mere practice of "keeping house" fails to manifest itself, when put to the test of keeping a boardinghouse. They have difficulties with their servants, difficulties with their bills, difficulties with their boarders, and no one "higher up" on whom to unload these difficulties.

Wherefore the pathetic failure of many of these necessary institutions, and the uncomfortable atmosphere of many more that continue to totter on. Mrs. Murray's establishment had been tottering during the six years Dr. Newcome had occupied its first floor, and that it still pursued its unsteady way was largely due to his presence there, not only to his cheerful encouragement and wise advice, but partly to his custom of paying board in advance, which made him regard her business as almost in the nature of an investment.

"Doctor," she said in an anxious whisper, "may I speak with you about something important?" and she advanced a plate of hot cornbread with two well-browned corner pieces as a species of preliminary tribute.

"Certainly, Mrs. Murray—go ahead."

"It's about Elma," she said, sinking her voice. "You know you wanted me to keep her—to sort of look out for her—but I'm afraid I can't."

Elma at this moment came in with the doctor's eggs, and hovered about for a moment, seeking to do something more for him.

"You needn't wait, Elma," said Mrs. Murray, and she departed with an adoring look at the tall man.

"She's going on with that young Battlesmith, I'm afraid," pursued her employer. "Not Mr. Gerald, *of course*—but his brother. I know he's only a boy—but I can't have it, you know, in my house. I'll have to send her off—let me give you some hot coffee."

Dr. Newcome stirred and sipped it. He had cream in his coffee, whatever the pitcher held for later comers.

"Now, honestly, Mrs. Murray, as between man and man," he smiled at her in a way she always found completely disarming, "which of these two young people does the going on? I ought to know that before I can advise."

"Well, of course, he's the active party, so to speak—but I can't turn him out, you know."

The doctor sighed. "No, of course you can't. I appreciate your position, Mrs. Murray. That child is too pretty and too light-headed to be safe anywhere. But if you turn her off, she'll find the same luck wherever she goes. I hoped, with your wide experience and good judgment"—Harry Newcome's years of "jollying" his patients had, it is to be feared, somewhat shaken his instinct for absolute veracity—"that you could shield her till she was safely married. Didn't you tell me the grocer's man was decorously attentive?"

"Oh, they're all attentive enough—I can't say how decorously—but, Doctor, I must do something!"

"Will you leave it to me another day? I can set Jim Battlesmith straight, I think."

Jim's brother entering at this moment, she could do no more than nod mysteriously behind him, and departed to the kitchen.

"Good morning, Doctor," said the newcomer gloomily, and put sugar on his small plate of blackberries with no great interest. Henry Newcome had known and liked Mr. Battlesmith ever since that summer when they had toiled as comrades bearing picnic baskets up steep hills. Himself a hard worker, winning his own education under difficulties, he had sympathized keenly with the boy's long struggle through college, and continued to sympathize during the later years, when a teacher's salary proved all too little to support comfortably the young man in Boston and his small brothers and sisters in Maine. Ten years had left him but one as wholly dependent, a boy of eighteen, bigger, stronger and far more strenuous in disposition than the brother who supported him. Gerald's quiet face was anxious, his pleasant blue eyes turned to his friend with a worried look.

But other boarders came in and he said nothing till Dr. Newcome rose, when he accompanied him upstairs.

"Can you give me five minutes, Doctor?"

"Certainly, come in—it's not 'office hours' yet. Fire ahead!"

But Mr. Battlesmith did not seem to find it easy. He walked around the office and looked at the pictures and books, coming back to the desk at last with a little shrug.

"It's Jim," he said.

The doctor nodded understandingly.

"He's not sick—that I know of; but Doc—I can't hold on to him anymore. He ought to be up on the farm, and he will hang on here.

He's got in with a gay crowd. He likes you, Doctor; he admires you. I wish you'd say a word to him. He'd have respect for what you say. I've got him to agree to listen to you, anyhow. He thinks you'd be on his side! Here he is now."

There was a brisk knock and the boy entered. He was a stalwart young fellow, rather heavily built, with a fresh color and an air of cheerful assurance, perhaps a little forced.

"Good morning, Doctor! I won't apologize—Jell has dragged me into this. And you can cut it as short as you like—the shorter the better."

Gerald particularly disliked this nickname, as his brother well knew, but he only said "Thank you, Jim," and went out.

The boy lounged forward and seated himself in the patient's chair, in a comfortable position. "Can you give me an anesthetic with the sermon?" he cheerfully inquired, "or put it in capsules?"

Dr. Newcome sat silent, turning his long paper cutter over and over on the green blotter. Then he wheeled his chair sharply toward his visitor.

"Tell me your side, first," he said.

This was a little discomforting. The boy had expected to be questioned, lectured, advised; had even hoped for a little high-handed, "man-of-the-world" encouragement.

"Why—I haven't anything to say, particularly," he said. "It's all Gerald's talk. You see, I'm grown up now"—he flushed a little—"and I've been—well—just been going with the boys some. And he's cutting up about it."

"Only with 'the boys'?" Dr. Newcome gently inquired.

"Oh, you know what I mean," said Jim, flushing a little more. "It's a question of a fellow's health, you know."

"Yes, I know it is," the older man agreed. "You have been reading Esterly and Hendling, and a bit of Greer, haven't you?"

"How'd you know?" the boy demanded.

"I was in your shoes some seventeen years ago, and I read them. It is easy to believe what agrees with your feelings, isn't it? I suppose you've tried some Nietzsche, too—and enjoy Wells—and Ellen Key?"

Young Battlesmith agreed, evidently impressed with the doctor's penetration.

"And how do you sum it up? What is your position?" His tone was even, his manner one of scientific inquiry. The young man was encouraged to proceed.

"Why, I think—of course—early marriages would be the ideal thing. With free divorce. But while economic conditions are what they are—why, a fellow has to put up with—has to get along the best he can," he concluded with less assurance.

"There are new men, good ones, who disagree with the books you've had. Have you read any of these?" asked the doctor, showing him a list of authorities of such weight that even this student knew their names. Then he laid before him facts and figures, showed plates, diagrams, statistics; clearly presented the later views of wider-visioned men, who teach that continence and health are quite compatible.

But Jim was at the age when the ego is strongest, both in body and mind, and preferred to believe what seemed to him convincing views on his own side of the case.

"There's a difference in men!" he burst forth at last. "Of course, there are some that don't have any trouble."

The doctor looked at him so steadily that his eyes fell.

"Yes, there is a difference in men—and there is a difference in the same man at different ages. My boy, this is not a question of men, alone, you understand. It is a question of women. And of children, and of the health of the whole population."

Again he showed the results to the world of what he was so lightly considering as a "natural indulgence," and again the boy fell back on the irresistible power of what he called the "life force."

"It's all very well for Gerald to talk," he said. "He's different. He doesn't know how I feel."

"I know," said Dr. Newcome. "I've been there."

The boy looked up at him. He had, as his brother had said, a hearty admiration for the tall, sinewy frame, keen mind, the high reputation of the man before him. He knew him, not only as a physician, but as a winner of cups and breaker of records in more than one line of athletics.

"I was just such a young fool as we all are," said the older man quietly, "plus the illimitable knowledge of a medical student. I knew it all, just as you do, son, and more. And went the pace."

He stood up and braced his broad shoulders.

"I was just a plain fool, Jim. You are just a plain fool. I learned better after the event. You may learn better, beforehand. There is only one small shade of advantage out of all that smear and stain behind me—I can with a better grace advise others. Now, if you wish to qualify as a signpost, at your own expense, at the risk of your own life, reason, health, and those of your wife and children—why, go ahead. If you have the sense I credit you with, quit. Quit beforehand."

"But old Gerald's such a granny," began the boy.

"Now, look here, Jim. That brother of yours is a *man*. He worked his way through college, which is more than you are doing. He has carried your mother and all you kids for eight years. The least you can do is to run straight till you're on your own feet, and if you're the man I think you, you'll keep on till you've cleared your score with him. By that time you'll get the habit."

The doctor smiled, that wise and winning smile of his, and held out his hand. "You want to see life, Jim—will you let me show you some? I'd like to take you about for a week or so. Will you come?"

This could hardly be refused, and they presently entered upon a course of social pathology together. Grave, silent, or with scant comment, the doctor showed him in sordid repetition the miserable lives of the lower grade of those women he had vaguely figured as creatures of gaiety and charm; told him their numbers, their proportion of disease, their sure and rapid death, their literal imprisonment, and the means used to recruit their decimated ranks. He showed them in the prison, in the hospital, in the morgue.

Elsewhere, he showed him what women must endure who bring forth a child.

He showed him men, too—men with locomotor ataxia, with paresis, idiots, lunatics, all the sequelae of a "life of pleasure."

Then he took him to a children's hospital, and exhibited the effects of the father's indulgence upon the third and fourth generation. Jim was an affectionate fellow, always fond of little ones, and this reached far and deep. He had seen only healthy babies before; these were a revelation to him.

"You see, Jim," said the doctor, "there are several sides to it. I'm not preaching morality to you; that's not my line of work. But I can set forth the facts for you to look at. On one side you have a plain, hard fight with yourself. What of that? What's your strength for? No man that is a man is afraid of a fight. Then, by and by, a wife, a home, children of your own. On the other side, you have—this."

The boy walked by his side, silent, shaken through and through with the heavy, drastic dose of naked facts. His young heart was sore with sympathy for those helpless, unwilling girl victims—sick with horror at the wrecks of manhood he had seen, and there were tears in his eyes from the thought of those patient babies, crippled and poisoned by their own fathers.

"These young fellows want to know life," said Dr. Newcome, after a little. "I wish they did. Better stay out, Jim; the water's not so fine, eh?"

And Jim stayed out.

Not only so, but he astonished his brother by asking a loan to take him to Kansas. "I'm going to work in the harvest," he said. "I'll finish college when I can afford it."

Little Elma was not long a problem. Dr. Newcome spoke, not to her, but to the grocer, and the grocer's young man, unexpectedly advanced in business, forthwith immured her in a small flat, and by means of the most flattering jealousy and much marital authority, kept her in safety till her charms were somewhat dimmed by continuous motherhood—thus adding quite unnecessarily to the doctor's list of grateful, but unpaying patients.

He worked steadily on, through the hot, monotonous days, and then, toward the end of office hours one morning a visitor surprised him, a young girl in cool, beruffled white. She rose as he stood in the doorway and came toward him.

"I'm not next, I know, Dr. Newcome, but I just want to say a word. Mama is coming later, and I thought I'd meet her here. You don't mind?"

"You're very welcome, Miss Briggs; just sit there by the table. What will you have to read?"

"Oh, anything will do; I don't mind waiting. Don't let me disturb you."

Miss Daisy's voice was not loud, but clear and high, and Dr. Newcome smiled to himself in his office as he heard a step on the stair and the voice of Gerald Battlesmith in the waiting room.

The last patient had gone, but the doctor still sat quietly in his desk chair. Finally Gerald brought Miss Briggs to the door. "I'm so sorry, but I have an engagement at twelve-thirty, to arrange for some more tutoring. I know you'll be glad to entertain Miss Briggs until her mother comes. So good of you to look in on us, Cousin Daisy!"

Miss Daisy came in rosily fanning herself.

"It *is* hot down here, after the mountains. I'm telling Cousin Gerald he ought to get out of town. Mother would have asked him to the camp, I'm sure, but we're expecting Miss Yale, you know, and her last surprising protégée. We shall be pretty full. But Gerald—there's the Barlow House. It's very pleasant there."

"I'm so sorry," said her cousin again. "I'd like to, you know how I'd like to! But I've got this tutoring to do, and I can hardly leave this summer."

He took himself off, with evident difficulty, and left his fair cousin leaning gracefully back in another chair the doctor had drawn out for her. She had started for the one beside his desk, but he said, "No, don't sit there; that's for the patients. You don't look in the least like a patient, Miss Daisy."

"I don't know about that," she said guardedly, pushing the point of her white parasol against the tip of her white shoe. "I've often thought I'd like a little—serious advice."

"Now's your time," he answered cheerfully, "and here's the place. You shall have any amount of advice, professional and friendly."

She did not seem in any haste to seek it, however, but applied the parasol tip to various lines in the rug beside her. "What seems to be the trouble?" he asked gently. "Is it physiological or psychological?"

"I guess it's both," she admitted. "Doctor, I don't suppose there's anything really the matter, but there are times when I can't sleep, and I don't eat, and nothing interests me. I get so depressed! I feel sometimes as if there was nothing to live for—as though I'd better be dead."

She lifted a perplexed, pathetic face to him.

"Will you pardon an older man, and a professional man, if he asks two direct questions?"

"You may ask anything you like, Doctor; I don't mind. I'm twenty-eight, if that's what you want to know."

"That much I did know, Miss Daisy. My terrible questions are these: First, why do you not marry? Second, why do you not go to work?"

Her chin was on her hand now, her eyes on the neat white shoes. "There are too many girls in Massachusetts for all of us to marry," she answered, with truth, if not with frankness. "As for working, I have tried, but Mother was always against it, and Father, too. They have only me, you see. They say a girl's place is at home."

He nodded, understandingly.

"Of course, they were willing I should study," she went on. "I went to Radcliffe, you know, and did some postgraduate work, and I tried a year in the art school, but I'm not artistic in the least bit."

"You like music better?"

"Oh, much better," she said eagerly. "I've worked hard on my music. They do say I'm an excellent accompanist."

Dr. Newcome smiled again. It occurred to him that Gerald, spending long, lonely evenings with his violin, often expressed a wish for an accompanist. "I don't see any signs of serious disturbance," he said, "and what you tell me does not indicate any need of treatment at present. But I would most earnestly advise you to take up some kind of work and stick to it. A full-grown woman with fifteen waking hours to fill has to do something to earn her sleep."

The bell rang again and Mrs. Leicester-Briggs entered, somewhat flushed. "What weather!" she panted. "Good morning, Doctor! I do not see how you stand it here in the summer. Daisy and I only came down on some errands and we are nearly dead. How long have you been waiting, Daisy?"

"Sit here," he said. "There's a little air. Have a palm leaf. And now that you've come so far, I want you to stay and take a boardinghouse lunch with me."

"I'm afraid we can't this morning, Dr. Newcome. You're very kind."

"I'm sorry your cousin is not here to add his invitation to mine. He was called away this morning on some business, but do stay and keep me company. You have only a hotel to go back to, you know."

"Thank you, perhaps we will. I'm sure I'm glad to rest after shopping. But first I must tell you my errand. You're not busy at this moment?"

She looked around, as if suspecting patients concealed beneath the furniture.

"Not at all," said he. "It is after office hours and before lunch hour, and as it happened I had no pressing visits to make this morning."

"That's good. Now, let me begin at the beginning and tell you all about it. You remember Mary Yale?"

"I remember her with pleasure."

"You know how queer she is—always adopting people."

"I've heard that she is a—sort of international benefactor."

"Oh, yes, benefactor, of course. But she has no settled home of her own, except her flat here in Boston, which she's hardly ever in. And I assure you these protégés of hers are sometimes a great care to her friends. You remember that little German boy, Daisy, that she left with us one summer?"

"Yes, Mama; he was a nice boy."

"Oh, he was a nice boy enough, but he came down with scarlet fever, Dr. Newcome, right in the middle of the summer, and there we were, way up in the Adirondacks, and couldn't move him. We had to get a trained nurse, and cancel all our invitations. It was simply dreadful! Well, now we've got another one."

"Another little German boy?"

"No, it's a girl—German, or French, or Italian, I don't know. She talks all three. Mary picked her up in Switzerland."

"She's a perfectly lovely child, Dr. Newcome," put in Daisy. "Bright as she can be. I thought you knew about her."

"Oh, the child is nice enough," continued her mother, "a little black-haired thing, very pretty manners, but, Doctor, I've had a telegram this very morning and that child is sick."

"I'm very sorry to hear it. Not another case to quarantine, I hope. Shall I get you a nurse?"

"Thank you very much. I thought you'd get me a good nurse, if it's necessary. But I haven't told you all about it yet. She sent the child over in the spring, with the Hallocks; sent her to me, and begged me to keep her this summer, so that she would be well and strong to go to school in the fall. Said she wanted her to go to American schools— I'm sure I can't imagine why. Mary, herself, is not in America half her time. She's fonder of this girl than any child she ever adopted, she says. Writes to me all the time about her, and now the worst of it is I'm expecting Mary herself in about a fortnight, with that young female prodigy of hers, and I can't have the child sick. Mary'd never forgive me."

"That is awkward," Dr. Newcome admitted. "Let us hope she will get well at once. You have a good practitioner up there?"

"That's just it," protested Mrs. Briggs. "We haven't. We haven't anybody. Old Dr. Jones in the village is dead, and there's nothing nearer than the Inn, twenty miles, over the mountains. Now, this is what I've come for. And I won't take no for an answer. You've got to come back with us and cure that child."

"Oh, how perfectly delightful!" cried her daughter. "You will come, won't you?"

Dr. Newcome hesitated. He had made other plans for August. This was a totally unlooked-for and sudden change.

Mrs. Leicester-Briggs saw him waver and pursued the attack. "We shall enjoy having you so much, for your own sake. It is a long time since we summered together. I'm sure you'll like the country up there. There's fishing, you know."

"Splendid fishing," urged Daisy.

"Miss Yale will be there later; she's always an attraction. And this last pickup of hers, who really seems to be a credit to her—you won't mind her, I'm sure. Or are you sensitive about women doctors?"

"Not in the least," he assured her. "You are really most kind, Mrs. Briggs."

"It will quite spoil our summer if you don't come, Doctor. You're so wonderful with children, Dolly will get well at once. And then I can face Mary Yale. You simply have to do it, you see. Just make your arrangements and take the night train with us."

"It is absolutely impossible," said Dr. Newcome. "But I'll do it, with pleasure. Thank you very much."

6. *Coming Home*

Up and down the windy decks she walked and walked—swiftly, steadily, by herself; sometimes more slowly, an older woman on her arm; seldom with any of the officers, or passengers, who so obviously stood about at strategic points, seeking that privilege.

She stood long by the rail, too, watching the white welter sliding by along the tall dark sides of the vessel, the wide heaving stretch of blue water, green water, gold water where the low sun blazed across it before them, silver water where the large moon made a palely tempting pathway behind them.

Now that her ten years of exile were over—the years of education, the years of study, research and practice, the years of tender joy and pride, of ceaseless heartache and remorse that motherhood had meant to her—Margaret Yale was coming home. As the long wet miles flashed by, as each day's record showed the distance shortening, her emotion grew more intense. In some strange way she felt as if she was coming back, not only to America, but to her own buried girlhood, to somehow face that shamed and terror-stricken child, Mag Wentworth.

In all these years little had ever been said about her past. Miss Yale told her when she heard that Miss Joelba Bingham had died of pneumonia one unusually severe winter; and had also occasionally referred to the days behind as being gone forever; but in general she had wisely trusted to the healthful oblivion of youth and time. With no one else could the girl ever speak of home.

She herself had early recognized the plain duty of forgetting; had steadily fixed her eyes on the future and refused to spend one thought upon the past—when she could help it. She had built wide and deep. The world of knowledge which had opened to her, the world of experience, the world of action, all these had helped to form a strong base of character, the new character of Margaret Yale.

But through it all ran like a crimson wound her throbbing motherhood, that open way, which she could never even wish to close, yet down which came at any time, straight into her defenseless heart, pain, loneliness and shame. As she longed for her child, and strove with all her strength to work for that child's future, she must needs remember that her baby's orphanhood was its mother's fault.

Blaming the selfish, thoughtless father was no ease to her conscience. The more she learned and lived the more she felt that no excuse could relieve the mother of responsibility. And yet, from the hard-won heights of her knowledge and experience, she must have some pity for that ignorant girl-mother, herself an unprotected child.

"If I had *known!*" she would groan to herself, in bitter, sleepless hours. "Girls ought to *know!* If I had only *known!*"

But her health was too good, her courage too high, her days too richly full of work and study, for those hard hours to come often. Four things she had built up in those ten years: a vigorous body, graceful, strong, alert, skillful in many ways; a fine mind, clear, well-ordered, stocked with knowledge, trained in high uses; a character whose strength was tempered to softness by that hidden pain, whose pride was always kept in check by memory; and beyond these, a reputation which was wider than the girl knew.

Mary Yale loved her as she had once hoped to love children of her own, with a deep congenial friendship which would have drawn them together if there had been no other tie, with frank admiration for her rich vigor, her all-around capableness, her genuine achievements in her profession, her vivid beauty; and besides all this she loved her with fond pride as a successful experiment. Few mothers personally enjoy the society of their daughters as this world-mother enjoyed her favorite child's companionship.

"Do come and sit down, Marguerite," she urged her. "You'll tire yourself out before you get there. You can't go any faster than the ship!"

"All right, Mother-friend. I'll come and sit by you for a solid hour." The tall girl pulled her steamer chair into closer alignment, arranged her Kenwood rug and buttoned herself in, turning a serene rosy face toward her companion.

"It is good to look at you, child," said the older woman. "You are 'a sight for sair een.'"

"It's lucky for my modesty that I've had to do my work mostly away from you," the girl replied. "You would have spoiled me over and over, just like any other mother!"

Miss Yale reached out a hand and found Marguerite's.

"You blessed child! I wonder if you realize at all—in the faintest degree—what you are to me!"

"Can't possibly, because my limited mind is too wholly occupied with what you are to me, Mother dear."

They were silent for a bit, hands clasped under the rug, watching the tossing splashes of wind-whipped spray that spattered the deck before them. Hovering persons, both men and women, looked at Margaret as they passed as if more than willing to stop if invited; and one man, emboldened by previous acquaintance with Miss Yale, did stop to speak with them for a little.

"She's the hardest girl to get on with I ever saw," he confided, later, to an older man in the smoking room.

"I don't find her so," his friend replied. "I've talked with her quite a bit. She seemed to me one of the easiest to get on with."

"That's just it. She's too easy—just like a boy! She's cheerful and good-natured and frank and polite and all that—and you *slide off it!*"

His friend laughed. "Perhaps you try to stick too close. I don't, you see. I always did enjoy coasting."

Another traveling acquaintance joined them. "Talking about that young Dr. Yale? Isn't she a stunner? I'd no idea a woman doctor could—well, not show it, you know."

"The ship's doctor thinks she shows it all right. He was much interested when he saw her name on the list. Says in Germany she's thought a wonder. She's a surgeon—actually. He had a lot to say about her."

"Jealous, I suppose."

"That's the surprising thing. He admitted that he was, at first, and disapproved of women doctors, and all that—but now they are as friendly as——"

"As any of us, eh? She's all right!" said the third man, heartily, and they all agreed.

After he had left them, Miss Yale began, quietly, "You're feeling all right about going to the Briggses now, aren't you?"

"Yes," said Margaret slowly. "I guess you are right about it. I must meet your friends, of course, and one time is as good as another. And Dolly is there."

"Dolly is there. You and she can have a lovely time together for some weeks. You will get well rested before we make our beginning in Boston. Then we'll find a good house on a good street, and hang out your little porcelain sign, and I shall be so proud!"

"And you have the next floor for yours, Mother-friend—and Dolly with us. Oh, it's too good to be true." The girl gave a long sigh of relief.

"It won't be all beer and skittles, child, you know that."

"I do, indeed. I have to begin all over again and make a place for myself. I have to work, hard and long. I'm willing."

"You have a tremendous start with your European reputation, but I'm afraid that will not mean everything for you in America."

"I know that, too," the girl admitted. "In many instances it will only make jealousy and suspicion. I have to begin."

"But there isn't the shadow of a doubt of your success, my dear, both professionally and socially. I was so proud of you, dear child, at Lady Raynor's."

"It was sweet of her to ask me. She only did it because she was so fond of you. Of course I did my prettiest for your sake."

"And your prettiest brought every one of them to your feet—not only the men but the women. That's what I admire so much about you, Margaret," she went on soberly. "Any girl as handsome as you are would have plenty of men admirers, in spite of your professional success. But to have both beauty and success, and yet make friends among the women, as you do—I *am* so proud of you, Margaret! And you have every right to be proud of yourself."

The girl was silent. Turning to look at her more closely, Miss Yale saw that her eyes brimmed with tears. "Dear child, what is it? Have I said it wrong?"

"No, no, Mother dear, you never say anything wrong. You may be as proud of me as your generous heart allows, but I shall—never—be proud of myself."

"Now, child, how absurd! You have ten times—a hundred times—the right to be proud that these sheltered ignorant young creatures have, that never knew danger, and never did anything worthwhile in their lives."

"Yes—I know," Margaret answered slowly. "In a sense you are right. And I might have grown almost to feel so—if it were not for Dolly. . . . You see, no matter how I rebuild myself, I cannot make up to her for the lack of a father, a home, brothers and sisters maybe, a family, a position. I could stand my own loss, my own suffering; I could even honestly feel that I could do enough good work in the world to make up for my own misdoing. But nothing can ever make up to her." She set her lips tightly and turned her face away. Miss Yale kept silent for a while. Then she spoke, gently.

"That is true, my dear, while you consider her as a child, as a girl. But she is growing up in as much happiness as most children have, with your love and care, and mine. By and by she will marry, I trust, and then she will have her own home and family, and never feel more than a sentimental regret for what after all she does not miss, because she does not know it. When Julie married again, she did grieve for her, but she was so little that she soon got over it. She loves me I think. She loves you dearly. And in another ten years' time she will be loving somebody else, still better, perhaps. Cheer up, dear child. I can't bear to have you feel so, when we're coming home."

Margaret smiled bravely, the kind hand held close in her own. "I'll be good," she said. "I won't do this again, I promise you. But, Mother, while we are on it—do you suppose I'll ever meet—him?"

"I'm afraid you'll have to, my dear, if you will persist in living in Boston. You know I'm perfectly willing to go to New York with you, or to California. Los Angeles is a fine place for a young doctor."

"Not another word about that, you immeasurable darling," Margaret interrupted. "We've argued that subject to a finish. I will not take you away from your home city, and I will not go away from you, unless you send me."

"Well, then, you obstinate child, you may make up your mind to coming face to face with that man, someday, among the other doctors. He stands very high in his profession, I hear—the wretch. But you needn't be in the least afraid of his knowing you—your mother wouldn't, scarcely."

"Have I really changed so much?"

"Changed? Why, you're inches taller; you are full and round. Dear me, what a scrawny little chicken you were, child! That red hair is copper-brown, copper-black-brown! I never saw such splendid hair. Your color is as different as a red rose from a pink hollyhock. And even your eyes—they say eyes do not change, but I could swear yours are darker. Perhaps it's the lashes and brows, they are so thick and dark, now. And your whole carriage and bearing—you really have a beautiful manner. Nobody would ever know you. And your aunt, poor dear, is gone. Oh, you're safe enough."

"I should hate to meet him, all the same," said the girl. "But don't you give another thought to my foolishness, best of women. I'm going to be a credit to you from this hour. We will drop my 'past' in this deep blue water, and I'll take the future standing."

When the dim blue line of land was sighted, Margaret found to her surprise a lump in her throat, a stir of tender feeling in her heart. She had not imagined that she loved her country in that vital sense. And when the tall towers of New York rose before them, unbelievable height upon height, she turned to Miss Yale with shining eyes.

"I'm glad to come home," she said.

7. *An Unexpected Arrival*

Before the blazing logs of the big fireplace of his Adirondack "camp" sat the Reverend Edward Leicester-Briggs, reading the last *Churchman*. He looked rather more reverend than when puffing up New Hampshire hills, burdened with baskets, or holding a necessarily casual position at the spare table of Miss Joelba Bingham; and the "Leicester" was now ungrudgingly added to the Briggs in all public mention of his name, though some still balked at the hyphen.

His book, after years of calm unhurried labor, had appeared, through an unexceptional publishing house, and held its place in reference libraries, and among other theological works of like character, with dignity if not distinction. Life had given him comfort, and as much honor as his unambitious soul desired, though not perhaps as much as the more ambitious soul of Mrs. Leicester-Briggs desired. She had long entertained a wish to appear in those disconnected announcements "the Bishop of Rhodeshire and Mrs. Leicester-Briggs"—which leave the uninitiated to wonder what this matron is doing with that bishop. As years passed, this hope receded with the dreams of youth, and her present ambitions were mainly maternal.

The soft breeze of a pleasant August afternoon came in at the wide door, opposite the fire, and at the open windows, fluttering the white curtains (Mrs. Leicester-Briggs would have had white curtains on a desert island) and the papers on the long table.

Mr. Briggs rose ponderously and closed the door, reseating himself in comfort. He liked the fire in all weathers in this mountain region. He sat with his back to the stairway at the hall's end, and did not see a small, curly-headed child, who peeped through the window beside it, and presently climbed in. With the utmost caution she stole up behind him, holding a long wisp of grass in her hand, a fuzzy-tipped slender spear, with which she delicately touched that reverend and somewhat bald crown.

He clapped his hand to it, and turned upon her.

"Now Dolly Yale!" said he. "I'm astonished at you! Little girls mustn't be rude, you know!"

The child drew back, abashed, but her big dark eyes still twinkled.

"Was that rude?" she asked, shyly.

"Yes, my little dear—you know it was. But I will forgive you. Come and be friends."

With a most benign expression of countenance, he held out a large white hand. The little girl sidled up slowly and laid her small brown paw in it for a moment, then skipped away again. She ran to the door, pushed aside the sash and looked out; then to the big window opposite the stair, from which the road could be seen for quite a distance; then back to stand by the fire and look at him, asking, "When will Aunt Mary and Sister Margaret come?"

He smiled at her again.

"Not for some time yet, my dear. You must not be impatient. You must trust, and wait."

The small bright face clouded, almost in tears.

He added, hastily, "Aren't you happy here in the beautiful hills? Don't you like visiting us? Better than your school in Germany?"

"Yes," she admitted, politely, but not with ardor. "But I want my Aunt Mary to come."

"You love your Aunt Mary very much?"

The child nodded emphatically.

"And Sister Margaret?"

The child nodded less emphatically. "Don't you love her, too?" pursued the benevolent inquirer, feeling now quite as if he was addressing a Sunday school.

"Oh, yes," Dolly admitted, "but I don't see her so much. She didn't 'dopt me."

"You love your adoptive mother best?"

"Yes."

"Do you love all your adopted brothers and sisters?"

She shook her head at this, with great decision. Her questioner could not but laugh at the bobbing curls, but recovered himself and declared:

"You should love everyone, my little friend, and especially your brothers and sisters. How many have you now, Dolly?"

"Oh, I don't know, they do not all live with Aunt Mary. Only just Sister Margaret and me. "

"And 'I,' Dolly," he corrected, and the child flushed a little. She was sensitive about her English, being more accustomed to other languages.

A firm step was heard on the gallery above, and the rustling skirts of Mrs. Leicester-Briggs brushed its balustrades and the broad treads of the stairway. She stopped on the lower landing, where the stair turned outward, and stood for a moment scanning the large hall with the housewife's observant eye; then continued her descent.

"Well, Dorothea, are you having a good time?"

"Yes, ma'am" replied the child, drawing herself up primly.

"Don't say 'ma'am,' Dorothea. 'Yes' is sufficient. Do you think you can change your dress for dinner all alone? Eliza has not come back from the village."

"Yes, ma'am—I mean, yes."

"That's right, my dear. You had better run along and begin; it will take you some time, I am sure."

The child departed rather slowly up the stairs, while her host, who had risen and stood with his broad back to the fire, waved his hand to her.

"She is really a very nice child, my dear, a very nice child," he said.

His wife agreed with him. "Yes, Mary Yale has better luck with her selections as she grows older. Though they do say, this young doctor is a wonder—and she's had her on her hands for some ten years or more."

She went to the center table and arranged the papers in neat equidistant piles, with swift precision; then closed the corner window by the stairway, drawing the curtain into even folds, and arranging the cushions on the seat below.

"Yes," said her husband. "Yes, I've just been reading an account of that special discovery of hers. It does seem surprising that a young woman like that should be so—so prominent."

"Oh, women do everything nowadays," she replied. "I confess I do not admire it, myself. It seems to me rather unfeminine! But dear Mary is as proud of her as if she were her own daughter. I simply *had* to ask her here."

"When do they arrive? Little Dolly is getting very impatient."

"I don't quite know. She wrote last from the other side—they meant to come earlier, but this young woman's work—or their English visits or something—has kept them."

She withdrew into the dining room at this, and presently reappeared with a tray, bearing pitcher and glasses, which she set down on a small table in the corner.

"It is really very kind of you, Laura, to have this child on your hands all summer. So much trouble."

She finally ceased to domineer over the furniture, and seated herself with a little sigh in the chair opposite him.

"It would have been no trouble—if she hadn't been ill. And no one can be blamed for that, I suppose." Mrs. Briggs seemed a little aggrieved at finding no one responsible for the child's illness. "However, that's all over."

"Besides," she added, after a moment's silence, "I would do a great deal for Mary Yale. I have a deep affection for her—as you know—in spite of her eccentricities."

"Yes, yes, of course, Laura. She is a fine woman, a very fine woman. And very fond of our Daisy, eh?"

"Yes, indeed. She always was. . . . It will be a good thing for the child, too—if she doesn't marry."

"Oh, she'll marry fast enough!" said the good man, stretching his legs toward the fire. "Nature takes care of that!"

His wife surveyed him with affection and a general respect, somewhat tempered by a critical view of this particular statement.

"I wish it did," she said at last, with a sigh that spoke volumes, "but really, Edward—I do think Dr. Armstrong is seriously interested this time."

"You don't say so! You don't say so! Lose our little Daisy at last, eh? Well, well! It is Nature's law. Nature's law."

His wife again considered him as if she thought his faith in Nature quite overdone and that in this particular instance other forces had been at work, but she said nothing.

He gazed at the fire, with a retrospective air. "I had thought—at one time—that Dr. Newcome fancied her. He is a good doctor, too."

"Yes, indeed," she assented, "especially with children. But he will never be more than a good practitioner. Dr. Armstrong, now, is brilliant."

"Yes, he is. He stands very high, indeed. And then he was independent to begin with. That is a great consideration, of course."

The parental conclave was interrupted at this moment by a quick step on the porch, and the entrance of Miss Daisy herself. She was a little flushed from her walk, and seemed to find the fire quite unnecessary.

"Dear me, Papa! Why *will* you have a fire in August? This room's a perfect oven."

She pulled off her gloves, kissed her parents with promptitude, and proceeded to frisk about the room, opening windows, shoving back curtains, and stirring up the papers on the table, as if looking for something, while her mother and father both regarded her with proud affection.

"Were the Hallocks in?" her mother asked.

"No, Mama, but I met that lady that's visiting them and the oldest Hallock boy, on the road, as I was coming back. They are all much excited about Miss Yale's wonderful protégée—want to know when she's coming, and did I know this and that and the other. They said there was an account of her in the last *National View*," and she pursued her search.

Her father regarded her fondly. "She will quite cut you out, my little Daisy."

"How absurd you are, Edward!" said his wife. "These 'advanced' women are never attractive to gentlemen. And doctors, especially—— What are you going to wear tonight, Daisy?" she added, rather disconnectedly.

Daisy looked at her with some amusement. "Why—the pink one I suppose."

"Why not your new one, dear, that Aunt Mary sent you from Paris?"

"I was rather saving that for some special occasion. It's so pretty. Oh, here they are!"

"They" were only Dr. Armstrong and Dr. Newcome, who appeared at the door, the former proudly carrying a string of fish, the latter the rods, basket and other impedimenta.

The reverend gentleman rose to greet them.

"Welcome, my gallant Nimrods," he said. "Or at least——"

"Tobits," suggested Dr. Newcome, and his companion added, "or Jonahs."

"How many, today?" inquired Miss Daisy, regarding the silvery victims.

"Don't bring them any nearer, please," her mother hastily protested. "I'll call the cook."

"I'll take them to her," said Dr. Newcome, and disappeared through the dining room door under the stairway.

"Daisy, do give Dr. Armstrong some lemonade. I have it all ready here—you must be so thirsty——" The good lady fairly beamed on him, and urged them both toward the small table in the corner. Dr. Newcome, returning fishless, she intercepted by the fireplace, saying, "Sit right here, now, and rest a little. Where did you go today? Edward, do bring Dr. Newcome a glass of lemonade."

"Certainly, certainly, with pleasure." Daisy poured it, her father brought it, and their guest drank it, with evident satisfaction.

"Thank you," he said. "We went up Potter's Creek—and over into Little Brook afterward—had pretty good luck—eighteen."

"And who caught the most?" pressed Mr. Briggs.

"I'll have to admit that I did this time."

"Have to admit—well, I like that!" The older man chuckled, and his wife smiled, too.

"I thought all men loved to brag about their success at fishing," she said.

"Yes, but some like it more than others, Mrs. Briggs. What excellent lemonade this is. May I have another glass?"

They brought him another one, which he consumed with leisurely appreciation, while in her corner, Miss Daisy politely inquired:

"How many fish did you catch, Dr. Armstrong?"

"Oh, ten or a dozen, I think."

"How men do love to kill things!"

"Not all the time, Miss Daisy," he answered, in a low voice. "For instance, I wouldn't have gone fishing this afternoon if you had been at home."

"By the way," said Dr. Newcome, suddenly rising, "we stopped on our way home and got the mail." He burrowed into various pockets, bringing out papers, magazines and letters which his hostess thankfully seized, and began to sort out on the big table.

"On our way!" said Dr. Armstrong. "That's a good one! He dragged me two miles *out* of our way to get that mail, Miss Daisy."

"Any for me, Mama?" asked that young lady, going forward to see. Her father punctiliously distributed them, and with mutual excuses, all began to examine their respective shares, till Mrs. Briggs suddenly burst forth:

"Why, Daisy—Edward! Look here! Here's one from Mary Yale. From New York—they've landed!" She looked hurriedly at the postmark. "This letter has been delayed! She says they're coming right up—that—where is it? 'We leave Monday night.' Why, that was yesterday! They ought to be here *now!*"

"Let me see!" said her husband, taking the letter, while Daisy looked over his shoulder. "Why, yes, they ought to have gotten here by now, almost."

"There must have been some delay on the road. But they'll be here at any moment. I'm so thankful you brought the mail, Dr. Armstrong!"

"Don't mention it!" said Armstrong with a wink at his friend, who smiled and said nothing.

"Dear me," cried Mrs. Briggs, "and their rooms won't be ready—and Eliza's out. Daisy, you run away and dress this minute—they'll surely be here to dinner."

Dr. Armstrong gathered up his rod and basket. "Is this the Infant Prodigy that's coming with your friend, Mrs. Briggs?" he asked.

She eyed him a little uncertainly. "Yes, Dr. Armstrong—but you won't mind her, I'm sure. They say she's really quite attractive."

"Not any of that kind for me! I prefer unprofessional ladies!" said he, bowing gallantly.

"I shall be glad to meet her, Mrs. Briggs," said Dr. Newcome, quietly. "She has made a remarkable contribution to science already."

"That is very kind of you, Dr. Newcome, really."

"Not at all! Come on, Armstrong. We'd better clear out and get ready for dinner," and they took themselves off accordingly.

"Just think, Edward! I hadn't expected them for another fortnight. This is going to be so awkward—having them all here at once!"

"No, indeed, why should it be? The rooms are vacant—and your house is always in good order, my dear. I am sure all these young doctors will have a nice time together."

A sound of wheels was heard crunching up the last slope of their own drive.

"They've come!"

"Here they are!" cried both, simultaneously, and rushed for the door.

8. Meetings

The lean mountain horses stood breathing hard after the last long pull. Their driver was a stringy, discouraging-looking man, who owned the nearest starveling farm, and did teaming in summer to make a living. He untied the straps and cords which had held the baggage in place in spite of Miss Yale's unconcealed misgivings, and carried the one trunk upstairs, while the passengers dismounted.

Much to the surprise of Mrs. Briggs she was greeted by a cheerful "How do you do, Cousin Laura?" and found Gerald Battlesmith one of the party. She met him with a confused blend of the cordiality on tap for Miss Yale, her old friendliness for her cousin, and a strong sense of the limitations of her bedrooms. Gerald laughed reassuringly:

"Don't you worry, Cousin Laura. I'm not coming in. Mr. Haines here is going to board me for a while."

"If you can stand bachin', or near it," grinned Mr. Haines, returning to his seat. His "near it" spoke volumes to those who knew him. He was a long-limbed, loose-jointed, hulking fellow, dominated unmercifully by an old and invalid mother who could do little for him herself, and refused to let any other woman into the house for fear Hank would marry her.

"I can stand anything that'll keep the rain off and prevent starvation," announced Gerald, cheerfully. "This air is enough to live on, almost!"

He drew in great breaths of it with heartfelt satisfaction while Miss Yale explained that she had overtaken him walking up from Shoreville.

"He went faster than we did, I do believe, and looked so superior that I couldn't stand it, so we made him ride."

"Many thanks, I'm sure—good afternoon. You'll see enough of me later," he said, and departed with Mr. Haines.

The others straggled into the hall in friendly confusion, making belated introductions.

"Well, Laura, here we are. I'm afraid we're a little late. And this is Margaret—Mrs. Briggs and Mr. Briggs—Dr. Yale." Miss Yale's expression was calmly triumphant, as she introduced her new daughter to her old friends. Her keen eyes were on the alert nonetheless, watching for the faintest symptom of recognition on the part of either. None appeared.

Margaret looked as calm, as modest, as simply at ease, as in the classroom, sickroom, ballroom, or anywhere else. Whatever fears she may have entertained before, she certainly showed none now.

The benign clergyman was much impressed with her manner; and his less benign wife, if not impressed—it was a little difficult to impress Mrs. Leicester-Briggs—was at least approving. She greeted the young woman cordially, for her, and Miss Yale with real affection.

The belated Eliza now appeared, running out to take the lighter luggage, and Mr. Briggs affably insisted on helping her.

"Is that all?" he asked, looking about for further labors.

"That's all," Miss Yale assured him. "Margaret travels with one trunk; I travel with these!" And she handed one of her two large suitcases to Eliza with evident reluctance, insisting on carrying the other herself.

"Well, well!" said Mr. Briggs, ambling amiably about. "Do sit down. Have a chair, Miss Yale—have a chair, Miss Margaret Yale! So this is the young lady we've been reading such wonderful things about!"

"Nothing very wonderful, I'm sure," the girl replied. Her face was quiet, but to Miss Yale's eyes, at least, she had the air of one waiting, listening, and not wishing to show it.

The sound of little feet was heard on the gallery above; a small, dark head bobbed beside the railing, and Dolly came scampering down the stairs, taking the last four in a flying leap into Miss Yale's arms.

"Oh, Aunt Mary! Aunt Mary! I'm so glad you've come!"

Her adoptive mother held her close—her real mother waited, the exquisite control of her fine face a marvel to see. Miss Yale loosened the child's arms and brought her forward.

"Here's Sister Margaret," she said.

Then Margaret could take her in her arms; could hold her close—close; could kiss her almost as she longed to—not quite.

But the child wriggled out from her embrace with a little "Ow! You hurt!"

Margaret pulled herself together. "Forgive me, dear; I wouldn't hurt you for the world——" There was a quiver in her voice.

"Now, Margaret!" Miss Yale broke in. "We must go and wash before dinner!"

"Yes, yes!" cried Mrs. Briggs. "You must be tired out. We'll go upstairs at once." She led the way with Miss Yale while her husband succeeded in capturing the other suitcase and bore it in the rear.

Dolly was for starting after them at once, but Margaret dropped to the floor by her side and caught her to her heart again with a smothered "Oh, my darling!"

The child submitted peacefully enough; she even kissed her in return, a nice, dutiful little kiss, but still pushed softly away.

"You hug me too tight, sister." Margaret relaxed her grasp, but held the little hands, and kissed them, over and over, the child standing looking gravely down at her.

"I haven't seen you, precious, for almost a year!" her mother said. "Are you well, darling? Are you happy? Do you like your friends here? Are they good to you? As if anyone could help it!"

A luminous idea struck the child. "Oh, Sister Margaret, what have you brought me?"

The mother looked at her with tender, brimming eyes, but a quizzical little smile flickered across her face for a moment. In all the tension of such a moment she could still feel the touch of absurdity in this blind game.

"Don't you love me, darling, without my bringing you anything?"

"Oh, yes—of course I do. But you always do bring me something."

Margaret opened her small hand-satchel, and took out a little package. "Here is one thing," she said. "It's not very big—but I hope you'll like it."

The child nestled close to her, sitting on the floor at her side, opening her little box with dainty curiosity. Margaret watched her, surreptitiously kissing the soft hair with passionate affection.

"Bless me!" said her host, from the gallery above. "What a picture of sisterly devotion!" Mrs. Briggs appeared on the stairs:

"Won't you come up, Miss—Dr. Yale?"

Margaret sighed softly, but rose to her feet with the swift grace of a deer. "Certainly, Mrs. Briggs—I'll come at once. You come, too, Dolly darling, and see what else there is!"

They went up hand in hand, Dolly hugging the little box.

Mrs. Briggs bustled down presently and bustled up again, bearing hot water. Eliza was heard setting the table with more noise than usual, which caused another descent of her mistress, followed by comparative quiet.

In some ten minutes Miss Yale came down, erect and fresh, in garments as uncompromising in cut as ever, though made of silk, and with more than one white corner peeping here and there from the pockets. She stood on the landing a moment, facing the wide, pleasant hall, with the air of one well pleased.

"It'll be all right," she remarked, in cheerful though enigmatic soliloquy. "I thought so!" She walked to the fireplace and stood with her hands behind her.

Mrs. Briggs emerged again from the dining room and came to her with genuine affection. "I *am* so glad to see you, Mary! It's ages since you've been home!"

"Why, it is some years, isn't it?" her friend agreed. "I knock around so I forget my bearings."

"It's five, at least, since you were up here. I did see you in Paris, of course, that summer. What a gadabout you are!"

"Yes. I'm a regular globe-trotter. The world is my country—and my family!"

"Your family! I believe you have a child in every port—like sailors' wives."

"Oh, not as bad as that, Laura! Really they are all off my hands now but little Dolly. Isn't she a dear? It's so good of you to take her up here for me! I assure you I *appreciate* it!"

"Nonsense, Mary! The child is no trouble. You certainly picked out a nice one that time. Where did you say you found her?"

"In Switzerland. Such a pretty baby as she was? You see we old maids love children just as much as if we had them ourselves— maybe more!"

"Do you know anything about the parents?"

"Oh, yes. I always make careful inquiries, you know. There was very decent stock on both sides. But circumstances make it advisable——"

"I see—I see! And this young wonder of yours! Really, Mary, she is most impressive!"

"Yes—isn't she? She made a tremendous hit in London, I can tell you! You care more for things like that than I do, but I confess I was pleased to see her bowl them over. Lady Raynor couldn't say enough about her. And that old lady has good judgment—and unlimited experience."

"Did she have many proposals?"

Miss Yale laughed cheerfully. "If she did, she didn't tell me about it. Margaret is a close-mouthed young lady—discreet beyond praise. But I can answer for two young Honorables and an elderly earl that if they did not propose it was because she would not let them."

"Let's see——" Mrs. Briggs counted reminiscently. "It's ten years or more that you've had her, at least. French, isn't she?"

"It's all of that. I found her in France—such a nice child—about sixteen. Poor, of course, and an orphan—absolutely without friends. I thought she had ability; talked with her; offered to educate her on the spot. She was very stubborn about it—wouldn't take my money. I told her she could pay it back, and if you'll believe me, Laura, she has!"

"What! Not all of it!"

"Every sou. She's twenty-six or -seven now, you see, and has been doing special work for a year or so—operations—she has a wonderful gift for surgery and gets big prices. She saved the life of a little High-and-Mightiness over there—and that placed her all of a sudden."

"How very gratifying it must be!" said Mrs. Briggs; "quite the most successful of all your experiments, isn't she?" yet so unenthusiastically that Miss Yale laughed outright.

"Yes—she'll be the stay of my declining years."

"What do you mean, Mary?" queried her friend anxiously. "You haven't lost your money, have you?"

"Not at all, Laura. There's plenty yet—little Daisy is quite safe! Why, where is Daisy?"

"She's dressing," said her mother. "She'll be down in a minute. She has been expecting you so eagerly!"

"I'm glad of that. Daisy is almost my first love. And you haven't succeeded in marrying her yet! Let me see—she must be nearly twenty-eight."

"You needn't dwell on that, Mary. She is as much of a child as ever. And besides—though I do not wish to be premature—I think someone is much interested in her!"

"Indeed! And who is the captive of your bow and spear this time?"

"Aren't you ashamed of yourself, Mary Yale! As if I wanted to lose my only child!" She lowered her voice confidently: "It's Dr. Armstrong."

Miss Yale tossed her head like an angry horse. "What! Not that man who was at Notchville with us?"

"And why not that man?" Mrs. Briggs seemed quite aggrieved at her friend's tone. "He's of an old family—the New Hampshire Armstrongs—very nice people, and well connected. He stands high in his profession; he's called one of the best surgeons in Boston—if not *the* best. And he has money of his own besides."

Miss Yale was thinking quickly as to what she might say and what she must not say. She remembered that her judgment of the man, on his own record, and her interest in Daisy, quite justified strong feeling, and committed her to nothing further.

"And you'd let that man marry Daisy!"

"Sh!" said Mrs. Briggs. "Not so loud. I don't know certainly yet, but I think he will."

"Why, Laura Leicester! You know he's a man of no moral standards!"

"I know nothing of the sort! He stands extremely well, socially. Mr. Briggs thinks very highly of him."

"But surely you must know—both of you must know—that he's the kind of man that—ruins young girls! Why, Laura," she went on, with freshening memory, "I made the same objection that summer—and it is still sound."

"Tut! Tut! Mary—I'm ashamed of you!"

"I'm ashamed of *him!*"

"No girl need be ruined who has any moral character," said Mrs. Briggs firmly.

"How about *his* moral character?"

"It's not like you to be so censorious, Mary. We know, of course, that Dr. Armstrong was a little wild in his youth—but then, most men are."

"Youth? Look here, Laura—I've heard things about that man within two or three years."

"Nothing—scandalous—I hope."

"Scandalous!" Miss Yale laughed bitterly. "Nothing that hinders his 'standing well socially,' I see. Merely the destruction of a girl or two, more or less. I suppose you think that's nothing. Why, Laura—the man's a criminal! You can't mean to think of him—seriously?"

"I will not listen to you, Mary. And I do hope you'll be polite to him."

Again her friend laughed, or rather sniffed. "I'm not likely to meet him, thank goodness!"

"Not meet him!" Mrs. Briggs stared at her for a moment. "Why, he's here—he and Dr. Newcome."

Miss Yale started violently; her firm, tanned face paled. "*Here!*" she cried. "Not *here*—in this house?"

"How absurd you are, Mary. Yes, of course, right here in this house. They are up here for the fishing. Dr. Newcome I brought on Dolly's account. I haven't told you, but Dolly was quite ill; I was afraid it was a fever or something dangerous—so I just *made* Dr. Newcome come up. He set her all right again in no time. You needn't look so worried—she's all right now."

Miss Yale did look worried. What is more, she was worried—she was frantic. But not on Dolly's account; Dolly was beloved, but her mind was now quite oblivious of the child; she was thinking of Margaret.

She was never good at excuses and was much agitated by the excitement of this sudden blow, following upon what, after all, had been some strain—this return among old friends with her transformed protégée.

But something must be done at once, and she started for the stairs with the banal excuse: "I must go up again—I've forgotten my handkerchief."

Mrs. Briggs was highly amused. "Nonsense! You've got two in sight—and dear knows how many more. Don't be a goose, Mary Yale. You've surely met men before that you didn't approve of."

"I *have!*" said Miss Yale with decision. "Many of them. It's not that, Laura—I must run upstairs right away."

"I don't believe a word of it," said her friend, seizing her dress. "You sit right down here and let me tell you about Dolly. She was really quite ill, you know—and I was so worried! But Dr. Newcome is splendid with children."

"In a minute, Laura—I'll be right down!" And Miss Yale freed herself with a firm hand and made for the stairway.

She was met, however, by Miss Daisy, flying down in joyful haste, the pretty Parisian gown fluttering about her slim ankles, and her eager arms outstretched.

"Oh, dear Aunt Mary! I am so glad to see you!"

"Yes, yes—glad to see you, child—delighted to see you! I was just running upstairs——"

But the girl drowned her protests with affectionate kisses. "In-

deed you shan't go upstairs. I was hurrying so—and I'm all un-
hooked. You must see this lovely gown you sent me—isn't it dear!"
And she whirled slowly about, slim arms outstretched between her
and the stairs. "If you really love me, Aunt Mary, you'll hook me up,"
she said, stopping short, her chin on her shoulder and roguish eyes
looking back.

"You get your mother to hook you up, child—I'll be back in a
minute, I tell you." And the good lady, growing more and more nervous as she heard resounding steps along the gallery, took Daisy by
the shoulders and turned her firmly aside, to make room for a dash
upward.

But the resounding steps descended, proving to be those of good
Mr. Briggs, who came ponderously downward, and stood directly in
her path, holding the newel post in either hand.

"Not so fast, my dear lady, not so fast! Let me get it for you. I'm
not so spry on my feet as you are, but my heart is in the right place.
What is it that you want? I'll be very quick."

Miss Yale felt a strong desire to lay violent hands on this amiable
bulk and hurl it from her path, but when benevolence, a sprightly,
teasing spirit and some two hundred pounds combine as an ob-
struction, removal is difficult.

She descended to pleading: "Now, Edward Briggs, do let me by!
Laura, can't you persuade him?"

The minutes were flying fast. She heard more steps above and
men's voices. In spite of her distracted conviction that she must get
up to Margaret at any price and warn her, she was still restrained by
the thought that a too wild insistence might arouse at least curiosity.

"Do sit down, Mary!" was all she got out of Mrs. Briggs, from behind the back of Daisy, whose gown she was fastening. And then Dr.
Newcome and Dr. Armstrong appeared above, and came down.

Then did Mr. Briggs withdraw his hands and step aside, his hos-
pitable soul well pleased.

"These are old friends of yours, Miss Yale—you remember our
pleasant summer in Notchville, surely? Dr. Newcome, and Dr. Armstrong—Miss Yale. Such a pleasure, these reunions! Such a pleasure!"

He stood there smiling cordially, rubbing his large hands together,
while Dr. Newcome shook hands warmly—he had always liked Miss
Yale; and Dr. Armstrong was at least urbane in his greeting—which
was more than could be said for her.

Mrs. Briggs was watching rather nervously, but her husband
seemed as pleased as if he had devised a special treat for his friends.
Then Dolly's eager little voice was heard, with soft steps behind her,

and Miss Yale cast an anguished look above, but could not even catch Margaret's eye—she was looking at the child—and they all silently watched the picture of the two descending. Not till they reached the lower landing and turned to face them did she see what was before her.

For one swift instant a shudder ran through her from head to heel; she caught at the newels on either side and stood motionless, a little fixed smile on her lips, her color ebbing. But it was only a second; her eyes never wavered; her cheeks warmed again; she drew Dolly more closely to her and came down serenely.

Miss Yale was dumb, first with sheer terror, then with breathless admiration. Daisy and her mother came forward to make introductions, but Mr. Briggs anticipated them all.

"Let *me* have the pleasure, Dr. Yale," he cried. "Allow me to present Dr. Henry Newcome, of Boston, and Dr. Dick Armstrong, of the same city. What a fine time all you distinguished professionals will have, to be sure! Talking shop! Talking shop!"

In the back of Miss Yale's mind burned a sudden wish that the Reverend Edward Briggs might be mercifully removed—at once—to a great distance. But Margaret came forward, calmly, graciously, making her graceful foreign little bow, speaking with her scarcely perceptible foreign little accent:

"I have heard of Dr. Newcome's beautiful work with children, and Dr. Armstrong's name is also familiar. But I think I can promise not to talk shop."

She stood there, quiet, queenly, all eyes admiring her, even to Dolly's, whose young heart had been rewon by loving gifts; and then the situation was relieved by the soft, chiming gong.

"Now we'll go to dinner," their hostess announced. "Edward, will you take Dr. Yale? And Dr. Newcome—Miss Yale."

Dr. Armstrong followed with Daisy, and Mrs. Briggs, still anxious lest her friend should be impolite to her possible son-in-law, followed them out.

9. *Developments*

The dinner was an excellent one, but the appetites of the ladies last arrived proved disappointing. Their amiable host, carving lavishly, grieved at their indifference.

"Don't worry them, Edward," his wife protested. "I don't doubt they're too tired to eat. I'm sure I should be."

"That is often the case," Dr. Newcome agreed. "A few days in this air will make a change, though. You've not been here in a long time, Miss Yale, have you?"

Margaret cast a swift, grateful glance at him, but he was looking only at his neighbor.

"Not for several years," she admitted briefly, seeming hardly better able to talk than to eat. Never in her fifty-odd years had she been placed in a position of such sharp anxiety, and if she felt it so keenly, what must it be for her beloved daughter! She watched her with feverish anxiety, yet tried not to appear watching.

Only Daisy was between Margaret and Dr. Armstrong. Miss Yale was opposite, and as she observed the two young women, with that man sitting between Daisy and her mother, a welcome guest, her long-felt sense of horror at ordinary social standards increased momently.

Daisy chattered sweetly, evidently favorably impressed with the young visitor, and Margaret responded with such steady quiet and good cheer that the heart of her adoptive mother lightened somewhat. Mrs. Briggs was studying Margaret; that, Miss Yale had expected. She knew her friend well enough to almost read her mind, and could note with pleasure its guarded approval—approval of the girl's quiet dress, her lack of jewels, her smooth hair that evidently sought to diminish its own beauty. She by no means outshone Daisy, who was particularly well dressed that night, and wore a flush of happiness that was most becoming to her. Neither did the distinguished young woman bear herself with any hint of the honors which had befallen her, nor yet—and here Mrs. Briggs kept careful watch—did she seek in the least to converse with either of the younger men, but devoted herself with gentle courtesy to Mr. Briggs on her left, and to Daisy on her right with real cordiality.

Daisy was unusually brilliant, too, her mother thought; unusually pleasant and gay with Dr. Armstrong and with Dr. Newcome as well; but her mother's satisfaction in this cheerfulness was not wholly unalloyed. Her main concern was with Mary Yale. She had not spoken once to Dr. Armstrong, but then, neither had he to her—it might be an accident. She was occupying herself in the main with Dolly, who sat beside her, and with Dr. Newcome, her other neighbor.

But good Mr. Briggs had no mind to let slip what seemed to him a delightful coincidence.

"To think ten years ago we were all around one table!" said he, smiling broadcast. "That is—all but these young ladies beside me."

Dolly gazed at him seriously over her spoon; Margaret met his eyes with a quiet smile. Miss Yale's heart gave a bound and sank ominously.

"Ten years is a long time," said Margaret, pleasantly. "And have you never been together since?"

"Not all of us, my dear young lady, not all of us. And there was one other—Gerald was with us then. It was a pity we could not ask him in, was it not, my dear?"

"Oh, Gerald understood. He always was a sensible boy," answered Daisy eagerly—too eagerly, her mother thought.

"Ten years ago!" persisted their host, beaming upon them like a well-fed Buddha. "And we were all eating huckleberries together!"

"Did you have huckleberries in Europe, Dr. Yale?" suddenly asked Newcome. "I have heard that the real huckleberry of our New England hills is found only in this country."

Margaret was not sure, but at least she thought he was right; still there were such abundant himmelberreen—and erdberreen——

"And gooseberries in England," Miss Yale broke in firmly. "Such gooseberries as you never saw! I remember a costermonger's cartful—purple and big as plums."

"In northern Siberia," said Dr. Newcome, "up there on the tundra, they have three kinds of berries at once—I forget their names—it's a regular bird boardinghouse. Did you ever hear of that inquisitive Englishman who tracked the migrating birds up there?"

They never had, and he launched forth upon that tale and many others, winning the heartfelt gratitude of two of his hearers, at least.

For an hour that dinner lasted. Margaret continued cheerful and ready; Dr. Newcome kept the conversation well diversified; Daisy, vivacious and friendly, tried to rouse her beloved "Aunt Mary" with affectionate pleasantries; but Dr. Armstrong seemed rather quieter than usual. Mrs. Briggs endeavored to cheer him, and to draw Daisy's attention in his direction, while Miss Yale, in the seclusion of her own mind, kept up a running fight over the incredibility of the situation. She answered questions at haphazard, making little Dolly gurgle in her glass of milk when Mr. Briggs asked how long she had been in crossing and Miss Yale replied tragically: "Ten years!"

Margaret darted a sympathetic glance at her and soothingly added: "I'm sure it seemed ten years to both of us. We had head winds—and something ailed one of the propellers, I believe. Do you enjoy ocean travel, Mr. Briggs?"

Mr. Briggs rejoined at considerable length that he did; that, furthermore, one could enjoy everything if one gave one's mind to it; and, lastly, that it was a duty—one of our chiefest duties—to enjoy life. "Except on occasions like the present," he added blandly, "when enjoyment is so inevitable that it can hardly be called a duty." This remark fell rather flat.

Then Newcome started a defense of Stoicism as against Hedonism, Armstrong in opposition, Daisy hopping from one side to the other with commendable agility, and Margaret partly siding with Armstrong, to Miss Yale's amazement. Around and around in that lady's mind ran the question: "Does he know her?" Generally she applied it to Armstrong, watching him, lynx-eyed; studying every glance, every tone, every gesture; trying to read his thoughts by what he said and what he did not say. Occasionally she turned her searchlight on Dr. Newcome, but he was so steadily cheerful and conversational that he gave her but little anxiety. Now and then the reverend gentleman at the head of the table made some remark that set an unerring finger upon the uneasy center of her thoughts, and she would fix her eyes on him in sudden terror.

But no, he was as bland and calm as a Hindu idol; his well-meant words fell upon spots sensitive and insensitive, guiltless of intention.

Mrs. Briggs was plainly unknowing; that was to be seen even in her evident watch on Margaret. She was not watching her with suspicion, but with the full acceptance of her present place, and a jealous fear lest she prove too attractive.

Daisy was evidently in the clutch of a swift and growing admiration. She listened appreciatively to Margaret's words, and as appreciatively studied her beauty, her changing color that paled and glowed with the shifting talk, her rich hair, her quietly perfect gown.

And Miss Yale, watching her also, caught her breath in aching sympathy again and again, as she saw her sitting there, confronted with all these she had known before in the crisis of her bitter girlhood, with her child, and the father of her child, unknown, at the same table.

It was a terrible dinner—for two, at least—but dragged on to its replete and decorous end. At last Mrs. Briggs rose, pushing back her chair, and they left the men to smoke. With a keen sense of relief the door closed between them; it was only a moment, but that was something.

They spread and moved here and there in the pleasant hall, Daisy still admiringly close to Margaret, while Mrs. Briggs made a place for the coffee tray, and Miss Yale planned for a way of escape. Dolly softly seized a book and sought the shelter of the corner beyond the stair, but without avail.

"Now Dolly," said Mrs. Briggs. "Here's your lump of sugar. Come and get it, my dear."

The child slid from the seat and came forward.

"Be sure and brush your teeth well," pursued the lady, "and then, bed!"

Margaret gave a little start. She had been meaning to go and sit in that corner, too, and continue her siege to the child's heart. "So soon?" she said, in spite of herself.

"Now, Dr. Yale, do not upset the child's excellent habits. It is kind of you, of course—but I must think of her."

"But it is such a pleasure to have her with us." It seemed to Margaret that she could not bear to have that little face look grieved, to have her go.

Mrs. Briggs smiled politely, but remained firm. "Ah!" she replied. "You see you are not a mother—we must think of the child's good."

Miss Yale leaned forward as if to shield Margaret from a blow. "Come, come, Laura! It won't hurt Dolly to sit up a bit longer. This is an unusual occasion. Come here, Dorothy—wouldn't you like to sit up a little longer, just for tonight?"

Miss Dorothy was greatly pleased with the situation. It was tempting to be allowed to sit up for a while longer, but it was also tempting to show how nobly virtuous was her soul. She looked from one to the other and calmly announced: "I'm going to bed. I can go by the clock, even if you don't tell me. And I can undress in *one minute*, if I don't have to wash."

"Good girl!" approved Mrs. Briggs. "You can call Eliza to help you."

"Do let me!" offered Margaret, starting forward. "I'll go with her—I'd love to."

"Oh, not at all," Mrs. Briggs insisted. "It's entirely unnecessary."

"I don't need *anybody*," proclaimed the superior young person from the stairs. "I can do it all myself."

"But you'll let—Margaret come—this time?" Her young mother stood below her, trying to keep her voice quite gentle and steady, and Miss Dolly graciously consented:

"Oh, yes, you can come if you *want* to." She began to ascend, taking two slow steps at a time.

Miss Yale, who had been walking up and down uncertainly, came forward to accompany them, but Margaret's murmured "No, dear—please—I want her so!" held her back. She nodded and stood still, watching the two go up together.

Mrs. Briggs stirred her coffee. "Well, Mary, I am glad to see that you have picked two successes—out of your procession of failures. Though Dolly is young yet to call her a success," she added.

"Why, Mother," Daisy protested, coming to sit on the arm of a big chair and dragging Miss Yale into it. "I'm sure Aunt Mary's Polish musician was very interesting—and that little girl who was so sure she could paint."

"And couldn't! Your mother is right, Daisy. I've made a lot of mistakes. But these two are good enough to make up for it. Margaret alone is."

"She is, indeed! I think she is just *lovely*, Aunt Mary. I like her *immensely*. I don't wonder you're proud of her. But you don't look as happy as you ought to, tonight, seems to me."

Miss Yale sat straighter at this, and laboriously brightened up. "Don't I?" she inquired. "I'm sure I ought to!" and she laughed rather grimly.

"She's tired, of course, Daisy," her mother interposed. "They are both tired. It is a very tiring trip up here—we will all go to bed early."

"I don't think Dr. Yale is tired," the girl persisted. "I never saw anybody so brilliant."

"A very clever young woman, undoubtedly," her mother agreed. "You must remember that she has had a good deal of experience, my dear."

"I wish I'd had some of her experience, then," protested Daisy.

"Time enough, child. You are young yet."

At which Miss Yale promptly responded: "So is Margaret!"

"Oh, well, Mary, you can't compare the two. Daisy has been so sheltered. Of course you have done what you could for Margaret, and done well—very well, indeed; but she was seventeen when you adopted her, wasn't she?"

"Near it," admitted her friend.

"And character is often pretty well formed at that age," Mrs. Briggs pursued. In the back of her mind rose the proverb: "You can't make a silk purse out of a sow's ear," and that horticultural difficulty about figs and thistles which Mr. Burbank had robbed of its terrors, but she did not in the least wish to offend Miss Yale, and neither did she consider Margaret as resembling either the animal or vegetable illustration.

Daisy was still a warm protagonist. "It must have been formed uncommonly well, then. *I* think she's just splendid, Aunt Mary. I'm in love with her already."

Miss Yale at this gave her an approving kiss. "You are a good child, Daisy—you always were. I thought you'd like Margaret—and I know she likes you."

The girl rose from her perch and flitted here and there from window to door.

"Let's come out on the porch for a while," she suggested. "There's a moon coming up—it's going to be lovely."

"Take a wrap, then," urged her mother. "And get one for me and your aunt. Right there in the window seat——"

Miss Yale stopped her. "Not for me," she said. "You two can parade there—I want some more coffee. No, Laura—I'll help myself—I'd rather—go along, do!" She put the shawl around Mrs. Briggs's shoulders and closed the door on them.

"I've *got* to breathe!" she said to herself, stirring her coffee with mechanical precision. "And I've *got* to get hold of Margaret—now's my time!" She set down her cup on the corner of the mantelpiece, and went swiftly but softly to the stairs, but a sound from above arrested her—a sweet and simple sound, low-toned and tender—a mother's lullaby to her child. The tears sprang to Miss Yale's eyes. "Oh, the poor thing!" she murmured. "It's harder when she's with her than when she isn't, I do believe!"

It *was* hard. Margaret had gone up with the sedate child; had tried to help her undress and found her offers disdained. Dorothy was friendly but firm.

"I can do it," she insisted. "I can do it all. I've been able to button and unbutton in the back since I was *five*—don't you remember?"

So her mother sat and watched her hungrily, admiring the erect, vigorous little figure, the neat attire so dexterously wiggled out of and hung upon chairs, and by no means appreciative of the child's evident desire to make a record.

"There!" said Miss Dolly, bouncing into bed with her nightdress still unbuttoned. "I'm in—and it wasn't two minutes, was it?"

It was two minutes and five seconds by the morsel of a watch Margaret had bought her, and she now solemnly wound it, delighted with the faint clicking and the "feel" of the little winder. Her mother showed her how to set it, in case it should happen to stop:

"But you must learn to wind it regularly, dear—every night or every morning—morning is really best."

"Why?"

"Because we get up at about the same time, but we go to bed more irregularly. Still you go to bed regularly enough, don't you, precious? So you can do it at night. You'll remember better perhaps when you take it off."

"Oh, I forgot!" cried the child, bouncing out of bed again. "Mrs. Briggs makes me say prayers—do I have to?"

Margaret smiled. "Perhaps we'd better while we stay in her home, dear. Is it the Lord's Prayer?"

"That's one—and there's a little one—'Now I lay me.' I can say them both." With a clear precision and evident pride she recited the two, her mother listening, very close to tears. There was so much she wished to do for her little daughter, had wished to do for all these years and never until now had there been any time when she could feel the child was hers. Yet even now she was only "Sister Margaret" to her.

"I have been sick," Dolly volunteered, as she nestled down in her bed again. "Very sick. They brought Dr. Newcome up to see me."

"Did they, darling? That was very kind. What was your sickness, dear? How long? Did you suffer?"

"Oh, it was not—serious," said the child gravely. "They thought it was going to be—serious, but it was not. It was only chicken pox. See this mark—I shall have that always!" She lifted the hair from one temple and showed a tiny dimple of faint white. "Dr. Newcome was very nice," she continued. "I like him very much."

"So do I—if he made you well again, dear Dorothy."

"He said I would get well again anyway," pursued the little one. "But Mrs. Briggs made him stay. She was so afraid it was going to be—serious."

Margaret held one small hand and pressed it to her lips. "I'm so glad it wasn't, dear," she said. "So *very* glad!"

"Now I must go to sleep," announced this paragon of infant virtue, and she shut her eyes in two tight white lines with a pinched fringe of curving lashes in the middle of them.

Margaret could hardly insist on her keeping awake. She sat still, hungrily watching the vivid little face, now brown and healthy again in spite of recent illness, and began to sing in her soft contralto a little German slumber song.

"That's nice," Dolly allowed, flashing sudden starry eyes at her, and closing them as suddenly. "Do it some more."

So Margaret sat, motionless, refusing to think of the trials that awaited her downstairs, feasting her eyes on the quiet, childish face before her, easing her full heart a little by the tender beauty of the song. She heard Miss Yale's step on the stairs presently, and went out softly to meet her, finger on lip.

"She got into bed in two minutes, and went to sleep like a little dormouse," she said triumphantly. "I even tried to keep her awake—and couldn't. Oh—she's so lovely!"

Miss Yale listened with divided attention. Her face was drawn and anxious. "She's a dear child," she said, "but it's *you* that I'm worrying about. I'm so upset that I can't think! What excuse can we make to get away? Of course I never dreamed *he'd* be here! It's awful!"

Margaret softly closed the door of Dolly's bedroom and they moved back toward the stairs.

"It *is* rather more than I expected," she agreed. "We must go down, mustn't we?"

"Not this minute—wait! Laura and Daisy are outside and those men have not come in yet. Thank goodness Edward Briggs is so slow! Here—come into my room for a minute." Miss Yale drew the girl inside and shut the door. "I tried my best to get upstairs and tell you before dinner. It was simply *dreadful* to have you come down like that without a word of warning."

Margaret smiled and lifted her fine head proudly. "As well one time as another," she said. "And really, I do not think he knows."

"Oh, I'm sure he doesn't—not yet, neither of them. But it's a terrible risk—a perfectly impossible situation! Of course we'll have to go away at once—and I confess I don't see how. After they've been so kind to Dolly, too! And Daisy has quite fallen in love with you—I knew she would. Daisy's a nice girl."

"She is a dear girl," Margaret heartily agreed. "A sweet, lovely girl. I am very much drawn to her. . . . Perhaps they will go away," she hazarded presently.

Miss Yale shook her head. "Dr. Newcome was brought up by force, as it were, to see to Dolly, and now he's having his vacation. As for *him*——" (She evidently did not refer to the last male mentioned.) "I'm ashamed to say it, but Laura Briggs has been after him for these ten years—to marry Daisy."

"Marry that child!" Margaret's color rose.

"Child! She's older than you are!" Miss Yale watched her with intense sympathy, wondering just what she was thinking.

"No woman is older than I am," was Margaret's solemn response. After a little she added earnestly, "Surely you won't let that happen. You can stop it!"

"I don't know how," Miss Yale answered slowly. "They both approve of him—her father and mother, I mean."

"Does he—love her?" asked the girl, her face turned away.

"Oh, he makes love to her. He does that to any woman who's on hand. That's his little way. And Daisy's a good deal of a fool, poor child. They've never let her know anything, you see. She may think he means it. Then Daisy's getting on—and her parents' influence— and long association. I'm afraid it's a go—that is, if Laura can make him. After all there's really no reason he should—unless he happens to want to."

Margaret was pondering deeply. "Do you think she loves him?" she asked in a steady voice.

"Oh, I don't know," answered Miss Yale miserably. "I hope not. She may think so. What does a girl like that know?"

"Could she be—happy, with him?" pursued Margaret earnestly.

"Happy!" Miss Yale exploded. "Happy—with that man! Why, he'd ruin her health, dislocate her conscience, and break her heart inside of a year. But child, it's you I'm thinking about. And I'm much too upset to think straight. How can we get out of this soonest—with any decency—that's my question."

Then Margaret rose to her feet. "I mean to stay," she said.

"Stay! Here! With that man!" Miss Yale was bewildered.

"He shall not spoil that dear girl's life if I can help it."

"What can you do, Margaret? You don't mean to *tell* her—surely?"

"Not unless I have to."

"But, child, it will kill you. You may be recognized any minute! The risk! The strain!"

"It is worth it!" said Margaret Yale.

10. *Further Developments*

The Reverend Edward Briggs had at last finished his second fat cigar, and his seventeenth story, to which one of his listeners had offered polite attention, and the other an air of barely repressed impatience; but Mr. Briggs was not sensitive. He rose at last, genially chuckling, and they came back to the hall.

"Very good, Armstrong, very good!" cried Mr. Briggs. "It's just as you say. Well, well, where is our coffee? Ah! Here you are, my dear!"

Mrs. Briggs reentered promptly. "Come in," she called over her shoulder, "come in!"

"Yes, Mother," but Daisy stood for a moment with Margaret and Miss Yale who had come down the outside stair, then entered without them. "They want to stay out for a little, Mama," she said.

"Very well—don't tease them. Everyone is free to do as they like here." Mrs. Briggs seated herself at the little table; put out the alcohol lamp, and poured coffee from the steaming percolator.

Her husband stood by the fireplace, gazing about him with the pleased expression he usually wore after a good dinner—unless the dinner was too good and he knew that he had sinned against the inner man.

"Here, Daisy," continued Mrs. Briggs, with her usual air of being the goddess in the machine, "will you give Dr. Armstrong his coffee? Dr. Newcome, may I trouble you to take this to Mr. Briggs? While the gentlemen drink their coffee you might give us a little music, Daisy— something light and cheerful. Perhaps Dr. Armstrong will sing for us later." Well she knew that Dr. Armstrong was especially proud of his deep baritone and that Daisy was an excellent accompanist.

Then, casting an observant eye on Dr. Newcome, who had disposed of his little cup very promptly and declined more, she inquired if he had seen the article on vivisection in the last *Moderator*. Dr. Newcome had not, and she was unable to rouse any interest on his part, though he came to her side with docility and turned the pages of the magazine for a moment or two.

Then he went to the piano where Miss Daisy was obediently looking over the music, and they fell to chatting of this and that melody, till Mrs. Briggs again begged Dr. Armstrong to give them something. He sang willingly enough, standing squarely on his feet, with a great deal of chest, and strong mouth well-opened, and Daisy followed in delicately perfect agreement, while Dr. Newcome turned the pages.

Miss Yale entered quietly under cover of the music; took a chair by the center table and fixed a disapproving eye on the article Mrs. Briggs had been discussing; presently followed by Margaret, who slipped softly in and seated herself in the window seat at the far corner.

Dr. Newcome turned the last page and strolled across to where she sat. The good Mr. Briggs, casting his eyes in the same direction, presently lumbered after him. Dr. Armstrong, having finished his deep-throated warbling, and paid Daisy one or two of the compliments which always came naturally to his lips in addressing a young woman, left the piano in an unostentatious manner, and made a third in Margaret's corner.

Daisy was quite unconscious of this secession, and turned to her with unfeigned cordiality. "Oh, Cousin Margaret, you've come in! If you are my Aunt Mary's daughter, you're my cousin, surely!" she urged.

"I'm delighted to be called cousin on any ground," Margaret replied, making room for Daisy near her.

Armstrong leaned forward, with his warm, impressive manner. "Might I presume on that and call you 'cousin,' too?"

She met him lightly enough. "I confess I was only thinking of Miss Briggs at the time."

"But one may have many cousins," he urged.

"Yes, one does," Miss Yale broke in dryly. "The more distant the more there are of them." She was quite sure that Armstrong had no suspicion to whom he was talking, and as she watched the beautiful gracious woman, cool, assured, completely mistress of herself, and compared her in her own mind with that poor little "brick blond" of ten years since, ignorant, awkward, at once shy and overbold, she began to feel safer. Yet to see them together was a constant terror to her.

"But some are very near," he pursued, and Margaret sweetly answered: "Yet many whistle in vain. I think one cousin's enough to adopt for an evening."

"Speaking of cousins," said a voice outside, and Daisy sprang to the door and opened it to Gerald Battlesmith.

Mrs. Briggs began to feel ill at ease. Her function with the coffee being ended, and the music having stopped prematurely, she cast about for other means of rearranging the company. It gave her no pleasure at all to see three men apparently contented to exchange light words with Mary Yale's too attractive daughter, and her own evidently contented with the fourth. Gerald was a good boy; she had a high esteem for him; but he would never, never do for Daisy.

She rose cheerfully. "Why do we all sit indoors this lovely evening? If our guests are not too tired I think it would be nice to go to our little summer house on the point—it is only a step. We do not always have as clear a night as this. The moonlight down the valley is entrancing!"

Several of her hearers were willing enough. Dr. Armstrong rose to his feet with a smile, and crooked an elbow. "An admirable suggestion—may I show you this special brand of moonlight, Miss Yale?"

Miss Mary Yale, who had been drawing closer to Margaret, now suddenly took his arm. "Thank you," she said. "You are very kind," and forthwith marched him out of the door.

Newcome and Gerald laughed merrily. "I guess he'll give her her title next time," the latter suggested. "Come on, Daisy."

"My wrap, Daisy," her mother broke in. "And Cousin Gerald—may I trouble you?" She annexed him firmly, while Newcome brought her shawl, and Daisy, piqued, sat down by Margaret.

"I'm not going a step unless we all go," she announced.

But Margaret begged to be excused. "Pray go," she said, "all of you. I am really a little tired and shall hope to find the moon tomorrow night."

"We will stay with you of course, my dear young lady," her host protested.

"Oh, no, Father—do come out. She'd like to be all alone and rest. I know just how she feels. Come on, all of you." And Daisy seized upon her father and Dr. Newcome and bore them away, her mother following with the helpless Gerald.

It was not as Mrs. Briggs would have preferred—but it was better than it had been before.

Margaret was left alone. She sat perfectly still in her corner for a little while. For all her trained strength, her unusual agility, she had the gift of sitting still, the long sweeping lines of her figure as motionless as a statue, the strong, delicate hands quite quiet in her lap. After a moment she rose and moved to go upstairs, but stopped herself, shook her head slowly and came back.

She chose a chair before the dying fire this time, and sat there, still quiet again, gazing steadily into the dull glow of the embers, listening to the soft whisper of dropping ash, and the murmur of the wind in the pines outside.

There was a whirling excitement in Margaret's mind, out of which one dominant idea after another thrust itself into the foremost place. Now it was Dolly, her own sweet little daughter; at last they were together to stay. The child stood out in her memory in a series of pictures, each yearly visit rising clear with its special growth and joy, and each one burnt in past forgetting in the long hungry months between. Always the happiness of being with her had the dark shadow of separation at the end—a shadow that rushed down upon her with growing swiftness as the days passed. Now she could think of her with a sense of peace. They had come home, to their own country, to live, to live together. That was a large contentment. With it was the rebellious thought that even now she could not be acknowledged in her true name—Mother. She could love the child, and win her love, but she could not claim what rightfully was hers. Dorothy thought herself an orphan—spoke of it sometimes—and here the mother's heart ached to claim her and could not. Again she reviewed the reasons, long since established, for holding to this course, and again, with a deep sigh, accepted it as right.

"Why shouldn't I suffer?" she asked herself, with a little wry smile. "I ought to. Anyway—I've got her!"

The meeting with the Briggses she had schooled herself for, and felt an easy confidence in their complete acceptance of her new position. The long years of foreign life, the familiarity with more than one language, the whole range of her experience shielded her in strangeness. Great pains had been taken in training her voice, which is so apt to betray to the ear when the eye is wholly misled, and with that special cultivation, and her careful, exquisite enunciation, there was seldom a trace of the slipshod, slangy, nasal speech of her girlhood.

Then, over her sense of confidence in this complete disguise, suddenly rushed the terror of that moment when she stood on the landing and saw Richard Armstrong not ten feet away. The sturdy strength of all the struggling years behind her was needed then—the instant shutting of the door in the face of emotion, the calling upon every faculty, and the prompt response of disciplined brain and nerves. But she shivered as she thought of it. He did not know her; she was sure of that. She had met his eyes, fairly, again and again; her own glance level and calm, courteous, but not too friendly; his with the same admiring gleam, warm, persistent, she remembered so well and had once found attractive, but without a flicker of recognition. She felt no terror, but a strange distaste.

Gerald Battlesmith had been completely dismissed as an anxiety, on their ride up the mountain. But what of Newcome? Did he? Didn't he? He had been courtesy itself, all interest and admiration for her present place and work, without the faintest hint of knowing more. But nevertheless—did he?

Then the thought of Daisy filled her mind: a sweet, wholesome Boston girl, a little overeducated, but still natural, almost conspicuously simple and girlish in manner and good to look at and to trust. She seemed so attractive to Margaret's eyes that she was ready to believe her so to anyone and felt a genuine terror lest Armstrong should fulfill the mother's evident desire. That he might have done so at any time during those ten years, had he chosen, did not occur to her; or, if it did, vaguely she put it aside with the assumption that Daisy had kept him off.

There was Gerald—if he had his way the girl was safe; and modern mothers have scant powers of coercion. Still Margaret was alarmed for her, and keen to defend.

The door, which stood unlatched, opened behind her, and Henry Newcome entered. She did not hear him, so deep was her abstraction; and he stood quietly for a moment, watching her. Then he latched the door, and, as she turned, remarked:

"Your cousin sent me with a message, Dr. Yale. She says she knows you're tired out, and too polite to admit it; says I'm to tell you—as a prescription, if you like—not to wait up for us; just slip off to bed."

Margaret flushed with pleasure. "How good of her!" she said. "What a dear, thoughtful child!"

He came forward and dropped lazily into one of the large chairs. "She does seem young," he admitted.

"It is so beautiful," pursued Margaret, following her own previous thoughts. "Girlhood growing up naturally, carefree, protected—I do admire it so."

"How about the other kind—yours?" he asked.

Margaret started—in the depths of her heart she started—but outwardly she was still.

"Mine? The 'other kind'?" She turned him a face of simple inquiry. His reply was reassuring enough.

"Yes, the brave, strong, achieving kind. You see I'm in the same profession, and I know a little of the work you've had to do—and the courage it took. There isn't a man of us but would be proud of your record—at your age."

"Oh—*that!*" She could not help the note of relief in her voice, but tried to cover it by a little airy gesture of disparagement.

"Yes, *that*, young lady. And don't you try to underrate it—you're too honest."

"I don't think I underrate it," she answered, quite seriously. "I have worked—but all the same, I do so honestly admire that sweet girlishness!"

He nodded, understandingly. "Yes, but you can't have your cake and eat it too, you know. Dissecting rooms and hospitals take out one's girlishness—and boyishness, too, for that matter."

"Yes," she agreed thoughtfully, her eyes on the ash-topped coals.

His were quietly bent on her as he continued: "But there are compensations, aren't there? I wouldn't be what I was at sixteen again, would you?"

The hand on the other side of her, the one he could not see, clenched tightly, but her face was quite calm as she remarked cheerfully: "Heaven forbid!"

"You're right," he agreed heartily. "You're worth a lot more now than you were then."

This had to be faced as well now as anytime. She turned dear, inquiring eyes upon him, asking:

"How do you know?"

But he replied lightly enough. "Why, anybody is—that isn't a fool. When our little grandmas married at sixteen they weren't half-ripe—just little green apples. Who wants a green apple!"

"Boys seemed to like them," the girl suggested.

"Yes, and a nice pain they get, too. Men can wait."

A silence fell between them. She felt a panic—something must be said. She rushed back to their former topic.

"Why don't men—that is, *a* man—how does it happen that such a sweet girl as Daisy Briggs is not married?"

"There are a great many such sweet girls as that in Boston," he lazily suggested.

She scorned this explanation, and made one of her own. "Perhaps she does not mean to marry."

"Lots of girls do not mean to marry—especially in Boston," he agreed.

"Aren't you rather—caustic?"

"Cauterization is very useful sometimes. But seriously, Dr. Yale, you are tired—even a doctor can see that. Why not take Miss Daisy's tip and slip off to bed?"

Margaret made no move of acquiescence, but rather argumentatively inquired: "Did I seem tired—at dinner?"

"Do you want me to stand up, click my heels together, and make a bow with my whole spinal column with a compliment as long? At dinner you were a sparkling refutation of that old idiocy that women have no sense of humor—and can't tell stories. But then—some temperaments do sparkle when tired—or under a strain."

"You are observing!" said the girl, herself noting keenly his pleasant, strong face.

"Yes, I have to be, you know. You've had a long journey—all this meeting of new faces—and old ones," he added with a whimsical smile.

Margaret did not meet his eyes this time, but coolly inquired: "Which are the old ones?" and held her breath for his answer.

"Well, I don't mean to be rude," he assured her, "but surely Miss Daisy's face is newer than her mother's."

"Oh—yes!" She drew a long breath of relief, and patted her mouth as if it had been a yawn.

"Hadn't you better slip off before they come back?" he suggested again.

"You *are* uncomplimentary! Trying your best to be rid of me!"

"Well—put it that way if you like."

"I won't go!" she said, smiling.

"Still a woman—however much a doctor!" He smiled too—that pleasant, understanding smile of his.

"Well, aren't you still a man—however much a doctor?" she flashed back at him.

"Why not?"

"And why not, too—or either?" she insisted.

"Or both," he contributed, laughing. "This is getting too subtle for me—— Ah, here's Armstrong!" And to himself he added: "I'm not surprised."

Dr. Armstrong did seem surprised to see him, however, and not overpleased. "You like sunlight better than moonlight—eh, Newcome?" he suggested. "So do I, Miss Yale."

"It must be a very poor light," Margaret replied, "for you will persist in confusing me with my adoptive mother."

"I beg pardon—Dr. Yale." He bowed impressively. "Or, Miss Margaret Yale, M.D."

"Very well—Mr. Richard Armstrong, M.D."

"She has my name already. I am complimented."

"Why not?" she answered quickly. "It is a well-known one."

Again he bowed. "Honored, I'm sure."

Newcome looked from one to the other and shook his head, smiling. "'And she began to compliment, and he began to grin!'"

Armstrong was a little nettled. "Nobody ever'll accuse you of complimenting, Newcome."

"No," said Newcome calmly, "they don't."

Margaret watched them, sensitive, observant; her nerves keyed tensely again from the moment of Armstrong's entrance. With the other she felt more at ease in spite of his having repeatedly touched so near the hidden groundwork of her thoughts. She gave him a friendly look.

"They like you nonetheless, I'm sure."

"Who are 'they'?" Armstrong inquired, jealously.

"Sensible women, of course," she replied.

"Oh!" he waved her adjective aside. "Who wants sense in a woman?"

"That's a lovely compliment," drawled Newcome. "Which end will you take, Dr. Yale?"

Margaret seemed to consider the question. "I think I'll take the one most pleasing to my self-esteem—that Dr. Armstrong does not want me."

Newcome chuckled. "You're up against it, Armstrong! Let's see how you'll crawl out."

"There's no need for crawling," he answered, unabashed. "I'll boldly state that the answer to my conundrum is: I do!"

"Bravo!" cried Newcome. "Cleverly done! How do you meet that, Dr. Yale?"

"I do not meet it at all," she replied, a little distantly.

"Do!" urged Armstrong. "Meet it halfway!"

Newcome lifted his lean height from the lounging chair.

"I have done my errand," he said, turning to Margaret. "Shall I tell Miss Daisy you are not as tired as you were?"

She smiled up at him. "Tell her—more so!"

"Oh, cruel!" cried Armstrong. "But of course you must be weary from your journey. Let me make you more comfortable. Sit in this chair, do—with the cushion—and your feet here—on this stool. Rest now—and let me amuse you."

She rose graciously and took the place he offered, placidly remarking: "You do, already."

Newcome stood at the door with a little quizzical smile. "Got the spotlight ready, Armstrong? I'll try the moonlight again." And he went out.

Margaret leaned back among the cushions, quiet and serene, her still face showing nothing of any thought or feeling that might be within. Armstrong watched her admiringly.

"He may have his moonlight—I will bask in the sun," he said, with a seriocomic air, and arranged himself on the long rug before the fireplace.

She watched him guardedly. His manner might mean anything or nothing—she was accustomed to admiration and to its sudden exhibition. His rather melodramatic intensity, his freedom of attitude, contrasted far from favorably with several years of not unpleasant memories. He seemed to her as somewhat strained and overblown, too long accustomed to his part, and she marveled, as many a woman had done before, that even in her starved and stunted youth she could have found in him an overwhelming charm. A sense of power and security rose in her, seeing him there before her, so near, and feeling nothing, not even dread of discovery.

"You are astonishingly graceful, Dr. Armstrong——" she began.

"Thank you," he interrupted.

"For a man of your years," she calmly finished.

"My gratitude was premature, I see. Yet, even as modified, I am thankful to please you."

"You must keep pretty constantly in practice—to do it so well."

"Practice?" he looked up at her inquiringly.

"Yes, lying about on rugs, in well-composed attitudes."

"It is my daily habit," he agreed, disarmingly. Then, studying her face, he asked wonderingly: "How have you managed it?"

"Managed what?"

"To go through all those weary studies and remain so beautiful."

"For a woman of my years?"

"I do not qualify my tribute," he assured her.

"And do you, as a daily habit, make these unqualified tributes to a stranger on an hour's acquaintance?"

"I cannot think of you as a stranger," was his answer.

Her heart jumped for a second, but she spoke calmly:

"No? Why not?"

He gazed upon her earnestly. "Because you are so like—so like——"

She met his eyes. Was it coming? Now? No; it was admiration she saw there, not recognition. "Well—like whom?" She held her breath.

"Like my Ideal!" quoth Dr. Armstrong, devotedly.

Margaret laughed outright. Across her mind flashed a picture of a certain dark Italian of noble lineage, who had so lain at her feet one summer evening—but whose conversation was on quite another plane. Also of a fellow student, a young Spaniard, the exquisite, finished grace of his devotion. And Armstrong did not lack for practice, surely!

"Well, well, Dr. Armstrong! A man of your reputation—with ideals!" Perhaps she laid a shadow too much emphasis on the words.

"What do you mean by 'my reputation'?" he asked.

But she replied pleasantly: "Aren't you one of the most eminent gynecologists in America?"

He smiled relievedly. "Oh—you do me too much honor!"

"No——" she slowly answered. "I don't think I do." But this time her voice was quite smooth and he felt no undercurrent of meaning.

"As you please," he said. "Only do not think that I speak to all women as I speak to you."

"I suppose," she mischievously suggested, "that even with your wide experience you have not met all women."

He did not in the least relish being made fun of by a handsome woman; he was not used to it.

"My experience?" he repeated inquiringly.

"Yes—experience. An eminent gynecologist has to have wide experience among women, doesn't he?"

"Professionally, yes," he agreed. "But it does not by any means follow that he is experienced in affairs of the heart."

This she admitted: "No—but—it sometimes precedes."

"How brilliant you are, Miss Yale. Never with all my 'experience' have I met with such wit—such humor—or such eyes!"

She began to be sorry for him—he played so badly—and foolhardily replied, looking straight at him:

"I am sure you must have seen just such eyes."

"Never in my life!" he protested. "Nor have I heard so rich and soft a voice."

Again she tempted fate. "Now, really, Dr. Armstrong, you must have heard just such a voice."

"Never," he protested. "Is it possible that you do not realize the unusual charm of your voice?"

They heard steps now; the others were returning, Daisy laughingly offering to see Gerald home, and being promptly taken at her word. Her mother cried after her that it was more than bedtime, but Miss Yale remarked that Daisy was certainly old enough to know when to go to bed—and further, that *she* was, in any case, and departed upstairs at once.

The days that followed were strange ones to Margaret. She grew more and more attracted to Daisy's simple sweetness and quiet strength.

"It's a shame that girl has not been allowed to do something," she told Miss Yale. "There's plenty of time yet—I know she would be happier."

"She won't be happy, to my mind, unless she marries that young Battlesmith," her friend answered. "I guess we made a mountain out of a molehill about Dr. Armstrong. 'You can lead a horse to water but you can't make him drink!' And he doesn't know you from Adam, Margaret. We might as well have our visit out—if you can stand it."

Margaret said she could stand it perfectly—that she was even enjoying it. She seemed in truth to derive a certain satisfaction from the complex possibilities around her, her confidence growing as the days passed; and her continued acceptance in her new character made it more unlikely that the old one would ever be recognized.

She spent long, happy days with Dorothy, walking on the steep mountain roads, picking blackberries and raspberries and thimble berries—though Dolly declared she did not like the last at all. "They taste like pink flannel," she said. In sheltered spots some huckleberries were left and the child was eager to show her the best places and to fill her little pail. This, too, was a pleasure to Margaret. No years of foreign fruit could obliterate her fondness for huckleberries. The very sound of the black shining stream of them as they poured thumping into the pan, their bobbing ebony spots in the bowl of milk, their endless deliciousness in cornbread and gingerbread, muffins, griddle cakes, puddings and pies—she could not have enough of them! And blueberries, too: little thick ground blueberries that knocked against her feet; big spreading thickets where one might sit for hours and pick quart after quart; and the very tall swamp bushes that one had to reach up to, with huge blue halls hanging overhead. She remembered the berries of her childhood's hills as lovingly as she hated balsam fir.

They grew very friendly together, little Dorothy and her "big sister"; but the child always seemed to draw the line at a certain depth of affection, or any note of authority. It was hard to tell what was going on in her youthful mind; but she evidently had firm ideas of her own as to the conduct appropriate to various degrees of relationship.

Dr. Armstrong sought Newcome's room one night, too full of new emotion to sleep. He was greeted hospitably and offered a chair, but waved it aside, and clapped his friend upon the shoulder with stinging emphasis.

"By all the Prophets, Newcome—I'm hard hit this time!"

Newcome turned and regarded him whimsically, rubbing his shoulder, and remarking: "So am I!"

Armstrong looked at him with sudden jealous suspicion, then laughed at his rueful face. "That's the only kind of shock you seem to feel, old man. But by all the Graces and Muses—*what* a stunner she is!"

Newcome agreed with an unenthusiastic "Um—hm," which by no means satisfied his friend.

"You old iceberg!" he rejoined. "Whatever has got into you? Anybody'd think you were ninety-five instead of thirty-five. How any man can look at that woman and not fall in love with her on the instant, I don't see. Such hair—such color—such a shape!"

"Such brains! Such courage! Such achievements!"

"Oh, hang the achievements! What do I care for achievements? She's a lovely woman—the loveliest I ever saw!"

His friend regarded him with quiet amusement, at least that was all that showed in his expression. "I thought you didn't approve of women doctors," he said.

"I don't," Armstrong retorted. "A woman is a woman, and that's enough. Anything beyond that makes her ridiculous."

"But it is a woman doctor you are speaking of so highly—isn't it?"

"Just the foolishness of youth, Newcome—nothing better to do. She'll outgrow it." With which sage pronouncement Dr. Armstrong seated himself in the most comfortable chair and lit a large cigar.

"She's been some time in growing it, Armstrong. Do you really imagine she would give up her profession even if she—married? No—I won't smoke, thank you."

"Give it up? Certainly—like a shot!" said the other. "As soon as she falls in love. Any woman would—that *is* a woman." He puffed a little, and added soberly: "What merciful power has kept her from it all these years and brought her to me, I don't know. But I'll take advantage of my opportunity, I assure you—and ask no questions."

"Questions? About what?"

"About anything," Armstrong continued. "Of course no woman of her splendid beauty could reach twenty without lovers in plenty—and she must be twenty-five, you see—by her record. I judge," this he put forth most seriously as one past master in the secrets of the feminine heart, "I judge she's had some early heartbreak or other—and renounced marriage. A girl will do that you know—and mean it too. It doesn't generally last so long, but then she might have been hard hit. Chap died, I imagine. No man alive could have left her. And to think of that lovely creature wasting all these years in this professional foolishness——"

"Her record is not a foolish one, Armstrong."

"Not if it were a man's, of course, Newcome—but anything's foolish for a woman except what the good Lord made her for. Well, she's been mercifully preserved, that's all I can say!"

"Mercifully preserved for you?" Newcome's tone was close to sarcasm, but it passed unnoticed. Armstrong's nature was not subtle. He was a straightforward, self-indulgent, powerful man, and such deeps as he possessed were now genuinely stirred.

"Perhaps!" he agreed seriously. "By heavens, Newcome, it may be. I never felt like this before."

Newcome leaned back his head and smiled broadly. "I've often heard you say so before," he remarked.

"Oh, of course—of course—I know that," Armstrong admitted, getting up and moving about the room. "I've been in love no end of times—that's nothing! This is different, I tell you. You never heard me talk of marriage on a week's acquaintance before—did you?"

This was freely admitted. "No, I can't say I did. But I've seen you raving about in much the same way—lots of times. There was that little Sayles girl——"

"Oh, pshaw! Lasted about three months!" Armstrong waved away the little Sayles girl as if she had never existed.

"Well, how about La Corona?"

This seemed to touch a more vital spot, for Armstrong paused and took a chair again, smiling a little. "Yes, I had it bad that time, didn't I? But bless me—every man I knew, almost, was gone on her."

"And Mrs. Bergsmith——" pursued his tormentor.

"She was a stunner, wasn't she?" admitted Armstrong.

"And a whole train I've forgotten the names of," Newcome persisted. To which his friend cheerfully added:

"I have too. Come, now, Newcome, don't bother about them. That's not the same thing and you know it."

But Newcome was not to be diverted. He went on in an even voice, his eyes on Armstrong's face: "Then there was that little rawboned, red-haired girl in Notchville that summer—what ever became of her?"

Armstrong sprang to his feet, and paced the chamber, evidently distressed. "God knows——" he said. "She ran away, I guess. Maybe drowned herself—they said so up there."

"Took it hard, didn't she?" his friend suggested, but the other retorted angrily:

"You shut up, Newcome! I'll admit you were right about that young one. I ought to have let her alone. But hang it all. There wasn't anybody else around—and she was *such* a greenhorn. I sent her money. I meant to take care of her, of course—but she sent it back. I was awfully sorry about her—really."

"I should think you would have been," said Newcome quietly.

"What in Hades set you to dragging up all this ancient history, anyway? Confound you, Newcome, keep your ghosts to yourself, will you? There's an end of all that foolishness for good now. This woman I mean to marry."

He relit his cigar, which had languished during these unwelcome reminiscences, and smoked valiantly. His friend gazed at him in a sort of admiration of his single-heartedness. "Maybe she'll turn you down," he quietly suggested.

"Maybe she will—but she'll be the first woman to resist Dick Armstrong—when he's made up his mind!"

"I always did admire your intellect, Dick."

"Oh, come, Newcome, don't be a lemon. You're a mighty good fellow and I've liked you too long to quarrel with you, but what are you rubbing it in for? Casting up my diversified past at me like this! You've had your own little episodes, but I never fling 'em at your head."

Newcome was leaning forward, his elbows on his knees, his eyes on the floor. "Yes—I suppose most men have tried a little hell. But when they see heaven they wish they hadn't."

"All men, Harry, all men—unless something ails 'em. But they're not sorry—why should they be? It's nature."

Newcome turned upon him, serious in face and voice. "Aren't you sorry now, Dick?—when you do really love at last? When you see the woman you want to make your wife?"

"No," said Armstrong shortly, rising to his feet. "I'm not. I never was at the time, and I'm not now. I'm sorry for that poor little tyke up in the country, of course, but for gathering roses while we may— never!" He walked about excitedly. "And now! Now! Why, everything I ever did—every other woman in the universe—every other memory is blotted out in this blaze of glory—this great, splendid, full-blooded woman! All light and fire and honey! I'll have her or I'll know the reason why!"

"I guess you will," said Newcome, quietly.

"Well, confound you for a clam, Newcome! The moon's more cordial than you are, tonight. I'll go outdoors for company!" Armstrong took himself off for a tramp in the hills, the large yellow harvest moon shining down upon him, his heart full of the lift and splendor of the deepest passion he had ever known.

Newcome stood at his window for a while, watching the sturdy figure swing along among the vivid black and white lights and shadows. He turned at length and paced softly up and down, his head bent low. Then, sitting down at last beside the lamp, he drew out a pocket case, such as a man carries for photographs of sweetheart, wife or child. In this was no picture; only some newspaper clippings, and a faded and creased piece of blue ribbon—that uncompromising blue so often chosen to decorate red hair. He turned it over in his hand, looked at the little "airtight" stove, and drew out his matchbox.

Then he put the matchbox away again, tenderly smoothed out the big blue bow, and put it carefully back in the case.

"I don't know," he said quietly to himself. "I don't know as there's any harm in my keeping this much!"

11. *Various Efforts*

Margaret Yale had a clear head, and she needed it. She had steady nerves, a trained mind, a strong, practiced will, a healthy body; she needed them all in the remaining days of that visit in the Adirondack hills.

Those blue distances and green foregrounds, the cool gloom of the forest, the heat of the stony roads and stonier pastures, the sights and sounds and smells of the place, brought to mind the experiences of her youth in a bewildering way. She was haunted as by a dual personality, an unwelcome intruder, bringing back the crude longings, the fierce sensitiveness, the limitations of her uncared-for youth. She found herself aware of feelings which she knew were not her feelings now, but shamefacedly remembered as having been her feelings once.

To this confusing and undesired rejuvenescence was added the sense of being a person in a play, as she moved, undetected, among all those who had known her before, and now seemed so utterly unaware of it. She had soon grown quite calm concerning the others, but with Armstrong there was always the astonishment that he did not remember; she had even sometimes an impish temptation to test his complete forgetfulness. And of Newcome she was not quite sure; still he never alarmed her, and though she saw comparatively little of him, he seemed to extend an atmosphere of calmness and goodwill that was very restful. Then, sufficient in itself to try any woman's strength, was that bittersweet campaign in which she pressed on ardently, yet with patience—the wooing of her own child's heart.

What love for a mother that calm young person had felt went first to Julie, for whom she still grieved at times, and second to her adoptive parent. Miss Yale she had always known as a sort of fairy godmother, hovering on the outside of her life, sending delightful presents, showering kindnesses on everybody. To cross the ocean and be with her to live, to be the adopted daughter of this high beneficence was a far more prominent fact in Dolly's mind than the coming of this grown-up foster sister.

But Margaret showed a patience beyond her years, far beyond the swift, embracing love with which she so desired to engulf the child. Hers was a hunger unknown to most mothers, a stored, accumulated hunger, a hunger that had unconsciously absorbed such other longings as these growing years might else have known. The self-reproach which she bore always within gave a desperate bitterness to her longing. Most mothers regard their children with fond pride, and a pleasant sense of duty done; but Dorothy stood, to Margaret, almost in the light of an accuser. She knew that she had robbed her, robbed her own child, of a home, a father, a name and place among other children, and even of a mother—to the child's knowledge.

Again and again her whole nature rose in fierce demand. She would claim the child as hers, face the world with her, force a place for them both. Then she would relentlessly look at the facts again, see how long and hard would be that struggle, not only for herself— she would welcome it—but for the little one. For the child's sake, for her home, her education, her associates, her ultimate marriage—her mother must pay the price. It would be no kindness to Miss Yale, to whom they both owed more than life, either to leave her, robbed and alone—or to force upon her problems she had not chosen.

So Margaret, with her aching mother's heart, remained the foster sister, and laid siege to Dorothy's young affections with careful skill. She must not go too far—too fast. Dorothy must never know she was being wooed. She must tempt—withdraw—be always kind, but not always within reach. So she took part in the mild gaieties of the household, and went walking and climbing with the others when she would have far preferred to be seeking flowers or berries with the little one. She would not hunt, though in a bout of pistol practice Armstrong got up for amusement, she showed astonishing proficiency.

"I pity the burglar when you wake up!" he said admiringly.

"Why so?" she asked him.

"I doubt his recovery," he assured her, with evident intent to compliment. But she only suggested:

"There is no death penalty for burglars, is there?" and continued to perforate their impromptu target with close-grouped dots of black.

They all praised her, but she laughed it off.

"That was all acquired in a season in Paris," she said. "It took a great deal of time, really, and I doubt if I shall ever need to use it."

"Did you learn to fence?" Daisy asked her. "I thought in Paris everybody learned fencing. I always wanted to."

"Yes, I took fencing lessons," she said, "and dancing lessons, too. There was so little real exercise to be had, you see."

Armstrong could fence, and fence well. He was more than anxious to prove his proficiency in her eyes, mastery if possible. Keeping his own counsel, he sent for his foils and masks. It annoyed him more than he liked to admit that she shot so much better than he.

"Why should you care?" Newcome demanded, amused at his continued grumblings. "A pistol is a woman's natural weapon, I think—a little lady-gun, just as sure to kill as a cannon, and much easier to carry. If they only knew it they might have been safe from all dangerous males ever since pistols were invented."

"Well, they're not," said Armstrong. "They're afraid of firearms—and they ought to be. It's natural."

"I don't think it's natural at all," maintained the other. "It's purely artificial—all this nonsense about female timidity. You don't see any timidity in a lioness, or a bearess, or any of those females. I think it's great to see Dr. Yale shoot—she does it so unconsciously."

"Pity she doesn't hunt," mused Armstrong, examining his gun. "It seems inconsistent."

"Oh, I don't know," said his friend. "She says she's willing to kill lions and tigers and things like that, if it is necessary, but she doesn't see the fun in killing little beasts that can't kill you—and don't even want to! What's more she won't fish. That leaves me out. But she certainly plays tennis well enough for two."

She played well enough to beat either of them, and this also was galling to Armstrong. He was highly skilled in many lines, not often bested by men and never before by a woman.

They played whist in the evenings, Miss Yale stoutly refusing to learn bridge; and again Newcome admired and Armstrong winced under Margaret's strong play. If she played with him they beat the others, and he was happy; if she played against him, he needed the best of cards and all his skill to save his game. From whist to tiddledywinks, which was Dolly's favorite, into which she always strove to inveigle her elders, Margaret played better than any of them.

Armstrong could not keep away from her. She had always some easy reason for not going off with him on any separate tramp or excursion, but he was near her for some part of each day and evening, and the more he saw of her the more intense grew that fierce desire for ownership, that overmastering hunger, which was his variety of love. If she had been weaker he might have felt a gentler affection, but she seemed armed at every point. Precisely because of his growing love he could not bear to have her master him, even in a child's game. He wished to help her, serve her, guard and protect her; he wished her to turn to him for strength, to lean on him, look up to him, admire him. She was quite kind and civil always, but he made no headway with her, and with her every easy victory in the small sports he felt as if he was losing ground instead of gaining it.

"I believe you would play a good game of chess, my dear," predicted Mr. Briggs, one evening, looking across the table admiringly, as they finished a triumphant rubber together. "I think there are some chessmen about. Armstrong and I used to play, I think—didn't we, Armstrong?"

Armstrong agreed that they did, years ago. Daisy obligingly hunted out the men and found a checker board. The Reverend Edward was reduced to smiling extinction very promptly.

"It's no use, my dear. I see you are far beyond me in this game. Time was when I could have made a better defense—been more worth your while. Come on, Armstrong, let's see you hold your own with her—if you can!"

Miss Yale stood by with keen enjoyment, quiet, but hotly interested, when Armstrong and Margaret sat down to their first game of chess one rainy afternoon. She could read his feelings fairly well, though unsympathetically. Only Newcome, glancing across from the long chair where he was reading, made pitying allowance for the double strain. He knew that that firm, delicate hand, hovering a moment, but never touching till the move was settled, then making the swift step, and snapping up a piece or pawn maybe, without touching or upsetting any other was more interesting than the game to her opponent. Armstrong forgot his plans in watching her broad, smooth brow, the shining satin and soft cloud of her rich hair, the dropped eyes, warm color, and serious, sweet mouth. His mind was haunted too by scraps of poetic memory about such scenes—"white hands among the ivory men astray," and bits like that. He was in no fair condition to play chess, but when she presently mated him, the blood flushed to his hair in angry surprise; he steadied himself and played better. When she mated him again he grew white about the lips; his pride rose and gripped him; even love was lost for the moment in the fierceness of conflict. He set his whole mind upon the game, played coldly, slowly, brilliantly—but she beat him the third time.

"It's not the game, merely," he explained to the patient Newcome that night. "I've been beaten, of course—I'm not such a hard loser. But, hang it, Newcome, to be beaten by a woman—and the woman I love!"

"I should think you'd be proud of her," his friend assured him, "glad and proud because she's so capable. She certainly is a wonder, that girl!"

He shook his head, meditating inwardly on the strain she was under, too, in all these days. But Armstrong was unable to be quiet:

"I'm out of practice," he protested. "I haven't played a game of chess—with anybody worthwhile—in years. Briggs doesn't count. And then, a man's at a deuced disadvantage when he's in love. And she knows it!"

Newcome glanced at him. "She played a very steady game, I noticed," he said soberly. "No 'nods and winks and wreathed smiles' about it."

"Oh, no, of course not—nothing so apparent. Trust a woman for not showing her hand. But I'll beat her yet!" He set his heavy jaw in utter determination. The instinct of the hunter was strong within him; the fire of battle seemed now added to the conflagration already existing.

Newcome was minded to give him a sharp warning, but remembered Margaret's repeated victories and thought better of it. He was minded then to joke a bit about it, but glanced at Armstrong's fierce, set face, and thought better of that, too.

Good Mr. Briggs, always kind, took a lively interest in these con-
flicts, and became a staunch upholder of Margaret's record against
all comers. His wife, while polite and congratulatory, showed no
such pleasure in her young guest's abilities; but told Daisy in private,
in answer to her rapturous acclaim, that she was really glad she,
Daisy, was not a phenomenon.

"In any case she does not compare with you in music, or in art,
my dear."

"Why, mother! I'm not jealous of her! I simply admire her beyond
words. And she's so nice about it. She hasn't ever tried to get up any
of these trials—it's always Dr. Armstrong. He likes to overcome anybody or anything, I think. It's lots of fun to see somebody overcome
him."

Her mother glanced at her sharply from under the scant tail of
hair she held firmly in one hand upon her crown, and brushed down
frontwards over her bent head. But Daisy showed no more pique
about Armstrong than about Margaret, and Mrs. Briggs heaved a
faint sigh behind the gray cascade.

"Gerald says she's a wonder—he never saw anybody like her," the
girl went on happily. "That she's as gentle and sweet as a woman
need be, and yet so tremendously able."

Again Mrs. Briggs glanced shrewdly at her daughter, but she
seemed not even jealous of Gerald, whereat her mother took hope.
That hope was baseless; Daisy was too sure of her cousin's long-
established affection to mind his praise of any passing wonders. The
two had had opportunity to settle many questions this summer,
among others the question of time.

"I've had such a good talk with Newcome, Daisy," Gerald had told
her, one quiet afternoon in the deep shadowy ravine. "He knows how
I'm situated and how long I've cared for you, and he asked: 'What are
you waiting for?' I told him about Mother, of course, and he said:
'Look at Hank Haines—do you think it is right that he should have
sacrificed not only his own life but some nice girl's just to gratify that
domineering old creature?' I was a little offended, but he said of
course he didn't mean that Mother was like that, but that all of us
children were grown up now, and she was only about fifty and quite
healthy. 'Why doesn't she do something for herself now?' he said.
And what's more, do you know he actually wrote to Mother and put
it to her—she thinks a lot of him, you know—and she said she'd be
glad to—always had wanted to—but was afraid the boys wouldn't
like it. And he wrote her another of his jolly letters and told her she
was free, white and twenty-one—she sent the letters to me—and

Daisy—she's going to! She's going to take boarders in summer, and she says she can make enough to come into Boston in winter and see and hear something."

"I think Dr. Newcome is just splendid!" Daisy told him. "I like him tremendously."

"More than you like me, Daisy?"

"Well, I don't know," she replied, looking at him with unexpected mischief in her soft eyes. "I only said 'like,' you know."

After which there was a pause in the conversation.

"Do you think you can live at all comfortably on a teacher's salary, dear?" he asked, and she told him she would rather live uncomfortably on a teacher's salary than luxuriously on a broker's.

"It's such noble work, Gerald—the very highest in the world. Even doctors are only tinkers, you see, but teachers *build!*"

Daisy was quite in earnest in her admiration, and together they announced their intentions to her parents. Her father was well pleased. He was fond of Gerald, and not fond of Richard Armstrong; also he felt that his little girl would be quite safe with her cousin. Mrs. Briggs received the news with as good a grace as she was able to muster, and, in spite of her disappointment, with a certain vague relief. She liked Gerald, too, in her heart, and, after all, Daisy was twenty-eight.

Miss Yale highly approved. "My best congratulations to both of you young people. You show good sense, Daisy; I always thought you had it. And if you never do anything better than lead several thousand boys in the right direction, Mr. Battlesmith, why that's a very commendable job."

To Margaret, harried and strained in her maze of feelings, this union was pure joy. Her fondness for Daisy was genuine, and she was relieved and glad to watch her quiet happiness. To see the light and wonder of their love shining across the broad base of friendship and long acquaintance gave her a pleasure so keen that it hurt, hurt in unavoidable contrast with her own strange case.

Newcome jested with them both in pleasant fashion, but Armstrong seemed vaguely to resent any man's winning any woman while he, Armstrong, was still unsatisfied. He paid fierce court to Margaret, so that she began to look forward eagerly to the visit's approaching end.

When the foils arrived Armstrong said nothing of his plans at first, but got Newcome to practice with him, early and late, getting home with his thudding button triumphantly. Daisy and Gerald came upon them one morning, stamping and lunging, with the rustling clash of steel, and the girl exulted hugely.

"Oh!" she cried. "Now we'll get Margaret to try—I do so want to see her fence."

Margaret, when found, declined. She was not fond of fencing— she had no costume—she much preferred to watch. Daisy's gymnasium suit was promptly offered, and Newcome, watching, wondered whether he had better "fall upon his sword" in such wise as to break it, or if she really did object to the trial. Miss Yale appeared, brisk and interested, and rather urged her on. "You're a fine fencer, Margaret, and you know it. Why not show us?" And Mr. and Mrs. Briggs came bustling up, she politely disapproving, he profoundly impressed and eager for the fray.

"Just the thing! Just the thing!" he cried. "I see that Newcome is no match for you—eh, Armstrong?"

Armstrong stood quietly, bending the foil, its button against his shoe.

"I'm quite at Dr. Yale's service," he said. "It will be an honor to cross swords with her—but of course if she does not wish to——" His eyes met hers, longing, dominant, fiercely desirous, and his firm lips wore a little close-held smile.

Then came a flying patter of little feet along the turf, and Dorothy burst upon them. "Is it a duel—a real duel?" she cried delightedly.

"Not a bit of it, Dollykins," said Newcome, swinging her to his shoulder. "I've been standing here and letting Dr. Armstrong punch holes in me, and now they want Dr. Yale to take my place."

Dolly, from on high, surveyed the scene proudly.

"Do it, sister," she commanded. "Please do it! And punch holes in him! You can!"

Whether it was the child's wish, or Armstrong's repressed smile, or sheer desperation among the conflicting impulses within her, Margaret suddenly agreed to try. She went off with Daisy, promptly reappearing in blouse and knickers, firm and light of foot, swift, graceful, sure. She scorned to make apologies, but Miss Yale had forestalled her in her absence.

"The girl hasn't touched a foil in a year to my knowledge," she explained. "So if our friend here does get in on her, there's plenty of excuse. But I'm not worried about *that*——"

Armstrong could not for the life of him have told whether love or rage was strongest in him. His cool opponent, her face hidden by the wires, her dress unfamiliar, her attitudes and action precisely those with which he was used to combat, seemed in no way the woman he loved, but an enemy. The presence of Gerald Battlesmith, that happy lover, and of Daisy, whom he long had thought of as his if he chose to ask, Mr. Briggs's friendly jeers, Miss Yale's relentless scrutiny, even little Dorothy's clapped hands and "Hit him, Margaret—hit him!"— wrought him to a furious determination. His wrist was strong, his eye keen, his foot steady, and he pressed fiercely to the attack.

But ten years of youth and clean habits count much in fencing, and while Margaret had no recent practice, she had had four seasons of it under the best teachers in Europe. If he was hot, she was cold; that still, concentrated mastery which held her hand firm when another life trembled beneath it held it now. She also felt that more was at stake than appeared, and gave her whole mind to the affair. She touched him once, and he paled under the light pressure. He touched her, and a dark flush rose to his face. Then there were a few breathless moments, the steel playing like fireworks between them, and then, with lightning swiftness and a wiry clatter, he stood disarmed, looking in dumb amazement at his fallen weapon.

She stood at attention, waiting for him; but Armstrong, without a word, walked over to his foil, broke it across his knee, and tossed the pieces into the ravine.

"Congratulations, Dr. Yale," he said in a somewhat strained voice, bowed to the group and walked away among the trees.

They were all silent but Dolly, who rushed to the victor and threw her arms about her in keen delight.

"I knew you would! I knew you would!" she cried in triumph. "You dear, splendid sister!"

Margaret looked down at the little face turned up at her with such rapturous admiration, and her lip quivered. She stooped to kiss the child, and turned toward the house with her. Newcome picked up the masks and foil, and followed silently. They all drifted back, trying with pleasant chatter to cover Armstrong's behavior.

"I'm astonished at him," persisted Mr. Briggs. "To be such a bad loser! I'm sure it's an honor—" he made a courtly bow to Margaret, "to be beaten at such hands."

"You surely are a wonder!" Gerald told her. And Daisy cried:

"Oh, I'm so *glad* you did it, Margaret—I'm so glad!"

But Margaret was not glad. She walked as one in a dream, a bad dream that grew more and more oppressive. That she should fight with the man she once had loved, with their child crying her on to the assault—it was too dreadful.

"Cheer up, my dear girl," Miss Yale urged that night. "We're going Saturday. *He* goes tomorrow I understand—'called away suddenly'— good thing! I guess you've seen the last of him, my dear. We'll have one restful day on the mountain, and then—home!"

But Margaret did not cheer up. She felt no elation. Dorothy's innocent triumph in her victory seemed almost wicked. He was her father.

She could not sleep that night.

Across the tangled web of feeling in which she found herself, a new thread was weaving itself from day to day, of a color so pure and brilliant that all the rest looked soiled and dim, a beautiful but inharmonious thread that matched with nothing there.

She drowsed at last, and fell to dreaming in terms of the same metaphor, seeing herself vainly trying to mend a terrible rent in a fair robe with that bright thread, and finding it tear out of the old cloth and leave a gap greater than before.

They were to climb Mount Huykill the next day, an easy trip, to which Dolly had looked forward with lively enthusiasm.

"I can walk all I want to," she explained to Margaret. "And when I'm tired I can ride on the donkey—and if I get *awfully* tired Dr. Newcome will carry me—won't you, Dr. Newcome?"

The excursion up Mount Huykill had been postponed to wait the full moon, and to this last day on account of previous cloudy weather, for the exhibition was to give them not only a view into Canada and across Lake Champlain, with Vermont and New Hampshire and their immeasurable beauties of river, lake and mountain around about, but the most sublime spectacle the world can offer—the moon and sun facing each other across the earth.

A night on the peak had no terrors for any of them; there was plenty of balsam fir for couches—Margaret made a wry face as she heard them extolling its attractions. Their hostess had no great fondness for the trip, but she would not for a moment admit less vigor than Miss Yale, and Miss Yale fairly ramped in the ease with which she ascended mountains.

"Where are your lanterns, Laura?" she demanded, casting a careful eye over the preparations.

"Why, Aunt Mary," laughed Daisy. "What do we want of lanterns? We're going to stay up all night, you know—and there's a full moon!"

Miss Yale made no further protest, but being a somewhat opinionated lady, she carefully tucked into her rucksack and Margaret's a small electric pocket lamp.

It was by no means a hard climb, shaded for the most part, and winding gently upward over sidelong slopes that hardly suggested ascension.

"I don't call it climbing unless I have to use my hands," Miss Yale airily explained, and flitted on in the lead as if she were fifteen instead of fifty.

Margaret would have been with her if she had not preferred to walk with Dolly, though indeed Dolly's young ambition was almost equal to her adoptive mother's and kept her well to the front.

A certain lightheartedness among the party seemed to show Dr. Armstrong as not greatly missed. Dolly indeed confided to Margaret:

"I'm glad he's gone—aren't you, sister?"

Her mother turned the question aside. The child's plain lack of liking for her father half-grieved, half-pleased her. To her straightforward disciplined mind it was most disturbing and unpleasant to be pushed and pulled this way and that by feelings she could not disentangle enough to pass judgment on. She looked forward eagerly to her work. There was something she was sure of, safe in, something which gave her the joy of power and the comfort of service.

Newcome, stepping out cheerfully under a heavy load, ranged alongside her in a downward dip of the trail that sent Dolly scampering with the leader.

"I wonder if you women who have real work know how to sympathize with the women who don't," he said.

Margaret smiled at him gratefully. The world of fact and thought he talked of, the large impersonality and free, respectful equality with which he met her, was an unceasing delight to her. Armstrong's manner, even when most anxious to please, kept always in sight the fact that she was a woman and he a man. Newcome reached across the gulf as if they were both too tall to mind it. If she had felt, sometimes, beneath his wide area of pleasant friendliness some touch of deeper concord, or if he did, it was mutually ignored.

"Most women work pretty hard, I think, too hard indeed—don't they?"

"Oh, they're busy enough, and tired enough," he answered, "but not with real work. I was thinking of the rest to the mind of having one large area fully trained and developed, and clean flushed with power. To have one part of you that is normal and in smooth running order, no matter what may be tangling up the other parts."

"Is that why men stand trouble better than women—if they do?" she asked.

He laughed with her. "If they do, indeed! As if they did! It is what makes them able to bear it at all—that and the conviction of superiority."

He had to go then and lay violent hands on the donkey, which had reached a brook that some inner conviction assured him he could not cross. Moral suasion, bribery and physical violence were used on him in vain, and at length they had to tie him to a tree and leave him to solitary meditation on a light local diet, while they divided up the rugs and blankets between them.

The last part of the climb was steeper; even Miss Yale had to put forth a hand now and then, being heavily laden; and Dolly was carried over the dangerous part by Dr. Newcome, who left her in perfect happiness, the first on the peak by a full minute, and came back for his burden of food and clothing.

Margaret thanked him warmly. "Some men would have taken the load up first and made Dolly wait," she said.

"Dolly wait! You couldn't make her," he cheerfully replied. "I think she clearly inherits from her adoptive mother's disposition."

They reached the top, tired but happy, and sat some time gazing as far as the still hazy distance would allow. Then there was much gathering of wood to burn and fir boughs for the beds. Two camps were laid, Miss Yale quite particular about the careful thatching of the fanlike boughs, Newcome and Gerald pitching theirs down in larger if less shapely heaps, while Mr. Briggs exhibited his skill in the building of a safe and efficacious bonfire.

They enjoyed their supper to the full, perhaps a little past that measure, but were forced to admit disappointment in the sunset. Doubtless it did occur, at the time set in the calendar, but a regiment of level gray clouds lay low across the west and hid it all. The rising of the moon was also obscured on the other side. They could see the pale, silvery glimmer of it here and there, but no full-orbed majesty of light.

"Never mind," Daisy cheerfully suggested. "We can use our imaginations a little, and in the morning it will be glorious."

Quite good-tempered and happy they sat about the blaze and told stories, so wrapped in dancing firelight that they forgot to look for stars—and then of a sudden, upturned faces, questioning hands stretched out—a sudden scramble to their feet—it was raining.

"It's only a shower," protested Mrs. Briggs, as if it could not presume to be anything else; but Jupiter Pluvius seemed quite indifferent to their needs or wishes, and the soft shower soon deepened into a steady settled rain. Then rose Miss Yale in serene triumph with her electric light.

"They won't hold out long enough to get us home," she said, "but they'll help us arrange for the night."

Descent in that velvet darkness was impossible—they must stay where they were. Margaret lent her light to Dr. Newcome, and the new-cut boughs were dragged partly into the only sort of shelter the rocky top afforded—a yardwide flat-bottomed crevice with a few bare poles stretched across it. A double blanket was laid across the poles and weighted down with stones; the women all crawled into this long bunk and lay there, spoon-fashion, in two overlapping rows, while the men sat outside and kept up the transplanted fire.

Mr. Briggs, who was subject to physical disabilities, not helped by a long chill wetting, grumbled in spite of himself. Gerald was helpful, but quite worried about Daisy, anxious to go down and get lanterns. He did try it a little way, but the electric spotlight made the dense darkness darker. He nearly lost his life in the one dangerous stretch of trail, and came back subdued, nursing a wrenched finger.

But Dr. Newcome seemed to find the occasion one of sustained hilarity. He heated stones in the fire and tucked them at the feet of the packed ladies in that long hard couch. They lay still perforce, because there was no room to move, but no one slept save Dorothy. She was warm in Margaret's arms, pillowed on Margaret's heart, and not all the cramped discomfort of that granite bed could mar the mother's happiness.

"Are you dry in there?" inquired Gerald, hearing Daisy giggle irrepressibly.

"Dry!" she answered gleefully. "It runs down beneath us like a brook. It drips down the walls in sheets. And the blanket hangs in pools—positive pools—and in the middle of each pool there is a round, unbroken stream that comes straight down on us. *Dry!*" And she giggled again.

Newcome produced from inner pockets various remedies and stimulants. "We shan't catch cold," he assured them all. "No influenza germs on Huykill Peak, I warrant you. But here's something for you, Mr. Briggs, that'll make you feel a bit easier, I think. And here are some lozenges if anybody wants saccharine comfort; good peppermint won't hurt anybody. Anything you'd like out of my pharmacy, Mrs. Briggs? Miss Daisy? Miss Yale? Dr. Yale?"

More cheering than his peppermints were the stories he told. As the slow, wet night wore on, and the stones and twigs seemed to grow harder hourly, he produced an unfailing series of jokes and anecdotes, interspersed now and then by contributions from Mr. Briggs and Gerald.

Gray and cloudy was the light that came at last. No setting moon shone upon that hasty breakfast; no rising sun glorified it. But the hot coffee gladdened their hearts, and the swift descent warmed them. A chastened spirit moved the damp donkey to bring home all the bedding in patience, and their baskets were light on their backs. Dolly held to Miss Yale's hand and hopped gaily beside.

"I think you'd better run a bit," suggested Newcome to Margaret. "You look rather chilly yet."

"Good idea!" She smiled gratefully at his thoughtfulness and was off with long, light steps. He kept beside her where the path allowed, behind her when it was narrow, and watched with a satisfying pleasure her perfect ease of motion as the downward miles flew beneath their feet. The sun came out at last; gold light and green shade flickered over her bright hair; the air was sweet and stirring; the woods dripped in diamond and emerald, and they raced down the glittering path like happy children.

12. *Questions*

When Richard Armstrong had planned to draw Dr. Yale with a fencing bout his motives were somewhat mixed. Her easy proficiency in so many lines had at first piqued, then irritated, and at last quite infuriated him. His love for her, intense and increasing, had in it no submissiveness. The more he loved her, the more he longed to conquer her. Submission, to his mind, was the woman's part. He saw himself, somehow, somewhere, coming out overwhelmingly ahead, and then, from heights of achievement, lifting her to his breast.

The usual easy ground of supremacy—professional standing—was undermined by her own. In vain did he assure himself that it was but temporary, the passing interest of a heart-hurt girl, to be relinquished when the heart was whole again. Even at that, to have made the position she had at her age was a record of which any man might be proud. If a girl could do that on the side, what might not an earnest woman do as a lifework?

He would make sure that it was given up.

Then this unwomanly ability at whist or chess, with racket or gun—whatever she undertook she seemed to give her mind to "like a man," and to succeed in it. Yet in the very face of his criticism she was so utterly a woman, so much more a woman than the devitalized, ultrafeminine invalids and half-invalids with whom he was perforce so frequently associated. More of a woman, too, than the carefully dressed and elaborately charming ladies of whom he knew so much, or the poorer and more frankly solicitous class with which he had also wide acquaintance.

The most striking impression Margaret gave to him was at least of womanliness. It was not only beauty, but that underlying sense of giving power, of rest, comfort, care, which means motherhood. Just to see her with little Dorothy would have convinced any man that she was first of all a woman—he said to himself. Also he wished to see her less with little Dorothy—the child was always in the way, always coming between them.

So he had planned a sort of coup, this crossing of swords in earnest, which would show her she had found her master. Instead of which, his foil had been whipped from his hand—by a woman—before spectators.

He had left the place as promptly as timetables would allow, and back to Boston with every intention of driving this infatuation from his mind. This he undertook to do by means well known to him and used before with success. He worked hard, he turned to his men friends with hearty appreciation, and to "lady friends" as well. Within limits he thought safe, he drank.

It did not work.

As the flamboyant word-painters of the early nineteenth century put it, concerning the perfidious Alonzo, "Not the most licentious scenes of folly, nor the vain splendors of pomp and parade could possibly dissipate the gloom which enveloped his thoughts." Whenever he was alone and awake and not under artificial stimulus he was back under the windy shade, his foot on rough turf, that light, masked figure before him, and his sword ringing to the ground.

Back of that tense movement was a shifting field of faces—always Margaret's: Margaret's laughing—she had a pleasant, honest, musical laugh; Margaret's smiling—she had a wide variety of smiles, each seeming lovelier than the last; Margaret with Dorothy—which touched all that was best in him, and, in a vague way, angered him as well. He wanted her love for himself; this fellow waif had no right to it. Margaret doing a thousand things, and doing them all well. Margaret ahead, overcoming—he felt again the surge of furious desire to have her somehow weaken, that he might be strong and lift her up. She *must* look up to him.

Presently the "lady friends" became unendurable, then the men friends as well.

There was still time for some shooting. At risk of professional loss he took himself off again. "A little run to the Maine woods," he said, and tried what solitude and pleasurable bloodshed would do.

They did not do much either. He was back in Boston before the end of November, and calling on Miss Yale and Dr. Yale as if nothing had happened. And neither of them seemed to think anything had.

Miss Yale had selected her house with the utmost care, studying localities, consulting friends, asking advice from professionals. The same motives which had decided Dr. Newcome's choice governed theirs, with perhaps one more.

"You are sure you don't mind having another shingle set up so near you?" Margaret asked him, when he promptly called, almost before they were settled.

"On the contrary," he assured her, "it is an advantage. Don't you know the 'dry goods district' is improved by each new store?"

He was unaffectedly glad to have them there, and was of good service owing to his knowledge of the whole region. In advising them about milkmen and marketmen, grocers and plumbers, he betrayed so wide and intimate a knowledge that Miss Yale nodded her fine head in strong approval. She liked the man heartily, and it had never yet been necessary for her to conceal her likes or dislikes.

But he was not their only friend by any means. The Briggses' home was not far off; the neighborhood abounded with old acquaintances, and greater Boston soon furnished many new ones.

"I wouldn't have believed, Margaret, that I should like it so much," said Miss Yale. "The house is really too big, but that's a good fault. Dear me! I've jogged about the world so long that I'd entirely forgotten how good it feels to be at home."

It was a little surprising. She was only about fifty, and had always expressed a determination to continue on the wing till at least seventy-five.

"I think it must be Dolly," she added, as if some excuse were needed. "Where there's a child there must be a home. Also it's you, best daughter. A professional person has to have a home, too."

Margaret went over and administered several well-placed kisses and an undiscriminating hug.

"It's just *you*, you lump of goodness!" she said. "But as you will mix up your goodness with elaborate reasons and concealed obstinacy, I shan't argue with you."

Miss Dorothy accepted the new conditions with calm appreciation. When she was shown her room—her own room—the first of her lifetime (and a child's life is a lifetime long and full of incident), she turned to Miss Yale with such heartfelt gratitude in her eyes that the good lady stooped and took her in her arms.

"*Thank* you, Aunt Mary—oh, *thank* you!" was all the child said, but her joy in the place was better thanks than all her small vocabulary could convey. She put on pretty airs of proprietorship, that child proprietorship which says "my home" long before it owns a cent.

Her school delighted her. There seemed to be some blended strain of old Bostonianism which came to the surface now, and made her feel happily at ease among the clean, safe streets, the highly modern schoolrooms, and the prim, neatly ribboned damsels with whom she associated. Her "dearest friend" chanced to be a Wentworth, and Margaret, watching tenderly, wondered if the child might not perhaps be a cousin. The more she saw of Dolly's satisfaction in her surroundings, her good health, steady growth and easy progress in her studies, the surer she felt that Miss Yale was right, quite right, in her handling of the situation and that her own mad impulse of maternal love and maternal jealousy was only selfishness. She must be content to win and hold the love of a sister; she must not ask, perhaps might never know, a daughter's love.

One early evening she came upon the child in the front parlor, quietly busy at something on the center table. Very pretty and sweet she looked in her white frock and the soft ribbons Margaret herself had tied for her before dinner, over the vigorous dark hair.

A big square box was before her, done up in a magnificent amount of white tissue paper, and tied with a particularly splendid string of gold and red. The child was printing on a large card, in big clear letters, very black: "*Sister Margaret, from Dolly, with Love.*" This card she affixed prominently on the box.

Margaret stood quite still, and then turned, not to surprise the secret, but the child heard her and ran forward eagerly.

"Oh, sister dear!" she cried happily. "I've got a present for you!"

"Thank you, darling," said Margaret, stooping to kiss her. "I shall love it."

Dolly pulled her toward the table. "I *made* it!" she said proudly. "Every bit of it—all myself!"

"I shall love it all the more," Margaret assured her with another kiss.

"Now you sit here!" The child drew her to a big easy chair. "And I'll sit in your lap, and you can open it."

She brought the big box in her arms, and planted herself in Margaret's lap with that firm proprietary wriggle which was always a pleasure to her mother. She read the card aloud, impressively, and held the child very close indeed.

"Do you really love me, Dolly?"

Dolly returned the hug with enthusiasm. She had quite surrendered to this wonderful wooer.

"Of *course* I do! You are the nicest big sister that ever was. You're *most* as nice as a real mother."

The face above her turned a bit white, but the eyes were steady.

"Would you rather have a real mother—than Aunt Mary—and Sister Margaret?"

"Why, of course!" answered the child frankly. "A real mother is better than anything—isn't she?"

"I suppose she is," Margaret agreed. "I never had one—to remember—or a father, either. Any more than you—poor childy. Tell me, Dolly—if you did have a father, what kind of a father would you like?"

"'Gzactly like Dr. Newcome!" was the prompt reply.

"Why not like Dr. Armstrong?" asked her mother, and held her breath to listen.

"Because I don't like him."

"But why don't you like him? And why do you like Dr. Newcome?"

"I like Dr. Newcome," said Miss Dorothy, in her most judicial manner, "because he's polite to me. And—well—he's nice. I like him *ever* so much."

"Isn't Dr. Armstrong polite?"

"No, *ma'am*. I think he's horrid!"

Margaret was startled, half-shocked, and yet half-pleased. She did not question herself as to this, only urged the child: "But why?"

Dolly seemed a little at a loss for words, and swung her slippered feet. "He's always taking hold of me," she said at length. "And he kisses me when I don't want him to. And once he kicked my kitty! My little, soft kitty—I saw him! I just hate him!"

Margaret caught her closer with a little cry.

"Too bad! Too bad! Oh, my poor baby! My little orphan baby!"

Dorothy put up a loving hand to pet her.

"Poor Sister Margaret, too. We're both orphans, aren't we? But we'll be good to each other!"

"We will—oh, we will!" answered Margaret, holding her tight.

"That's why I made you the present, all myself," continued the child. "'Cause I love you."

"The dear present!" said her mother, and opened the box. There lay a cushion of balsam fir, and as its distinctive fragrance rose about her, she sat silent, staring at it.

Dorothy was triumphant. "It's balsam fir!" she cried. "Don't you love it? *I* do. I picked it all myself last summer up in the woods, and dried it, and broke it up so small. And I hid it away 'cause I had to work the cover. That took ever so long! I can keep a secret. I didn't even tell Aunt Mary!"

She chattered on, and her mother sat staring at the cushion, the past rising about her with its odor.

"Don't you love it?" urged Dolly, and lifted it to her face.

Margaret rose hastily and put the child down, the cushion falling to the floor as she moved away.

"What's the matter?" asked Dolly, astonished. "Why, you've dropped it!" Her voice was grieved.

Margaret turned hastily, knelt and took the child in her arms, with tender kisses. "I had a pain, dear—forgive me!" She took up the cushion and patted it admiringly. "What lovely work—how well you've done it!"

Dolly nodded complacently.

"And such a pretty color," continued Margaret. "It's a charming cushion, darling. I thank you so much for your dear love."

Still Dolly was not quite content. To her mind a major virtue had been overlooked. Again she held up the cushion, urging: "But don't you like the smell?"

And Margaret smiled that wry little smile of hers, that could see humor in a death warrant, if it was there. "It is very fragrant, dear. I never heard of anybody who didn't like it, did you?"

At which point Miss Yale entered the room. She stood for a moment, watching with intense satisfaction the pretty tableau before her—the eager child, offering her precious gift, the older woman, stooping lovingly to receive it.

"Dollykins—it's eight o'clock."

"Yes, Aunt Mary, I'm coming. See the present I made for sister."

"How pretty that is. You are getting to be a very good needlewoman, little girl. And sister was pleased, I know." Then she caught the look on Margaret's face, and the odor of balsam fir. Fond as she was of it, she had never had such a cushion with her when she was with Margaret. If the child had not been so triumphant in keeping her secret she could somehow have saved this—but it was a small matter at best, and it was done, anyhow. "You're a dear child, Dolly," she continued smoothly. "I'm proud of you. Now see if you can't break the record getting into bed."

"Yes, Auntie—good night. Good night, sister dear." She kissed them both, and skipped happily off.

Margaret sat limp and exhausted, with piteous eyes on Miss Yale, who came to her side at once.

"That's pretty hard, isn't it?" she said understandingly. "I know just how you feel, dear. It's so exquisitely painful that it's almost funny."

For once Margaret failed to see the humor. "She made it herself—for me—because she loved me!"

"Yes, I know, I know. And you hate that smell more than anything on earth—for reasons good. Funny—how smells and memories stick together!" She laid the offending cushion back in the box, covered it, and set it away from them, opening both windows for a sweep of fresh wintry air to take away the cruel odor. "We'll arrange to lose it somehow, my dear, without hurting that dear child's feelings."

Margaret shook her head silently. She laid both arms on the table, put her head down on them, and cried. Miss Yale closed the windows again and came back to her.

"Now my dear child!" She laid a loving hand on the bowed shoulder, tenderly stroking the proud young head. "My dear, you mustn't! After all this time!"

Margaret lifted a despairing face to her. "A lifetime won't end it!" she said.

"You're not well, child. You're doing too much. This summer was a terrible strain—and you're feeling it now. And all the effort of starting your practice here."

"I'm well enough," said the girl with the same quiet despair.

"Oh come, Margaret, cheer up! Think how well everything's going. You are only twenty-seven—you've made your splendid position in the world—and nothing can shake it now. Last summer proved that. You are established, my dear. You've *done* it—all that you undertook to do."

The bowed head did not lift.

"Margaret, dear—think! You can earn a very handsome living and serve humanity in a way it most needs. You can help women who need it. You have youth and health and beauty. You have the dear child with you, and she's given you her heart—and—you have me."

Margaret lifted her head at that. She turned and held the older woman close, crying: "I am an ungrateful brute, dear. I know it. You have made life all over for me; you have saved me from ruin— shame—death—and what's more you've saved her! Please don't think me heartless. I know all that you've done—and I love you almost as well as you deserve. You've saved me from all the usual consequences of—what I did. But you can't stop my—Punishment!"

She slipped down on the floor now, on her friend's knee, and sobbed passionately. Miss Yale looked down on her and patted the firm white hand that clutched her own so tightly with all a mother's tenderness. She guessed the reason for this new stir of grief and wild remorse. Years of wide living had taught her much. Perhaps her own life held more knowledge and experience than her friends imagined. She had watched Armstrong's eager advances, divided between a fierce wish to have him disappointed and the irresistible conclusion that in his present infatuation lay the way out of all Margaret's difficulties. Here would be reinstatement beyond the world's cavil. Married to Armstrong, Margaret could place herself and her child in safety. But she had also watched the steady growth of friendship between this daughter of her heart and Henry Newcome. He wore no airs of the suitor, brought no gifts, paid no "attentions," but he had been useful to them both in a hundred ways; he came often and spent long cheerful evenings with the two of them or took them both to the theater. If he "made love" it was to Dolly.

And here was Margaret, sobbing uncontrollably, and talking about "punishment." *She* knew.

"I wish I could bear it for you, blessed girl," she said.

Margaret sat up and wiped her eyes. "I know you do—you heart of gold! You've done more than anybody did before to save a woman from ruin. But you can't save her from her own heart. What do you think that dear child said to me just now?" She faced Miss Yale squarely, but her lips quivered so that she could hardly force out the words. "She said—that I was almost as good as a real mother! A real mother is better than anything, she said! Oh, my baby! No real mother! No real father! No real home! And all my fault! My fault!"

She tried hard not to break down again, sitting very straight and rigid, but the tears ran down. Miss Yale started to her feet stormily, and paced the floor. "It's *not!*" she said. "This is nonsense, Margaret! It's about one-tenth your fault, I should say—and nine-tenths his!"

The girl could not surrender her burden so easily. "It is the mother's duty to foresee—to protect her child——" she began, but her friend took her up sharply.

"Now look here, Margaret, I thought you had that all threshed out and off your mind long since. It wasn't a fair game at all, and you know it. It's all very well to talk about 'the mother's duty,' but what did that empty-headed child that was you—then—know about motherhood? You can't blame yourself for your ignorance. It was not your fault. You were foolish, and rash, and too sure of yourself—child's faults, all of them. He was ten years older, and a doctor already—*he* knew! And it didn't cost *him* anything. That's what makes me so furious—all the pleasure and none of the risk. I tell you, the fault is his— almost all of it!"

Margaret strove to recover her self-control. "Yes," she said, "you are right. As a matter of fact, I suppose it is. We owe this to him— Dolly and I! But while I can see that the fault was mainly his—the fault I suffer for is mine."

Miss Yale shook her head. "No, it isn't. You pile up all this misery—I don't say it isn't there, dear—though we've got it pretty much out of sight now—and then you *feel* as if you were responsible for all the child has lost. Besides——" She stopped in her walk and looked at Margaret steadily. "I don't see but you can give all those things to Dolly now—if you want to—a real mother—a real father—a real home."

The girl met her look with honest eyes. "Yes—I could."

There was a silence. Miss Yale mended the fire, patted the sofa cushions, straightened the pile of magazines on the table. "It might be better—for her," she said at length.

"Yes, I—have thought of that," Margaret responded. "But she hates him."

"Hates him? I knew she wasn't particularly fond of him, but—are you sure?"

"Yes. He's always trying in a jocose sort of way to make friends with her. But he doesn't go about it in the right way. He does not respect her. Dorothy has a good deal of character, but he doesn't see it. No—she has a real antipathy to him. Besides, do you think he is the kind of man to have authority in the bringing up of a young girl? She is *my* child now—even if I can't own her."

"Yes, she's your child, dear. I didn't legally adopt her, you know. When her mother wants to claim her she may—you're safe there, and as you say—he's not really what I should choose for that child's manager. Well, well, my dear, you certainly are in a hole!"

"You don't know how much of a hole I'm in," the girl replied sadly. "Nor how bottomless deep it is. It is not only for the child, dear. I'm a selfish woman—my heart is breaking, too!"

"I know, my dear, I know."

"Oh Mother dear—you know? *That's* the utter hopeless misery of it. Don't you see? It's not only the past, but the future! I cannot be like other women. I cannot be honestly loved and married as they are. I have this dreadful thing behind me."

Miss Yale came swiftly to her side. "Now look here, child—don't take that position. Keep it behind you! Don't ever refer to it! Why, my dear, you're better worth marrying than thousands of fool girls. A man never tells what he's done—why should you? Keep it to yourself, and take your happiness if it comes to you."

"And deceive a good man who trusted me? No. There is no happiness coming to me, Mother."

"I can't blame you, but I do think you are a bit morbid tonight. Can't you see it more reasonably? You are a strong, beautiful young woman. You are no worse than a widow—a widow of ten years' widowhood. You'll make a better wife rather than a worse."

Margaret smiled a little at that. "As they used to say, 'A reformed rake makes the best husband.' He might not see it that way."

"You shan't slander yourself," cried the other hotly. "Why, you poor deceived child—you never as much as *wished* to do anything wrong. You were just bamboozled as so many girls are. You shall not compare yourself to a man who makes a business of being bad."

"Well—I withdraw the comparison—to please you. But all the same no such woman as I am is a fit wife for—a good man."

"Why not?" demanded her friend sharply. "Suppose, for the sake of argument, that he never knew it—then what difference would it make to him?"

"He would know it," said the girl stubbornly. "I should tell him."

"Now, look here! I don't care how badly you feel—it needn't obstruct your reasoning faculties. Please meet my question fairly. If he never knew it, what harm would it do him?"

"It would do him the harm of having a miserably double-faced, guilty wife who never could meet his trust—or deserve it."

Miss Yale was deeply chagrined. She had striven for all these years to strengthen and develop the character, widen the outlook, increase the knowledge, of this beloved daughter; but this particular point had arisen between them. If she had thought of it at all, she had assumed that the girl's strong reasonableness would see it as she did. What she had not allowed for, with all her wisdom, was that strong reasonableness is a scant dependence when the reasoner is in love. She looked at Margaret and shook her head sadly.

"Dear," she said, "please don't do anything rash. Please wait—and think of it some more."

"I've no opportunity to do anything," the girl replied with an attempt to smile. "So far I am quite safe, you see. I surely do not have to tell things to—a friend."

A firm, swift foot ran up the steps. The doorbell rang. They listened, startled, and heard the voice.

"Oh please," said Margaret, "do see him for a little while."

"Excuse yourself, my dear—don't come down at all. I'll tell him you're engaged."

"Bless your heart, dear! No, I'll come down. I think he wants an answer—and I think it's time he had it."

Dr. Armstrong entered and swept the room with a swift, determined glance. He had come with exactly that purpose, and resented her absence.

"Good evening, Miss Yale," he said. "Is the lady Margaret not in?"

"Yes, Dr. Yale is in, and will be down presently. How you do hate to give her her professional title!"

"Frankly, I do. Professional titles do not belong to women," he said, drawing his gloves through his half-closed hand.

"No? And why not?" she asked easily. There was not the slightest pretense of friendliness between these two, but of politeness, abundance. He had never liked her. Single women, to men of his type, are to be pitied, if their estate is involuntary, and to be blamed, if it is held by choice. For women over forty he had no place in his mind, except that of mothers and grandmothers to real men and women. "Manhood," to him, was a permanent condition, lasting from twenty to eighty or so; but womanhood he measured on strictly physiological grounds, and its brief span was between fifteen and forty. After that these petticoated persons were officially nonexistent, and ought to act as if they knew it.

Miss Yale's large, continuously happy and useful life had always annoyed him; that she should piece out her childlessness with other people's children seemed almost dishonest. He never talked with her if he could help it. But she was Margaret's nearest friend and he must bear with her—for the present.

"It is no use arguing with me," he said. "Men look at these things differently."

"Fortunately all men do not look at them from the same point of view."

"No man—that is a man—would be willing that his wife should have a profession."

"Some men will go without wives then."

"Not in Massachusetts," he replied significantly.

"Oh, if *any* woman will do—perhaps not. But if it is one particular woman——"

"No true woman would hesitate for an instant between a profession—and Love," he stated dogmatically.

"Why should she?" inquired Miss Yale, with an enigmatic smile.

"Why, indeed?" he remarked, in profound distaste, and strolled to the piano. "Do you mind if I sing?" he inquired.

"By all means, do." She would always rather hear him sing than talk.

So Margaret, returning, saw his broad back, and heard in that rich voice:

> *"From the desert I come to thee on*
> *a stallion shod with fire,*
> *And the winds are left behind me in*
> *the speed of my desire!"*

13. *Answers*

She stood between the curtains of the back parlor, her eyes dry and clear now, her color high, her mouth quite firm. Miss Yale smiled approvingly, rose without disturbance and went out under cover of that rolling melody. It ought to stir any woman's heart—that profession of love and faith.

> *"Till the sun is cold,*
> *And the stars grow old,*
> *And the leaves of the judgment book unfold."*

He turned, sprang to his feet, and approached her eagerly.

"Good evening, Dr. Armstrong! What a beautiful song that is!" She seated herself and motioned him to a chair.

"It gives you pleasure?"

"Yes, it always does. I had a friend in Paris who sang it— overwhelmingly."

Now this was not at all to the taste of Dr. Armstrong. The amount of wooing which seemed to have surrounded this lady, and her friendly acceptance of it as a matter of course, appeared to discount his own. Perhaps his skill had deteriorated by association with the wholly inexperienced, or with those who had known perhaps the admiration and attentions of honest Americans only.

Here was a woman who was as frank and friendly as any other American girl, yet who seemed to sit on some inner height from which she mentally compared the ardent expressions of many nationalities. He wished to show her only his own real feeling, and he was constantly hampered by a facility in expression too often used. One can imagine something of the same hindrance and contradiction if true love came to the heart of a woman of the town.

He looked at her, sitting there so serenely, in her richly quiet evening gown, a big soft feather fan to serve as a fire screen, waiting for him to speak when it pleased him.

"Yet you were not—overwhelmed?" he suggested.

"No, but I enjoyed it. You sing it very well yourself," she added politely.

"I ought to—I feel it." He wanted to say much more, yet whatever occurred to him to say seemed wrong.

"One has to feel a thing to express it well, I suppose. Yet some actors say not—that the part should be conceived intellectually—that they should not feel it themselves, but make the audience feel it."

"I wish I could make my audience feel it!" said Armstrong huskily. "Make you feel it! By heaven, I will!" He started toward her with an odd mixture of pleading and violence in his expression.

She met him with smiling, steady eyes, and clapped her hands softly, murmuring, "Excellent! Excellent!"

He stopped short, his hands falling to his sides. "Have you had so much experience torturing men who love you that you have learned to do it with such grace?"

She answered serenely: "I have learned not to misinterpret the too tempestuous gallantry of Europeans."

"I am not a European. I am a plain American man—and I love you. Will you marry me?"

It was out. It was said. The question was asked, and not at all— oh, not in the least—as he had meant to have it. It was his settled theory that a man should make a woman love him first, and then he had but to claim his own. Now he had told this woman that he loved her; he had asked her to marry him, and she was only looking at the fire.

"Are you quite sure that you love me, Dr. Armstrong?" she said at length, adding gently—"Enough?"

"Enough!" he burst out. "Listen! You shall listen at last!"

She was listening, but he poured forth his tumbling words as if to force a hearing.

"I am a man of thirty-eight, strong, vigorous, in full health—or I was until I met you. I have lost twenty pounds. I cannot do my work—I see your face day and night—I hear your voice—I dream of you when I sleep—and your lovely, mocking, cold smile drives me mad—mad!"

She wore it still—a sort of man-to-man professional little smile. "You must pardon me if I suggest that you have doubtless suffered all these symptoms before."

He walked about uneasily, stopped and faced her again.

"I have no wish to deceive you. You are not the first woman I have been in love with. But by all that is Holy—" his hands trembled as he held them out to her, "you are the first woman I have loved!"

"I begin to believe you," said Margaret.

"Oh, you *shall* believe me! You must! I love you from that rich soft hair down to your feet—every inch of you. I love your soft, white hands, your glorious eyes, your proud, red mouth. I would give my life this minute for one long kiss." He took a step nearer. "Will you marry me?"

But she merely asked: "Does not my profession stand in your way, Dr. Armstrong?"

"Surely not!" he replied. "If you love me—I can make you love me—you will throw it aside as gladly as I would throw aside life for you!"

"You are mistaken," she calmly replied. "Even if I loved you as genuinely as I begin to think you love me, I should never give up my work. I am a physician—and a physician I remain—married or single."

He stood still, took an uncertain step or two, trying to find words to reach her.

"But think—consider—if there were children——"

She met him frankly: "I could take care of them better for being a physician, surely. At any rate, that is final I keep my profession."

If an overmastering love is any virtue Richard Armstrong was ennobled by his. It was the strongest feeling he had ever known, not the pleasure of a part of his nature, but the master of the whole of it. He felt the whole mass of long-established conviction pull at its moorings, break loose, and drift before the tide.

"Very well," he said at last, his voice quivering with earnestness. "You may make what terms you please. Keep your profession—I can bear anything—to hold you in my arms!"

Again he came to her, but she rose and stepped back.

"Wait!" she said. "There is something more. You know, doubtless, that I was adopted by Miss Yale in Paris when I was sixteen years old?"

"I know," he said. "I do not care where you came from, whose child you are. You are you—and I love you!"

"You also know, perhaps—you certainly should know," she continued ruthlessly, "that there are certain rumors passed about—reflecting on my good name. What do you make of them?"

He snapped his fingers triumphantly. "I make that of them." At last he had a chance to prove his feeling. "Only be my wife—and no one shall ever breathe a word against you."

Again he came to her with arms outstretched, but she stepped back and said with level eyes: "What if these rumors are true?"

He stopped, stared, a cold horror seizing him.

"They are true," she continued quietly. "I am the mother of a child."

He struggled blindly with the horror, held it back, beat it off feebly: "I did not know—that you had been—married."

"I have not been married."

He swayed a little on his feet and stepped back, groping, to a chair, dropped heavily to the seat, and sat there, his face buried in his hand. To have one's idol own to being clay—one's queen descend. His first mad impulse was to rush out—away—anywhere—to escape; then came the thought of losing her, forever; then a wild rush of feeling that now at least he could secure her, damaged and soiled, but what remained, his at last; and then some little touch of the ennobling affection which strove to force its way upward through a nature ill-tuned for nobility.

She sat, in almost breathless calm, and waited.

He rose, white and trembling, and came toward her once more, throwing wide his arms, with "Even that I can forgive! You will marry me now—won't you?"

Now Margaret sat so that behind her head the big yellow globe of the piano lamp lit the soft halo of her hair to vivid red. As he threw out his hands he chanced to knock the cover from the white box on the table, and the fire-warmed fragrance of the balsam fir rose around him. The shining hair—that odor—and the very words she had used to him when they last met—and he remembered.

"My God!" he cried. "Mag!"

"Yes—Mag—good-bye, Dr. Armstrong."

She stood to dismiss him, but he did not go. His world swung around within him, till time and space and all things else seemed jumbled beyond recognition; but through it all his desperate desire for her held like a chain, and he strove to bring the right ideas to bear, to find new reasons for his wishes.

"Why, the—why, it's all right!" he cried, a confused sense of victory growing through all the contradictions. "Then there is nothing between us after all! You will be mine—you are mine! I can make it all right—why, it's little Dolly!"

He was getting it straight now, and a great burst of hope came to him.

"I can give her a name—a home—ah—for the child's sake, you will—you must!"

Then Margaret rose and seemed to tower before him as if she had gained in bodily height.

"Shall I shelter my child by living in shame? By marrying a man I do not love—nor even respect? I am *not* yours. The child is *not* yours—she is mine—all mine, by the very laws you men have made to shield yourselves! You shall not have her—and she shall not wear your name." She paused a moment, continuing more calmly: "I will not marry you, Dr. Armstrong, because I do not love you. What is more the child does not love you. She dislikes you—she is afraid of you. Do you think a man can live as you have lived and win the heart of a child? For her sake I could have sacrificed my life—perhaps—if she had even liked you."

Armstrong listened, stunned, bewildered, not grasping Margaret's points at all clearly.

"But her name—her reputation—yours——" he urged.

"You should have thought of that ten years ago," she answered, with a cold gentleness worse than her first outburst. "As for my name—Miss Yale has given me hers; for reputation—I have built my own. And the child is mine." As she thought of her baby she felt a touch, almost of tenderness, for the man before her. "For her," she said, "I can even thank you—but I hope never to see you again—go!"

He turned and went without another word. She heard him fumble at the door, heard it slam behind him. She stood there, glowing with a sort of cold fire, triumphant, yet shaken more than she knew.

Then the doorbell rang again. She started, listened; a sudden weakness seized her and she hesitatingly dropped into a chair instead of leaving the room as she had intended.

Henry Newcome entered.

"Good evening, Doctor," he said cheerfully, going to the fire to warm his hands. "My word, as our cousins say—but a fire feels as good as it looks in this weather."

She murmured something of welcome, and he seemed quite satisfied.

"Do you mind if I poke it? You know there are two things everybody can do better than anybody else—mend a fire and unlock a door. If it's the door, you stand on one foot while the other fellow fumbles, and then you say—just barely polite—'If you'll let me take the key——' If it's a fire—you poke it whether or no."

He poked it with conscientious thoroughness, with artistic precision. He got all the ash and cinders out below, started a clear blaze above, and put on, with delicate accuracy, a large lump of cannel coal atop, hitting it one neat tap with the poker, so that the flames might leap along the line of cleavage.

"It's a treat to find you in, Dr. Yale," he continued. "There are so many other people always wanting to see you. Speaking of other people—I met Armstrong on the steps. On the run, too. Nearly knocked me down. He looked as if he'd seen a ghost."

"He had," said Margaret, before she could stop herself, and bit her lip. She must regain her composure.

"Speaking of ghosts," he rambled on easily, his long legs stretched toward the fire, and his eyes upon it. "I always wonder why people are so afraid of ghosts. Ghosts don't bite. Lots of things I'd be afraid of before ghosts. Mice, for instance."

"Mice!" She was amused in spite of her preoccupation. "A man afraid of a mouse?"

"Why not?" He turned a merry smile on her. "Women generally are—aren't they?"

"Yes, but that is on account of their clothes."

There is nothing like a light, impersonal argument to steady the nerves. Plainly Dr. Newcome was aware of it.

"That is what looks so unreasonable to me," he continued, easily. "Why, a woman could harbor a dozen white mice among her flounces—a whole merry-go-round of mice—and never know it. But a man! Let a mouse get up a man's trouser leg—and he's about crazy!"

"It would be rather annoying, I should think," she admitted with an irresistible little laugh.

"Annoying? Well, rather! I had a friend—excitable fellow—a little inclined to hysteria. Men do have hysteria, you know, in spite of the name's derivation."

She nodded. "Yes, I know."

"He was in a hotel in New York; sat in his room one evening very quiet, reading, and a mouse ran up his leg. Well—he raised the roof. He brought out two fire companies. It took three policemen to separate him from that mouse."

Margaret laughed in spite of herself. What was it in this quiet man that always put her at her ease? A moment since and she had been ablaze with nervous excitement, all wrung and trembling from the intense experience. Now it had all ebbed away; her tense muscles were relaxed; she sat there comfortable as if nothing had happened, quite naturally amused by that mouse moving the mountain.

He wore his usual easy air, as of an old familiar friend.

"You women doctors have done a lot to help other women out of their foolishness," he said musingly.

"Yes, it does help," she admitted. "They will often speak more sincerely and frankly to another woman."

"Of course, of course. Suppose it was the other way. Suppose a man had to go to a woman doctor—rather a young one, maybe, and attractive. Women doctors often are attractive, you know." He turned to her with a half-inquiring, half-quizzical look.

She solemnly replied: "I have been told so."

"I don't doubt you have," he answered heartily. "Often told so. Well—I'm telling you again. Where was I?"

Then Margaret laughed a pleasant, friendly little laugh, and leaned toward him, a grateful light in her eyes.

"You were in the midst of a very graceful, pleasant, subtle bit of mental therapeutics, Doctor. You were trying to put a tired and excited woman at ease—and you've done it beautifully."

He shook his head admiringly. "How clever you are! No use trying to play tricks on you!"

"Just as useful—if they work," she told him. "Thank you very much. Now I'll be sensible. And shan't I call Miss Yale?"

"Don't be as sensible as that, please—not yet, at least. I have something I want to ask you about." He took the poker again, and split the big cake into three flat fragments, making a jolly blaze. "I've got a business proposition to make to you. Fact is I have two—one business and one—well, I'll tell you——"

"Yes? I'm listening."

He did not seem to see his way quite clearly, even by looking down the poker with careful sighting. He put it back in the stand and turned to her.

"It is simple enough—and yet there are complications—a complication. I hope it won't stand in the way. It is really two propositions, but not absolutely dependent on each other. You might accept one, and you might accept the other—and you might accept both. I can't tell."

His tone was friendly and sincere, his manner quiet. She felt as she always did, at ease and at home with him. Perhaps the reaction from the excitement she had been through rather dulled her perception of any further appeal to the emotions. At any rate she felt only a warm interest in his two propositions. In all the months of their acquaintance he had never once shown her anything save a steady friendliness, but that friendliness was so broadly efficient, it met and pleased her at so many points, that she had grown to accept it as a part of her life—a very pleasant part indeed—long before her own heart had wakened to a deeper feeling. This feeling she had never faced but once—that very evening, with Miss Yale; yet now, in the atmosphere of strengthening peace he brought with him, she unconsciously put aside everything else and merely rested.

She had liked him first for what he had done for Dolly, and because the child herself was so frankly fond of him; and upon that had grown a steadily increasing admiration for his fine qualities, as well as this deep personal content. Vaguely she felt that, whatever might hold them apart, they were still friends and that this friendship was enough—if there were nothing more.

He returned to his propositions.

"Be sure you remember," he said carefully, "that the first one stands—whatever you may say to the second. And if you like the first, and don't like the second—why, you take the first and I'll never say a word about the second—see?"

She was naturally a little bewildered. "I can't say that I see very much yet, Dr. Newcome."

He turned to her with decision.

"Well, here goes for the first. You know you have a tremendous reputation, but not a very large practice—yet."

She met this with more than admission. "In point of fact I haven't any practice yet. I've not even started."

"Yes, exactly. Now I haven't much of a reputation."

"You have, indeed," she eagerly interrupted. "The best kind of one. I don't think I've ever spoken to you about it, but I do want you to know how much I appreciate your beautiful work. And it is so close to mine—overlaps, in fact, for I try to treat children, too, you know. But you have a special genius for them."

He waved this aside and resumed solemnly: "As I was saying when I was rudely interrupted—I haven't much of a reputation, but I have a pretty good practice—good size and good sort—mostly G.P.'s, you know——"

"G.P.'s?" she questioned.

"Oh, you're not on to our American slang yet? Grateful Patients. The lighteners of a doctor's life. Pay their bills and then give him affectionate presents. Brass umbrella holders, cut glass, gold-topped inkstands, pearl pins—all sorts of premiums."

"Oh, yes, I know. And I don't doubt you are furnished, decorated, and gentleman-outfitted by them."

"Not as strong as that, Doctor Yale! It's nothing like as bad as wedding presents—not much worse than Christmas. Seriously, though, it is a comfort for a fellow to feel that he has done something now and then and that some people appreciate it."

They sat in pleasant silence for a little while. The fire glowed softly; the little French clock struck its veiled musical note. He glanced up at it—only ten. He almost hated to break the silence to disturb this atmosphere of peace and homelikeness with what might put an end to it.

She sat content for the present, free from the bitter thoughts which had so overcome her earlier in the evening. He watched her tenderly, yet with keen discernment. Was he too soon? Would it be better to wait yet for a while? Or would she be happier for having this settled one way or the other? That was what he had made up his mind to before coming, and he would abide by it.

"My first proposition," he began briskly, "is that you and I go into professional partnership. *Newcome and Yale. Yale and Newcome, M.D.'s.*, looks rather well, I think. You see, as you say, our work touches and overlaps. You have the women and I'll take the children, and between us we can undertake any men that come along, too——"

"Undertake!" she cried. "Oh, Doctor! What a damaging admission. You don't propose to add that business to the partnership?"

He laughed good-humoredly. "Well, no—we'll keep that up our sleeves. But I mean this very seriously, Dr. Yale. I've thought it out carefully. I should consider it a great honor."

Margaret was wholly earnest now. She was deeply touched by this evidence of esteem and appreciation from a fellow practitioner. It meant real help, too, in these years of beginning over, to have an established practice to draw upon, and she felt sure too that she would not be a drag on him; she knew that her work was good.

"You quite overpower me, Dr. Newcome. I don't think you realize what a great—what a very great honor, and what a practical help you are offering me."

"I appreciate what it would mean to my business," he answered heartily. "You don't seem to see what a solid advantage it would be to me. Let us speak quite honestly, Dr. Yale. I am a plodder; I do good work with children—shall do better, I hope. I think my practice will grow and that I can earn a fair income and fill an honorable place in the profession. But I shall never do anything spectacular—and you will. You are a brilliant young specialist—you'll go far. But I think I can be of enough service to you to make it worth your while—especially at present. And further than that——" He had sat leaning forward, elbows on knees, considering his boots, while making these statements, but now he lifted his face to hers, full of the frankest friendship and admiration. "You are such an extremely good fellow, Dr. Yale! I should so enjoy having you 'round! You're a square businessman, as well as a good surgeon. You will consider it now, won't you?"

"I certainly will!" cried Margaret, heartily. "I must think a little, and I must speak to Miss Yale. I don't know how to thank you——"

"All right—all right—don't try till I've really been of some service to you. But now for number two."

She waited, listening, but he did not seem to find number two so easy to unfold.

"Well?" she said, at length.

"If you can be patient for a moment while I get this off my mind," he began slowly, his eyes on the rug between them. "And then—if you don't like it—just forget the whole business—consider it unsaid. I give you my word of honor that I will never reopen the subject. Of course you might—possibly—but I won't."

"I'm all ears," she assured him. "And full of curiosity. What is your second proposition? As to a suite of offices?"

"No," he said slowly. "It's not about offices." He turned to her again, with an entire change of manner. His heart was in his eyes, in his voice, in his whole earnest appeal, yet he sat quietly. "I love you—with my whole heart," he said. "Will you be my wife?"

Margaret stared at him in such astonishment that she could not for the moment grasp his question. Then it reached her, more through the look in his eyes than the words. And with it there rose, and swept over her again, all that bitter tide she had striven with but two hours since. She started to her feet, looking at him as if a widening gulf had opened between them, suddenly turned away, and burst into uncontrollable tears.

"I was afraid so," he murmured to himself, then went to her and put a brotherly arm around her shoulders. "Now, my dear girl, don't—don't! I see how it is. Please don't cry. See—we'll be the best of friends for years and years. I won't ever annoy you with that proposition again. Forgive me if I've hurt you."

"Oh, it's not that!" she cried softly. "It's not that!" She let him hold her for a moment, resting her head on his broad shoulder, and sobbing as if her heart would break, while he patted her as if she were a crying child. Then she drew off from him. "I'm ashamed to make such a fuss," she said, trying to smile. "But I've been through a good deal tonight. Dr. Newcome, you have a right to know. I do love you—I will not say how much. But I cannot be your wife."

"You do love me?" he said, incredulously. "You love me! Oh, my Marjorie! That is enough!" And he came to her, the light rekindling in his eyes.

She moved away from him.

"No—it is not enough. Don't—oh, don't be so good to me! You don't *know*——"

"I don't want to know," he declared briefly. "If you love me, I don't ask anything else." And again he would have taken her to his heart, but she held him off. Miss Yale's advice was ringing in her ears.

Why tell him? Here was love waiting for her; here were happiness, home, real rest and joy at last. And Dolly loved him too. How could she not only crush her own heart but hurt his?

But Margaret Yale had not lived hard and true for ten long building years to be false to her own ideals now. With one long shuddering sigh she put that tearing grief beneath her feet and faced him calmly.

"I do not deserve your love," she said in a low, dead voice. "I am not fit to marry. I have—sinned."

"So have I," he said, and took her in his arms. "Now, Marjorie—my Marjorie—be still and stop trying to tell me things. Bless you, child—don't I know! Why, dear, I've loved you for ten solid years! Look here—I'll let you have a look at the only comfort I've had all that time——" and he took out that wrinkled, faded bow of ribbon with one long, curly, glistening hair tied into it.

She looked at it—at him—wonderingly.

"Oh, my dear," he went on, "my little girl! I loved you then—but it was too late. You wouldn't look at me—and I couldn't save you. But sweetheart——" He held her off and feasted his eyes on her happy face, where the rich color glowed and changed like roses pink and crimson. "You'll have to love me very hard indeed, to catch up."

In spite of her happiness she still clutched at that receding sea of shame and pain.

"But how can you love me—after——" Her head was down on his breast again.

He held her so without a word for some quiet moments, kissing one of her hands. Then he asked, "Marjorie, dear, do you like your new name?"

"Nobody ever called me that before. It's your name, and I love it——" she said softly.

"Well, my Marjorie, let us talk our little ghost to death, and bury it—shall we?"

She nodded, without lifting her head from its resting place.

"All right—when you were barely sixteen, uneducated, unprotected, alone, you were fooled by a man ten years older, having both knowledge and experience. You did wrong—admitted. He did wrong—and why didn't I drop him and hate him and cast him off? Why, Marjorie—I had done wrong too. Not so cruel a wrong as he perhaps—but far, far worse than any fault of yours, poor child. Why, my darling, my brave, strong, suffering darling, there is hardly one man in a hundred who has the right to blame a woman like you. Now do you see? Ethically we are even, except that you are less to blame than I."

"But that doesn't alter—the facts," she murmured.

"What are the facts? You are to me like a beautiful widow—if I think of that at all. And as to main fact—which is Dolly—why, I love the child. It will be an honest pleasure to have her with us. I don't hate her on Armstrong's account, you see. In fact," he added slowly, "I am almost a little sorry for Armstrong. He deserves all he's got and more, but he's suffered enough and will suffer enough, I fancy—to make any man sorry for him."

"You think I was too cruel?" she asked hastily.

"Cruel? You cruel—to him? Why, my darling girl, you couldn't in a thousand years make the account even. Don't ever reproach yourself for that! I judge that you turned him down—and that he realized who did it—a nice situation. And I held my hand till you had done it, too. I was terribly afraid that you might consider it."

"I did—for a little—on her account," she murmured.

He nodded understandingly. "I know, my dear. It seemed as if he ought to have that chance, and as if you might possibly—prefer it—so I waited."

She lifted her wet eyes to his with adoring love. "You are better than seven angels, I do believe!" she said.

"Thought you were going to say seven devils—as it usually goes. Well, where were we? Now I, being honored above all men, marry a lovely young widow. We have Dolly with us, but we keep the status quo—for her sake, if you choose. If not—just as you decide. We have our work together. And there won't be anybody in the world as happy as I."

"You don't—really—mind it?" she asked incredulously.

"Do you mind what I did when I was a boy in college—before I loved you? Worse things, you understand?"

She pondered. "Why, I'm sorry, but I can't say I *really* care much," she answered slowly. "It seems so long ago. If you kept your health—" she glanced at him with a second's apprehension—"and you love me now."

"I kept my health," he answered, eye to eye, "and I love you, now and always. Shall we call it square and bury it—forever and ever?"

"Forever and ever," she agreed, her hand in his. Then she said suddenly, "But oh, my mother—my more-than-mother! It's going to be hard for her!"

Newcome smiled his hearty, friendly smile. "Why, I thought," he said, persuasively, "that as this house is so big, and even better situated than mine, that maybe she'd let us have our offices here, to-gether. There's lots of room on the ground floor. And I thought fur-ther that all things considered, perhaps she'd let me board here too. Then we shouldn't have to upset anything."

Margaret drew back and looked at him with a face of such radi-ant adoration that he fairly caught his breath.

"Oh!" she breathed. "If there is anything that I can do—in all my life—to make you happy!"

"There is something you can do right now," he softly suggested, "that will give me a piece of heaven. Marjorie—my Marjorie! You haven't kissed me yet!"

And she gave him heaven.

WON OVER

1

Why should unoffending children be forced to carry on from age to age the names of their ancestors and collateral relatives?

That was one of the first large questions which formed itself, vaguely, in the inquiring mind of Esther Ella Challis. She did not see it quite as widely, nor express it as fully, having in view only her own case and that of her friend Algernon Edward Hughes, who hated his name more deeply far than she hated hers. She had heard him insist on "Jerry," passionately insist, securing that name by force of arms whenever possible; but he could not thrash the big boys, nor the little ones, nor all those of his own size at once, so they called him "Algy" in drawling, tender tones, and "Al-ger-nonny," and even "Eddy-nonny," with all the other variations possible to ingenious youth.

She came upon him one day, actually blubbering in the depths of the backyard, behind the big tree, after the big boys' jeering chorus as they tramped across the lot beyond. Algernon Edward was only eight.

"Say—Jerry—" she suggested, "here's a cookie." He was comforted by the cookie, and by the willing concession of the name preferred.

Seeing him calmer, she remarked: "They named me after aunts, two of 'em, great aunts. I think it's mean."

He eyed her, still sullen, over the serrated fraction of brown cookie. "Mine's after my father. I hate it," he admitted.

"When I grow up and have children I'm going to name 'em new," she ventured dreamily. Esther Ella always escaped from the positive troubles of the present by solacing herself with a rosy future, but Jerry found no comfort in her remote purposes. He made his protest with his fists, and in due time passed out of Esther Ella's range entirely, growing up to contented manhood as "A. E. Hughes," and even in later years condemning his own son to the same burden. But she remained questioning.

That was when they lived in Mendon.

Esther Ella was a lonesome child. Her mother was a stern-faced

151

widow, having buried no one knew what dreams of hopeful youth, what sad realities, with the young husband who had died so soon. Some of her friends said that the time was well chosen; even some of his friends privately agreed that it was just as well Challis dropped out so early. He had been admittedly a disappointment to many, both in literature and general behavior. Mrs. Challis never admitted it. She erected a suitable monument, wore suitable mourning, showed, if not wild grief, at least a lasting sorrow. To her daughter she said little as to what she had lost, but the child used to sit long, studying her father's portraits, early ones in the big album, the last one or two more modern and expensive, the least satisfactory of all, on the south wall in the parlor.

He was handsomer than her mother, that was clear. She liked the bright, sweet, little boy face of him, standing brave though stiff in an attitude evidently dictated by others. She felt a stir of warm admiration for the one that looked straight at you, and had such an impressive little mustache—all the later ones were clean-shaved. Naturally she had no means of reading either the boy's promise or the man's fulfillment, but she let her empty little heart fill and run over with love for the father she never knew. If he had lived, she thought, she could have sat in his lap after supper; he would have liked to hold her; she would have felt the strong, warm arms around her; he would have let her kiss him; he would have said: "My little girl!"

She had long cherished a secret longing to be called "my little girl," but her mother never called her anything but "Esther Ella." Not that Mrs. Challis was unkind, or even lacking in affection. The sleeping child never knew how close her mother held her, what tender names she murmured, under breath, in the dark hours. Once or twice she did waken, dreamily, to that sweet surprise, and after that she tried her determined little best to keep awake till mother came. But a healthy child can hardly remain awake from half past seven to ten or eleven o'clock, even with the aid of pins.

If she had had a brother or a sister to play with, or if her careful mother, as aristocratic as she was poor, had allowed her to play with the neighbors' children, there would have been less loneliness and less dreaming. Even the associations of school life were rigidly sifted and scrutinized; she must not accept invitations to parties because she could not return them; she must not go to this little girl's house because they were too "common," nor to that one's because they were too "rich."

Mrs. Challis's distinguished relatives paid her no attention whatever, being permanently displeased with her marrying what they pleased to describe as a "low-bred newspaper man." Even Aunt Esther and Aunt Ella, beyond each sending a book at Christmas to the young namesake, seemed indifferent to the compliment paid them. But in spite of years of coldness the watchful mother always hoped that someday her sister who had married so well, or her brother, who was somewhat recognized even in New York, or the aunts themselves, would "take up" Esther Ella. So she watched over her studies and associates as carefully as might be, and if she could not afford to give her the society she approved, she would at least not allow any that she disapproved.

Little Malina Peckham, whose father taught Latin in the school, and whose mother apparently had as hard a life as Mrs. Challis, was at times allowed to come and play. Esther Ella was not at all fond of Malina, but anyone was better than no one.

"She is an extremely well-behaved little girl," said Mrs. Challis, "and most appreciative."

Malina did appreciate the cookies; there were none at home.

That was in Saunderstown.

When Esther Ella began to realize life at all clearly, being at the advanced age of sixteen, they went to live in Springfield, Massachusetts. Aunt Esther and Aunt Ella, at last wearied of "companions," and having previously exhausted more acceptable relatives, had offered Mrs. Challis a "home," and Mrs. Challis had accepted the offer—for the child's sake.

The house was big and old with a stationary atmosphere of fifty years' standing. The sisters had inherited it when they were twenty-five, and made no changes since. They were hale old ladies, wearing costumes of evident cost, if not of evident beauty. Pious were they, with the religious habits of an untroubled lifetime; one inclined to learning, the other to missionaries, both with the opinions of their long-deceased parents and early teachers still dominating every thought.

Mrs. Challis heaved a long sigh of relief when she was left in the big back bedroom that would be henceforth hers—hers always—if she was wise and careful. She knew her aunts well.

Esther Ella also heaved a long sigh, but not of relief, as the door of her room closed upon her. This, her mother said, would be "home" now, and always—if she was "good."

It was a small room, low-ceilinged, with a visible rafter on the side, cluttered with old furniture, valuable, no doubt, but not, to the girl's eyes, pretty. There was a deal of curtain and valance, of stuffed chair and high-piled bed. There was a bookcase, before which she dropped eagerly on the floor. Row after row she read the titles, but with all her passionate delight in reading she turned away with another long sigh. This room, she judged, must have been sacred to visiting missionaries.

Disappointed in the bookcase she went to the window, opened it, leaned out. Ah—this was better! A garden, a real garden, such as she had read of and seen pictures of, but never seen before. Box! Somehow she knew the smell from description. Big, old box hedges along the graveled walks. Roses—she smelled them clearly, white ones she could see—roses in beds, on arbors, up against her very wall. Yes, by reaching as far as she dared, she could touch a cool, soft cluster of crimson ramblers. Trees, too, tall and shadowy, giving an air of mystery and guardianship. In a far corner she caught a glint of reflected light, the faint tinkle of a fountain, and above, higher than the great elms, shining down on her with all the witchery of eternal romance, a soul-stirring, brilliant moon.

She set her chin on her crossed arms and looked and looked. A moon like that always made her heart leap with the hope, almost the promise, of joy. With such a moon still shining on the world something must happen, sometime.

Nothing did, however. If possible, less even than before. Esther Ella, to be sure, was now being educated with the utmost accuracy and precision. Her school was a small one, an exquisite product of the intellectual inbreeding of New England. The teachers, the books, the pupils, were so thoroughly "select" that a composite photograph might have been taken of either group with clear results. The girl's eager mind was cautiously supplied with the diet deemed suitable for her age, sex and station, and trained in a series of faultless exercises. Her home reading, if she found time for any, was also supervised. In association with the young ladies who studied and recited beside her, she found as the most daring soul an intellectual rebel who had read *Aurora Leigh*.

Mrs. Challis showed a ceaseless anxiety to have her daughter "do well," a restrained pride in observing that she did "do well," both in school and in such company as they saw from time to time, industry and patience in preparing her wardrobe, and more self-restraint and heroism than was suspected in maintaining her position in the household—"for the child's sake." That position was by no means easy for any woman, much less for a Livingstone.

These two sisters, who had lived together as joint mistresses of the big, old house for so long, had never yet agreed on any single detail of its management. It was theirs, indivisibly, with a rigidly tied-up income to maintain it and them; but each, in the nascent house-wifery of her individual soul, longed to manage it in her own way. That the original furnishings should remain, honored and well-pre-served, was undisputed, but where each piece should stand, and when, how, by whom, each article should be cleaned—these points remained open to discussion from year to year, from decade to decade.

In the matter of food a still broader field was open. Members of the same family, the same church, the same social circle, may yet dif-fer as widely as the poles in the matter of dietetics. When it is said that Miss Esther Livingstone was a fixed believer in the "Salisbury treatment," and Miss Ella Livingstone a vegetarian in general, with fluctuations toward "unfired food" and Fletcherism, enough perhaps appears to indicate the amenities of household management in their behalf.

Mrs. Challis was acting housekeeper, without either sister ever ceasing to order when it pleased her. She must engage servants with care and pains, to find them discharged at a moment's notice, or leav-ing with startling suddenness on their own initiative. She was, of course, the table and parlor companion, treated almost as a child her-self, and Esther Ella as a babe in arms; but after the babe was sent to bed the mother must remain, busy with tireless fingers, or perhaps reading aloud from books of soporific tediousness, or of such stimu-lating incentive to argument that the sisters would wrestle over them till welcome bedtime.

Mrs. Challis felt in her conscientious heart that she earned the "home" that was offered her, but she begrudged no effort, no en-durance, to hold this precious "setting" for her child.

Now Esther Ella had to love something. Her first love in the school was the teacher of mathematics, a grave, remote, pale young lady, with a soft wreath of fine black hair. Her eyes were blue, clear blue, and gentle, and the girl wove fiery romances about her in the wide spaces of her young imagination. Very shyly and gently she pressed closer, and when the teacher, scarcely more than a girl her-self, quite frankly met her friendly advances, it was as if a queen had accepted tribute and granted audience. Of the audience, however, lit-tle came. Miss Lester turned out to be a young woman of extremely moderate ambitions, teaching school as a stopgap, and hoping only, in a delicate, undefined way, to "marry well."

Esther Ella was vaguely disappointed.

Her next enthusiasm was for the music teacher, Sara Holliwell, not overhandsome, but possessed of a fine figure and a finer voice, who sang in the choir and was of a highly devotional temperament. In her society the earnest girl grew deeply religious, took a class in Sunday school, attended all services both Sundays and weekdays, began to feel a "vocation" for joining some sisterhood. But when Miss Holliwell quite patently flirted with the unmarried tenor, and also with the married basso, and then, when even schoolgirls had heard of her gaieties, suddenly eloped with a very ordinary young man who belonged to a brass band, her young admirer's heart cooled almost to a stone.

The girls she could not fully feel at home with. They knew more than she did, in their uninterrupted course of schooling, but they had read less, and thought, apparently, not at all. The repressive habits of her girlhood counted also, though no present objections were made to her having intimate friends among these extremely select young ladies.

It was quite a pleasure to Esther Ella to find in the beginning of her second year a familiar face in the classroom—that of Malina Peckham. Malina appeared there in a period of temporary glory, her mother having come into a small legacy, and disappeared the next season, owing to the rapid exhaustion of said legacy in her father's unskillful handling. While she stayed she was, at first, a source of considerable comfort to Esther Ella, who had a hidden capacity for staunch devotion which life so far had not encouraged. But in spite of her sense of established friendship and the protective tenderness she soon developed for the newcomer because the other girls unanimously disliked her, it soon became painfully apparent that Malina was not a "nice girl." She strove to curry favor with the daughters of wealthy parents; she flattered the teachers and took advantage of them at every point possible; she picked up school gossip as "pigeon peas" and retailed it broadcast with skillful twists and turns of her own contriving.

She clung like a limpet to Esther Ella, praising her "wonderful brain," prophesying great things of her in the future, laying an unerring finger on the most secret chord in the girl's heart—a never-told ambition to "do something," to "be somebody"—and twanging it till it thrilled again.

It was a good brain, though not in the least wonderful. The compositions she presented were quite the best of the class; others, not brought forward, were still better. Malina begged to hear them, listened in rapt silence, volubly admired. When her own last effort in the same line for the spring examinations showed so many earmarks of Esther Ella's work that even the teacher suspected borrowing, Malina stoutly denied it. Most of the girls were eager for her downfall; even the teachers were not sorry to have a tangible fault to show in a pupil not at all popular among them. But Esther Ella, called upon to state whether or not Miss Peckham had appropriated her work, stood quite pale but determined, feeling as she had once when she rescued a most unattractive kitten from a crew of yelling boys.

No, she said, not a paragraph, not a sentence, not a phrase, not an idea, of her work appeared in Malina's.

This was rigidly true, but it was also true that Malina's product was so near to the originals that several of Esther Ella's best papers could never be used, in that school at least.

Afterward Malina assured her with tears of gratitude that she had never seen such nobility, such generosity, such magnanimity, in her life.

"It's your style that did it," she said. "I never dreamed of imitating you, but your style is so impressive that it influenced me in spite of myself—I couldn't get away from it."

Next fall Malina was not there.

Seventeen, eighteen—Esther Ella "finished" in the Soper Academy for Young Ladies, and faced the bitterest denial of her life.

She wanted to go to college.

No one ever knew how much she wanted it. Grown people, old people, seemed to want things as they want their meals at the usual hour, and get right over it if disappointed, as one does if one misses lunch—not thinking of food again until dinnertime. But young people want things with the passionate hunger, the burning thirst, of the shipwrecked, dying slowly. And their disappointments bite as with acid, leaving scars.

To be eighteen, to be ambitious, to have a keen, active, willing brain, eager for larger work, to view the knowledge of the world as a banquet, and the possibilities of life among other students as a paradise of romance and excitement, to know that this may happen now, only now, and never again, and then be denied it—this is hard to bear at eighteen.

She was good to look at, if one knew much of "points" in human beauty. Not the round, pink type, blossoming richly at an early age, and then, as life passes, steadily falling away from that fresh bloom into a formless softness of well-girded flesh, or unintelligent wrinkles; but the kind that lasts half a lifetime in full power, and then— if the life has been well spent—leaves a strong and gentle splendor behind it. A tall girl, well-proportioned, with good features, a clear, dark skin and brooding eyes; eyes that looked weary for so young a face; the mouth a little set, a little sad, perhaps, but mouths may mend, with time.

School life had closed. College life had not opened. What could she do? What, indeed, could her mother do, even if she had wished to fulfill her daughter's hope? Aunt Esther and Aunt Ella, strong in unaccustomed agreement, put their feet down, a solid four, of quadrupedal firmness, in final refusal. As they paid Esther Ella's bills, and her mother's, there was no shadow of a chance, unless she ran away and "put herself through college," which seemed beyond any reasonable determination.

A whole year went by, one of those endless, priceless years of girlhood without anything happening, a year that seemed to the quiet girl, with the patient mouth and the smoldering eyes, equal to any ten. She read within the lines allowed her. She played decorous ladies' tennis with the Dacy girls next door. She visited, solemnly, in the family carriage, with her mother or one of her aunts, sitting quietly in dim parlors and making artificial conversation. She had her church work, and found some faint resource in that, but her "vocation" no longer called.

Every year for two weeks in August they all went solemnly to the White Mountains to a small old-fashioned hotel in a little-frequented valley. The rest of the year was spent in the cumbrous routine of the big old house, where three house servants and a "man," who came by the day, did the work, where Mrs. Challis "managed" and both the old ladies interfered, and where there was no single glimmer of interest or occupation, amusement or hope, for a young girl.

Then Morgan Widfield came.

The Dacy girls next door had a cousin in town who went to Harvard; the cousin had a friend who visited him. Both came to call on the Dacy girls—and Esther Ella happened to be there. Mr. Widfield played a set of tennis with Esther Ella as partner, and a warm color lit her quiet face. They won, he praised her playing, and the dreamy eyes waked up in merry flashes.

He said good-bye to her last. He held her hand a shade longer than was necessary—how a girl's mind weighs and measures these tiny things. That night the garden seemed a wilderness of fragrant mystery; a slim, young moon rode proudly, triumphing over swift hosts of flying clouds; there was a stir and a glimmer to life after all.

The Dacys saw a good deal of their cousin and his friend, and

Mrs. Dacy, whose motherly heart had a warm though conventional corner for the lonely girl next door, and whose daughters were, one engaged, and the other flatly refusing to be, saw to it that Esther Ella was counted in as often as possible.

Mrs. Challis observed keenly and with satisfaction. Having learned much wisdom in her precarious position, she presently animadverted upon young men in general and Morgan Widfield in particular, so that both the aunts became interested. They solemnly called on Mrs. Dacy and made due inquiries; they solemnly arranged a tea party, and invited Mrs. Dacy, both the Dacy girls, the young man one of them was engaged to, the Dacy cousin, and Morgan Widfield.

Old mahogany, old silver, old china and old glass shone brightly; the menu of that old-fashioned "supper" involved neither meat nor vegetables and therefore no acrimony; the conversation ran light and merry among so many young people; and Esther Ella glowed and sparkled with gentle happiness till both her aged relatives nodded sagely and concluded that the child was really growing up.

Other mothers in the always undermanned and overwomanned town gave little parties too. There were small picnics and excursions, visits to vaunted hills, and rowing trips, where young men showed bare, brown arms and sturdy necks, and young women unfurled rose-lined parasols behind fetching hats, and trailed rosy fingertips in the water.

Young Widfield was a general favorite, but so, to her surprise, was Esther Ella, now. Her quiet beauty was illuminated from within, her habitual repression was lifted, and she flashed and sparkled as wittily as any of them. Her talk was richer, too, from its wide background of books and years of dreaming. She became, in a modest local sense, a belle. Before she knew what was happening to her Julius Dacy proposed, and to her startled little cry: "Oh, no! I am so sorry—but I couldn't!" he demanded sharply: "Is there another man?"

"You have no right to ask," she told him, but she knew that there was another man, who had not asked her, who was even now bending low beside the minister's daughter.

She turned cold again, cold and still, quiet of mouth and eye, going home early from that picnic with Olive Dacy, the determinedly single one. She could eat no supper, found enough of a headache to excuse her stealing away early, and from the closeness of her little room slipped softly into the fragrant dusk of the wide garden. Down at the very end was a tiny summerhouse, shadowed with heavy vines, and there, leaning across the little table, she laid her head on her white arms and sobbed as if life had closed on her forever.

A movement in the vines and bushes against the Dacy wall, a jar on the gravel—someone had jumped down. Before she could catch her breath to cry out she heard the one voice in the world close beside her.

"I thought it was you," he said. "I heard someone—you're not crying—not crying when I love you so! Oh, Esther—will you marry me?"

"How can you love anybody with such a horrid name?" she asked him by and by.

"It's a lovely name," he said. "Esther Ella—Estella—Stella—my Star!" And the load of a lifetime rolled away with his words.

"Oh!" she breathed later. "I've been so long—alone! So miserably alone! There wasn't—anybody."

"I was coming," he assured her. "I was coming as quick as I could—are you glad to see me?"

"I feel as if I'd just got home!" she told him.

And then he put his arms around her, both arms, and held her close, and said:

"My little girl!"

2

It was characteristic of Esther Ella Challis that she had never herself sought to alter the clumsy name bestowed upon her by ruthless relatives. She scorned such pretense as she scorned artificial aids to beauty. No powders, creams and perfumes were on her toilet table; in reality she never had a toilet table; the top of a high old "bureau," with its two little drawers and limited center space, sufficed her. Her mother had always despised nicknames, and passed on to her the same attitude. But when Morgan Widfield rechristened her as "his star," the girl's whole soul went out to him in exquisite gratitude.

That he *knew!* And he *understood!* This was what overwhelmed her.

There is no deeper longing in the heart of youth than that for appreciation. It is not approval only that young people desire, though that is balm to their souls, but recognition—to be known for what they are. They will stand harsh criticism, severe condemnation if discerning and intimate, better than neglect and indifference.

As we grow older and lose so many of our delicate distinctions, learning to curl up what are left and hide them safely, we no longer seek so earnestly for that unattainable pleasure—full understanding.

As a matter of fact, Morgan had never given a thought to the girl's feeling as to what she was called. He had been greatly attracted to her on their first meeting, and when he learned her name the consolidation of syllables was pleasantly obvious. He had called her "Stella" in his own heart from the first, not because he thought she would like it, but because he did.

He was a fine, vigorous, unimaginative young male, healthy and clean of body and mind, already making good in his business, which was leather. His people were from the South, a large family, cheery and kind. He loved them all, but his main interests were naturally those of his business. Aside from all the efforts, hopes, cares and ambitions of his working life, however, he had always kept a fair place in his heart for wife and home.

When he found Stella that place was filled. He delighted in her grave and quiet beauty, in the delicate radiance that glanced about her when she was vividly happy, in the quality of her mind, as far as he could test it.

Now this fair Stella of his adoration, little as he or anyone else suspected it, and in spite of all her honesty, had a "hidden vice." Not to her mother, her minister, or her nearest girlfriend, Olive Dacy, had Esther Ella ever confided her secret sin. To her lover she longed to confess, but dared not. She made tentative approaches, asking him if he had read *In the Days of the Comet*.

"No," said Morgan, shortly, "and I don't want to. I don't care at all for that pseudoscientific nonsense, and I hope you don't. Besides— some of his books are unfit to read. I hope you agree with me— dear?" he added, noting the shadow that clouded her white forehead.

"I hope I shall agree with you always," she said, and slipped from the works of this author to the discussion of others less likely to offend. Especially they talked of poetry by the hour, and read poetry to each other with an appreciation that was more than literary. He brought her gifts of verse as well as flowers, small, richly bound books, works, many of which, for all those hidden misdemeanors, she had never seen.

This was Stella's sin. In spite of her rigid upbringing, in spite of her decorously perfect education and strictly revised associates, in spite even of her own delicate and steely conscience, she was a reader of forbidden books. This by no means refers to books under the ban of libraries—such she had never seen—but to an eager omnivorous reading of all she could reach in the well-governed public library of the town and in the bookcases of her friends. Her young mind was filled with a far more catholic range of literature than her mother and teachers knew. She had held to this indulgence defiantly, with some of the demand for freedom of thought which had brought her ancestors to this land, and with, perhaps, some of the extra enjoyment which belongs to forbidden fruit.

From this wide, unknown land within she now came forth, eager and happy, to greet her lover and share her inner life with him. But before they had gone far together she found that his inner world was different indeed from hers. It was not only that his college training had familiarized him with sterner work, and a fuller classical knowledge, but that his home background, the big library he grew up in, had made him more familiar with the great men of the nineteenth and even the eighteenth century than with the uneasy heterodox thinkers of today. On the other hand, he knew the practical affairs of his time, the movements of business and politics, with a fullness which seemed to the girl almost omniscient. It is easy to attribute vast wisdom to one who speaks easily on subjects of which the hearer knows nothing.

Over the happy intimacies of lovers a special angel watches. Each longs to please the other, and every subtle instinct urges forward the thought, word, action that meets agreement, and draws back into temporary oblivion whatever makes for difference. It is not dishonesty. There is no faintest wish to deceive. With voluminous soulsearchings each seeks to exhibit the inmost, the utmost, to the other, and yet only succeeds in bringing forward what the other wishes to see. This is a beautiful provision of nature for the furtherance of the immediate end.

They were very happy. There was no opposition to their marriage. Mrs. Challis, severe and concentrated mother though she was, could not disapprove of this irreproachable young man. Mrs. Widfield, genial and diffuse in her rich maternity, took the girl to her heart, and Stella, with a queer sense of disloyalty, felt as if she were an orphan who had found a home.

The aunts experienced an absorbing interest in the affair. It was a long time since they had had a wedding to prepare for, and discuss. In the first days of Mr. Widfield's visible attentions, they had made it their business to look up his family, and had deputed a prosperous nephew to report as to his business. Both proved desirable. The good ladies then devoted themselves to the matter of the trousseau and the wedding gifts, and prepared for it with a voluminosity as to linen, and a heaviness as to silver, of an almost pre-Victorian savor. The whole Livingstone connection seemed suddenly aware that the "little Challis girl" had grown up and was about to be a credit to them.

"She is marrying very well," they said, "one of the Maryland Widfields—his mother was a Royal of Virginia—very nice people indeed."

Wherefore the linen and the silver increased, with clocks, bronzes, jewels, and other treasures, which accumulated in the long, dark Livingstone drawing room to an appalling degree.

Stella looked them over almost with terror. She had never occupied her mind with dreams of housekeeping, and never had any to do in reality. Now her blossoming hopes were all for a small, sweet home, intimate, dainty, utterly hers and his. This incursion of other persons' tastes and opulences upon her own first home jarred subtly. She was grateful, too; it seemed strangely sweet to have so many persons care for her—persons she had scarcely known, some she had never met. It all became part of the undulating, rosy atmosphere in which her old life, so long and cold and dark as it looked, disappeared to a vanishing point as rapidly as the track behind the observation car.

Morgan was having his share of new sensations, too. The whole sweet reverence of man for woman made him her loving slave. The whole long habit of conquest and possession made him her loving master. New hopes, new ambitions, tendernesses, a sense of overwhelming consecration, astonished him as they spread wide within. Life looked new to him, too, beautiful and holy. He despised his own lower moments, and was fully honest when he vowed he was not worthy to touch her velvet-bowed slipper.

And she bowed her smooth head with overflowing eyes, and said: "My King!"

Nevertheless there were times when Stella felt a little sense of loneliness and hunger in some corner of her mind that he did not seem to see. She even mustered courage as their wedding loomed nearer to disburden her conscience of its one guilt.

"Dear," she said, "I'm not quite what you think me. I have to tell you something. It is very hard."

He lifted his head for a flashing moment and looked at her, then laughed lovingly.

"Tell me the worst!" he said. "Your worst is better than my best!"

She refused to be so comforted, and laboriously explained that she had not confined herself to the range of reading allowed, but had read everything she could reach—even books of which he disapproved.

"Such as——" he suggested evenly.

She named her most appalling list, and he drew her to him and kissed her fondly.

"You dear!" he said. "You precious little silver-souled child! Just because I don't care for those fellows is no reason you shouldn't read them if you want to. You haven't been feeling badly over *that*, have you?"

That she had, made it all the sweeter to be so shriven and absolved.

The girl approached her marriage with ambitions so luminously high as to be beyond human attainment, but that she did not know.

She would so live, she vowed in the still moonlight, kneeling by her window with the warm night wind stirring her soft hair, that he should never have cause to blame her. She would never criticize him, never say a word unjust or unkind, never oppose him in anything that was right. And he would never ask of her anything that was not right—that she knew. She would be faithful in thought, in feeling, in the last extreme of delicate reticence. No other man existed in her world. She would so love him, so serve him, so surround him with comfort and tenderest care, with companionship and sympathy and unfailing love, that when they were old together, he should say: "My wife—you have always made me happy!"

The tears ran over, the happy tears of deep, unutterable love.

Vaguely, behind all this, in deeps within deeps, glowed the high hope of motherhood.

They were married in October.

A wedding journey is a strange preamble to married life. Some long-surviving instinct of a nuptial flight, some impulse dating from the time of "marriage by capture" must actuate us in this custom. We will not speak of those sad little journeys in which the road to heaven plunges suddenly, and irrevocably downward, or even of those wherein the heaven-kissing hills turn out to be an endless, flat, hard plain, not overflowery—the kind so well portrayed in an old *Punch* picture, where the dreary pair sit on the dreary beach and the bored lady says:

"I wish some friend would happen along." To which the bored gentleman replies: "Yes, or even an enemy!"

The happier a wedding journey is, the less it prepares for the practical life to follow. The girl is taken from the surroundings to which she has always been accustomed, and enters upon a strange world—steamships, railroad trains, hotels, a whirling change of scene, of which she knows nothing, and in which he takes every care of her. He is her guardian, champion, "guide, companion, and friend." He devotes himself to her; her will is law; his time, strength, his interest and attention are hers. They two are together, unutterably happy, and the rest of the world is merely a place of amusement and observation.

Then they go to housekeeping.

How can a girl from Springfield, Massachusetts, choose a home in New York City? She knows nothing of the social values, or even the mere topographical conveniences. She would never dream of the difference one block makes to the average New Yorker—one block from that necessary evil, "the L," or the unnecessarily evil "subway."

Morgan had chosen; Morgan's mother and sisters had furnished—largely with wedding presents, and had even engaged the maids, colored, of course—they had never had any others.

So with love and good cheer, with all the necessary and usual adjuncts of married life, Stella Widfield began housekeeping.

She was just twenty.

Since Morgan had come—and she had known him six months—he had never been long away from her. In all the wistful, hopeful, fearful days before he spoke, she had thought of him almost continually, having, for that matter, no other business. Since they were engaged he had been with her almost daily, and on that dreamlike flight by sea and land he had been wholly hers.

Now she was planted in a new home in a strange, great city, with a totally new business to learn, and to practice while she learned, and Morgan was not there. Of course he was there nights. He was there evenings except on rare occasions. But he was not there, with her, in her new business. He had his own business, it appeared—a thing which he had hardly mentioned before, which she had never seriously considered as an opponent or rival, yet which now seemed suddenly to swallow him up, and take him away from her.

A whole group of new conditions confronted the girl, and she faced them as reasonably and courageously as any girl could. A boy of twenty, suddenly placed in new surroundings, cut off from every previous association, and given serious responsibilities, may face them with courage and reason, but he is only a boy. Of the girl it is expected that she shall adapt herself to new conditions, to her husband, to her business, and, in most cases, to the swift approach of the greatest responsibility of all—maternity, at an age in which we only say of her brother—"boys will be boys."

Stella did well. She was not too limited in money. If she ordered absurdly Morgan could afford to laugh at her. When she realized her deficiencies and wanted to take a course in household science up at Barnard, he could afford that, too. She learned a deal of chemistry and economics, something of the science of nutrition, and a little about cooking, and presently she put her own shoulder to the wheel—selected books, read, attended lectures and by the end of a year was forever exempt from the jokes about brides.

That was easier than to get along without Morgan. When he went away in the morning, each inexorable morning, and the elevator closed on him—she could not watch him down the street except by craning from the window, and then he was only a strange dot with far-reaching legs—it was bad enough, but what really made her sense of utter loneliness complete was that he went into another world.

In one of Charles Reade's novels Stella had read of a noble heroine who, though "they were married forty years, had never once asked him what he would have for dinner," and had then and there determined to be as noble should she marry. Proudly she made up her strong young mind that she would not unload on him the small cares and annoyances of her day. All her efforts and disappointments, her hopes and struggles in the housekeeping line, she kept to herself. Therefore her life, her daily occupation, was unknown land to him.

On the other hand she found that her deep desire to be a refreshment and a comfort to him in his work and trouble met small encouragement. He was not in trouble, not in the least discouraged. He was a hardworking, ambitious, successful young businessman, and this work in which he lived with such enthusiasm was unknown land to her.

In the evenings they were very happy together, as happy, that is, as two persons can be whose ground of union is that of small talk, and the discussion of books and pictures. Morgan admired his young wife, loved her tenderly, approved with many compliments of her evident progress as a manager, but his approval was that of the man who says: "Yes, you look fine!" and does not really know which gown you have on.

Stella asked eager questions about his business for a while. She even "read up" on leather, as far as she could. But she found that leather was one thing and business was another. He tried to answer her, tried to explain, to some degree, at least; but the whole technic of the business world, its code of honor, its purposes and methods, were quite outside her range. It was not a question of knowledge, but of a totally different type of mind.

Somewhat debarred here from her hoped-for usefulness, the young wife turned her efforts toward being charming. She took great pains with her costumes, which delighted him—when he noticed it. She deliberately read, visited, and went about to gather material for bright conversation. If she could not talk to him about her work, nor he to her about his work, they must needs talk about some other matters, of less concern to either.

Before the year was out a new interest appeared, a most vital interest; they named it Morgan Challis Widfield.

Again Stella faced new conditions, strange, important, without knowledge or experience. Again she found herself, for all practical purposes, alone. Morgan senior loved Morgan junior—they soon called him Junior for distinction—with both pride and devotion. He was willing, or would have been willing (had it been necessary) to walk the floor with him for uncomplaining hours. He was willing, and anxious, to buy him everything he could possibly need or want. Beyond that he made far-reaching plans for what the boy should do, in college, and after college. But for the daily work, the tremendous task of rearing that sturdy young body and aspiring soul, Morgan had nothing to offer except to back up his wife's authority, or to urge "send for the doctor."

Stella loved her home because it was Morgan's, loved her child largely for the same reason, and resented, in a faint blind way, the strange fact that both home and child seemed to come between them.

In three years' time there was a little Royal Livingstone Widfield, to play with Junior, to fill the young mother's heart and hands and time.

The proud possessor of two healthy children, of a husband who loved her, of a pleasant home, and of enough money to live on, ought to be perfectly happy. So, at least, it is generally assumed. Stella assumed it, too, and at times she was.

The next few years, five or six of them, were filled with the efforts and perplexities, the lonely labors and joys of child care. Here, as in the housekeeping line, Stella used her brains. She read what she could find, and thought on what she read. She found, as Junior grew older, a good kindergartner and learned much from her. It was easier with little Roy; she had learned something from his brother.

As these cares lightened, as the baby came triumphantly through the dreaded "second summer," and grew on from kilts to knickerbockers, the young woman, his mother, began to look about her again, and most of all to look for her husband.

Stella was now more beautiful than in her spare girlhood, stronger, too, and wiser. Her household gave her small trouble. Her children, now at school or kindergarten, were a joy. Then she began to realize this large, patent, unescapable fact—that eight from twenty-four leaves sixteen.

Few of us sleep more than eight hours. Add the laziest undressing, the most elaborate morning toilet, it is not over nine and a half; two and a half hours for meals, and you have twelve. Twelve hours from twenty-four leaves twelve. A twelve-hour day is long. Take from this the evening for amusement, after dinner, eight to eleven—three hours more. There remain nine hours to every day to work in, or to play in, or to be bored in.

Stella did not go at it in this arithmetical way. She was not analytical nor philosophic. She only realized that even housekeeping and motherhood, well-fulfilled, left her with two lacks: she was insufficiently occupied, and she was lonely.

"You must get acquainted more, my dear," said her husband heartily. "You've been shut up so long with these kids that you've forgotten how to visit. We must go out evenings, and surely you've got a lot of nice friends. Here's Cousin Alicia right in the building—you like her, don't you? And who's that nice woman across the hall, Mrs. MacAvelly? I think she's very pleasant."

Stella agreed. She stood watching her tall, handsome husband in the little dressing room between their chambers; she loved to help him with his studs.

"Oh, yes, there are plenty of nice friends," she agreed. "But it's you that I want, Morgan."

He smiled at her over the towel, rosy, clean and genial.

"Well, you've got me all right, my dear—got me for keeps! You'll never get desertion as a cause! I can tell you that!"

He went to look for the boys, a little visit before dinner, and she finished her toilet wondering why she was unsatisfied. Friends there were, new and old, in plenty, as she had said. But one old one, lately turned up, gave her small satisfaction.

This was Malina Peckham, who made her a most unexpected call. Malina had grown thinner, sharper, harder. She was dressed in a way both tailorish and dashing, and proudly owned to being a reporter.

"Yes, I'm on *The Evening Lookover*—got a pretty good job, too. I do society notes mostly and some space work—it's great!"

Stella asked for her mother.

"Oh, Mother's dead—lost my best friend—I know! And Father's dead, too. We went west, you know. Poor old Father always thought he could do things and never made good. I've been on my own for five years now. I've worked on San Francisco papers, and Chicago, and now I've got to little old New York. Don't you like it?"

She chattered on cheerfully, her sharp eyes taking note of the pleasantly furnished apartment, the books on the shelves, the pictures on the wall, and every detail of her hostess's costume.

"I knew you'd see me," she went on. "It's not like you to turn down an old friend, even if she does work for her living. You were mighty good to me in the old days, Stella."

Stella did not like her any better now than she had as a child, but the appeal to magnanimity always held her, and Malina called when she saw fit.

Alicia Cushing was a cousin of Morgan's, a young widow. She was now living with her father-in-law, who seemed devoted to her, in an apartment above their own. Plump and pleasant, blond and rosy, soft of voice, of eye, of hand, with nice manners and engaging Southern accent, Cousin Alicia was really a very attractive person.

And there were others, plenty of them.

But Stella wanted Morgan, and somehow, as the years passed, he seemed farther and farther away.

3

Three long rooms, opening into one another by wide archways discreetly closable with sliding doors as well as portieres, had Mrs. Widfield to promenade in.

They were very pleasant rooms, arranged with that careful dovetailing of beauty and ease which comes of long usage, good taste and a sufficient income. The glassed bookcases tempted like a walled garden, and repaid as well. There were few pictures and little bric-a-brac, but much restful space and soft color, with a wallpaper which was as unnoticeably comforting as one's mother.

Up and down the three long rooms walked Mrs. Widfield, now slowly and meditatively, now swiftly and nervously. She stood at one rain-streaked window and watched the wet, shining street so far below, with its clanging yellow-roofed surface cars, and the black, gleaming tops of taxis and limousines scuttling along like darting beetles. She walked the length of the apartment and stood at another window watching the river, vague, foggy, mournful and loud in veiled hootings. She stood at the middle window— a wide one, slightly bayed, and looked up and down the clean quiet side street, showing only hurrying husbands with umbrellas.

Mrs. Widfield was growing anxious.

It was time for Morgan to be at home, three minutes—yes, five minutes late. She had telephoned the office earlier in the dismal afternoon, and been told he had left for the day. Then he might come any minute—and she had been waiting now for an hour.

Morgan was always so thoughtful; he would surely have sent word if he were to be detained. There must be a block in the subway—perhaps an accident—her heart stood still.

There was nothing she could do. He had left the office, he had not come home, and between home and office lay the black terrible miles of New York, where men, women and children die daily in the streets from a score of dangers. The surface cars, the motors with their swift attack and swifter flight, murderers worse than criminal in their callous carelessness, these were bad enough, and worse on wet days. But that undying worm which perforates the long city, that culture tube of all communicable diseases, that horizontal- and swift-moving Black Hole of Calcutta, in which courtesy and decency are lost, comfort unhoped for, and danger ever present—the subway was her real horror.

They had been married fifteen years.

Stella was a gracious woman of thirty-five, her gentle distinguished beauty increased by the softer outlines, the richer color of maturity. Her fine hair was as softly dark as ever, and as plentiful, her straight figure still slender, though more rounded.

Both of the boys were at school now; they had just left home again for the autumn term, and their mother had been reckoning up the years of their coming absence. Three years more of school—four for the younger—and then four of college and then the medical school, or the law school, or the technical school—it would be ten years and more before they were "educated."

And then, she forced herself to recognize, they would not come home. They would never come home—they would promptly set up homes of their own. She had lost her boys, except for vacations. Even on vacations, they often went visiting—yes, they were gone.

She had only Morgan.

Again she looked at the clock. Fifteen minutes—and Morgan was never late! She pushed the swing door in the dark paneling of the dining room, and passed through the clean, light pantry to the white-tiled kitchen.

Her efficient cook sat, rosy, by the window; everything was "on," and it was not time to "take up" yet. The equally efficient waitress, white-capped and aproned, was upholding her religion against that of the cook, while she crocheted a cap for one of her rapidly accumulating blonde nieces. Hedda was a Lutheran, well versed in scripture, and Mrs. O'Mally a convinced Romanist.

Mrs. Widfield brought them out some magazines, and rather wistfully ventured a hope that Mr. Widfield would not be late.

"He will not, ma'am," Mrs. O'Mally reassured her. "I've cooked here these siven years, and he was never late without sendin' ye word."

"It's a bad night," said Hedda, rather gloomily.

Then Stella went to her own room, turned up both lights at the dressing table and seated herself before the wide mirror. She loosened the waves of her hair a little, changed an ornament, tried the effect of a big velvet rose on her bosom, at the girdle, on one side and the other.

She surveyed the back of her dress in the cheval glass, deriving some pleasure from its graceful lines, the delicate curves of the white neck above, and the clean-grown, fragrant hair. Then she heard the elevator and ran to open the door, before he could get his key out.

"Oh, Morgan, dear, I've been so worried! Where have you been? I telephoned at four, and they said you'd gone for the day."

He kissed her affectionately, and hung his coat on the rack, set his umbrella in the tall blue jar, and turned toward his dressing room.

"Why, I had to go over to Jersey City to see a man—and then I came home. Got here about as usual, didn't I? I'd have sent you word if I'd been delayed, of course."

She looked reproachfully at the clock.

"Oh, 'tis over time, isn't it? Well, you see, I got to the house about as usual, but I had to see Alicia about those stocks of hers. I didn't realize it would take more than a minute."

Stella's face clouded a little but she only said, "Well, dear—dinner's ready now."

"I'd have left it till after dinner," he added, sensible of a faint reproof, "but Alicia does take so long about things, and I'd rather have my evening with you." He kissed her again, a friendly indiscriminating kiss, and they went to the table.

It was a good dinner, the kind of dinner he liked, and he ate heartily, pleasantly conscious of the rosy lights, the shining silver, the fresh-aired warmth, the satisfying food.

Stella was not hungry. Her anxiety had been very real. As for Alicia, she knew her dawdling ways, and was really glad that Morgan had attended to his little business before dinner rather than afterward. She had nothing to blame him for, except not letting her know he was in the house, and she could easily see how natural that was. Yet for all her careful justice and her lack of jealousy, she was not happy.

"What's the matter?" he asked presently. "You're not eating anything. It's a bully dinner."

She smiled back at him.

"Why, I was so worried, Morgan."

"Worried! What nonsense, Stella! You can't lose me so easily. I believe that is your only weakness—worrying about me."

"It's not weakness, Morgan. You know very well that after you leave the office and before you get here you might be—killed—and I should never know it till I saw the morning papers."

"Oh, pshaw, my dear—that's absurd. I carry a card case. You'd know soon enough. I'm particularly careful to let you know when I'm delayed."

There was a shade of annoyance in his tone. She met it with prompt admission of his constant thoughtfulness, blamed herself for worrying, and began regaling him with small happenings as had punctuated her day. There was a letter from Junior—the boys were both well but did not profess great happiness in lessons—not much of a letter. The electric heater was out of order; the gas bill seemed to be moderate; her dressmaker was a week behind again.

When dessert arrived he absorbed it with evident pleasure, but she fell quiet, and sat with her white elbows on the table, making pale reflections in the smooth mahogany, her chin on the backs of her interlocked fingers, regarding him wistfully.

They heard the doorbell. Hedda silently closed the doors, and presently announced "Miss Peckham."

Also they heard Miss Peckham's penetrating voice: "Tell them not to hurry. I'll make myself at home."

"I shan't hurry, at any rate," observed Mr. Widfield. "I'd like some more of that—whatever its Bible name may be. It's mighty good."

Miss Peckham, left to herself, seemed well content. She loosened her coat, and pulled off her gloves, all the time stepping quickly and quietly about and making mental note of everything in the room.

A large photograph, wasteful of heavy paper mounting, stood on the mantel. Malina took it down and read the signature. "Cousin Alicia—h'm," said she softly. Another photograph stood on the piano. "Cousin Alicia again." She turned to the center table and stood, nodding her head sagaciously. "And once more, Cousin Alicia! If I were Stella Widfield, I'd stick one of myself up somewhere. Cousin Alicia's too much in evidence, *I* think—and too handsome."

As she stood looking at the pictures, a voice at her elbow startled her and she wheeled sharply about.

A quiet, pleasant-faced, middle-aged lady stood there murmuring gently: "Oh, excuse me—you see I live just next door and run in and out quite freely. My name is MacAvelly."

"Mine is Peckham, Malina Peckham, of *The Day*, formerly on *The Lookover*. Say, I've heard your name. You're a friend of the Van Tromps, aren't you? You can tell me the facts in the Van Tromp story, as well as Stella, I guess. Now *did* Katy Van Tromp—or didn't she?"

Mrs. MacAvelly smiled her gentle smile.

"You remind me of the little green grasshopper creatures—Katy did! Katy didn't! Do you remember that lovely thing of Holmes's about the Katydid?

> *Thou 'mindest me of gentlefolk—*
> *Old gentlefolk are they;*
> *Thou sayst an undisputed thing*
> *In such a solemn way!*

And speaking of Holmes, have you read his awful snake story?"

Miss Peckham regarded her with sharp, steady eyes. "Snake story?" she queried. "Is he one of those nature fakers?"

"Very good!" applauded the visitor. "You newspaperwomen *are* so sharp! Why, no. This story is something almost occult. Are you interested in the occult?"

"Not much," said Miss Peckham with truth. "I'm interested in the concrete. You know the Widfields pretty well, don't you?"

"Fairly well. They are delightful people to know."

"I've known Stella Widfield over twenty years." (Malina did not like to say thirty years, it seemed too confining.) "Went to school with her. And I think she's an unhappy woman. What do you think?"

Mrs. MacAvelly smiled brightly. "I always love to see loyalty to friends," she said, "especially among women."

"Oh, I'm loyal to women, all right," Miss Peckham cheerfully agreed. "But I hate men. You can always tell when a woman's unhappy. Most of 'em are. What do you think of this, now?" she suddenly demanded, wheeling about and pointing out the photographs. "And this, and this?"

Mrs. MacAvelly loosed her eyeglasses from the little gold hook on her shoulder and went about examining the pictures.

"Very handsome, I think," she declared.

"Very numerous, *I* think," amended Miss Peckham. "I don't see any of Stella, do you?"

"Speaking of her, she knows those Van Tromps, I think."

"Yes, I know she does. That's what I'm here for—I want the facts."

"I used to know Dick Van Tromp when he was a boy at college," pursued Mrs. MacAvelly reflectively. "Seems to me I used to have a picture of him——"

"Oh, did you? Have you? Do let me see it! *The Day* is wild to get a picture of him. He's too well known to fake it."

"If you'll come to my apartment I'll let you see it, if I can find it. The Widfields are dining, you see."

"All right—thank you," and Miss Peckham briskly followed her out.

In the quiet dining room Mrs. Widfield was idly stirring her coffee, while her husband sipped his appreciatively. She watched him in silence for a while, then rose, with a little, impatient gesture, and went to the back of his chair. She bent over him affectionately, threw her arm around his neck and held him close, her cheek upon his head.

It was a pretty picture, but he seemed uneasy, and struggled out of her embrace, fingering his collar. She stood up, moved away a little, and spoke with rather a forced cheerfulness.

"Now you sit still and read your paper, dear—as long as you want to."

"Thank you, my dear," he said with alacrity. She turned with rather a hopeless look, and he sprang up to open the door for her. Returning with a lighter air, he poured himself another cup of coffee, lit a cigar, opened his paper, and settled himself luxuriously.

She stood in the doorway, holding the curtain aside with one jeweled hand, smiling at him, but he did not notice. He was quite unconscious of her gaze and showed every sign of contentment. She turned softly away, and glanced about the pleasant parlor. It seemed chilly—these early storms before the steam heat was on always made her shiver.

Her latest joy in the perfecting of their home was an electric heater, a pretty thing, which glowed cosily even when unlit, and was a fire from heaven, lighted—all soft glow and warmth, no dirt, no trouble to replenish. She turned it on, and crouched a moment by it, watching the pink light through her fingers as she warmed them.

Starting to her feet at a slight sound, she turned to greet him—no, he had not risen. She pulled the cushions about on the divan near the fire, and arranged herself gracefully upon it—for about one minute. The cushions were not right, there were too many "candles" on in the heater. She passed here and there, arranging and re-arranging things, and going now and then to look at him.

"What is it, dear?" he said, with a preoccupied air, turning slowly from his paper.

"Oh, nothing," she answered precipitately, and let the curtain drop again. The long mirror over the mantel held her eye for some time; she could not but admire the fine face, pink-lit from the electric glow beneath her.

Cousin Alicia's photograph caught her eye; she stood it up against the glass, beside her own face, and studied the two, gravely.

Suddenly she saw something that seemed to startle her—leaned forward. Yes, it was one fine shining thread, a white hair. She carefully pulled it out, set back the impressive photograph and turned to walk again, her head bent down, her hands behind her.

Then, shaking off oppressive thoughts, she busied herself arranging his favorite chair, setting by it the small stand, the "gooseneck" light he preferred, the new eyeshade that was all gleaming green celluloid—no wire nor elastic, the footrest at the right distance, a magazine, a new book on the table near.

And every moment or two, a look through the portieres—was he never coming?

At last Mr. Widfield rose rather hastily, crushed his newspaper in his hand, and came in, with an air of cheerfulness that savored faintly of resignation.

"Now then, Stella, my dear, what is it you want?"

She stood waiting, eager, affectionate, her clear eyes on his. "*I want you*," she said intensely.

"Well, you've got me fast enough, haven't you? I'm quite in your hands for the evening."

"Oh, the evening!" She turned away with a quick, sensitive movement. "Don't stay in on my account, please."

He smiled, easily. "I am staying at home for the pleasure of my wife's society, as I not infrequently do."

She brightened at this, and ran to kiss him.

"You dear. Now let's sit down and talk! Here's your chair and here's mine." She brought a little stool and nestled down close beside him, looking up at him with loving eyes. "What have you been doing today, dear?"

"Nothing particular—just business."

"Oh, business! You might talk to me about business, then."

"Now my charming wife—there is nothing in my business that interests you, and we both know it by this time. I don't ask you to talk to me about your business. "

"I haven't any business," she answered slowly. "And I know you would not care to have me talk to you about what I do."

"Then why talk?" he suggested, with intent to amuse, and gently stroked her hair, but she dropped her eyes evidently hurt. Then, looking up brightly, "Would you like—have you seen that article on 'The Evils of the Leather Trade,' in the last *Uplift*?"

"No, thanks—and I don't mean to. Those muckrakers don't know anything practical."

She kept her light air, and suggested, "That's a fine story they are running now—don't you think so?"

"Have you known me fifteen years and haven't found out yet that I never read serials? Guess again."

But she was silent, studying her fingertips, and he looked around for a book, his hand on her shoulder. She looked at him rather grievedly, then rose and hovered about, arranging his footrest, putting on the eyeshade, with a little kiss for the thin spot on the top of his head. She leaned forward softly and laid her cheek to his; and he reached up to pat it rather perfunctorily. She drew back gently but hastily and walked to the window.

After reading a few minutes, he looked around, saw her attitude of patient resignation, and laid down his book with a sigh, rising and going to her.

"What's the matter, Stella, dear? Aren't you feeling well?" His voice was kindly.

She turned to him at once, bravely and sweetly. "Oh yes, dear, I'm all right. I'm reading an excellent novel."

So saying, she established herself by the table, and began to read intently. He was relieved, and after watching her absorption for a moment, went to the bookcase and brought back a thick book. He pulled his chair about a bit, turned the light differently, pitched the cushion to the divan, kicked away the footstool, and settled down to read.

The room was very still. At times the rain swept across the windows, and the distant clangor of passing cars rose fitfully. Presently he caught the sound of a little sigh, and looked at her. Her head was on her hand. Patiently he laid down his book. Patiently he spoke. "Well, dear, what is it?"

She closed her book, ran to him and dropped by his side, burying her face on his shoulder.

"I know I'm a suicidal goose—but—O Morgan! Why don't you love me anymore?"

He smiled a little wearily, holding her closely. "My esteemed, admired, beloved wife! How old are you?"

She drew back sharply. "Old?"

"Young, I should have said. About sixteen, anybody would think. Well, young lady—sit up and listen. One, I love you. Two, I love you. Three, I love you. Four, I love you. Five, six, seven, eight, up to say forty, I love you. Will that do for one evening?"

She rose and withdrew, softly but decidedly, resuming her seat on the other side of the table, saying, "Thank you. It will do for a long time." And she read determinedly.

"Well of all——" he began. "Stella—I believe you are ill."

"I wish I was!" she burst out passionately. "I'd rather be ill! I'd rather die than be so miserable!"

Quietly her husband rose and came to her, laying a strong, gentle hand on her shoulder. "My dear little girl! I know you must be ill, for you were always so reasonable—and now you are so unreasonable."

"Unreasonable—that's what men always say," she retorted.

"Is it any wonder!" he said softly. "Now really, my dear—what makes you miserable? What have you to complain of?"

"I'm not complaining."

"You certainly said you were unhappy. What does ail you, my dear?"

"May I tell you? Will you listen? Will you try to understand?" Again she clung to him, looking up earnestly into his face.

"Of course I will. I'll be thankful to find out. I haven't said anything—but I have noticed that you didn't seem to be as happy lately as you were before. It's nothing that money can get, is it?"

"No, indeed!"

"The apartment satisfies you? You don't want to move—or refurnish, or anything?"

She shook her head. "Oh! it's not that!"

"The boys are all right. You're not pining for them, are you?"

"Of course I miss them," she admitted, "and I was thinking that they're really gone for good. We never shall have them again, Morgan, not for our own. There's only you left."

"And I'm sure I've given you no cause for complaint," he concluded triumphantly. "So you must be ill."

"I am *not* ill," she protested with sudden vehemence.

"Then it *is* me you are not satisfied with."

He brought a chair and sat facing her, taking her hands in his. "Now dear, out with it. Please explain."

"I'm ashamed to."

"Oh, go ahead. I may be to blame without knowing it. As you say, there are just you and I left now, and we don't want any misunderstanding. Tell me all about it."

"It's no use telling you," she answered slowly. "When I tell you what I want—and you give it to me because I tell you—because you think it's your duty—then—— Oh, then it isn't what I want at all—and never can be."

Mr. Widfield rose and walked the floor.

"Mother of Pearl!" he protested. "If she says what she wants—and gets what she wants—it *isn't* what she wants—and never can be!"

He wheeled about suddenly and faced her again. "Look here, Stella! It's not—you can't be—*jealous!* I do believe you're jealous of Cousin Alicia."

She looked up at him with clear, honest eyes. "No, Morgan. It's not that. I am a little bit, sometimes, but I know that's foolish. The other is real."

"Tell me 'the other,' Stella."

She bent her head. He came closer, stooped nearer. "Come tell me, dear."

She whispered in his ear.

"Stella Widfield! I 'don't love you'? You—you foolish child. What on earth do you expect me to do to show I love you? You know I *do*. You know I *have* for fifteen years—and am likely to for forty! Unless——"

She looked up quickly. "Unless what?"

"Nothing. Of course I will, dear. You are my wife, and a good one. I've no criticism to make of you—except——"

"Oh, 'unless' and 'except'"—she burst forth. "I knew there was something! Oh, Morgan! Can't you see how it crushes me? To feel you grow cold and indifferent—impatient."

He smiled his steady smile. "You really think I'm impatient with you?"

"Oh, you're horribly patient! It isn't patience I want—nor duty—nor kindness. I want your love!"

"And do you think this is a good way to get it?"

"How cruel! When I know—only too well—that there's no way to get it—that I've lost it! Oh, Morgan—you know I think of you every minute of the day."

"I wish you would occasionally think of something else," he suggested quietly.

"You know I'm always here waiting for you when you come in—ready to pour your tea—to go out with you—to stay in with you. You know I care for nothing on earth but you——"

She had risen and come closer, appealing, reaching her hands to him. He took them and stood looking at her tenderly, and yet with a weariness he could not wholly disguise.

"And I don't care for tea—and haven't time to go out with you—and staying in does not seem to satisfy you. Stella, my dear, it would be a lot easier if you did care for something on earth besides me—had other interests in life."

"Such as what?" she demanded pathetically.

"You have your home. I thought you enjoyed it."

"I do—so do you—that's not enough."

"You have your children——"

"Yes—and they're grown up as far as I'm concerned. They don't need me anymore."

"You have friends—amusements—books——"

She shook her head. "I don't want any more things—or any more people, Morgan. I want your love—all of it. It's all I have in the world—all I *had!*"

"Cheer up, my dear. You've got it yet. I *do* love you—and I don't love anyone else, but I confess——"

She drew back, waiting—"Well?"

He looked at her quizzically.

"I confess there are times when I find Cousin Alicia—restful!"

4

Malina Peckham, always keen for fresh information, eagerly studied Mrs. MacAvelly's pleasant parlor, while the photograph was being looked for with cheerful assiduity. She saw nothing unusual, just a harmonious quiet room, ordinary but agreeable.

"I must have been entirely wrong," said Mrs. MacAvelly, coming in from her bedroom. "I can't find it anywhere. It is too bad to have lured you here on false pretenses, Miss Peckham. Now won't you tell me a little about your work. Do you enjoy it?"

Her manner was quiet, but attractive. Malina's alert defensiveness relaxed for the moment.

"Why, yes—I enjoy some of it. There are lots of interesting stories to be hunted up. I always did like to find out things."

"Have you ever made a scoop—one of those big stories I've read about?" asked her hostess. "I should think you'd be just the one to succeed where a good many would fail."

Then the newspaperwoman almost forgot her errand, while she chattered about the various adventures and achievements of her career.

"But I really mustn't waste any more of your time—and mine," she said suddenly, starting up with a jerk. "Bless me! How long I've stayed!" and she whisked back to Mrs. Widfield's door.

Mr. Widfield was by no means pleased to hear her hard voice speaking to Hedda in the little hall.

"Here's your childhood friend again, Stella! I thought good Mrs. Mac had saved us!" He sought to make a stealthy escape, but Malina entered.

"Now you needn't try to run away, Mr. Widfield. You're the very man I want to see! Good evening, Stella—I want to see you too, of course."

She laid aside her raincoat and umbrella on a chair, and whisked out her notebook.

"I know you'll help me out on this, Mr. Widfield. I just *have* to get the facts—or I'm fired! Now you can tell me all about this Van Tromp story, I'm sure."

Morgan Widfield was most displeased with Miss Peckham on account of the jarring mixture of feelings she aroused in him. He liked to admire a woman, and she was not pretty. He liked to take care of a woman, and she was patently able to take care of herself. His feelings about women formed, taken altogether, that vague roseate nimbus, half-reverential, and half-patronizing, which so many men have; such a feeling as one might have for an angel with a wooden leg. And here was Malina, whom he was forced to respect as a keen efficient worker, yet who jarred on all his "finer feelings." As a man he might have spoken of her as a "clever fellow"—"does capital work"—"sure to get on"—"honest and able." As a woman, he simply didn't like her.

So Mr. Widfield excused himself courteously but firmly, covering his retreat with the technical defense of some business he must attend to.

"Men are so mean! They'll always stand up for one another, and never tell a woman anything! How are you, Stella? You don't look yourself."

If Mrs. Widfield was not her usual gentle courteous self, she felt there was reason good. It was always a little difficult for her to be patient with Miss Peckham. She had tried to be helpful and loyal, sometimes had been of very needful service; and the more obligation she laid on Malina, the less she felt able to be cold to her, lest she seem to remind her of it.

"I am well as usual," she answered. "But I really cannot tell you anything about this Van Tromp affair."

"I thought they were friends of yours."

"They are. That is why I cannot discuss them."

"Oh! I see. Well—I wish I could afford a sense of honor like that! I'd have to tell tales on my own mother if the old man sent me. Never mind. It's good to look at you, anyhow. I've always admired you, Stella, since we were kids. And you've been mighty good to me! You're not one to go back on a friend, just because she has to work for a living."

"I have a great respect for the women who work," Mrs. Widfield answered her. "I wish I could."

"You *could*, easy enough. You always were clever. Why, those things you did in school were *gems*, Stella, absolute *gems*. Why don't you write? But then, why should you? You don't have to. Nobody need talk to me about the dignity of labor. *I'm* quite willing to be 'supported.'"

"But you haven't a good opinion of men, you know."

"Indeed I haven't! You just work in an office—a woman alone, and you learn what men are! I hate 'em."

"Yet you'd marry one?"

"I can't marry anything else, can I? And when I do marry—if I do—I'm not going to be the downtrodden one I can tell you. I'll do some down-treading myself!"

She sat leaning forward, elbows on knees, swinging her stout worn gloves, her keen eye on her hostess.

Mrs. Widfield thought she heard Morgan go out of the hall door—and showed it.

Miss Peckham spoke out sharply.

"Stella Widfield—you know you're unhappy!"

"Unhappy? I——?" Mrs. Widfield turned a quiet noncommittal face toward her friend.

"Yes, you. You may not know it—or you may not want me to know it—but it sticks out all over you. I know men. They're mighty mean to women!"

Her hostess laughed lightly. "You are entirely mistaken, Malina. I thank you for your concern, but there is no occasion for it. Tell me—how are you getting on with this paper? Do you like it as well as the other?"

"Yes, thanks. Better, if anything. But that red herring isn't strong enough. Look here! Haven't you got *any* friend to stand up for you? Isn't there anybody to see how thin you are—and how worried looking? Your boys are all right, aren't they? You have money enough. Your conscience is clear—and you're not sick. You're just unhappy—miserably unhappy. And eliminating all other causes, it's got to be your husband! *I* know."

Mrs. Widfield looked at her with an expression of cordial amusement. "What a champion you are, Malina! But you are quite too sympathetic—and too prejudiced against men."

"Maybe I am—but I think not. I remember poor Mother's life—and lots of her friends. And since I've been at work, I tell you I've seen things." She idly buttoned one glove to the other, watching her hostess. "You haven't by any chance a photograph of one of those Van Tromps, have you?"

Stella stiffened a little. "No—I think not. I seldom keep photographs."

"Except Cousin Alicia's."

Mrs. Widfield could not help flushing, more at the suddenness of the attack than anything else; but she answered calmly enough. "Oh—Cousin Alicia, of course, she is so handsome."

Malina laughed, shortly. "Are you a bat, Stella? Can't you *see* what's happening to you—right under your nose? *You* didn't ask for all those photos and stick 'em up everywhere, I warrant."

Stella rose quietly. "That is precisely what I did do, as it happens. You mean kindly, I don't doubt, Malina, but I cannot let you talk to me like this. I think I must ask you to excuse me. I'm tired tonight."

"All right—I'll go. Sorry if I've made you feel bad. I do care about you, Stella. You've certainly been white to me."

She took herself off, and Stella, left alone, raised a window and cooled her hot cheeks in the wet air. A spatter of rain struck on her white throat and she closed the sash again. Malina was gone, but the room reeked of her insinuation. Stella longed to forbid her the house, but felt unable. There was the old acquaintance—a goodwill she had no occasion to doubt—and the weight of obligation on the wrong side.

She shrugged her lace-covered shoulders, and went to look for Morgan. Yes—he had gone out, probably to Alicia's—why not? Perhaps to Mrs. MacAvelly's. With a strange feeling of complicated unrest she tried in vain to settle to books or music, and presently rang for Hedda.

"If Miss Peckham calls again, you may tell her that I am not at home. And, Hedda, when Mr. Widfield comes in, say I am at Mrs. MacAvelly's—and will he please come for me." She pushed the ivory button of the door across the hall.

Morgan was not there, but Mrs. MacAvelly was, and unaffectedly glad to see her. In that warm, fresh, restful room Stella's sense of confused distress slipped from her. She took a low seat near her hostess, with a little sigh of relief.

"You always make me feel rested," she said. "I'm hoodooed tonight. Everything goes wrong. And you somehow take out the puckers."

"Have you been 'interviewed' against your will?"

"Oh, no, not so bad as that. But you know some people *don't* rest one."

"No, they certainly do not," her friend agreed. "Now you just pretend I'm your grandmother, lay that smooth, nice head of yours on my knee—and 'just set' a while."

"That's good. I've done the 'setting and thinking' too long I guess—or not long enough."

They were silent for a little. Mrs. MacAvelly's fire was of coal. It glowed red and steady among the soft-hued tiles. Stella's eyes wandered about the room. She noted anew the variety in chairs, and studied it a little.

"You've got chairs for the Big Bear and the Middle-sized Bear and the Wee-Wee Bear, haven't you?"

"Well—people's legs are happily constructed to reach from their bodies to the ground, but not always from their chairs to the ground. I have one friend now—a dear little woman, who is short anyway, and what height she has is all in the body part. She says that thing you're on is the most comfortable seat she knows. And I have another friend—I always feel that he had a narrow escape from acra—acro—what is that giant disease?"

"Acromegaly?" her friend suggested.

"But his head's far too good for a giant. Anyway he's mostly legs, and he says that brown chair over there is the most comfortable seat he knows. I'm quite vain of my chairs."

They chatted on in little pleasant spurts, and remained silent for long intervals, while occasional dashes of the driving rain outside made that red fire a precious thing.

Stella turned her wedding ring slowly on her finger—turned it around and moved it a little this way and that, as if it hurt her.

"I had a pleasant call on Mrs. Cushing, this afternoon," said Mrs. MacAvelly. "We were speaking of the work they're doing for the city babies now. Your cousin was quite interested."

"She would be, of course. Alicia's very kindhearted. And very pretty. Don't you think so?"

"Extremely pretty. Fortunately some men like other types better."

"Not many, I'm afraid," said Stella, a faint note of sadness in the tone she tried to carry lightly. "Alicia's very attractive."

Her friend touched her fine hair with light appreciative fingers. "I'm glad you are one of the sensible women," she said. "Some I know would be foolishly jealous."

"Jealous!" She spoke the word with gay scorn as if it was quite unthinkable.

"Yes, jealous—very foolishly. But you have no occasion to be, and sense enough to know it. I've known you two a good while, my dear, and if ever a husband really appreciated his wife, it's yours."

Stella's eyes lit up. "Do you think so?" she asked quietly.

Mrs. MacAvelly laughed. "I know so. Little things he lets fall—the way he looks at you—his admiration for your intellect."

"Oh—my intellect!" Stella spoke as if her intellect were a last year's gown.

"Now don't run down your intellect. A woman with brains wears better than any amount of mere beauty."

"Wears a man out, I'm afraid."

"It wears a woman out if she doesn't use it. Now my dear Mrs. Widfield, I've a proposition to make. I really want you to be interested in a young protégé of mine. It will do you good."

"Another working girl fleeing from temptation?"

"No, it's a man this time, with a touch of genius."

"What kind, musical?"

"No. Literary. He's writing a play."

"Oh dear!" Stella was momentarily amused in spite of her preoccupation. "That's no mark of genius, surely."

They were quiet again for a few little moments, Stella dreaming, her sad eyes on the fire, till her friend said, "You don't look happy, Mrs. Widfield."

Then she rose to her feet swiftly, and looked down at the other woman, with new determination.

"If you'll let me, I'll talk. I'll talk it out. There's nobody else I could talk to—but you somehow make me feel safe, and vaguely comforted, like a big tree."

Mrs. MacAvelly smiled. "You'll be saying my bark is worse than my bite next! By all means talk it out. I'm a quiet person and truly interested."

Stella hardly knew why she trusted this friend so completely. They had lived near each other for three years, which is a long time for New York neighbors. They had been friends, quietly intimate, for most of that time, and never had Stella known her to repeat any talk of others, any gossip, any personality. But she was not thinking of this now, only of the troubles in her heart, and the sense of some possible comfort here.

So she unburdened herself, more fully even than she at first intended, going back to her girlhood, touching on those vague young aspirations, those half-formed ambitions to do something, somehow in the world.

"I suppose other girls feel so—I don't know. And I suppose it all goes away and turns to loving when that really comes. One grows to love a person so, so very much, when they are good, as Morgan is. After the babies came, I just loved him more. And now that they are gone—you see they *are* gone, Mrs. MacAvelly—gone for good, practically—why, there's just nobody in the world but Morgan!"

"Well, there he is, isn't he? He has nothing in the world but you, too."

Stella laughed, a little bitter laugh.

"Oh, he has everything else, you see, men do; he has his business and his politics and his friends and all his clubs and—and everything. I know you'll say I have my friends and clubs and things, too—and I have, of course—but I don't care about them. I only care about Morgan."

"Well?"

"Well! He doesn't care about me as he used to! I'm losing him! I can feel it—see it—clearer all the time! Of course I'm not young anymore. I suppose that must make some difference, to a man. . . . He's *good* to me. I don't want you to think for a moment that he isn't just as kind as a husband can be—but there's a sort of strain. I can feel it. I believe he's tired of me—and just doing his duty now!"

Her face was set and tragic. A strong, sweet, earnest face, with this deep gloom upon it as if life were over for good and all.

Mrs. MacAvelly watched her, silent, sympathetic, far too wise to set up hasty superficial denials against such real grief as this.

"You feel as if he did not 'want' you as he used to—as if it were a relief to him when you were not there? Just a weariness, a growing away? You don't think it is anything else?" she asked.

"No, I don't, not really. Of course there's Alicia Cushing. She's always in and out, and he does drop in there pretty often. She's his cousin you know, and she's always asking his advice about business matters in spite of her father-in-law being a lawyer. But I don't honestly think he cares much for her—yet."

"I wish I could help," said Mrs. MacAvelly, gently.

"You can't, nobody can. I've just got to keep on living. There'll be the boys now and then—till they grow up, and the little outside things—but I want—Morgan!"

Her head was down on the other woman's knees, now, and she cried quietly, with little shaking sobs now and then; cried herself into a more peaceful mood at last, and rose to go home.

"You *have* done me good," she said. "I just had to have somebody to cry on—for once. I won't do it again. Good night and thank you."

After she had gone, Mrs. MacAvelly returned to her chair and sat quite still a while. Her quiet face showed no signs of concentration, except for the eyes, in which there grew and deepened a look of steady power.

They were clear, frank eyes, of a grayish hazel, eyes which faced you squarely and showed no reserve. Yet as one looked into their still depths, the soft-blended hues that made one think of a brook, a mountain brook, running level long enough to be still and show the color of its bed, there was an indefinable sense that the water might be deeper than it looked—it was so clear.

She was running over in her mind the position Mrs. Widfield had revealed to her, quite unnecessarily as it happened.

"I had to let her talk it out," she mused. "That is always a relief. But bless me, it was no news. No—I don't think it's Alicia. That would be easy enough." She smiled her gentle, tolerant smile. "Alicia's a nice girl, too—lovely heroine for Locke or Bennett! But what is Stella going to *do?*"

She reached for the telephone on the table beside her. "Beverly 4268—yes, please," and soon got her friend, Miss Woodstone, of the Clam Street Settlement.

"Good evening, Mary—glad to hear your voice. Tell me—is that young Smith about the place tonight? Yes—I'll wait."

In a moment or two, a deeper voice answered her.

"Oh, Mr. Smith—could you come up here some night of this week—and bring your play? . . . Yes, I want you to read it, some of it at least—to a friend of mine—rather an influential man, and a woman, too. I think one or both of them could be of advantage to you. . . . I can't say certainly—will let you know again. . . . You see I wanted to make sure of you before I asked them. . . . Oh no, not at all. Thank you. Good-bye."

Then she got Stella on the phone—with apologies for her stupidity in not remembering to settle the date for that young playwright when she was there, and arranged it tentatively. "I want to make sure of Hamp Tillotson," she explained.

Then with her best notepaper and a long-nosed stub pen she wrote an irresistible note inviting to dinner one of the most caustic critics of *The New York Day*.

5

Mrs. Alicia Cushing was still slowly sipping her after-dinner coffee when Morgan Widfield entered. Her father-in-law, Colonel Charles R. Cushing, of the State Militia, had finished his long since, and was reading the evening paper, partly to himself and partly aloud.

"Have you followed this discussion, Alicia, about those crazy English women?" he had just asked, and Alicia, smiling sweetly both at him and at her cousin, replied, "I read some of it, Papa, and I saw you had a letter to the editor, yourself. Do read it to us. I'm sure Morgan will enjoy it. Coffee, Morgan?"

"No, thank you. Do go on, Colonel Cushing. I'll smoke—if I may, Alicia?"

"By all means—you know where things are."

Stella would have made a dozen errands, to open the humidor, to select a cigar, to bring the ashtray, the matches, the little tabouret at his side to put them on. Alicia never stirred. She was cozily curled among a heap of cushions. One silken foot was tucked under her, one hung daintily in its high-heeled shining slipper, one of those exquisite creations which are undeniably beautiful so long as you do not associate them with any attempt to stand or walk; further than that, imagination could not go, so far as running, for instance. Perhaps one ground for admiring these objects is precisely that they so preclude activity, suggesting peace—and helplessness. But as the arbitrary vaselike curves follow out and supplement the curves of a graceful foot, such a slipper is undeniably pleasant to look at, and Morgan looked at it.

Colonel Cushing was delighted to have his audience increased. He was extremely fond of Alicia, and Alicia's views, in so far as she had any, fairly reflected his own; but Morgan was a man, a fellow being. He would undoubtedly feel the weight, the cogency of these arguments of his.

He cleared his throat. "It is only a little thing, just a few words. But one simply has to say something. With your permission——"

He read, with evident relish, some third of a column of well-rounded sentences, each and all of which sounded like a wilted echo of the similar but more violently expressed ideas of the past century.

Alicia evidently did not listen, but sat playing with the soft ears of the little dog who was trying to sleep on the sofa beside her. Still she was ready with an appreciative smile when he had finished.

"It's good, Papa. What you say is so wise, and so—well, so reasonable—don't you think so, Morgan?"

Now Morgan knew that the arguments of his host were palpably weak and unconvincing, but he agreed with the spirit of the effusion, and said so.

"What a memory you have for proverbs and old sayings," he added. "I often wonder where you find them all."

"In my reading, Mr. Widfield. I read rather extensively in ancient history, as you know, and the literature of the ancients is full of proverbial philosophy. The wisdom of Solomon we now know to have been based upon the gathered wisdom of centuries. "

"Those ancients seem to have been profoundly ungallant, I must say. What was that comparison with asinine acrobatics?"

"When an ass climbs a ladder you may look to find wisdom in women."

Alicia smiled her placid little smile. "I don't think it matters," she said. "I don't think men want wisdom in women—do they? Any more than donkeys on ladders?"

"Wise head! I didn't know you did that much thinking."

She took no offense. One of her strong points was a lack of personal sensitiveness, a steady sweetness of temper. It was no fun to tease her, because she would not be irritated, but Morgan was always trying.

"Oh, well, feel, then," she answered, still smiling. "A woman's feelings are more valuable than her thoughts, seems to me."

"Right you are, Alicia!" agreed her father-in-law. "It is better to marry a quiet fool than a witty scold."

"Dear me, Papa, how you do run us down! One would think there were only two kinds of women to choose from."

The Colonel was quite in his element. He leaned forward, cheerfully rubbing his hands.

"Four kinds, my dear, four kinds. 'Fair and foolish, dark and proud, long and lazy, little and loud.'"

Morgan laughed outright. "It's no use. I've been up against your categories before. You have a proverb to fit every occasion. And when it comes to women, you are merciless."

"Why don't you get Stella in and we can play bridge?" urged Alicia presently.

"She's engaged," Morgan answered, his irritation rising once more. "That newspaperwoman is there again."

"What a nuisance," his cousin agreed, and the Colonel demanded, "Why don't you refuse to see her?"

"She's an old friend of Stella's, you know—and, what's worse, she has done things for her now and then—and just because she has put the woman under obligation she won't turn her down, you see."

"How splendid of Stella," murmured Alicia, but Morgan was too much displeased with Miss Peckham to agree with her. He did not think it splendid of Stella but rather absurd; on the other hand, he felt it distinctly nice of Alicia to see it that way.

"We might play dummy bridge," the Colonel suggested, but Alicia broke in with "Oh, no—let's play solo—wasn't that it? That game you learned out West somewhere, Morgan—if we haven't forgotten it."

The Colonel protested that he had no head for new games, but Alicia was up at once, feeling about with a plump shining little foot for the dropped slipper, and going to bring the card table. Morgan was before her, but she insisted on helping and brought out her new packs of cards, counters, poker chips, paper and pencil.

"Is there anything else?" she asked, looking over the array, and reassuring her father-in-law in affectionate asides, "Oh, yes—you'll remember, Papa—you beat us last time. I can remember that! And I shall be a victim for both of you."

Alicia would have been an ideal partner but for her deficiency in the science of the game—of any game. She would have been an ideal opponent if her very sweetness and placidity had not somehow robbed victory of half its excitement. There is really no sport in fighting a blue-eyed lamb.

But the Colonel made up for this by the extreme vigor of his play, his acrimony displayed in defeat; and in conquering, he showed the modest reserve of a Roman Triumph.

That night fortune was cold to Colonel Cushing. "I've had enough of this," he announced after he had been cruelly extinguished three times in succession. "You two can play cribbage or dominos or jackstraws. I'm going to smoke."

"It's too bad, Papa!" Alicia comforted him. "Try again. The games are so short——"

"They're liable to be hours long, my dear. No, you'll have to excuse me!"

"Never mind, Morgan," she amiably agreed. "You needn't play jackstraws. Come sit over here and smoke, or talk if you want to." She reestablished herself in her sofa corner, where the light was just right for reading or needlework or for a becoming idleness, settling into the cushions without an unnecessary motion, a picture of peaceful repose.

Morgan watched her with a subconscious expectation of some nervous rearrangement of the pillows, some alert starting up to get something. She continued placid and motionless, her white hands relaxed in her silken lap.

"You are a most comfortable person, Alicia," he remarked, idly noting her graceful lines. "It's restful just to see your placidity. Seems to me all the women nowadays have some kind of jumps."

Alicia smiled her friendly little smile, and said nothing at all.

The Colonel had sunk back into his favorite chair with *The Nation* at hand, his usual soporific. His cigar went out for lack of due attention; his breathing grew more insistent. The gas logs purred softly, and the scent of roses was in the air.

Alicia did not care for "plants"—they were so much trouble, she said; but cut flowers she had always about—the maid could arrange them. It was no Japanese longing for beauty on her part, nor that half-aesthetic, half-maternal instinct which makes New England winter windows into hospitals for defective geraniums, but merely a love of sweet odors.

She herself was sweet enough, with a modest taste for perfumes, and she liked the house about her to be warmly fragrant.

Morgan stretched his long legs toward the fire, let his head rest on the smooth stuffed back of the chair, and drew a long breath of utter relaxation.

It certainly was comfortable with Cousin Alicia.

Nothing but a growing sense of duty, a feeling that Miss Peckham must certainly be gone by this time and that his wife would be wondering where he was, waiting up for him, worrying about him, made him rise at last and say good night.

Only a flight of stairs lay between this home and his, but it was with a strong impression of changing climate that he opened his own door.

Stella was waiting as he had supposed.

Stella had been crying, and had tried to conceal it, he could see that. She met him with a bright cheerfulness that clearly showed a lack of the full, sweet understanding which allows some margin for protest.

"She's gone?" he asked in a whisper.

And Stella said: "Yes—come in, dear," instead of "Gone hours ago—where *have* you been?" She did not ask where he had been, which made him feel obliged to mention it, and that again made it seem as if she thought he had something to conceal, which was utterly untrue.

In five minutes his nervous mood came back, his forced patience, the mingling of pity and affection and weariness which was making their life so tense and strained. But when she came through the cedar-closeted dressing room to say good night to him, in her shimmering white-ribboned negligee, and stood in the doorway for a moment, her rich soft hair in two long braids that hung long over her shoulders before her, like those of some Merovingian queen, the affection rose to dominance, and he gave her good-night kisses of genuine tenderness. He fell asleep with a feeling that he had a good and beautiful wife and two fine boys, a comfortable home—and—— Oh, well, women were queer, but that couldn't be helped, and life was hard, anyway.

She did not "fall asleep" at all, but lay for hours trying her best to climb into it, sidling up to take it unawares, striving to deceive it, shutting her eyes and breathing deep, long, steady breaths that sleep might think her overcome and make it a fact, unnoticing.

6

Mrs. MacAvelly's dinners exhibited no special luster of decoration, no "pecuniary canons of taste" in provision or serving. A soft-stepping, clean-gowned colored woman changed the plates and brought the dishes, and those dishes contained mere food, plain, commonplace American food, of singular perfection. It was not made apparent how, living in New York, she contrived to furnish her guests with roast chickens which could be carved with easy abandon, yet which sent up a tempting savor, instead of a steaming breath from the long past; which had the tenderness of youth instead of the flaccidity of age and impending dissolution. She never discussed her own household methods, though listening with sympathy and patience to the recitals of her many friends; never complained of the incompetence and expense of servants, yet condoled sweetly with those who did.

There was a firm, round table, chairs comfortable to sit in, glasses easy to hand and lip, silver which was no tax on one's muscles, a clear soft, becoming light, which was not on the table, a simple decoration that interposed nothing between face and face, and never too many guests for general conversation—in a word a dinner which offered good food, allowed good talk, and resembled neither a florist's and confectioner's display nor an exhibition of arts and crafts.

Colonel Cushing regretted that he could not come, a dinner of his State Society preventing, but his daughter-in-law was there, also Mr. and Mrs. Widfield, Mr. Tillotson, and—observed with varying interest by all the others—Mr. J. Smith.

Mrs. MacAvelly placed Mr. Widfield at her left hand and Mr. Smith at her right, between her and Stella, then the journalist with the gently smiling Alicia between him and Morgan, and they began what promised to be a pleasant meal. So far as five persons could make it so the promise was fulfilled, but the grim insurgent face of Mr. Smith was darkly irreconcilable.

Mrs. MacAvelly had asked her friends not to wear evening clothes on his account, and he, on their account, had halved his dinners for a week to hire a dress suit. Now he was torn between two suspicions—that he had denied himself under a mistake and was wrongly dressed, or that they had discussed his poverty and dressed down to him.

He was inwardly planning a bitter article for one of the "labor papers" for which he wrote; satiric periods formed themselves in his mind; the very fact that he had so far considered their conventions as to wear this strange, ill-fitting garb added venom to the shafts. As he swallowed his soup in labored quiet, he was thinking: "They so utterly overestimate the value of their silly customs that when they condescend to invite a working man to their bourgeois banquets they say to themselves, 'We must not wear our dress suits—lest he be overawed! We will wear our ordinary clothes and put him at his ease.' They forget that their ordinary clothes are so superior to his in cloth and workmanship that a sharper contrast is shown than in their waiter's costumes." The last phrase pleased him, and he smiled.

Mrs. Widfield noted the smile and saw possibilities in the dark face. "They tell me you are doing good work, Mr. Smith—work that promises greatness."

"I am," he replied, facing her squarely. "Who told you?"

"Mrs. MacAvelly heard it at the Clam Street Settlement, you know. Miss Woodstone is a good friend of yours, I am sure."

Again he smiled, a sort of Assyrian smile of calm, unquestioning pride. "She is. Miss Woodstone has some critical ability."

Stella studied him with interest. Here was one who had at least no false modesty, whatever of the true he might conceal. She glanced across at Morgan to see if he had heard, but Morgan was exchanging calm remarks with his hostess.

Mr. Tillotson gazed on the young man with a guarded twinkle in his eye, and Alicia looked at him with approval.

"We've all heard about your work, Mr. Smith, and we're very anxious to know more of it," she said. "You're going to read it to us, aren't you?"

"I am to read a portion of some small part of it," he replied. "A fragment of a play—as yet uncompleted."

Morgan did not like him. He had the not unusual American dislike of foreigners, and this man did not look to him as if his name was really Smith. All nations, in their ignorance, are apt to look down on other nations; we inherit from England that unshakable insular pride, the deeper for its narrowness; and beyond that comes the peculiar misfortune of our country, that the majority of our foreign immigrants are recruited from the poorest classes of other nations. His Southern blood had English prejudice unimpaired, and he possessed plenty of later ones as well. But also he was unshakably polite, even to Malina Peckham when he had to talk to her, so now he courteously inquired: "What is your play about? Is it a problem play?"

Mr. Smith eyed him a little resentfully, replying: "It treats of the old problem between men and women, and of the new problem between rich and poor."

"Haven't we been rich and poor almost as long as we have been men and women?" Mr. Tillotson inquired.

"Aren't they the same thing?" suggested Stella to him aside, whereat his twinkle grew perceptible as he smiled at her.

But Mr. Smith was not smiling. No one should jest, before him, about poverty.

"They are by no means the same thing," he sternly contradicted

Mrs. Widfield, "although some of the problems of sex are governed by economic conditions. But the growth of riches and of poverty— together, the dual disease of a bourgeois civilization—is the overwhelming problem of today."

"How can you bring it into a play?" asked Mrs. MacAvelly. And Mr. Tillotson gravely suggested: "You must have wonderful power if you can dramatize world issues as a legitimate background to personal issue."

Then it was Stella's turn to give him a swift little shining smile, but Mr. Smith merely replied: "I have."

Alicia was visibly impressed. "Have you been writing long?" she inquired, her soft blue eyes roundly open.

The young man was suspiciously resentful of a possible patronage on the part of Mrs. MacAvelly, and of a possible criticism on the part of Mrs. Widfield, but here was simple goodwill and admiration; here was the eternal feminine with no hidden sting.

"I have been writing always," he burst forth. "I learned to read before I can remember. I read always, everything I could reach. I went to school before I was big enough to work, to night school after I was at work, and to college—working always—and writing always."

"Miss Woodstone told me how wonderful you have been," said his hostess. "It must be a great joy to her—it is, I know—to be part of that helpful work down there. You did find it helpful, didn't you?"

He swallowed hastily, evidently regarding the dinner as a bar to conversation. "The Settlement furnishes an infinitesimal fraction of the necessities of growth to an infinitesimal fraction of the poor. It is, as you say, helpful. But the horror of it is that a few people can go arbitrarily to live among the miseries of the poor, and find comfort in distributing these doles."

"'A fragment of sponge cake in a bucket of ink.' Sinclair called it, didn't he?" offered Mr. Tillotson, impartially.

Alicia showed a gentle continuity:

"Have you written much?" she inquired.

"I have written many words," he answered her, "many columns, pages, sheets. But no books yet—only the newspaper work, the petty perishable work that one must do to live. The great work that might be done—the noble work the world loses because of poverty—we shall never know."

Mr. Tillotson smiled like sunny ice. "You see nothing great in newspaper work then, Mr. Smith?"

"If newspapers were free they could do great work," he answered calmly, "but what can we expect from a commercial bourgeois press?"

Then Mrs. MacAvelly asked him a question about the drama in Russia, and paid such attention to his opinions that he turned to her with relief and pleasure, while Morgan began teasing Alicia, or trying to, about her interest in the arts, and Stella listened with pleasure to her other neighbor.

But not all the intelligent sympathy of his kind entertainer could keep Mr. Smith from hearing the cheerful lightness of the others. When they laughed he felt an inner conviction that they were laughing at him; the gay little intimacies of the cousins he suspected to mean something more, and lowered at them with dramatic intensity. That Mrs. Widfield should prefer talking to Mr. Tillotson to talking to him he resented, and in any case, though he might utter epigrammatic criticism in four languages to Mrs. MacAvelly, the others were not listening. So he folded his arms, ignored the ice cream, and sat back in his chair with Jovian hauteur.

The worst of it was that no one seemed to mind; they chattered amicably to and about and across him, and presently were all gathered in the other larger room with their coffee at hand. The percolator flashed and bubbled in a tray in a safe corner; the sugar and cream and cognac were there, and anyone could help himself or herself at will.

"You are the only person I know, Mrs. MacAvelly," said Mr. Tillotson, seating himself near her, "who has a chair for everyone, and everyone in his chair. How do you do it?"

"I don't always," she sadly replied. "Do you see that tiny rocker over there?"

"I see it. It's a frail, delicate hardwood thing, palpably intended for small-sized old ladies—opinionative, straight-backed old ladies, I should think," he replied with a critical glance.

"And do you see that one," she continued, "the dark-blue one yonder?" This was a chair for a lazy giant, a person whose femoral bones might have been a yard long and be still comfortable therein. "One day two men called on me. One was from Maine, very long and very heavy, all bones; the other was a diplomat from Central America, about half-size and plump as a sausage. Do what I would, they sought to thwart each other and insisted on taking each other's chairs. The little man sat on the front edge of that blue one like—like——"

"Like a tourist looking at the Grand Canyon," he suggested to her smiling delight.

"Yes, exactly. And as for the other—the Maine gentleman's knees stood out like a katydid's. I had to send that chair to be repaired next day. It has never quite recovered."

"She's a fine creature—your Mrs. Widfield," he observed softly, dropping sugar into his second cup. "A woman of brains evidently. But she doesn't look contented, somehow. Why are our American women so discontented—tell me that, won't you?"

"Here are three of us. I'm quite contented." She gave him a most flattering smile. "And look at Mrs. Cushing."

Mrs. Cushing certainly seemed the picture of silken ease; her beaded scarf gleamed over rounded outlines, her fair placid face serenely pleasant, in spite of Morgan looking patently bored on one side of her, and Mr. Smith looming haughtily on the other.

Stella was trying to reach some sort of understanding of the playwright's point of view. She was so patient and calm under his sharp replies that Morgan grew restive.

"You mustn't object," Alicia told him. "Women don't mind being taken up like that—when they respect a man."

"I don't see why she should respect that person," said Morgan aside.

"Oh—of course she does! He's a writer, you know—a real writer. I respect him immensely." She turned large eyes toward him. "Oh, Mr. Smith, aren't you going to read your play to us?"

Mrs. MacAvelly answered for him. "He certainly is, Mrs. Cushing—if he will be so kind. Have you all had coffee?"

They had, and grouped themselves comfortably, to listen, or as far as Morgan Widfield was concerned, not to listen, to the reading.

"It is only a part of a play," Mr. Smith explained, unfolding a manuscript. "It is not finished. I cannot get time to finish it." He gazed somberly at them as if they were somehow to blame for his pressing necessities. "Besides, I need more knowledge of how the other half lives—the half I do *not* belong to. That is why I was willing to come," he added, almost to himself.

Tillotson grinned, sitting safely out of range, and shot an appreciative glance at Mrs. Widfield, but she was gazing at the stern lean face of the young enthusiast with every appearance of interest.

Mrs. MacAvelly placed at his elbow a solid little table with a shaded drop light, and a glass of water, and they all sat silent.

In a voice that was harsh and strained at first, moving his ill-shod feet awkwardly on the soft rug, and taking refuge in sudden gulps of water now and then, he began.

There was some exaggeration, there was evident limitation in experience, there was a strain of pronounced bitterness, but, to the sharp astonishment of Mr. Tillotson, and even the reluctant admiration of Mr. Widfield, it was a strong and gripping piece of work.

When he finished the first act they sat, a little breathless, waiting for him to go on.

He remained silent, however, and slowly folded the paper into a tight packet again.

"You're not stopping, are you?" asked Mr. Tillotson.

"That is all I have completed," he replied. "The rest is outlined only. I must see more, know more—I cannot get it from books."

There was a burst of congratulation from the ladies. Mr. Widfield told him he was much impressed by the opening, and the critic offered sincere compliments in a very different tone from his previous one.

So warm was the atmosphere of approval that the young man quite relaxed his defensive attitude. These seemed to be real persons after all, and able to somewhat appreciate good work, in spite of their class. It needed but a few words now to set him talking, really talking, as he loved to do. He looked about for more coffee; Mrs. MacAvelly supplied it. With a succession of cups beside him, and the flicker of burnt brandy in his nostrils, with cigarettes uncounted freely at hand, and with five more or less appreciative listeners, Mr. Smith launched forth as if in his favorite café or club room.

He talked of the drama in Europe and America, of numbers of authors, some of whom he had apparently met, though he gave no details as to the incidents. He talked of various European countries, always from the underside, from a background of poverty and oppression. And having entered upon that ground he held it, speaking with fire and passion, and a half-veiled biting irony.

At first they took some part in this discussion, or tried to. Alicia's amiable questions, sometimes a little aside the mark, he tossed aside like leaves upon a flood. Stella was more discerning; she reached him in light keen comment and query, but he merely poured forth more fully and overwhelmed her.

The hostess sat smiling and silent. Morgan relapsed into his attitude of quiet dislike again. Only Mr. Tillotson held his ground, seeking to defend Mrs. Widfield's position, and to make some protests as to his own.

Nothing but an opposing group of equally loud and earnest enthusiasts could have checked Mr. Smith, however. He was accustomed to unsparing interruption, to opponents who held against his flailing words a steady guard and were ready with cut and thrust and counterrush at a second's pause.

Mr. Tillotson shrugged his shoulders and desisted. The ladies sat silent, perforce. Mr. Widfield covertly looked at his watch, but Mr. Smith had the floor—and there was none to call him to order.

It was brilliantly interesting for a while, but by and by Alicia's pink mouth twisted in careful suppression of a yawn, and Stella began to wear that strained look her husband dreaded—she would be tired out for days. He went near her and showed her the time—but she waved him away. Tired or not, she was deeply stirred and excited, not convinced by any means, but shaken to the depths by this blazing picture of life she did not know, the raw, ragged painful life of millions. She felt the gaps in his logic, and had agreed fully with the objections advanced by the journalist, but he, to her regret, had withdrawn from the combat.

As for the orator, he seemed to see in them now mere types of the oppressors of whom he spoke. "It is easy for you to be indifferent now," he bitterly declared. "But a time will come when you cannot be indifferent. A time will come when the lines will be drawn, when the classes will be sharply divided, when the enormous overwhelming numbers of the proletariat will be organized at last, when the upper classes will seem but a handful, and even the bourgeoisie, the grossly contented, blind, selfish, middle class, will see their weakness. A time will come——"

Mr. Tillotson rose to his feet.

"I am sorry to interrupt you, Mr. Smith, but a time has come when I feel that I must tear myself away. Mrs. MacAvelly, I have to thank you for a very pleasant evening."

He made his adieux with pronounced deliberation, lingering especially with Mrs. Widfield, and hoping that he might have the pleasure of seeing her again. "There are many things I should like your opinion on," he told her. "I have seen, even in this limited opportunity, that you can think."

She was bright-eyed, flushed, still keyed up by the unusual onslaught of ideas. "Come and see us by all means," she urged. "Mr. Widfield will love to have you, I am sure." Her husband added most cordial assurances. He liked Tillotson for himself, admired his work, and could have offered him a loving cup for breaking up that interminable evening.

Mr. Smith sat forward in his chair, looking from one to the other, expecting the others to sit down again, but with thanks and compliments they all withdrew, even the sympathetic Mrs. Cushing.

Mrs. MacAvelly returned smiling from her door. "If you will excuse me one half moment, Mr. Smith, I have a favor to ask you." She withdrew, leaving him alone long enough to look at his dollar watch and realize the hour. It was not late for him, or for his usual companions, but his uneasy sense of unfamiliarity with their conventions had returned to him, and she found him standing when she came back.

"Just a letter to post," she said. "I ought to have asked Mr. Tillotson—the others all live in this house—you don't mind?"

He took it awkwardly, placed it with great care in the pocket of his hired suit—and never thought of it again, which was of no great consequence as there was nothing in the envelope save a blank sheet of paper.

"It was worth two cents," thought Mrs. MacAvelly.

Alicia bubbled over with amiable enthusiasm as Morgan took her to her door.

"Wasn't he splendid!" she said. "Absolutely he seemed like a prophet of old."

"If the prophets of old were like that, I don't wonder they were stoned," he told her. "You are too amiable to live, Alicia. Good night."

Stella was walking the floor of their long rooms, her head up like an alert antelope's, her eyes shining.

"I feel like Dante!" she said. "As if I'd been taken through the infernal regions. Morgan, is it true? Is *any* of it true? Are people worked like that—and housed like that, and treated like that, and paid like that?"

"Oh yes—in some cases—in some countries," he assured her. "But those fellows come over here, into a free country, where every man has a chance—and bring their old prejudices with them. There's no need of such talk here. It's absurd!"

"But he told about Pittsburgh—and Chicago—and the children in the Southern mills. Some of it was here—some of it is our fault."

"It'll be my fault if I let you talk any more tonight. Come, let's go to sleep as soon as the Lord will let us."

"Talk any *more!*" she smiled. "When have I talked tonight?"

He laughed with her. "That's so. You didn't have any show at all, did you? Even Tillotson was knocked out in a few rounds and he can hold his own pretty well. I never heard such a word wrangler!"

"Mr. Tillotson is very interesting, isn't he? I hope we shall see more of him."

He seconded the hope, and suggested that they both have a glass of milk to sleep on.

Mr. Tillotson, going home to his bachelor apartment, took from the ammonia-piped refrigerator in his porcelain-lined kitchenette, not a glass of milk, but several glasses of beer with wheaten wafers, and sat a long time over them, thinking in words, as a writer is apt to: "Pretty woman—Mrs. Cushing," he meditated. "Ought to be Cushion. Alicia Cushing—what a feathery name. She's the kind to rest on—if that's all a fellow wants. . . .

"As for Mrs. Mac—that woman's a genius. I can't read her. She never shows her hand—not a card—not a single pip. But I'm convinced she's a genius; her simplicity is too perfect. Nice woman, I love to go there. She knows how to make you comfortable and never seems to try. . . .

"That confounded windbag's a genius too, for all his talk. Awfully good stuff, that act he read. We'll hear from him yet—at a safe distance, I hope. . . .

"Widfield's a nice fellow enough, but as for Mrs. Wid—I've got to see more of that woman. Brain and heart and energy—and not a thing to do, I warrant—all on edge. People certainly are mighty interesting. . . ."

And having finished his third glass of cold comfort, with many a crisp biscuit, he betook himself to the orderly, well-furnished, unalluring bedroom of his expensive pseudo-home.

7

When Stella Widfield opened her eyes next morning it was with an unusual sense of well-being. She had slept, really slept, and her mind, instead of focusing at once on the thought of Morgan's fading affection, was occupied with several fresh images.

The bright chintzes and soft colors of her pretty room looked fresher than usual; the soft air that stirred the white curtains felt good to her; there was sunlight shimmering on the floor. She lay quiet for a little, smiling to herself as she thought of the torrent of fierce words so dexterously checked by Mr. Tillotson, then sobered as she thought of what the words had shown.

"I'll go down to see Miss Woodstone," she determined. "She'll tell me what to read. If what he says is so——" This did not come to any definite conclusion.

She was up and dressed and out to the sunny breakfast table, for a wonder a little late. Morgan was surprised not to find her before him, with every detail of his possible wants anticipated, but not displeased; he rather enjoyed a few minutes to read the paper before she came in. As she chatted brightly over the coffee cups he felt, without analyzing it, a lessening of the strain of that soft, indescribable tension which had been growing between them.

She told him how interested she was, how she had determined to find out for herself how much of those lurid horrors were true, and though he by no means shared her enthusiasm he was glad to see her eyes shining impersonally upon him.

"That's a good idea," he agreed. "Miss Woodstone's a good sort—she'll straighten you out."

While not much in sympathy with any radical movements he had great respect for the work of Social Settlements, considering it to be high-grade modern philanthropy of considerable use, and quite suited to occupy the energies of benevolent unmarried ladies, and of some few men whose minds, while unquestionably able, were unequal to the supreme task of achieving success.

"What an awful bore that fellow was!" he said again.

"Why, I don't think so. One might be very weary of a typhoon—but I shouldn't call it a bore, should you?"

"I call him one—unqualifiedly."

"Oh, Morgan, bores have to be slow, and dull, and uninteresting!"

"Not a bit of it. There's a fellow at the club. He talks like a mill-race; he's so bright he makes jokes in every sentence. He's a newborn encyclopedia for fresh information—but everybody ducks. It's a tax on the mind—awfully wearing. But if you like this chap, have him up—have him up. Personally I like Mr. Tillotson better by a thousand miles. Ask him to dinner—without Smith—won't you?"

"Yes, I want to see more of him. He is certainly most attractive. But that poor boy does appeal to me tremendously."

"Boy! He's well over thirty!"

"Oh, I dare say—but he seems so young, so inexperienced, with all he's been through."

"He's inexperienced in good manners—that's pretty clear. However, you be Mrs. Ponsonby de Tompkins all you want to. If it amuses you it's all right."

It annoyed him a little to have her so attracted by a man he did not consider a gentleman in any sense of the word. But on the other hand he was glad of her bright looks, even of a little opposition, for a change, and when she said good-bye to him at the door she did not look as if his kiss was only a payment on account.

The Clam Street Settlement was necessarily located in a poor neighborhood; on the outside were ravening wolves, as it were, but inwardly it was white as snow. The serene grace of its casts and photographs, the comfort, space, and beauty of its well-appointed rooms, Stella thought must seem to the huddled inhabitants of the surrounding tenements as cold water to Dives. Some of them, to be sure, could enjoy these pleasures for small fragments of their time; the place swarmed with them when they had free hours to spend there; but the fraction of the poor thus reached seemed only to make the contrast sharper with those beyond its reach.

Miss Woodstone was a tall, pale person with a penetrating eye. She looked willowy and lax, but her years of efficient work in that region proved the contrary.

"How do you *bear* it?" demanded her visitor. "How can you stand seeing it—and hearing it—and smelling it—all the time?"

"If I did not, would it be any less unpleasant?" she answered.

"Less unpleasant for you, yes," insisted Stella. "Couldn't you work for them if you wanted to, and not live in it?"

"Perhaps I shouldn't care as much if I did not live in it. Perhaps I should forget."

"Oh no—I am sure you wouldn't—you would care, always. How splendid it must be—to care so much."

Miss Woodstone smiled her patient smile, giving one the impression of a person several hundred years old but still kindly interested. "Don't you care about anything—you who have so much?"

"Not about outside things."

"Outside of what?"

Stella smiled a little guiltily. "Outside of my own affairs, I suppose. But I want to—I do, really. I was tremendously impressed by that young man, Smith. He doesn't *look* like a Smith."

To this Miss Woodstone agreed. "He surely is a power. He's crude yet; not so young in years, but young in his limitations. And his Socialism is still in the bitter stage; you wouldn't wonder if you lived in the bitterness."

"Are you a Socialist?" asked her visitor.

"Of course. I do not see how anyone can help it, who knows conditions—and is not too blind."

Stella was a little surprised. She had long known Miss Woodstone, distantly, as a power for good in the city and even farther, and had admired her tall grace at some of those semi-civic banquets in which New York abounds. And knowing her for a person of balanced judgment, universally respected, she had not supposed her to be one with a party always believed in her circle to be madly revolutionary.

"But don't they want to break up everything—to destroy all our institutions? Wouldn't it mean real danger and chaos?"

Miss Woodstone's expression was more motherly than ever. "I'm afraid Mr. Smith has alienated as well as interested you. It is too bad they will see it that way and put it that way. But you cannot expect unbiased judgment from the underdog, you know."

"Or from the upper one, either, I suppose," said Stella, suddenly enlightened.

"Precisely. You see, the poor of today are for the most part lineal descendants of the poor of all the ages behind us. Their families are as 'old' as ours, you know, though they have no records. Their 'bitterness,' which some of us find so offensive, seems sweet as milk when you study their age-old grievances."

"But aren't they better off today, in all ways, than they ever were before? Better educated and everything?"

"They certainly are. That is precisely why they are becoming so aroused. Don't you see? When they were absolute slaves or sodden peasants, tied to the soil, they were too utterly crushed to lift their heads at all, and too utterly ignorant to know or care about the condition of one another. Now they are thrilling the world over with a sense of solidarity; they begin to feel their common wrongs—and their common power."

"But—is it wrong? That is, isn't it a necessary evil? Won't some men always be masters?"

Here Miss Woodstone balked, shaking her head with gentle firmness. "I am no propagandist," she said. "If I begin to hold forth at length on this topic I should never see you again, I'm afraid. But I'll tell you a book or two to read, if you care to."

"I do—I care immensely. If this movement is *right*——"

"There speaks New England! Well, you must prove all things, you know. Paul was wise in that remark, anyway. I'm going to give you two easy ones to begin on; easy, I mean, in that they are strong, attractive books, not too violently doctrinaire. Get *The Citadel* by Samuel Merwin. Mr. Widfield will like that, I think—enough to read it anyhow. It is not 'Socialistic' in any specific sense, but it shows the way intelligent native Americans are waking up as to the vicious folly of present methods. Then read Wells's *New Worlds for Old*—that is the best book I know to start a thinking person with."

Stella's mind swept back to the time when she had asked Morgan if he had read *In the Days of the Comet*. She had not touched a book of Wells's since.

"Isn't he—rather dreadful—Wells?" she asked.

"He has his limitations, like most of us. But a more finely sensitive, high-keyed social soul I do not know. And the power of him—the sheer power! The way that little bunch of battling Englishmen are laboring to shake up 'all the obese, unchallenged old things which stifle and overlie us'—it is a splendid sight to see them."

"But wasn't *Ann Veronica* really—disgusting?"

"It disgusted some people. But surely, Mrs. Widfield, you can be thankful for the power and glory that is in a writer, in spite of his open defects, can't you?"

"I'll read the one you suggest, anyhow, and the Merwin book. Tell me some more. And incidentally, tell me some more about Mr. Smith."

"The short and simple annals of the poor" in this case were quite long and varied. There was travel and tragedy involved, heroic labor and self-denial, phenomenal progress.

"We think him here quite the strongest of the younger men. But he does need to know more of life—the general life of the world. It is difficult, I know, for those of us who have been for so long conscious and vocal, able to read, write, associate freely and exchange ideas, and to whom 'the masses' have just been that—mere indiscriminate masses, without personality—it is hard to turn the tables and see that from the point of view of the poor we are just such a mass, smaller, but just as indiscriminate and impersonal. We are 'the rich,' unknown, misunderstood, and now regarded with growing malevolence."

Stella nodded earnestly. "I see, and it is immensely important that a man like this should know whereof he speaks. Well, Miss Woodstone, if I may serve as 'the rich' in this case I will do my best to introduce Mr. Smith to our alien mysteries."

"You'll be doing something worthwhile, and I, for one, shall feel personally obliged to you."

"Oh, you needn't, I assure you. I can't say that I like the man, but I begin to see what he stands for—and it's worth helping."

"Exactly. And a woman can do it—a woman like you, not a girl, not personally at all within its range, and yet able to smooth the way for him as no man could."

"I'm sorry, but Mr. Widfield has taken a dislike to him, I'm afraid——"

"That's too bad. But there are husbandless hours—afternoons—teatimes——"

"Yes, and I can interest some other people."

"It is no use patronizing him," Miss Woodstone explained. "I have tried, as delicately as I knew how, to get some nice people to 'take him up'—but he won't be taken. The reason I think you can manage it is because he approves of you." She was amused to see Mrs. Widfield's expression. "'Approves' is just the word. He was in here this morning on some newspaper errand, and took occasion to tell me so. 'I have been dining with some friends of yours,' he said. 'I dare say I have you to thank for it—if it is anything to be thankful for.'"

"He's a gracious person, isn't he?" Stella suggested.

"'Gracious' is exactly the word for him. I told him he needn't have gone unless he wanted to, and he said he went because of his play. I think he hoped something of Mr. Tillotson, perhaps—was he nice to him?"

"I think Mr. Tillotson was interested, really—and impressed. We all were. But as to being nice to him——" Stella laughed at the recollection. "We were lucky to escape at any price! Such violent eloquence!"

"You'd get hardened to that if you worked with us a while. Violent eloquence is the breath of their nostrils. But he told me that you appeared to have some mind—I think that's the way he put it."

"Very kind of him, I'm sure!"

"Wasn't it! But seriously, Mrs. Widfield, if you can put up with his rudeness and ignorance in consideration of his real ability, and help that fellow to a better understanding of life, you'll be doing real social service."

"I can try," Stella answered slowly. "But you've no idea how I hate to do anything Mr. Widfield does not like."

"This is not anything he would really object to, is it?"

"Why, no—not seriously. Of course he does not interfere with anything I want to do, but I never want to do anything that does not please him."

"He must be devotedly fond of you."

Stella said nothing.

"Perhaps—really—he'd be fonder if you did do something you wanted to now and then."

At this Mrs. Widfield stiffened a little, and Miss Woodstone asked if she would not like to see some of their rooms.

"We haven't much going on until evening, except for the children, but the nursery is always in full swing—and the playground."

"I'm afraid I can't stay; it's later than I thought. I shall be late for dinner, as it is," and Mrs. Widfield excused herself.

She started home with her head buzzing with new ideas and purposes. She had meant to stop and buy those books, but there was no time now. That place always took longer to reach than she allowed for. There was nothing for it but the subway, and at that she would be late for dinner. With an idea of getting an express at once she took a surface car to Brooklyn Bridge. A crowded, smelly car it was, full of the kind of people she had come down there to find out about. She did not like their looks. Every delicate, well-bred sense was offended. Making the universal error, she blamed them for their appearance—

as if they had chosen to be so born, so reared, so dressed, so over-tired, underfed, and perceptibly unwashed. Why they should be so dirty especially troubled her. Like most people who have convenient bathrooms, hot and cold water, plenty of time, no heavy labor, a clean environment and an intensely critical social atmosphere, she found it hard to understand the lack of cleanliness in those others around her. She had never used her imagination in following out the daily lives of these millions, and as she gazed upon them now, the swarms in the street, and the pushing crowd in the car, the big woman in a wig who breathed so hotly beside her, the slouching, pale-faced old-young man on the other side, the general stunted look of all of them, and the hard, haggard faces, a sense of horror grew within her.

"They don't look like people—it's a nightmare. It does not have to be like this," she told herself, and eagerly escaped to take the subway.

In her easy, guarded life, warned by her husband and friends, able to choose her hours, and generally taking a surface car or a taxi if their car was, as at present, out of order, she had known only by hearsay of the "subway crush." Before she realized it she had dropped her ticket in that cavernous glass box and was borne along by the hurrying people down the stairs to the platform. Finding there a solid swaying mass, malodorous, and ruthless in determination to get on the already well-filled trains, she at first thought of return, but a glance at the numbers between her and the stairs, and at the solid wall coming down, appalled her.

"I can stand it for once," she thought. "They do. People ought to do their shopping earlier." And then she had sense enough to laugh at herself—these people were not downtown for pleasure. They could not choose their hours. Behind them was a long day's work. Before them—at an unwalkable distance—their families and something to eat. They must go as quickly as possible.

So down the stairs they poured, making a "saturated solution" of the already packed crowd, and when the trains drew in, there was need indeed for those gray guards. Such as desired to come out had to fight hard for the privilege. The mass obtruded itself against the doorways and was pressed in like a paste, pushed from without re-sistlessly, moving their own feet only to keep standing. Some, find-ing the whole space filled, strove to resist those behind them, but after the car was filled it was packed, and after it was packed it was jammed, and after it was jammed Mrs. Widfield saw a burly guard use his whole force to ram an unresisting man into the side door, find it a physical impossibility, and pull him off again as a dentist might scrape off an unnecessary bit of filling.

In sheer terror she hung back and waited for a train or two, but the crowd steadily increased, and at last she was borne forward and forced against a humanity-packed entrance. She could move neither forward nor back, but a gentleman several persons farther in, seeing her plight, reached forth a long arm and literally pulled her on board, so that the door slid shut behind her.

In that impossible compression, occupying less space than she would in her coffin, Mrs. Widfield did some thinking. There was a strange uncomfortable excitement in being part of such a solid human substance. She could see, had to see, details of necks and ears, of chins and mouths and collars, such as had never before been forced upon her ken, and she must feel as well as see, to her shuddering objection. The grossness of men's clothing affected her strongly, such heavy cloth, such continuous wear, such impossibility of cleanliness in that material, part wool, part cotton, part sheer dirt. And against the women she registered a heavy protest in the matter of hats. A stiff quill jabbed her cheek as the car lurched; a bristling bunch of feathers affronted the other ear; and she saw, just beyond, a straggling "willow plume" tickle a man's face till his expression changed from angry offense to a more offensive pleasure.

Men and women, black and white, young and old, they were pressed solidly against one another in the thick warmth, and, swaying with the swaying cars, joggling back and forth as they stopped and started, experienced a physical intimacy closer than that of ranked steers in a cattle car. One sharp-voiced girl remarked: "And they don't want women to be jostled at the polls," to the amusement of those who heard her.

As they thinned a little in the uptown region, Mrs. Widfield saw, in the corner opposite her, Mr. Tillotson, reading a newspaper in closely folded sections. He joined her as soon as it was possible, and they stood for a moment, glad to merely breathe again.

"Why do you do it!" he protested. "This is discomfort and degradation for men—it is impossible for women."

"There seem to be a good many of them," she answered, "and they seem to stand it—literally—as well as the men. I suppose they have to."

"But you do not have to, surely. I hope it was only a temporary aberration."

"Exactly that," she agreed. "You see, I was so stirred up by that young iconoclast last night that I have been down to see Miss Woodstone and ask more about him—and about what he told us."

"Now that you are quite safe and comfortable above ground,

needing no assistance whatever, may I not 'see you safe home,' Mrs. Widfield?"

"Why, as you say, it is not in the least necessary, but I am glad of your company. I must hurry, though. See here, Mr. Tillotson, won't you come in and have dinner with us tonight—not a party—come just as you are."

"You are very kind. I am really tempted to accept. But I suspect you of self-defense."

"Self-defense! You'll have to explain——"

"Why, you are nervous about that dinner. Only pressing haste would have driven you into that black hole of New York. Before you looms a hungry husband, reproachful, ravening, but if you bring me in he will have a new cause of offense and not upbraid you for being late!"

"You surely are a mind reader, Mr. Tillotson! And even further— if you are there, dutifully eating cold soup and burned roast, and saying how good it is, he cannot condemn the dinner so unsparingly. No, seriously, he told me last night to ask you to dinner—not specifying today, to be sure, but really wanting to see more of you."

"That is very fortunate—I want to see more of him. I accept with pleasure."

Mr. Widfield showed no offense at a belated dinner and a missing wife, but did seem a little annoyed that she was so profuse in apology and explanation.

"Glad to see you, Mr. Tillotson. Perhaps tonight you and I can say something. Cape Henry! What a talker that fellow was!"

"Unparalleled intellect!" he exclaimed. "You have invented a new oath. Do you always swear geographically?"

"Frequently. Got the idea from that old tale of the quiet, pious Englishman abroad, who noticed that the swearing diners were always waited on first, so he brought his fist down as they did, and bellowed, 'Northumberland, Cumberland and Durham!'"

"It did the trick, I've no doubt. May I keep you hungry a moment longer while I remove a layer of subway deposit?" begged Mr. Tillotson.

"You have deceived me, Mrs. Widfield," he protested later. "The soup is hot, the roast perfect. Is your cook a mind reader, too?"

"Not at all. But to tell you the truth she is a slow person, and unless I am here to hurry matters, is apt to be behindhand."

"What a delightful arrangement! If you are on time, so is the dinner; if you are late, the dinner keeps step with you. Being a bachelor I find much pleasure in my friends' dinners, Mr. Widfield."

"Glad you do. Let me give you this piece—it's hotter," and he served his guest bountifully. Morgan liked to have people in to dinner, especially in this informal way. Stella was too careful, he always felt, too elaborate in preparations. What he enjoyed was openhanded hospitality—to the right sort of people. The conscientiousness, the intellectual power, the tireless patience with which his wife had studied and mastered her household problems he had never appreciated. To his mind women were housekeepers by nature. Given a wife, with a husband who was a good provider, and a home was the natural result. If the home was not smooth-running, comfortable and pleasant, it was the fault of the wife of course, reflecting in a general way upon her womanhood.

The difficulties of the first years of housekeeping to the young bride were as invisible to him as was the easy monotony of the later period, when the not impossible task is mastered, and the hours of the day grow longer.

In his own life the enlarging business kept pace with his enlarging abilities. He had as much exercise for all his powers today as he had when he married—more perhaps. With his world widening and changing about him, with the responsibilities and interests of politics beyond those of business, he naturally expected of his home the same high level of beautiful comfort and relaxation. And of late years here was Stella growing more tense and anxious instead of less. He was especially glad now of friends and visitors, and said as much.

"I wish you'd drop in often, Tillotson," he said. "There's always something to eat, and it's a favor to us. We're very much alone, now that the boys are gone."

"You won't have to urge me much," the visitor replied. "Down in our hearts we all of us like hospitality better than entertainments—don't you think so, Mrs. Widfield?"

Mrs. Widfield did think so. She liked this man, liked to hear him talk, was immensely pleased to see that Morgan enjoyed his society.

Her worry about being late had all faded away; it did not seem to make the least difference. She smiled affectionately at her husband across the table, found a chance to kiss him, unnoticed, when they gathered in the other room, and found the evening restful as well as enjoyable.

After the guest had gone there was a little quiet time when they sat talking of Mr. Tillotson and what he had said, Stella vivid and appreciative, Morgan enjoying her bright color and cheerfulness.

"We must have more company," he said. "It does you good, my dear."

"It's not only the company—it's being so interested," she replied. "I've got a list of books to read. I'm going to find out things."

"Find out anything you like—be as interested as you like—but don't ask me to be. I'm interested in seeing you look happier, though."

She was happier already.

8

The laborious daring of those who seek to photograph the wild beast in his lair, pushing their impudent cameras into the seclusion of leonine family circles, and spying on the siestas of elephants, combined with the patience and firmness of those who train performing tigers, was now manifested by Mrs. Widfield in her dealings with the refractory Mr. Smith. Rooted and deep was his prejudice against "the rich," profound his ignorance of every condition and result of riches. She could hardly have borne with him at first, but for that illuminating comparison of Miss Woodstone's; and when he seemed most unreasonable she drew a hasty parallel in her own mind between his attitude towards the friends and circumstances she knew so well, and her own toward his friends and circumstances.

Presently she found a strong sense of interest, as of exploration in strange lands, or of keen laboratory research. His lack of what, to her training, was common courtesy carried offense at first. But she soon found that he meant no offense and that while her delicate shades of disapproval were quite lost on him, he was not sensitive to frank criticism and suggestion.

Against his torrent of discourse, which ignored any faint hint of would-be interruption, but which ruthlessly interrupted her whenever she did find a chance for a few words, she finally made flat protest. "See here, Mr. Smith, do you really want to deliver a series of lectures to me—or one lecture in serial chapters? Or are you willing that I should have some opportunity to say what I think?"

He was leaning forward fiercely, ignoring the curving comfort of the big chair, and, as usual, talking continuously.

She had made an opening by suddenly rising to her feet, a motion not followed by his automatic imitation, as would have been the case with every other man she knew. He was not in the least concerned to have her stand before him, not in the least offended by her sharp demand, but for the moment he hesitated, because her question was quite aside from the subject they, or at least he, had been discussing.

She followed up her advantage swiftly, having learned the necessity. To converse with Mr. Smith was like launching a lifeboat in heavy surf; one must watch opportunity and rush boldly in.

"You would not come here if you had not something to gain by it; that something is knowledge of and experience in the habits and customs of an unknown species. If you are to write intelligibly about the master class, the bourgeoisie, the oppressors and exploiters, you've got to know something about them. In the interests of your work you come here for wider experience—and then you talk all the time."

"There is something in what you say," he admitted, not in the least mortified by her charge, but recognizing that he was missing something of what he had come for.

They got on much better after that. By constant vigilance she succeeded in holding her own for about one quarter of the time, and in the wary contest her own mind grew keener, quicker, stronger.

His flat contradictions staggered her at first. There was no tradition in his mind that one must not contradict a lady. He would have contradicted an archangel unhesitatingly. She reeled back at first, as from a rain of blows, under the sharp words with which he demolished a weak position, refuted unsound argument, knocked to pieces false premise. But in time she learned to "take punishment" without losing temper; learned to sidestep and counterthrust, and grew to enjoy the game as a game. For all his fierce tenacity he had the sense of logical conclusion, and was to be held up at any time by strong clear reasoning.

Like an athlete under training she grew "harder" and stronger, and after she had rubbed her bruises and returned to the combat after many defeats, she had at last the rich delight of fairly beating him. She was advancing the claim of economic independence for women, largely driven to it by his intolerant attitude. With German thoroughness, with technical glibness, with the sweeping fervor of a Single Taxer, he had waved the whole proposition aside on the ground that the strength of women was all expended in "maternal energy" and there was none available for "economic energy" without injury to motherhood.

With eager eyes she laid her plan of attack: "If an unmarried woman is working as a servant for wages, ten hours a day, is she not using economic energy?"

This he must needs grant. "If she marries, but has no children, and continues working as a servant, though without wages, doing the same work, for the same hours, she is still using economic energy, is she not?"

This, too, he had to admit.

"Now, when she has children, she gives to their bearing and rearing her maternal energy, but she continues to do the work of the servant—more work as a servant for each additional child, and that, you have already allowed, is economic energy. A woman who is a mother has more work to do than a woman who is not—and she does it. These are the facts."

Mr. Smith had cut short the interview that day and taken himself off, but Stella never again felt browbeaten and timid. She had won her spurs.

Moreover, besides the rather drastic training, she did gather from his flow of fiery words a wider knowledge of literature, a new understanding of the drama, a sense of pushing power. Feelings and hopes that had not stirred for many years stirred now. To her deep and wondering joy as of one long barren and now hoping motherhood, she began to feel again the impulse to write. The coming of love had meant so much to her that its splendid tide had washed away all more personal ambitions. The fulfillment of love, and the cares and labors we have attached to it, had taken the very power. Her life had been so richly filled by husband and children, had flowed so thickly in domestic joys, that all those earlier buds and shoots had been forgotten.

Now that the rich petals of girlhood's beauty were necessarily less softly brilliant, now that the children had already branched off sharply from the parent stem, she who had been feeling so lonely and deprived, so grieved for the falling of those sweet petals of early joy, began to know strange prickings and stirrings of new life—not towards flowers or fruit this time, but the equally natural law of growth that "makes wood."

Mr. Tillotson came oftener than Mr. Smith, and proved as valuable. When she met him on an evening, bruised and breathless still perhaps from some rough-and-tumble encounter with the Socialist, he brought balm for her wounds and the sweet stimulant of appreciation to supplement the sharp tonic already taken. Mr. Widfield always enjoyed him, and Stella began to recognize a peculiar effect of the presence of this new friend. When he was there her husband talked more freely, not only with them both, but even with her than when they were alone. The third mind seemed to enlarge the area common to all. Strangely enough she felt nearer to Morgan, more at ease with him, when Mr. Tillotson was there. Even when they were alone together she found now a new sense of comfort, a feeling that was not so insistent in its demands, as had been the case a few months since, and was more satisfied.

What Morgan felt he did not say, but he did seem happier, less near the verge of irritability. He responded also to that clearer atmosphere when this friend was present, and did not at all object to the fact that when Tillotson called in the afternoon or spent an evening with his wife when he was absent, the comradeship grew apace between them.

A quiet man was this hard-writing editor, hiding under his cheerful air of gentle cynicism much deeper springs of feeling. He was not young, not handsome; his thin hair was graying fast; his work, even in power and steady in volume, was known far and wide through its publication; but there were only one or two of his closest friends who knew the man inside.

This knowledge was now opening to Stella.

However much one loves one person, there remains the possibility of some interest in others. When the other person brings the new wine of sympathy in work, in thought, in inner purpose, even the closest love can spread its wings a shade, extend a few feathers to the newcomer. Not for a moment wavering in her heart from deep allegiance to her husband, Stella did reach out a warm hand to this new friend who brought so much to her.

"Have Tillotson around," Morgan would say. "I've got to go to Pittsburgh tonight—be back Thursday." Or, "Can't we get Tillotson up to dinner—he's not been here for a week."

"He's been twice," Stella would say.

"Well, I haven't seen him. I'll call him up now."

And Tillotson generally came.

He abounded in new books, freely lent and given, in theater tickets also, and when Mr. Widfield could not go, and he himself was too busy, he would send a cheerful young reporter to accompany her.

A rich and varied diet this, with the rigorous exercise of eternal combat with Mr. Smith, and the sunshine and fresh air of new friendship.

Stella grew apace.

Her letters to the boys changed subtly in tone and substance. She was no longer Rachel mourning for her children and refusing to be comforted, but a mother proud of accomplishment and looking forward to the further flowering of her work.

"It does my heart good to see you looking so much brighter," Mrs. MacAvelly told her, dropping in for a quiet talk one evening when she was alone. "You do feel better, don't you?"

"Oh—*immensely!*" Stella answered. "Things look so different somehow. Of course I miss the boys still, but I'm getting to see their side of it—their end of this great business of growing up. I suppose I was holding on so tight I could hardly detach myself enough to consider them. And they are really doing nicely. Morgan, Jr., writes delightful letters now—and Roy is getting quite ambitious."

"It is a pleasure to watch things grow, isn't it?" her friend agreed.

"I should say so! And I'm beginning even to watch myself grow, Mrs. MacAvelly! That young man you—unloaded on me is a liberal education—in some lines."

"You do find him interesting? I hoped you would."

"Interesting—very. And drastic! But when I have sense enough to overlook the three sets of artificial sensitiveness—of personality, sex, and class—I do find him instructive and valuable."

"He has real promise, don't you think so?"

"Unquestionably. That play of his has big things in it—if he'll ever learn to mitigate the class prejudices a bit."

"How does he get on with it? He hasn't been to see me much since you have let him come here. I'm a sucked orange, I fear." Mrs. MacAvelly smiled cheerfully, and Stella with her.

"You are more comfortable than the orange still under pressure," she agreed. "As to the play, he's got a tremendous scene on. You know he's pulled it all to pieces and done it over more than once since that reading."

"Yes—he did tell me that, the last time I saw him."

"And now we are fighting over the proper attitude of the heroine. I use the word advisedly—talking with that man is not only hard labor but combat."

"You have thrived on it at any rate."

"Yes——" Stella laughed lightly. "The female of the species was more deadly than the male once, at any rate. I'm tremendously proud when I can stand up to him."

"Does Mr. Widfield like him any better?"

Her face clouded. "No—rather worse if anything. Now your other friend, Mr. Tillotson, Morgan delights in. I never knew him to be so pleased with a new friend. But he can't bear to have me mention 'Alias Smith,' as he calls him. So I just don't mention him."

"He doesn't really object to his visiting you?"

"Of course not! Morgan's not so narrow as that. He's always said that I could have any friends or visitors I pleased, so long as he didn't have to see them. He always dodged poor old Malina, you know."

"She has not been annoying you lately, has she?"

"She has not! I've told the girls not to let her in, you see—I got so angry with her last time. But I can understand about her work, and even her—horridness—since knowing Mr. Tillotson."

"Another liberal education?"

"Yes—far more liberal. You've no idea—or rather you have, and I never had before. What a pleasure it is to have a man friend. You have a lot, haven't you?"

"Yes—and appreciate them. But then I am a good bit older than you, you see."

"*That* hasn't anything to do with it!" Stella insisted. "It's because you are—broader, somehow. I've been so absolutely wrapped up in Morgan that I've had no time or room or inclination to think about anything else."

"And you have now?"

It was a very quiet question, scarce more than acquiescence. Stella meditated over it conscientiously. "Why, yes—I have. You see, really, I have oceans of time. The boys are gone—the house runs itself. I don't really see what I would have done this winter without these new things to think about. I've done so many new things, you see. Those excursions you took with me—the Settlement evenings—all that horridly interesting time with the prisons and asylums——" She shivered. "Oh, I've learned a lot, and such different books! You can't think how sudden and queer it is—that tempestuous Socialist person hammering on one side and the calm emotional mind shining on the other!"

"Like the Sun, the Wind, and the Traveler," Mrs. MacAvelly suggested.

"Exactly. And the Sun wins, as before!"

The visitor smiled softly to herself. Several times she had come within speaking distance of what had been so deep a grief in their last close talk together, and each time Stella had launched off briskly on the boys or her new interests, not as one avoiding a painful subject, but in genuine enthusiasm.

"Let sleeping dogs lie," Mrs. MacAvelly said inwardly, and began to talk of the play of the season.

Mr. Tillotson was announced, and they both met him cordially.

"Where's 'himself'?" he asked. "Still going to Pittsburgh?"

"Cleveland this time," Mrs. Widfield explained. "I do not understand why leather should require so much traveling—nor why the heads of the business should have to do it."

"Not so much leather as politics, I fancy, or at least organization," he suggested, settling into his favorite chair. "I'm glad to see you, Mrs. MacAvelly. You still find life interesting, I trust."

"I find it more interesting than ever—don't you?"

"Well—yes. All things taken together, I think I do. I'm the richer by two friends, thanks to your kindness." He rose and made her an elaborate bow. "And the better amused because of that literary waterspout you turned loose upon us."

"Does he use you too as 'material'? Not in office hours, I hope."

"Not exactly that. My friend here is his favorite prey at present, I believe." He waved a well-kept hand toward Stella, who leaned back, watching them both with contentment.

"I keep him posted, you see," she explained. "At first I used to run to him to be comforted. You see I couldn't complain to Morgan—he can't bear the man. I'm afraid he'd have said—'The more fool you!' or its polite equivalent. But Mr. Tillotson quite understands why I put up with him, and, I imagine, takes a sneaking satisfaction in the punishment I get."

"Oh no, no. My dear lady! Not 'sneaking,' I hope. I do confess to something of that 'stern joy' that—shall I say—parents feel when their children are getting good, although perhaps painful, training."

Mrs. Widfield protested violently. "Parents indeed! I won't hear of it for a moment! No, Mrs. MacAvelly, it is the secret triumph of his sex in seeing a woman 'get hers' at the hands of a tyrant man."

"A man has to have some satisfaction in these days of overturning all natural supremacy. Before long we shall be hearing that 'a *man*, a spaniel and a walnut tree—the more you beat 'em the better they be.'"

"It has done me good, anyhow," Stella admitted. "I can see it myself. I can see things more clearly, think more clearly, and talk more clearly—can't I, Mr. Tillotson?"

"I do not know to what depths of fog and murk your mind was previously accustomed—but you certainly can do all you say at present."

Mrs. MacAvelly looked from one to the other with her quiet, faintly humorous little smile. "And can you write more clearly, too?" she asked Stella.

"Write? I write?"

"Why not? Everyone writes today."

"I fancy you would write better than most, Mrs. Widfield. Perhaps you do——?"

She was looking from one to the other with something of a blush, and something of a smile, rather shamefaced on the whole.

"Oh well—*that!*" She said it as if writing in this sense were common as breathing. "As you say, Mrs. MacAvelly—everyone does a little."

"Now, Mrs. Widfield!" The editorial eye was sternly upon her. "Is this the hideous bar which now interposes between our previous happy days and that eternal friendship to which we were looking forward? At least—to which I was looking forward?"

"I don't see any bar," she answered, a little hurt by his manner.

"Alas for the innocence of women—and more especially for their unprofessionalism! Do you not see, my dear lady—I know Mrs. MacAvelly does—that if you take to writing you must either do it well or ill. If you do it well—which is the most probable case—then rises professional jealousy and stalks between us. In place of the free exchange of thought in which, so far, you have furnished me with a fluttering throng of valuable suggestions—you've no idea, Mrs. MacAvelly," he said in a mock aside, "how much my work has brightened up since I knew Mrs. Widfield—instead of this peaceful interchange we shall come to regard one another with covert suspicion, to hide our ideas as so much copy, to check—oh, I beg of you not to do it!—to check the crisp epigram, the clever turn of expression—lest the other profit by it."

"You needn't be afraid," she assured him. "I promise never to do that."

But he was not to be consoled. "You must have heard complaints from the unthinking of the loss of finished brilliancy, of quick spontaneous wit, in the men writers of today. This, I am convinced, is due to the evil habits of our modern women. Whereas in times past they were flattered and grateful to have their brilliancy and stimulating thoughts appreciated by their men friends, now they have the sordid custom of selling the same at so much per word. It is a great loss—a great loss."

"Admitting this sad prospect for the sake of argument, what are you afraid of if I write badly?"

"That will be even worse," he answered, sadly shaking his head. "In the first case we could at least maintain an armed equality, and I could still glean a stray sparkle now and then, but in the second—what friendship can stand when one is asked to give an opinion on poor stuff? You will come to me in all the young enthusiasm of the beginner, with such a proud glow of enjoyment in your tender bantlings—and I shall cease to be your friend in reverting to my other self, the editor."

"That is a ghastly prospect," Mrs. Widfield agreed. "In spite of Mrs. MacAvelly's fond belief in my capacities I see but two alternatives. I must either not write—or not let you know it." She looked at him mischievously but most kindly. There was something very attractive to her temperament in this quiet man. He made no claim on admiration by exhibition of strength, no claim on sympathy by some engaging weakness. She had never known much of men. There were few in her memories of childhood or girlhood, and Morgan was *sui generis*—she had never compared him with any other. Since that dinner party of Mrs. MacAvelly's her range had widened, not only in these two who came so often, but in many others she had known through them. Of them all this one stood easily first in her esteem, yet so quiet was he, so undemanding, and uncommunicative that she was sometimes puzzled to account to herself for her strong liking.

And she had tried. It was one of the expressions of her new impulse to do, to work, which had set her at bits of description and analysis. She had covered many stray sheets with rough sketches of the violently earnest Mr. Smith, a practice which enabled her with better grace to bear that violence and even to draw him on to fuller expression. Other sheets were devoted to most friendly description of this quiet friend, and further to an effort to understand and to explain his atmosphere of strength and comfort.

Mrs. MacAvelly excused herself early, stating that with the weight of advancing years she found herself waking up earlier and earlier every morning, so that unless she went to bed with equal recession she should have no sleep at all.

Very trim and capable she looked as she said it, but neither ventured to contradict her.

"You remind me of the logical extension of the old rhyme," he said, rising to open the door for her. "You remember the beginning, 'He that would thrive must rise at five'?"

"Well—what next?"

"It is perfectly obvious: 'He that would thrive more must rise at four. He that would still more thriving be must always leave his bed at three. He that all others would outdo must be prepared to rise at two. He who would never be outdone must briskly leave his bed at one. He who would flourish best of all must never go to bed at all!'"

"That may do for editors but not for me, Mr. Tillotson. Good night, Stella. I only meant to stay a minute and it's been hours."

He glanced at the clock.

"Nonsense," said Stella. "We've only just begun. And you know you 'never go to bed at all.'"

"You'd like me to stay a bit longer?"

"Of course—do sit down."

"On one condition—you have to pay for the privilege of further companionship."

"What *do* you mean?" She was laughing but puzzled.

"You have to show it to me."

"Show it to you? Show what?"

"Your work, of course."

She dropped into a chair and looked at him with such childlike eyes, so big with astonishment, and a funny sense of guilt discovered, that he laughed aloud.

"Bring it out," he commanded. "I will eat all my words. Good, bad or indifferent, I want to see it. And I think you can trust me to be editor and friend too."

"I confess you tax my credulity," she said. "I know at least enough to realize that a man in your position cannot—possibly—want to be bothered with any more word stuff than he has to handle every day." She regarded him with puzzled eyes. "You must think a good deal of me," she said.

"I do," he assured her. He tossed the cold end of his cigarette into the fire, and stood before it. "I will own, frankly, that I have very little interest in what is written outside of the pile I have to work through. But I have a very great interest in you."

She leaned back on her cushions and regarded him with a most girlish interest. His tone was quite matter-of-fact, wholly impersonal. It carried no faintest hint of any further feeling than the interest he owned to. And that met so fairly her own interest in him that it gave her a peculiar pleasure.

"Why?" she asked.

"Why am I interested in you?"

"Yes."

He looked at her in a critical estimating way, as if she were so much "copy" instead of a very attractive woman.

"I've no objection to telling you," he said. "You interest me, have interested me from the first, as having potential energies as yet untouched. I think you have it in you to do something—— You see——" He hesitated. "I know it is a poor compliment to praise one woman at the expense of others, but—your harp has a thousand strings, we may put it—and theirs have only one!"

"Oh no, no!" she protested hotly. "I won't stand it. Women are not like that!"

"Most of them are," he insisted stubbornly. "Now, see here—I'm not making love to you. I'm not praising your peerless beauties and graces—I've seen handsomer women."

Thanks to her apprenticeship with Mr. Smith she took this without the quiver of an eyelash.

"But these 'beautiful dolls' are tedious—little as they think it," he went on. "Of course a man knows his weaknesses—none better. But he can see when he's being led by the nose—even when he follows—and he does not respect the process."

She was still displeased. "But there are hundreds—yes, thousands and millions of women today who are not like that—women with big brains and warm hearts, who would be ashamed to play that old one-stringed harp the whole time—or anytime!"

He chuckled a little. "That's another difference, my friend. They'd be ashamed to play that string—anytime. Most likely they haven't it—never had—or it's broken. You've got it all right—but there are others. And I suppose I'm man enough to like a woman 'as is a woman' even when she's none of mine. Come now, don't let's talk personality anymore. Get out your manuscript and let's see what you can do."

9

Mrs. Widfield's quiet living room held a new piece of furniture, a large, imposing piece of furniture, an object of beauty and of undeniable and evident use, yet somewhat incongruous with the general tone. It was a darkly polished, high-standing rolltop desk of rich mahogany. Stella had bought it with the first check she received for work—that is, with the first check that was big enough.

All her life she had secretly hungered for a desk like that, her small correspondence not giving her the faintest excuse for possessing one, but now, without any conscious effort, the seven large drawers, the two little ones, the fourteen pigeon holes, square and long, the twelve letter boxes, were all occupied, if not filled.

She regarded that desk with more pride than her piano, with more affection than her entire wardrobe; dusted it sacramentally with a silken cloth, adorned it with smooth clean blotting paper and a careful selection of the various implements of her new occupation.

Stella was at work.

Perhaps the discovery of one's natural work, when eager, blundering youth is passed, may result in an enthusiasm similar to that of which we pityingly remark, "There's no fool like an old fool." Of all the thousands of people who were writing in New York, no burning young genius from the South, starving in order to follow the gleam, was happier in the work than this quiet, comely married woman, no longer young.

No longer young in years, that is, in the smooth, bright-eyed bloom of girlhood, in the vision of a hoped-for love that should out-shine all others.

That youth had quietly, softly, slipped away, with the reasonable fruition of most of its hopes.

Love, marriage, motherhood, a home of her own—all these had been hers, were hers still. In all her earnest conscientious fulfillment of duty—and she had neglected nothing of her cycle of sweet labors—she had never felt the peculiar personal satisfaction that now refreshed her tired nerves.

"This is *mine*," she thought, tipping softly back in the swivel chair; "all that I've had was the joy—and the duty—of a 'girl,' a 'mother,' a 'housekeeper'—this is the joy and duty of Stella Widfield."

Mr. Tillotson had casually looked over one of her neatly paged manuscripts, his kind, rather amused and affectionate expression hardening, as she watched, into the coldly professional, and then kindling into a restrained enthusiasm.

He ran over another, glanced at a third, and then laid them down on his knees and looked at her for a while in silence.

Her eyes were eager, timid, hopeful; she did not speak.

"You'll have to let me take this stuff home," he said; "it's better than I thought. Not masterpieces—don't let me deceive you—but it does look as if you had it in you to do something."

That was four months ago.

He was perfectly right. The little things that Stella did were not masterpieces, but they were distinctive, original, new, and caught the popular taste more suddenly than many a greater thing. Little sketches, scarce more, delicate but strong, describing common things, people and feelings, so that the average readers felt as if they had written it themselves.

One or two in the "magazine section" of his paper, two or three in a popular weekly, and two taken, with warm praise, by a "real magazine," as she called it—in four months, and with checks coming in that astonished her.

But the difference inside was what astonished her the most. It was as if a cramped and overtended house had suddenly spread to a palace, a narrow city garden opened to the mountains and the sea.

When she woke in the morning she had that cheery feeling of something new and pleasant, before the definite memory of it awoke, the always open prospect.

At first she had brought all this bubbling joy to Morgan, as a matter of course, but to her puzzled surprise, he took only a perfunctory interest in it.

"I'm delighted, my dear, of course—delighted. Awfully proud of you," he had said. "But I don't need any new cause for being 'proud' of my wife—I was before."

And while he was never openly indifferent, his interest seemed so halfhearted, almost forced, that in spite of herself she drew off a little and solaced the hurt in the joy of working.

"Why should he care?" she thought, philosophically; "I don't care about leather—not really, only on his account. I'll not bother him anymore."

She told him, of course, of each little triumph, each fresh upward step, and he had to admire the desk—though he seemed somehow to resent it, too.

In some way his dislike of the "wordsmith," as he called him, was connected with the desk; and Stella's frequent mention of Mr. Tillotson, her gratitude for his advice and help, did not shake this arbitrary idea.

Associate feelings cling close in spite of facts.

Morgan came in one afternoon, a bit early, his hands full of letters and papers.

"Mail enough for an editor!" he rather resentfully thought, depositing it on the desk. "Stella! O Stella!"

Stella was not there, evidently. He looked in her room, in the dining room. She was not in the house, apparently. The tea table stood there in all its careful imitation of the English meal, and he regarded it gloomily.

"No wife—and no tea. Well, I'll make it myself," he muttered a little irritably.

He was a trifle tired that day—things had been going a bit awry. He had had to cordially agree with various warm praises of that last thing of Stella's, and somehow found it difficult.

He wanted to say to them, "What difference does it make? Anybody can write good stuff nowadays. But she is my wife—and that's enough." He did not say these things, even to himself, but that was the way he felt.

He dragged out the wicker table, tried to light the spirit lamp and found it empty; filled it from the little long-nosed copper can, and managed to spill some on the rug. This he hastily mopped up with his handkerchief, lest it discolor the hardwood floor, and Alicia coming in, in her neighborly way, found him squatting there.

"O, Morgan, how nice!" she said with an air of pleased surprise.

He continued to wipe up the wet spot, remarking dryly, "What's nice?"

"To find you in, of course, and also a chance to be useful. Let me—please."

She was going to seat herself in Stella's pet rocking chair and pour the tea for him, but he forestalled her.

"No, thank you, Cousin Alicia; I'm doing very nicely. You shall wait on me when I call at your house. Allow me——"

He offered her biscuit—cake—thin bread and butter. He made tea, wiggling the fat little tea ball in the cup, and gave her some.

Alicia scorned it. "It's not hot," she said. "The kettle hasn't boiled."

He received this suggestion with indifference. "Oh, well. It will boil sooner or later—then you can have some that's hotter. Just wait a bit."

But Alicia was not pleased.

"Indeed, I'm not going to. You don't deserve to be visited—you're not a bit nice. I'll go up and make some good tea in my own little teapot."

She stood a moment, lingering prettily, her hand on the back of the chair. "You'd better come up and have some of mine," she suggested.

"Thanks," he said, poking at the wick of the lamp, "I think I'll stay down."

She came a little nearer. "It'll be very nice tea!"

But all she received was, "This is good enough for me, thank you."

Then she sat down again, plumply.

"Why, Cousin Morgan! What is the matter with you lately? You used to be so nice to me—and now you are so—so——"

"So what, Alicia? Here—it is boiling now." He filled the teapot and offered her some.

She waved the cup aside. "So unkind. You used to sit by me and talk—or not talk. You used to say I rested you!" Her big blue eyes were quite wet, her soft, amiable mouth drooped pathetically.

"So you did, Alicia," he agreed pleasantly.

"And now I don't? Is that it?" she persisted, with such apparent distress that he hastily reassured her.

"Why, you're all right, my dear cousin—always were. If I've been rude to you, I'm sure I'm very sorry." And he put sugar and cream in the cup she had rejected, and tasted it approvingly.

"Oh, no, you're not *rude*—but—" (he was sipping his tea calmly) "but I feel as if you didn't care to have me rest you anymore!"

"My dear Alicia!" Morgan sat up, looking a little nettled. "Don't be absurd! You can't expect a man to want to rest—or be rested—all the time, can you?"

"Oh, you *are* cross!" she protested; "I'll take myself off till you are better natured." She started up, still rather reluctantly, and looking back.

"Just as you say, my dear Alicia!" he placidly agreed. She went out with some feeling, and Morgan, still sipping his tea, glanced over the evening paper.

He heard the bell, and looked up eagerly, but it was only Mrs. MacAvelly, whom he rose to greet.

"All by yourself?" she said cheerily. "Stella is more uncertain in her habits than she used to be, certainly. How often I've found her at this time, sitting in that very chair, waiting for you! And you're making tea all alone by yourself—how clever of you."

"Not at all," he replied almost tartly; "I'd much rather my wife made it for me. But she is so—busy these days. I've had to learn how."

She gazed at him in kindly amusement. "Do you good, Mr. Widfield, do you good! Men are much happier for not being fussed over—for having to wait on themselves."

"Well, I don't know," he demurred. "There is great comfort in being waited on."

Mrs. MacAvelly praised his independence, however, and went on, chatting agreeably of her admiration for "dear Stella's work."

His sympathy was a little constrained, but he agreed that she had certainly shown unsuspected talent.

"And she has done wonders for my friend, Mr. Smith," pursued his guest, with a momentary glance that showed her quite clearly his lack of enthusiasm in that direction.

"Yes, I dare say she has," he dryly admitted. There was a somewhat inimical silence, which was broken by the sudden and cheerful return of Cousin Alicia, Colonel Cushing rather protestingly in tow.

"You wouldn't come up and take my good tea," cried Alicia, "so I've brought Papa down to have some of yours, even if it is bad. Isn't it a shame, Mrs. MacAvelly—the poor man having to make his own tea!"

"She would have it so, Morgan," Colonel Cushing was protesting. "Women must have their wills while they live because they make none when they die," and he bowed to Mrs. MacAvelly as if offering a compliment.

"That old saw is certainly a back number, Colonel Cushing—you'll have to drop it," said Morgan, as he drew up chairs and offered cups of tea, the first cool and strong from standing, the second hot and weak from a sudden influx of hot water. "Make yourselves comfortable. Stella'll be in a minute, I'm sure."

But she did not come, though they lingered, conversing amiably, until Mrs. MacAvelly spoke of a huge book on the City of Minos she had received, a surprising present, and urged that they come and look at it. Colonel Cushing was the only one who accepted this invitation, and he looked rather as if he did so to "oblige a lady."

"Thus are we led about, Morgan, my boy," he said, putting down his cup. "Women's wills and winter's winds change oft, eh?"

"I don't think that's a very nice one, Colonel," the lady objected. Whereat he offered to amend with "Women, wind and fortune are ever changing."

"If I were you, Mrs. MacAvelly, I'd change again, and cancel my invitation," suggested Morgan, lazily.

"No, indeed; that would only prove him right. Come along, Colonel—perhaps you will find some ancient Cretan proverbs against women."

Alicia watched them go, nibbling a little cake with small, childish bites around the circumference.

"Now we are cozy again," she said.

At this he looked about, dispassionately replying, "Yes, it is a cozy place, I think."

"It doesn't seem so homelike with that great desk in it, though. Looks like an office!" She rose and drifted about the room with an air of gentle curiosity, touching Stella's heap of mail matter with a pink inquiring finger. "What a lot of letters!" then drifting back again. "I shouldn't think you'd like to have your home look like an office, Morgan."

To this he paid scant attention, merely, "I don't mind—I don't think it does, really," and turned a page of his paper.

She sat watching him for some moments. They were on terms of almost lifelong intimacy. She had always insisted that he should read and loaf and do just as he liked—that she did enjoy seeing her friends comfortable. But she also enjoyed comforting them, and there was a new sense of indifference about this pleasant cousin. She was very fond of him, and had grown of late years to believe that certain unexpressed roughnesses in his path of life were smoothed by her light touch.

Alicia was not in the least analytical. She had never tried to define just what the strain was in Morgan's life, but she felt that there was one, and had tried in all good faith to make things pleasant for him. Possibly this habit, followed by the vague sense of his withdrawal, now urged her to more feeling than she had herself suspected.

"One," she remarked, distinctly, but in a low voice, as the minutes passed. "Two," he did not notice her in the least. "Three," a little louder. "Four!" this rather explosively.

"I beg your pardon, Alicia." He started to his feet and suggested, "Have some more tea?"

She laughed her soft laugh at that.

"Indeed, I won't submit to any more of your tea!"

"Have some bread and butter, then—some cake——" She refused them all, with some lessening of her usual good nature.

"O, all right. Just make yourself at home then." And he dropped back into his newspaper.

"Thank you, Cousin Morgan, I will—but in my own." She moved to the door. "Come and see me when you are feeling pleasanter— when you're tired of being left alone." And Alicia departed almost petulantly.

"Good-bye, Alicia," was all he said, and that absentmindedly. The paper no longer interested him any more than she had. The more he had turned to her for solace and companionship, the more eagerly and freely she had offered it, and to his gradual surprise, he found himself wearying of steady sweetness. Stella, now, was more refreshing when she was not so everlastingly nervous. Of late that nervousness had largely disappeared, the worrying, overinsistent affection, all that had worn and worried him. But then—so had Stella!

He walked about the room and looked out from one window and another. He rang, and interrogated the stiff-faced Hedda. "Did Mrs. Widfield say when she'd be in? No? Very well. When she comes tell her I'll be back before six." And after a few more futile paces up and down, and study of the remote streets, he departed.

She came in but a few moments after, very brisk, trim and cheerful, looking younger by years. Her dress was as carefully chosen as ever, but touched a new note, had a sort of business air about it, not pronounced, but visible. From her face that look of strain—of a concealed and denied hunger, as of those awaiting the last belated guest at a dinner party, had disappeared.

Just as those who suffer from "genteel poverty" strive painfully to look well dressed in spite of all deficiencies, so do many women's faces wear that brave assumption of happiness which is evidently maintained by constant effort.

But now Stella looked frankly and easily happy, and young, because she had begun again, opened a new chapter. She went straight to her desk and seated herself with a brisk air, rapidly opening the mail and sorting it.

One big envelope contained proofs. She read the note with it asking for immediate return and glanced at the clock. Another letter was even more imperative, begging that a certain promised article be mailed that night.

She settled briskly to work—the proofs she could do before dinner, the article could get itself finished, somehow, in the evening. It was not a very important one—and was nearly done, she thought. And this sense of work being wanted promptly, of having to do things at once—whether she liked it or not—pleased her through and through.

While her blue pencil poised and darted, with an occasional stop to consult the little book she had with "Signs Used in Correcting Proof" clearly described and illustrated, Hedda opened the door and admitted a dressmaker's girl.

She was a spare little person, in a too short skirt, a jacket that did not fit her, large worn shoes and a hat which flopped down over her eyes, a hat whose eccentricities rather held the attention.

She pushed past the maid even as she announced her, and came in, remarking in a high voice:

"Here's your gown, madam."

"Gown?" Mrs. Widfield was annoyed, interrupted in her hurried task. "I'm not expecting any gown. You've come to the wrong house, child."

Hedda had discreetly retired, and the girl laughed as she saw Mrs. Widfield look for her.

"Stung!" she cried gaily. "I thought I could fool you! That maid was too easy."

"Malina Peckham!" cried Stella.

"The same! I came twice, and she said you weren't in. Now it's my regular business to get in where I'm not wanted—I have to, or lose my job—so I thought I'd practice a bit. This is an awful easy one. Say, don't be mad, Stella. I know I'm a nuisance; but this time I want you to help me out—really. I've got a big chance here, a Sunday story, 'Society Women who Work,' and you are my trump card. It'll be worth twenty-five dollars to me if you'll talk a little."

Mrs. Widfield swallowed her anger. The appeal for help was one she was never able to resist, and her own new activities gave her a keener sympathy. But Malina's methods and manners had become increasingly hateful to her, and she did not wish to be "interviewed," especially about this new undertaking.

"I'm not a society woman," she said shortly.

"Oh, yes, you are—or were. You are yet, in spite of your literary successes. Say, Stella, how did you ever get it over like this—so quick!"

"I have done very little, you know that," Stella answered. "Just a little newspaper work, a few things in that weekly and two magazine articles. It doesn't amount to much all put together."

"It amounts to more than most of us ever get to, I can tell you that. You've hit it—everybody's talking about you."

This was too much, even for the new recruit. "Nonsense, Malina. You're overestimating the whole thing. This is just a flurry, a small local interest. The work is of no real importance."

"I've heard you got five cents a word for that thing in the *Columbian* all the same—and that you're snowed under with orders."

This recalled to Mrs. Widfield's mind the immediate pressure. "I have one or two—and hurry orders at that—but it's only a fad of the public——" She took up her long blue pencil.

"No such thing," protested Malina. "You're turning out good stuff, all right. How on earth do you do it, and keep up all your other things? I don't see that the house looks neglected any."

Stella smiled amusedly. "Why should it? The maids are not affected by my new occupation—as far as I know."

"You certainly do look better—and happier," pursued the inquisitor.

"Oh, I am—it certainly agrees with me—being busy. But Malina, I *am* busy—now."

"Yes, I know. I'll go in a moment. But see here! Do you know that Mrs. Widdall, who's gone into chickens? Makes lots of money they say—furnishes all her friends. I've got to get hold of her. And those three Garonne girls, who run that tea room just for fun—and sell their old tea! I tell you it makes me *sick!*" she broke off in sudden heat.

"The tea makes you sick, Malina? What do you mean?"

"I mean exactly what I say," the girl burst out. "Here I am, having to work for my living and hating it like poison! Precious poor living I get, too! And here are you, just turn your hand over and make a big success! And you didn't need it."

Mrs. Widfield rose and spoke earnestly. "That's where you're entirely wrong, Malina! I did need it. I needed it as much as any starving woman in New York. There's more than one way of starving."

"You think so!" snapped the other. "You haven't starved, that's all! Well—I've got to go after the Chicken Lady now. Much obliged, Stella."

She took up her big paper box, and added, with instant return of the high girlish voice, "Did you say I was to take it back, ma'am?" and let herself out, laughing.

Stella turned slowly to her desk, much irritated.

"What a fool I was to talk to her—to see her at all! She'll have it out tomorrow, 'Mrs. Morgan Widfield says she was starving'!" She heard the maid in the dining room, and spoke to her. "Hedda—that was Miss Peckham you let in just now. Please notice carefully and do not let her get in again." She returned to her beloved swivel chair and found peace in intricate blue streaks and dots.

Her husband came in while she was in the midst of it.

"O, Morgan!" She looked up with a loving smile. "Just a moment——"

Presently she laid down the proofs and came to him where he stood near the fire watching her, his gloves in his hand.

"Now, dearest, aren't you going to take off your things and stay?" She kissed him and tried to take his gloves, but he held them.

"I was hoping you could make that call on the Spateses with me before dinner," he said. "It's only next door; you know we ought to——"

"Oh, I am sorry," she cried, and she did hate to refuse him. "I just *have* to finish these proofs! But Morgan, dear, *do* you know what day it is?"

"The fifteenth, isn't it? Tuesday——"

"Yes, it's the fifteenth. But it's something more—it's somebody's birthday! And I've not forgotten it. See what I've got for you!"

She was smiling, flushing, eager as a child. From a tiny hidden drawer in the desk she brought a little box, a dainty, pretty thing, and offered it to him. He turned it over curiously, opened it, his face a little shadowed, and took out a scarfpin.

"That's a beauty," he said constrainedly. "What is it?"

"It's an opal, a black opal." Her eyes were shining.

"Why, Stella! A black opal? You mustn't give me such expensive presents."

"Mustn't I?" She was almost dancing. "Oh, Morgan! That's the first real present I ever gave you. *I* paid for it, dear! *I* earned the money! My own self."

"But—you mustn't spend it on me."

"That's the beauty of it," she triumphed. "I can. I can spend it on anything I like. And you mustn't say 'mustn't' anymore."

He turned it about gravely. "Well—thank you, my dear. Thank you very much. I'm glad you're enjoying it," he added, securing her look unsatisfied. "You must be earning quite a bit."

"It isn't much," she said in a quieter tone. "But it's mine. I never had any money of my own before in all my life. It does feel good."

"Why, Stella." He spoke almost sharply. "Haven't you had money enough?"

"Oh, darling—I didn't mean it *that* way. Of course, I have. You have always been more than liberal—with the housekeeping—and the bills—and giving me presents. But I couldn't give you presents, you see. And I like it."

A little silence slowly rose over her enthusiasm, and while they stood there, in came Alicia for the third time, with, "Oh, Stella, you have got home then. I've been in twice to find you."

"Why, yes, I've been here for some time. Sit down, Alicia. And will you excuse me for just a moment. I have a bit of work that must be done before dinner."

Morgan put out a hand to detain her. "Can't you do it later, Stella, and give me fifteen minutes for that call on the Spateses? There's just time. Alicia won't mind."

"I am sorry," she said, "awfully sorry—but this has to go off tonight, and—as to later—I've an article to finish after dinner."

"Why, that's an outrage," he protested. "Here I've brought home tickets for *The Pale Pretense* this evening. You said you wanted to see it."

"Oh, Morgan!" Her face clouded. "I *am* so disappointed! I wouldn't have undertaken this thing if I'd known they would hurry me so. But Mr. Elderstone writes that he must have it tomorrow morning. They've changed the issue it's to be in."

Alicia sat graceful and still on a cushioned divan, looking from one to the other with her gentle smile. "How technical you are, Stella, and how businesslike and efficient! I do admire it so." She did not look as though she admired it in the least. "Now here am I, hopelessly unbusinesslike and inefficient, with not a thing to do. I'd just love to call on the Spateses. I'd be charmed to see *The Pale Pretense* tonight."

Morgan did not seize this opportunity with any alacrity, but his wife did.

"There you are, Morgan, all provided for. You take Alicia. You will both enjoy it."

Short of pronounced rudeness there was no escape. "We'd better start at once then," he said, without enthusiasm, and they went out together.

Stella bade them good-bye with a cordial smile, but it faded instantly. She stood for a moment, quite limp and sad, then went swiftly back to her desk, with straight-held shoulders and head erect.

"Anyhow, I've got my work," she said to herself, shutting out all other thoughts.

10

Alicia asked for "a minute" to put her hat on, and was so long about it that when she appeared, unusually pretty and quite pink from her haste, her cousin flatly refused to go.

"It's quite too late now," he said. "Besides, Stella ought to do it. They've been to see us twice, and Mrs. Spates has been very kind. Never mind, sis, I'll 'phone to Stella and stay here to dinner if you'll let me—she's too busy to eat—and then we'll go to the show."

So he telephoned to his wife, half hoping that she would remonstrate, but she answered cheerfully that it was an excellent idea, and hoped they would have a very good time—that she had no time to eat.

That ought to have pleased him, but did not, singularly enough. Alicia's dinner was excellent; Alicia's good nature quite returned; she was beautifully dressed and unusually charming. Also the good Colonel cheered up amazingly, and rehearsed many of his tales and saws on the inexhaustible subject of feminine deficiencies.

"Do you know they wore corsets in Crete!" he told Morgan triumphantly, full of recent information. "Corsets and high-heeled shoes, Morgan, my boy! In ancient Crete! There are plain pictures of them. I tell you women are women!"

"Didn't they do other things too?" asked Alicia with unusual acumen. "I think I heard Mrs. MacAvelly telling somebody that there were wonderful women athletes, doing something with the horns of cattle—weren't they?"

"Bull-grappling!" her father-in-law explained, so pleased with his new knowledge that he overlooked the mitigating circumstances of feminine achievement. "Those gigantic wide-horned ancient bulls, Morgan—quite prehistoric and extinct. Must have had cows too—terrible creatures to milk! Perhaps the cows had no horns though. But this sport of theirs—it was not bullfighting, mind—they turned somersaults over the beasts apparently, and between their great horns, six feet across or so. Tremendous!"

"Tremendous women, I should say," Morgan remarked, and Alicia smiled upon him.

Smile as she would, and good as was the well-served meal, he was not happy. The sudden flare of success which had befallen Stella had given him such a mixture of feelings as was quite distressing. He did not like mixed feelings, especially about a woman, most especially about his wife. In his clear, strong, settled scheme of life women held a fixed place, separated of course by the great demarcation between good and bad. The bad had no demarcations, but the good varied as stars in magnitude, and his mother, his sisters, his wife, were of course among the best.

That his wife possessed a talent for writing did not materially add to his admiration, or at all to his affection for her. A gift for music would have been of more domestic satisfaction, and if it was a great gift—if she had been a potential operatic star with a proud career before her, and had given it up for him—that would have held a poignant sweetness. He had been quite thrilled as a young man by reading of this supreme renunciation in certain novels.

But this writing could not be confined to him apparently, and then he had no subtlety of comprehension in literature. He admired her cleverness, genuinely, but took no pleasure in having the public admire it. She had taken no "pen name" and he disliked seeing his own thus widely acclaimed for work not his.

Worse than all was the money. He had money enough. He had always given her money enough. To have his wife, Mrs. Morgan Widfield, publicly earning money was in no way pleasing to him.

Besides all this came the new claims upon her time, her interest. Here is where his feelings became doubly contradictory, and caused irritation. He could see that the new work gave her pleasure, and was glad. He could see that it improved her health, and was glad. He felt the relief from that exigence of overprominent affection which had so webbed him about with incessant giving and asking; there was now a fresh aloofness about his wife, a place of withdrawal where he could not come, and the more she withdrew the more he wanted her. There rose in him a recrudescence of feelings long since satisfied and outgrown. Here was not a woman wholly his and always wanting to be more so, but a woman getting out of reach and seeming to like it. She was like a girl again, a young free creature; and as she vanished he desired to pursue—and could not.

Then he was undeniably and crudely jealous of young Smith, and frankly ashamed of himself for the feeling. He trusted his wife absolutely. He had never seen the slightest cause for any suspicion. He did not in the least believe there was any. Yet he was sullenly jealous. Perhaps he felt, in hidden rivalry, the ruthless selfish power in the young man, the fact that he was using Stella as a study, the further fact that he visibly had had an influence on her life, her work. Possibly again, so circuitous are psychological channels, he confused Smith's influence with the strong, stimulating friendship between her and Mr. Tillotson. This man he appreciated and liked; he had no shadow of feeling as to his visible goodwill for Stella, or hers for him; nevertheless, much that was really attributable to the influence of this keen-minded critic, he most illogically laid at the door of the young playwright. Sentiments have little to do with logic, in either sex.

Colonel Cushing rambled on about the palaces of old kings with their amazingly modern systems of drainage and waterworks, and Alicia was ease and smiling patience itself, but Morgan was not content. Nevertheless he made what show of it he could, and took his amiable cousin to the play.

Stella worked fast and hard. Strong emotion, well-restrained, is a good stimulant. In the back of her mind all these months was an aching desire for Morgan's approval, for his appreciation of her work. She wanted him to like it, to enjoy it. It was pleasant to have other people pleased, her friends, her boisterously proud boys, who called her stories "bully," and showed them to their much impressed schoolmates; she frankly enjoyed the praises of the editors, the visible effect on the general reader, and the cautious commendation of Mr. Tillotson was very precious to her. Even Smith's grudging "not bad stuff—for a beginner" gave her pleasure. But the one thing she absolutely hungered for—almost as much as she had once hungered to be called "my little girl"—was to have Morgan really impressed by her work—and say so.

She had found him once reading something of hers when he did not know she had come in, and had stepped back, watching, eagerly, delightedly. If he would pause, and read a bit of it over—if he would look back—if he would turn at the end and reread any of it! But when he laid the magazine down, it was with a little sigh of impatience, and he had instantly taken up the newspaper as if to take out the taste of her work.

She had not asked him how he liked it.

Besides this inner loneliness she felt now increasingly uneasy about Alicia. At first she had seen with joy how her own awakened interest had freshened her beauty again, given her life and sparkle, and had hoped before it was too late to regain the ground lost during those years of too much asking. But now doubts had overwhelmed her rising confidence, until she felt at last that her work was not a bridge to bring her husband back to her, but only a life preserver to keep her up, alone.

All this was stirring uneasily within her, demanding recognition, but she refused it absolutely and focused all her growing power of thought on the work before her. The proofs were done, and well done, before dinner, and that lonely meal took very little time.

"I can work better if I don't eat," she thought. "I'll have something afterward." And she took only a little soup and bread, and a cup of coffee, rigidly keeping her attention on the pages of her nearly finished manuscript instead of on Morgan's chair.

Then she settled determinedly back to the work and found herself able to cut off everything else, taking a certain grim pleasure in that power.

"It's no use my 'feeling' anything," she told herself. "If he does not care for Alicia it would be all wasted. If he does—well, I shall need my work!" And she did it.

It took much less time than she had allowed, to her surprise. "That's saving the dinner hour," she thought, as the two big envelopes went flying down the chute, and came back to find the soft-belled clock chiming only the half hour after eight.

The little strain of forced effort was over. She felt tired and unstrung. Those denied thoughts and feelings were knocking very hard now. Half past eight—the whole evening before her to *not think* in. She was appalled.

"Mr. Tillotson," announced Hedda.

Stella rose to meet him with such evident joy as brought a flash into his quiet eyes. She held out both hands to him and he held them a moment.

"Oh, how good of you to come!" she said. "How did you know I wanted you?"

"I have never dared to suppose so," he answered, "—before." And the second's pause made the word a shade impressive.

But he sat down quietly with his usual dry smile and added, quite as caustically as ever: "Neither am I overflattered. It is painfully evident that you only wanted me because you had nobody else."

As this was exactly the fact, and seemed not only rude, but a betrayal of her inmost feelings, Stella flushed and turned away.

"You mustn't think that," she said constrainedly. "It's just that I got through some work—too soon."

He noted the little flush, the shade of constraint.

"That is not exactly illuminating," he urged.

If ever in his life he had found a woman alone and lonely—it was this one. And if ever in his life he had longed to comfort a woman who was lonely—it was this one.

But he neither looked nor said it.

"Morgan still wearing out good leather in the pursuit of better?" he inquired.

"Oh, no," she answered with elaborate frankness. "He's gone to the theater with Alicia, instead of me. Isn't that cause for grief? You see I had a hurry call from two editors this afternoon, and just *had* to finish some stuff—and he had tickets for this evening. It was too bad—but of course we didn't want to waste the tickets."

"Not in these days of managerial syndicates, assuredly. But how, then, do I find you on flowery beds of ease, as it were? Where is this work, my all-too-popular young author?"

"It's done—all done and gone down that glass hole in the hall."

"You must have developed the speed of a night editor. I am becoming more and more jealous," he protested.

But she explained hastily that it was not so much speed on her part as the saving of a whole hour of dinnertime—instantly regretting the admission.

"No dinner! And did your husband stand for that?"

Then she was forced to explain further, going almost beyond the limits of her rigid truthfulness, showing that it was a real advantage to her to have Morgan "off her hands" when she was driven like that.

"Alicia's such a dear," she added with cheerful heartiness. "She and Morgan have been more like brother and sister than cousins, always. They grew up together, you see."

He made no comment, and she went on, flattering herself that her manner was absolutely disarming.

"He likes the Colonel too, even with all his absurd pose about women. I think it shows Alicia's sweetness that her father-in-law should be so fond of her, and she so content to make a home for him."

"I should think she would have made another for herself long since," he suggested candidly. "She is certainly a very attractive woman. But quite aside from all these husbands and cousins and fathers-in-law, the fact most pressing on my mind is that you have had no dinner!"

"I did eat some," she protested.

"Some what?"

"Some soup—and a piece of bread—and some coffee. It doesn't matter, really. What is one dinner?"

"One dinner is a good deal to one Little Mary," he insisted. "Now my suggestion is that you spend ten minutes putting on your bonnet and that you and I go forth to a wild exciting cabaret, and refresh ourselves with wine, woman and song."

"Haven't you dined either?"

"Oh yes, to a certain extent. But man is an insatiate animal and a restaurant meal more or less does not matter so much."

She regarded him with an appreciative smile.

"How do you manage to conceal—from most people—the kindest heart in the world under that hypercritical manner of yours?"

"That is an evasive answer," he promptly replied. "You know the tale of how the Englishman asked the American, 'Why do you Americans always answer one question with another?' and our compatriot answered, 'Do we?' Your ten minutes are shrinking."

"I'll tell you what's better," she said. "If you really have the remnants of an appetite—and as I plead guilty to the rudiments of one—we'll have a chafing-dish supper all to ourselves."

"Admirable! But my suggestion is that you let your wholly excellent cook do the chafing."

"You rude thing! My wholly excellent cook and coldly superior maid have both had special leave of absence—it was a good opportunity for them, you see, with so few dinner dishes—so you'll have to put up with my chafing."

He tried to persuade her that she'd much better come out with him, but Stella had vague objections to being taken out in that way by anyone but her husband. Also, though she did not frankly face the fact, she was unwilling to have the gentlemanly colored boy in the hall see Mr. Widfield going out with his cousin and Mrs. Widfield promptly following suit with a friend.

"You'll have to take the risk here," she insisted. "I don't feel like going out."

"All right—I'll take it!" He said it with a tone of defiance, and added in a half-earnest voice, "but you'll be sorry if it doesn't agree with me!"

She was used to his quips and turns, his wide range of joking, from the biting wit of his work on *The Day* to his crackling brightness in common conversation. She used that phrase to him one day, meaning it as a sincere compliment, but he had answered: "See Ecclesiastes VII, sixth." And when she had seen she apologized.

"You'll have to help," she told him gaily. "Come on—we'll see what is in the refrigerator. The French have their *pot-au-feu*, but we have our box-of-ice."

He bent his long legs and they both peered into the cool porcelain crypt.

"Cold chicken—cream—and, I do believe—mushrooms!" She was quite triumphant. "And there's lettuce if you want it." Then a further survey of resources was made. "Here's cake—good cake—and fruit, too. We'll have a real good supper."

It was good, all the better for having to prepare it themselves. She begirt him with a large apron, gave him a tray to carry, showed him where things were. They set everything together on the dining room table, and she creamed the chicken, with grave intent eyes and chary tastings.

For a man with all the hereditary instincts of the home, who had lived without a home ever since the unfortunate but mercifully brief marriage in his rather quixotic boyhood, the intimate domesticity of all this was more compellingly attractive than all that New York had shown him in twenty years.

What is called the "brute in man" may be reached by physical beauty, or even, lacking beauty, by the "come hither in the eye." On what is also popularly known as the "higher plane" he may be appealed to by grace, cleverness, wit, all manner of "accomplishments," not to say virtues; but between these upper and nether fields is a range of domestic attractions with an appeal deepened by centuries of association.

This was not the coolly graceful hostess of the drawing room, or candled dinner table, with her facile wit, her pleasant cordiality; it was not the fledgling author, of whose young flights he was in secret inordinately proud. This was a housewife whom he had never seen, setting the table, preparing the food, in gay intimacy—for him.

Somehow, in this atmosphere he began to notice details of soft color, little tricks of the hand, a quaint severity of compressed lips as she stirred and waited till the precise moment to take off the steaming dish. The age-old "way to a man's heart" is not merely gastric—it is along a blended network of little paths, all smoothly worn by long, long use.

Whatever personal attraction might have stirred within him before had been rigidly defined as "friendship," and "professional interest." If ever he had told himself he was playing with fire, he had also rested in the security that he was the only one to get burnt—and the game was worth the candle. But tonight he had felt for the first time a hint of loneliness and appeal in her, and it beat about within him almost beyond his power of repression.

In spite of which inner tumult he sat there by her—she had not given him Morgan's seat, but one cosily near, with their picnic array spread in a convenient semicircle before them—and showed practical appreciation of her skill so far as he was able.

"I withdraw my cruel remarks as to your cook," he told her solemnly. "She is no longer wholly excellent to my mind, but a nice understudy, tolerated in order that you may have time for higher things—if indeed there be such!"

She smiled on him without reserve.

"I am so glad you came!" she told him. "If you hadn't I should never have known enough to eat—should have just sat there and grizzled. Now you've made me feel all right again."

And this, as far as it went, was true. There was a region far within her heart where all was not right, but in his always pleasant companionship she had become able to get that door shut tight again.

"No, indeed——" for he was now proposing to wash the dishes. "The Wholly Excellent will do that without a murmur. We'll leave things right here—all but the soiled ones, and shut the curtain."

So they had further merry traffic with plates and dishes, and settled back at last in the big easy chairs, Stella looking forward with enjoyment to a "real good talk," Hamp Tillotson facing with reckless delight an evening he knew he should be wiser to flee from.

A preliminary pause, pleasant to both for its outer peace, and to him for its prickling inner hint of danger, was broken by the doorbell.

"Dear me—who's that?" she said with some annoyance. "And the girls out——"

"Let 'em ring," he suggested mischievously. "They'll think you're all out." But she had gone already, spurred by a flicker of her old New York fear—that something had happened to Morgan.

She was not wholly pleased to find Mrs. MacAvelly and Mr. Smith, but her feeling was an Arab hospitality compared to that of Mr. Tillotson.

"So glad to find you," Mrs. MacAvelly told her. "I wouldn't have come in so late, Stella, but I saw Mr. Widfield on his way out, and thought it was a good chance for my friend here. Mr. Widfield is not much interested in drama in the making, we all know."

Neither was Mr. Tillotson that night. Nevertheless he grimly felt that he ought to be thankful—that by this interposition he had probably been saved two friends and had lost nothing but a dangerous opportunity. In which frame he took himself away as soon as he decently could, urging his ever-present work in extenuation.

Mr. Smith, who had invited himself to dinner with Mrs. MacAvelly and had talked the two other guests out of the house before ten, was glad of three hearers for the scene he had brought with him. He rather resented Mr. Tillotson's departure, but work, especially literary work, was fair excuse for any man. As for the time, ten o' clock was but the dawn of the evening to him, and as for any possibility that Mrs. Widfield might have preferred her earlier company to his, he neither thought of it nor would have cared if he had.

"You've upset this thing so many times already," he told them both, "that I mean to get a sidelight on it before I go farther. May I smoke?"

This was great progress in his study of the manners of the despised bourgeoisie, a concession which he made in a surly, protesting tone, and always accompanied by the lighting of his cigarette.

"Certainly," said Stella gravely, remembering how Morgan disliked his tobacco, and how he was sure to stay too long for her to air the room.

"I have been obliged to put this away for some months," he explained. "There has been miserable translating to do—with the publishers snapping at my heels." To Mr. Smith any work which was not his own preferred writing was not only an evil but an insult. His attitude toward those who employed him was far from grateful or even patient. Yet there were not only his own meager wants to be met, but those of an old mother and a struggling family of sisters who had cheerfully starved themselves so that the brilliant boy might be educated. So he did work, hard and well, neglecting the real children of his brain as might some want-driven wet nurse.

"You will remember the first act," he said, and regardless of their assent he proceeded to review it at some length and then plunged into an introduction to his second.

In this a young Russian, Oscar Panin, employed as secretary by Mr. Williams, a rich Chicagoan, had fallen in love with Mrs. Williams.

"It is evening," the author explained. "The husband was called by a telegram, but has ordered the secretary to wait. 'I shall be back,' he tells him, 'at eleven.' Panin is working at his typewriter. Then comes in the woman." He read with gestures.

"*Elaine*: 'Is not my husband here?'

"*Panin*: 'He was here. He will be here again at eleven.'

"*E.* (glancing at the clock): 'At eleven.'

"*P.*: 'Yes—and it is only nine now. We have two beautiful hours.'

"*E.*: 'You will have your beautiful hours all to yourself, Mr. Panin. I am going out.'

"*P.* (rising): 'No—you are not going out. You are going to stay here—with me!'

"*E.*: 'You seem very sure!'

"*P.*: 'I am sure. I know you are strong and proud, but love is stronger than your strength—even stronger than your pride.' (He seizes her hands. She cannot resist him. She weakens, trembles.)

"*E.*: 'But my husband trusts me. He has never dreamed that I could care for anyone else.'

"*P.*: 'Let him dream on. You are awake at last—you know that you love me.'

"*E.*: 'I admit it. I love you.' (She throws herself into his arms.)"

At this point Mrs. Widfield interrupted, being quite used to the necessity with Mr. Smith. "Not so fast," she said. "I remember Elaine Williams. You know I told you in the first act that you had made her too—tropical. This is an American woman."

"What of that?" he demanded. "An American woman is a woman, isn't she?"

"Some of our American critics seem to think not. But anyhow—you are showing the influence of this hot-blooded young foreigner, how he has been slowly breaking down the principles of an American wife, and I say she would not collapse like that—would she, Mrs. MacAvelly?"

Mrs. MacAvelly agreed with her, and asked quietly if she would excuse her if she slipped away presently—that she was very tired. Stella hardly heard her, but nodded, for Smith was off again.

"Women are women the world over, and when they love, they love! You must remember that these two have been long together—often alone together. This is the moment of culmination."

"Yes, yes, I understand. That is all right. I admit that she loves him. I don't see why she should—but she does. Therefore she would take thought for the morrow, and plan for a respectable divorce—and how to marry him!"

"Ah, yes," he scornfully agreed. "You cold-blooded people! But at this moment they are alone together—he is making his appeal—his demand as a man—she cannot resist him. She must give herself to him!"

"She would do nothing of the kind. Now see here—let me show you." Stella rose and beckoned him to her desk. "You be working here, and I'll be Elaine. Mrs. MacAvelly shall be the audience, and I'll show you a love scene *à la Americaine*."

Mrs. MacAvelly took a chair near the door, and Stella, retreating to the dining room, entered as Elaine, with—"'Is not my husband here?'"

There is something of the actor in most of us, children show that; and this position was not a difficult one. The dramatist threw himself into the spirit of Panin, and it was with a look she had never seen before in his intolerant eyes as he answered: "He was here—he will be here again at eleven." Stella remembered the earlier lines readily enough, but when he came forward to seize her hands, she drew back.

"Now here is where you are wrong, Mr. Smith. There will be no seizing. She will argue this out with him. Let me look at the manuscript. Now here she withdraws firmly—you go on from—'I am sure.'" And she laid it down on the table.

"'I am sure,'" said Mr. Smith, and he looked it. "'You are strong and proud—but love is stronger than your strength, stronger even than your pride.'" He came nearer, but she stepped away from him, answering with sorrow and amazement in her voice:

"'But my husband trusts me. He has never dreamed that I could care for anyone else.'" She neither heard nor saw the entrance of Mr. Widfield, who came in quietly through the dining room, thinking she might be asleep, and now stood in the parting of the curtain.

"'Let him dream on,'" said Smith with passionate intensity. "'You are awake at last. You know that you love me.'"

"'I will admit it,'" said Stella in a steady voice. "'I do love you'— but wait!"

He took a step toward her—she turned—and saw her husband.

Her face changed instantly. "Why, Morgan—come in! I was just showing Mrs. MacAvelly how——" But there was no Mrs. MacAvelly in the chair by the door. "Oh—she must have gone out."

"Obviously," said Mr. Widfield. "Pray, do not let me interrupt you, Mr. Smith."

But Mr. Smith was intensely annoyed. He had been getting precisely what he had come for, the very tone and accent of the life he did not know of, the kind of woman he had chosen to put into his play without any sufficient acquaintance. And here was his heroine dropping all interest in his work the moment her husband appeared.

"I am used to being interrupted," he replied with grim pretense of patience. "Good evening, Mrs. Widfield. Good evening, sir."

He went out, Stella polite, Morgan quite motionless. She came back from the door, still a little confused, and annoyed as well as amused at Mr. Smith.

"I am glad he had the sense to go, for once," she said.

Morgan walked to one of the windows and stood looking out, his shoulders square and black against the panes. She watched him, puzzled at first; then in sudden horror her quick brain showed her the thing he might be thinking, the disgraceful absurdity of his thinking it. She drew herself up. "I hope you have had a pleasant evening with Cousin Alicia," she remarked quietly. To which he coldly returned: "I hope you have had a pleasant evening with Mr. Smith."

Then the bell rang softly, and Mr. Widfield, going to the door, let in the two maids.

11

With neither reproach nor explanation, in perfect quiet and with mutual courtesy, Mr. and Mrs. Widfield bade each other good night and retired to their rooms.

Stella was too angry to think out the situation fairly; Morgan was too angry to try. She was upheld by a burning sense of injustice, not only of injustice, but of insult. That he should dare!

She could not but admit that the situation he had chanced upon was almost farcically compromising, but that very thing should have shown him at once the impossibility of thinking—her cheeks burned in the darkness.

That her husband, who had known her for so many years, her *husband*—who knew she loved him so intensely that it had even become a weariness to him—that he for one swiftest second should imagine her as personally interested in any other man, least of all such a man as that! If he had been jealous of Mr. Tillotson now, she would not have been so surprised, nor so offended; for jealous, as one friend of another, he had some right to be. She certainly was fond of Mr. Tillotson—but not in that way—not for a moment.

There may have been, in this stage of her thinking, a certain vague consciousness of a trifle different feeling, at least on Mr. Tillotson's part, that evening—a feeling which might almost be said to verge on "that way," but she put the idea from her, and even farther the idea that she had been at all moved thereby from her dispassionate friendliness. Anyway it had nothing to do with her present cause of indignation. In the case in hand she had but a bare tolerance for the man, an intellectual interest only, tempered by much criticism and some absolute dislike. As to that "situation" she flushed again, from anger solely.

"*The idea!*" she flung out softly into the darkness. "Does he imagine that if I did love any other man I would talk like *that!* Doesn't he *know!*" But the words said themselves over to her relentlessly, with Smith's flashing eyes, his rich compelling voice at once softer and stronger than she had ever heard it.

"'You are strong and proud'"—how much had Morgan heard? "'But love is stronger than your strength, stronger even than your pride'"—had he heard that?

Then her own voice—she had tried to speak as a woman would in such case—a woman almost surrendering: "'But my husband trusts me. He has never dreamed that I could care for another man.'" Oh, but Morgan *must* have seen how it was! And then that low, barbaric, exultant: "'Let him dream on. You are awake now. You know that you love me!'" And her admission—her definite admission!

Still, Mrs. MacAvelly was there—she had *said* that. Of course he believed her. She had never lied to him in her life. And yet Mrs. MacAvelly was not there when he came in. . . .

Stella got little sleep that night, and Morgan less.

If she was stiffened with cold anger at his suspicion and hot with shame for him—that he should have sunk to it, he was torn with the same feelings in more furious form. His was not a delicately analytical mind. He read little fiction and made no dissection of what he read, nor did he minutely discuss the actions of his friends, much less his own. Of course if he had had to testify on oath: "Do you suspect your wife of this thing?" he would have denied it, denied it honestly. He did not believe it of her. He did not really believe that she even cared for the man. Indeed he went so far as to tell himself: "It's that cursed play of his!"

But this he did not work out clearly; it was only a theory advanced to meet the facts, and the facts were overwhelming. He had been so sorry for his overworked wife, so remorseful for ill temper, for leaving her at dinner, for going off with Alicia in that way. Alicia had not been half so stimulating a companion as Stella would have been at the play—she certainly was tiresome at times. And he had let himself in so softly, meaning to tiptoe to his wife's room and see if she was asleep. He had seen the table laid for two, the signs of a little supper, and then that light between the portieres, and the voices—such voices!

He told himself that he was a fool, that he was making a mountain out of a molehill, that he knew Stella through and through—the thing was unthinkable. Against that rose a sort of devil's advocate within him, presenting the case in circumstantial evidence: "She knew it was my birthday and that I was going to take her to that play. She fairly threw me at Alicia—I didn't want to go with her. She didn't care if I stayed out to dinner. She certainly stated that she had work to do. Then this fellow comes—probably telephoned before-hand—and they have supper. She must have got it for him herself—the maids were out! It was not their night out. She must have sent them away!"

And Morgan rose and walked the floor in long swift strides, making no noise however.

The days that followed were coldly quiet. There was no break between them.

Morgan waited for Stella to explain to him what he felt sure, in spite of all that damaging evidence, was explicable.

Stella waited for Morgan to apologize to her for a suspicion she scorned to discuss.

In pride and courtesy and calmness they remained apparently as before, conversing perhaps a little less, yet without acrimony.

Mrs. O'Mally and Hedda felt the difference, though they could scarce have defined it.

"There's some trouble between them," said good Mrs. O'Mally. "I would not speak of it to any outsider, but you must have seen it."

"They don't quarrel," Hedda replied.

"Oh, quarrel, is it? There's many a man and his wife quarrels from mornin' till night an' are as lovin' as turtle doves all the time. 'Tis not quarrelin'—'tis the black frost has settled on them. I wish the boys was at home."

But it was some time yet to the next holidays.

Only when Mr. Tillotson came did they both unbend and seem more like themselves, Morgan because he liked the man and was glad of a friend, Stella because somehow she did not feel willing for that friend to know how gray and desolate her life had turned. Finding himself so cordially welcomed he came frequently, and was not sorry to learn that among their common interests her work came more into prominence.

Under the whipping stimulus of Mr. Smith's arrogant and merciless attacks and ignorings, he knew she had gained much in mental vigor. In the gentler atmosphere of his own penetrating criticism and sincere approval she had quite bloomed, but now he felt a new stage had been reached. There was a detachedness, a full concentration, which he knew to be essential to the best work, and had not found in her before. She began to read more intensively as well as extensively, so much indeed that he wondered when she slept, and told her she was studying too hard—that she would break down.

At which Stella smiled, a hopeless drawn little smile that told him there was something deeply wrong. He had little idea of the stark devotion with which she had plunged into her new labors, nor of the immense consolation she found in it. Without that resource she would indeed have broken, for the wall of ice between her and her deepest love remained unmelted.

The luckless playwright she could not bear to see again, blaming him the more bitterly that she could not justify the feeling. Someone had to be blamed, and she could not, in spite of effort, keep up her anger against her husband. As she remembered all the circumstances, those cumulative damaging circumstances, she saw that any man must have been shocked into suspicion, however unjustifiable. But if anger failed her, pride did not. He gave her no opening, made no advance, nor did she ask it.

Her children were out of reach; hearty, sturdy boys they were, full of their own interests, making few calls on her. Her home ran smoothly as before. And when she faced each gray morning—the brightest sun did not lighten them now. The thought of work to do, real work, was her only comfort.

A proposition came to her to furnish short articles for a daily paper, only a thousand words or so, but mounting up steadily into three hundred and sixty-five thousand in the year, equal to a considerable book. She accepted it eagerly. In fear of falling short she wrote feverishly, doing two or three a day to have enough in store. To keep up a variety she read widely both in current events and among such sources as would give a background of fuller knowledge to her comments. When she had a sufficient accumulation of these trifles she would take enough time for some longer work, throwing herself into it without reserve.

To her growing wonder and new joy she found in all this not merely what she sought, the oblivion to pain, but a fresh delight, something life had never offered her before. It was not pride; that had been pleasant enough in her first sudden wave of popularity. It was a growing satisfaction in the work itself, in doing it, and in the mighty brotherhood of workers among whom she found herself. There was something in life then, after all, besides love. . . .

If Morgan could forget his trouble in a violent immersion in business, so could she forget hers in business of her own. She felt a new pity for certain friends of hers: little Mrs. Warren, whose husband drank, and who sat at home, mourning, or mourned abroad, growing paler and grayer and less effectual daily; and Cynthia Deveraux— those who knew her husband did not blame her for her counterflirtations, but what good did it do to him, or her? All poor Cynthia's dainty dressing, creaming and massaging could not hide the reckless grief that drove her on. Even Mary Franklin, whose children were rather overworked, as an occupation, seemed to fall far short of the content she strove for.

Stella did not pretend she was fully contented. She suffered deeply, constantly. There was that inner ache, that trouble never quite forgotten. But while that part of life lay behind locked doors, other doors opened, and she grew strong in contact with the broader issues of world-life outside.

If she had known how this quiet, uncomplaining attitude affected Morgan, her joy would have been keen indeed, but he said nothing. As day by day he saw the woman by his side walk steadily on, achieving, learning, growing, treating him with steady courtesy and kindness, making no explanation and demanding none, he felt a new sentiment toward her, a feeling he had never known before, that he had not supposed he could have for a woman—he respected her as he would a man.

He respected her for her work.

This did not make her seem like a man—which rather surprised him. She was never more womanly. Her quiet grace, her beauty, and the inner call of her love-hungry heart—all these drew him to her far more strongly than when she had constantly shown him these and nothing else. In spite of all dogged reiteration of the justifying causes for his anger he gradually lost faith in it. But he was proud as well as she, and not only proud, but stubborn. Surely the least she could do was to explain.

Hampden Tillotson came and went; talked deeply with Morgan, grew to know him well, and liked him in spite of a growing resentment, a feeling that in some way he must be responsible for the trouble in Stella's eyes.

She took great comfort in his companionship. The accords and discords which draw men and women together or keep them apart play on in a dim region where neither reason nor principle hold sway.

This man was within range on that wireless system which makes some unions possible and others impossible. If she had met him in her youth instead of Morgan she might easily have loved him. If she had not loved Morgan, fully and satisfyingly, with the deep foundation of physiological accord and the rich superstructure of their happy years together, their interwoven memories and interests, their well-loved children, she might even have loved him now. As it was, in the cold and darkness that lay between her and her husband, following that long period of nervous strain which had gone before it, and with a growing jealousy of Alicia which she strove against continually, but which would not down, she found almost her only rest in the atmosphere of quiet unspoken affection with which her friend surrounded her.

Unselfish woman though she was, she never gave a thought to what it might cost him. It had not once occurred to her that, as Mr. Smith had said, even an American wife was a woman and a man might love her.

He watched and studied her, feeling vaguely that something was wrong, yet unable to place it, now hotly wishing that he might be the cause of that trouble, and then cursing himself for a brute that he even wished it.

And all the time she hoped and hoped that he, unprompted, would tell Morgan of that too short evening together, and how far from pleased they had been to have Mr. Smith descend upon them.

But he never referred to that evening.

If she had continued alert and happy he might perhaps have been able to fight down this growing longing for her presence, her voice, her serene yet vivid spirit; he might have had the strength to go away, as he sometimes felt he must. But she seemed far from happy in spite of her new strength; not only that, but she seemed to brighten when he came, to need him somehow—and he stayed.

Morgan was glad of his visits, glad now, of anyone's visits; he went out frequently, and when Stella alleged work and would not go out with him he took to "dropping in" on Mrs. MacAvelly a little, and on Alicia a good deal. Also his business journeys seemed more frequent.

Stella was much alone. One night, one of the many nights when Morgan was not there and Mr. Tillotson was, that gentleman left his gloves on departure, came back and found the door still open— Hedda was mailing a letter. He went in, glad of the chance of another look at the gracious, earnest woman he had left so reluctantly, left because their talk had verged on the theme of a recent novel and the principles involved in it, and he had felt that he must go—or say far more than he had meant to. She had stood so tall and graceful there, saying good night in such a friendly voice—he could hardly find strength to leave.

And now, as he entered, all that serene quiet was gone; she had sunk on a chair, laid her white arms along the back and bent her head on them; she was shaking in a passion of tears.

He closed the door; he was beside her, stooping, kneeling:

"Stella—what is it? Tell me—I won't have you suffer! If you *must* cry," he added with an effort at his usual manner, "let me help!" And he gathered her into his arms like a child.

For the moment she yielded to the comforting arms, to the tender voice, the cheek against her hair; it seemed so near to what her heart was aching for. But only for a moment. With swift revulsion of feeling she tore herself away—this was not Morgan.

"Forgive me," she said tremulously, "and thank you. You are heavenly kind—but you mustn't."

"Why mustn't I?" he demanded. "Look here—we are full grown, you and I—we know each other. I know that you are unhappy—have been this long time—and you know I love you."

She dropped her hands to her sides, turned a white tearful face upon him. "You *love* me?" she said.

"I certainly do! What did you think it was? Come—you are honest, the honestest woman I ever knew—you know I love you, and I almost think you love me—a little."

He took one of her hands and held it close in both his, drawing her toward him.

"Wait a minute!" she said, rising suddenly. "Just a minute!" She pointed to the clock. "I'll be back in five minutes—I promise—but I must have that!" And she fled to her room.

He counted those five minutes, refusing to think, and met her, when she returned, with a settled intensity of feeling that was almost terrifying. But she had used her short respite well. Water, cold running water on face and hands, deep breaths of cold night air, a hurried desperate prayer—it was a different woman who came back to him.

"You've had your five minutes," he said grimly. "I'm going to have one—if I die for it." He took her in his arms again, with passion, not compassion, this time, and kissed her forehead, her shut eyes, her cheeks, then turned her face till the red mouth was near his. "Now—will you give me one?" he demanded.

She opened her eyes, standing quite still in his grasp, and looked at him, with kindness but not love. "No," was all she said.

He let her go.

He turned without another word to leave.

"Will you go away somewhere and get over it—and must we lose one another altogether?" she said quietly. "Or do you think you can fight it out—and let me keep the very dearest friend I have?"

"Men are not made like that," he remarked with some bitterness.

"Neither are women," she answered dryly.

He turned with sudden suspicion—or hope.

"I'll be perfectly frank with you," she said. "Not only as to you, but as to what is my real trouble—if you wish it. As to loving you—I really think I should, if I didn't love Morgan better. And as to tonight, honestly, you nearly swept me off my feet altogether."

He took a step toward her eagerly.

"No, it was not the real thing," she told him. "But I was so lonesome, and you were so heavenly kind, and we are just male and female of course, under all our intellects and moralities."

"But you are lonely, you say."

"Bitterly. If you can bear it, I'll tell you about it. If you feel that you have to go away, I shall understand. But if you'll let me prescribe—how about a five-hundred with the battle door?"

This was a favorite bit of home exercise with Stella. She had loved it in her girlhood, had played it with the boys, with Morgan when he would, and had long since impressed this friend to the service.

He stood and looked at her, his tense expression slowly softening to a smile.

"Well, you *are* a wonder!" he remarked. "I'll go you."

It was rather amusing to see this twentieth-century distressed wife and ardent lover now concentrating eye and hand and all coordinate nerves on a little flying feathered cork and two light-netted battle doors. The thing dropped many times, but each grew grimmer, steadier, and at length they made their score, and stood a little breathless.

"Now if you'd like to wash your hands and 'lave your fevered brow,' you have full permission," she said smiling.

Presently he returned, cooled and steady, remarking briefly: "Fire away!"

She told him the whole matter, blaming herself, or rather, not herself, but the emptiness of women's lives.

"I don't really find fault with him at all," she said. "Not till that night. And even you will admit he had excuse."

"He had no excuse. No man would ever have excuse for getting tired of you," he protested.

She smiled on him like a mother.

"Didn't you ever get tired of any woman?" she asked.

He admitted that he had. "But that was different."

"Not a bit different. Any man—or any woman for that matter, gets tired of too much—too much of anything. The reason women do not get as tired of men, as a general rule, is that few men are as dependent on one woman's love as most women are on one man's."

In her new wisdom she saw far; but, her wisdom being limited, she did not see all the way. He said nothing to that effect, however, and she went on sadly.

"The trouble now is pride. I can see that. But I can't bring myself to take the first step—I *can't!* Surely—surely he had no right to *dream* of such a thing."

"But you say yourself it was a pretty clear case. It did look queer —now didn't it?" Then an idea struck him. "Look here, I can tell him about the supper part."

She shook her head. "No. I wanted you to, at first, awfully. But of course you never thought of it. If you told him, and he came around, that way—it wouldn't be the same thing. He didn't trust me—in the face of circumstances. Having it explained wouldn't alter that."

"What are you going to do*?"* he asked.

"Just wait," she said. "It is hard, but not impossible. I have my work, you see. That makes all the difference in the world. And I did have you. I've been very selfish, I can see that. You see a woman brought up as I was never imagines things."

"I see," he said dryly.

"And you've been going on getting fonder and fonder of me, and I've not helped you one bit!"

"No, I can't say that you have," he admitted.

"Well—what are we going to do—really? I do hate to lose you— but I deserve it. If this is going to be such a bother that—that it'll be too hard for you, perhaps we'd better say good-bye. But I hate to face it."

There was a silence between them.

"I'm not really blaming you," he said at length. "I can see just how you felt—and didn't feel. You didn't have many lovers, I gather?"

"Never any but Morgan. Oh—there was one who proposed, but he didn't count."

"You mean you didn't care for him?"

She laughed. "I suppose that's it. But you do count, you see, be-cause I care for you so much."

He took this like a man. "The situation is practically clear now, at any rate," he said. "That's one comfort. I love you. You don't love me. Small satisfaction to me to think that you 'might have'! You and Mor-gan are all right—but for this ridiculous affair of the unspeakable— (though not unspeaking!) Smith. I believe I'll clear that up whether you allow it or not!" he added doggedly.

"You can't!" she told him quickly. "You can only account for that supper table—not for my ill-advised histrionics—and the girls being out and all."

"That's so," he agreed. "Looks as if you'd have to just wait, as you say. But I imagine you have lost interest in the drama."

They both laughed, and in that mutual understanding reached a clearer ground.

"You don't think," he added presently, rather hesitatingly, "that— he's running any risk?"

"Oh, I don't know! I don't know!" cried Stella, her worst fear rising irresistibly. "Of course it's possible. Sometimes I think it's probable—sometimes I think it's so! But then Alicia's almost like a sister to him. I think it's just habit, and—lonesomeness."

"Lonesomeness is a very dangerous factor, remember." He was looking at her with his old expression, humorous, wise and tender.

"I know it—it certainly is. But," she drew herself up at this, "I will trust my husband even if he did not trust me."

He admired her, loved her, nonetheless for her determination, and went away presently, walking the long stone miles between her home and his apartment, his lean, nervous hands in his pockets, his head bent as he faced the wind.

"As soon as she's out of the woods I'll take leave of absence," he determined. "He'll come around sooner or later—Morgan's a good chap. And when he does she won't need me. . . . But I'm not so easy about the Cousin Alicia end of it, not so sure as she is—and she's not really sure. Cousin Alicia is a mighty agreeable sort of woman—most men like that cushiony kind. I don't! But I've no earthly objection to scraping acquaintance a little—just to see how the land lies. . . . May take up my mind."

12

Alicia was her gentle, pleasant self to Mr. Tillotson, restful and attractive, as she was to many men. How a woman so genuinely popular had remained so long without remarrying was a puzzle to many. Stella, when she considered it, felt always a sharp revival of the stinging suspicion she so resolutely refused to harbor.

She had always accepted Alicia as part of the family, had been sincerely glad when she came to live in the apartment house, and had mourned with her when her always fragile young husband had died there. That was eight years ago. For the young widow to remain where she was, with the father whose only child had been taken, was perfectly natural; that she should grieve and wait for some years was natural also; but Alicia showed no signs of grieving now.

Why should she wait so long? What was she waiting for? Stella felt at times a sickening sense of being in the way. Before this dreary "coolness" between herself and her husband she had never been really anxious about Alicia. Now she goaded herself into feeling that perhaps Morgan's happiness depended not on his wife—but on his cousin.

Even an unacknowledged suspicion may add intensity to other feelings, and the pride of that sundered pair held out with stern endurance.

Meanwhile the amiable young widow found her evenings more attractive for the occasional calls of Mr. Tillotson. She had a genuine admiration for "literary people," and had often expressed the vague wish that she could "write," the process seeming to her an accomplishment to be learned, like playing the piano. It puzzled her gentle soul that her cousin did not seem to share her pleasure in the increasing frequency of Mr. Tillotson's visits. She knew Morgan liked him; he had said so to her more than once, and she had perhaps hoped that to have a "real writer" among her friends would make her cousin respect her judgment more than he usually did.

But the more Mr. Tillotson conversed with her on Literature, Art, and Music, all in capitals, the more Morgan surreptitiously yawned, and the earlier he departed.

One rainy evening neither of them had come, nor any other friend. The Colonel dozed over his paper, and Alicia wearied of her embroidery.

"Oh, I remember!" she thought. "They were going to the opera tonight. I'll go over and borrow a magazine."

Hedda let her in with as near a smile as her prim blonde countenance easily attained; Mrs. Cushing was a generous giver of pretty bits of adornment.

Alicia made herself at home. It was too late to hope for callers, and she was tired of the company of a sleeping father-in-law. Stella's room was a change, at least. She sat in various chairs, turned the lights up and down with careful study of effects, looked over the music and played a little air or two. Then gazing about the room with an air of criticism and suggestion, she casually began to rearrange certain small movables, cushions, flowers, chairs.

As she bent over, patting up the sofa cushions, Mrs. Widfield entered and stood watching, a slow color rising in her cheeks.

Alicia heard some movement and turned with a start. "How you frightened me, Stella," she said with soft reproach. "I thought you were hearing Caruso."

Mrs. Widfield let her gleaming evening wrap drop from her shoulders. "I was," she said. "But my head ached, and I took the liberty of coming home. Pray don't mind me," she added, trying hard to sound sincerely kind.

"Now don't be sarcastic, Stella. There was nobody in tonight. Papa's asleep, as usual, and I just ran over to get a magazine or something. You've always told me to make myself perfectly at home here," she added, not pleased with Stella's silence. And then, as the silence continued: "I'm sure you are welcome to my place anytime—only you won't take the trouble to come up!"

"That's all right, Alicia. I'm cross because my head aches. Yes, I have always told you to make yourself at home here. And you have."

"Of course I have. I do—anywhere. I love the home feeling." She sat down among the newly heaped cushions.

"So do I," agreed Stella, a little wearily, dropping into one of the rearranged chairs.

"I shouldn't think you would," Alicia urged, with an air of wise argument, "now that you have all this work to do, and are getting so notorious."

"Notorious!" Stella opened her eyes wide.

"Well, not exactly notorious. You know what I mean—noted, notable, noteworthy—everybody talking about you."

Alicia's attempts to be censorious were apt to be like the scratching of very small kittens, kittens whose claws were not stiff enough to really prick, but Stella was perhaps more sensitive than of old.

"What is everybody saying about me?" she demanded.

"Oh, about your success, I mean. What wonderful things you write—and what wonderful prices you get—and—and——"

"Well? And what, Cousin Alicia?"

"Of course I wouldn't tell you if you hadn't asked me. But you won't mind, I dare say—you're so strong. They say it must be rather hard on Mr. Widfield—and that it's quite evident you don't mind that."

The kitten quite triumphed. Even soft claws may hurt on tender places.

Stella's voice was level. "What is so hard on Mr. Widfield?"

"Why—having his wife work, of course!"

"What harm does that do him?"

"Oh, well, I can't argue, but you know it reflects on him, of course. No man likes to have his wife work. It looks as if he was no good—and couldn't support her. Or as if he was mean—and wouldn't."

Stella seriously meditated on this. She had not had it presented so concretely before.

"I don't really believe Morgan minds it," she said at last.

"I'm sure he does." Alicia had felt this for some months, finding no opportunity to say so. "But it's none of my business," she hastily added.

"No," said Stella, shaking her head with a slow smile. "It is none of your business, Alicia."

"Well! You needn't take me up like that!" She listened to a clicking latch. "Here's Morgan now!" She turned with her soft, engaging smile, adding: "Let's ask him."

Mr. Widfield came in, somewhat wearily. He was no longer dreading an overemotional welcome, a pouring affection that he should have to play up to, but he was conscious of a distinct lack in not meeting it.

Alicia, sitting low among the cushions, he did not at first discover, but was surprised to find his wife. He checked a look of pleasure before she saw it, observing: "I thought you were at the opera."

"I came home because my head ached," Stella explained. "I am sorry."

"Sorry for your headache—or for coming home?" There was a forced lightness in his tone, as when one makes conversation with a casual acquaintance.

"For both," she answered, a little impatiently. "Here's Alicia."

"Oh, good evening, cousin." He was unenthusiastic.

She looked from one to the other with faint mischief in her blue eyes. "Yes, I'm here, as usual. Stella and I have been quarreling."

"Quarreling?" He refused to be interested, but as she said no more, perfunctorily inquired, "About what?"

"About you," she answered, as if it were the most natural thing in the world.

He looked annoyed, sincerely annoyed, and his wife watched him with a queer nightmarish feeling, as if something dreadful were going to happen and she could not stop it.

"Yes," Alicia continued easily. "And I'm going to ask you to settle the matter."

"Ask away," he said carelessly. "I'll tell the truth."

But his wife made sudden protest—

"No, don't Alicia! I especially object."

Alicia rose and came to her with pretty apologies. "It's a shame to tease you, dear. And you do look badly. You'd better take that headache right to bed. Good night."

She was gone, and Morgan turned to his wife with sudden concern.

"Do sit down. You look horribly tired."

She replied with repressed intensity, examining her close-held fan: "You told me you had a business engagement—you couldn't go to the opera with me."

"That was true." The cold politeness had dominated his voice again. "The man failed me, however. I waited an hour—he sent a messenger boy to say he could not be there. So I came home."

She said nothing, and he added quietly: "Why do you question me? I do not question you."

"I beg your pardon." Her manner was as remote as his own. "Is there anything you wish to question me about? I am perfectly willing to answer you."

"No. I do not wish to question or discuss. You have a right to your own life."

"And you to yours. I shall not stand in your way, Morgan."

There was a strained silence. The faint hidden bell of the clock rang softly. The radiator murmured with a soft shrill sound like distant locusts.

The pain in her woman's heart drove her to expression. She came to him, her hands outstretched:

"Morgan! Is it too late? Can I do nothing, say nothing, to change it now? I know I have been to blame, dear, but just wait a little longer. Give me time—try me—see how different it will be!"

He stepped back from her, holding up a protesting hand. "Stop, Stella—for heaven's sake, stop! Have more self-respect! For your own sake—for mine!"

She stood frozen by the harsh bitterness of his tone. She did not know with what fierce pain he misunderstood her honest self-reproach.

"You are right," she agreed, regaining her poise. "I am sorry I said anything. . . . Won't you sit down?" she added presently, as if he were a visitor.

"Thank you," he responded with careful courtesy. "I will go and smoke in the library if you'll excuse me."

Left alone she stood white and silent, made a swift movement to follow him, but drew back.

"It is too late!" she cried bitterly, under her breath, walking about in her agitation. Then stopping short again. "Perhaps even yet—if I try—— There are the children to hold him." She knew in her heart that if she could not, neither could they. "And the home," she thought, clutching at straws in her distress. She looked around the pretty room and perceived what Alicia had done. This touched the springs of rage. "Not yet! It is my home *yet!*" she breathed through tight-set teeth, and fell to rearranging everything as it had been before, with swift sure touches. When all was to her mind she stood looking about at it with gathering tears. "My home! My *home!*" she murmured to herself.

A light tap at the door broke upon her hopelessness. It was Mrs. MacAvelly who bustled in affectionately.

"I've brought you my menthol pencil," she said. "It was a shame for you to lose all that splendid music."

"It was a shame for *you* to—why didn't you stay as I told you?"

"Of course I wouldn't let you come home alone. The idea!" She sat down by her, and saw the keen distress in her face. "Why, Stella, dear child, what is the matter?" She gathered her into her motherly arms. "Can't you tell me about it?"

"It is nothing but what you know. What everybody sees now, I suppose."

"Sees what, my dear?"

Stella dried her eyes and straightened herself with an attempt at calmness. "I might as well face it," she said slowly. "And I'd just as soon say it right out—to you. We've talked before. . . . Why, it's simple enough—happens often, I'm told. My husband loves another woman."

"Oh no, Stella—he doesn't—I'm sure he doesn't!"

"If you don't mind I will tell you about it. You have been so kind to me this winter, Mrs. MacAvelly. You are a wise woman."

"I wish I was, my dear," said her friend simply.

Stella sat brooding a moment.

"It's a very simple case," she said presently. "I had the best husband in the world—and I wore him out and threw him away."

"Absurd, my dear! You have a good husband now, and he loves you—I'm sure he does. You don't feel well tonight, dear—you exaggerate."

"I exaggerate nothing. You see I know now how I used to torment him. I can see now what a lazy, idle, selfish, morbid, empty-minded, irritating little beast I was!"

"Nonsense, Stella. You never were anything of the kind!"

"Oh yes, I was!" She forgot the keen grief of the moment in retroactive self-reproach. "I had nothing to *do*, you see. Nothing to think about but my own emotions. No life, no real life. And I just drew on him for everything."

Mrs. MacAvelly patted her hand comfortingly and held it in her own strong warm ones. "If it does you good to blame yourself, my dear child, go ahead."

"I will. I'm trying to see the whole thing clearly, and then decide what to do. You see I love him very much—always did—and I used to think of nothing else but him, practically."

"Very proper, my dear. Any man should be glad of that."

"Very *improper!* Any man gets sick and tired of it. And he was so good to me—so patient." She buried her face in her hands.

"Don't be too hard on yourself, child."

"I can't be," said Stella determinedly. "I deserve all I'm getting. The long and short of it is that I wore out his patience and his love. . . . No wonder! . . . Alicia is beautiful and womanly—she is right here all the time. . . . I do not blame him a bit. . . . I do not blame Alicia—much. She isn't at all a 'designing woman,' but she's lonely herself, you see—and was always fond of Morgan—and then when he got no rest at home——" She smiled bitterly. "Why, it is the most natural thing in the world!"

Her friend shook her head with conviction. "You're wrong, Stella, utterly wrong. He's fond of his cousin, naturally, and I dare say has found some amusement and perhaps relief with her, but he loves you—I know it."

Again Stella smiled that hard little smile. She rose, moved about restlessly, turned over the papers on the desk.

"The pity of it was," she said, coming back slowly, "that things were getting so different. You see I have really waked up at last, and got hold of life. I've got something to do now, something to think of besides Morgan."

"You don't mean that you think less of him?"

"*Less!* More than I ever did, having more intelligence. I've got a kind of—perspective on him. You see a man can't bear to have a woman yearning and longing after him all the time. He wants—well, he wants to want her!"

Mrs. MacAvelly smiled appreciatively, and agreed with her: "I think you are right about that."

"Then you see I was just finding myself, just learning how to be more self-contained and desirable. A little more time and I think I could have won him back. . . ."

"But, Stella, surely it's not too late. I have been noticing a good deal all this time; I'm sure that is exactly what has happened. He thinks more of you than he ever did."

"No—it's too late. You don't know! But there's one thing——"

Stella was quite fiercely determined now. "I can set him free if he wants it. You see I can earn my own living now."

She looked so young, not girlish, but rather boyish, in this high-minded boast that the older woman had almost a mind to laugh, but did not.

"Aren't you forgetting the boys?" she urged gently.

"No, I'm not forgetting the boys. But I was thinking more of him. A man's life is not finished so early as a woman's. Alicia is younger than I am. . . . But if he does not wish to change—if he prefers me to stay here, to go on as we are—I can bear even that, I suppose—now that I have my work to do."

"Do you mean—" the older woman was studying her earnestly, "that in all this bitter trouble you find the work a compensation?"

Stella nodded gravely. "You can call it a compensation, or a counterirritant, or what you please; it is an escape from pain, and a source of power. If I hadn't that——" She stretched out her arms with a gesture of desolation. Then with sudden intensity: "It's no wonder a man gets tired of a woman who is nothing *but* a woman—and always womaning! Suppose a man was fussing about all day and all night wondering if his wife had 'ceased to love him'! She soon would!"

"Then you do not believe that women need more love than they get?"

"They think they do! They don't know love when they see it, that's all. They think they're perishing with loneliness when really it's just laziness that ails them. . . . Oh, if I'd only learned it in time."

Both were a little surprised to hear the bell, the voice of a stranger, slow, drawling, affected. Hedda brought in a name: "Mrs. A. Freyling-Huysen. She says she knows it's late, but begs to see you for a moment, ma'am—says she's forgotten her cards."

A woman followed her in—a showily attired woman, redolent of the latest fashion and the most delicate scent, with an air of overamiable apology, a large-figured veil pinned snugly about her face, and a lorgnette.

"Shockingly late to call, I know! Hope you'll excuse the informality, but I simply *had* to see you about that dinner tomorrow before it was too late."

Stella rose coldly, studying the stranger. "I am very sorry," she said. "There is some mistake. I know nothing of any dinner tomorrow—and I have not the pleasure of your acquaintance."

Then the imposing stranger threw herself into a chair and laughed triumphantly.

"Stung again! Oh, Stella, don't be mad! I know you don't want to see me, but every once in a while I just have to see you."

Mrs. MacAvelly rose with her pleasant negative smile. "I'll run home, Mrs. Widfield. I've stayed too late, I know. You must be tired—and with that headache, too!"

Stella tried to detain her. "Don't go, I beg of you. Miss Peckham will not be long, I am sure."

If Miss Peckham had possessed any natural sensitiveness, or had not entirely lost what she possessed, in her professional experiences, she would have been very short indeed—would have needed no further hint. As it was, she merely leaned back smiling with an air of "*Je suis; je reste*," and Mrs. MacAvelly went away. Stella followed her to the door.

"What shall I do with that woman? I've told her again and again not to come here—and she's always getting in on some ridiculous pretext—like this."

"Suppose you remain standing?"

"That would not trouble her at all. I doubt if she would notice it."

"Suppose you excused yourself and went to your room?"

"She'd come too. It will take a policeman to get Malina out. Oh dear!"

Returning, she stood looking at her undesired visitor, who smiled back at her serenely.

"After what you put in the paper about me the last time, Malina Peckham, I wonder you dare come here again."

"That's one thing I came for. I knew you'd be mad—and I don't wonder, but I got my raise on that thing. It was a real help to me. And it hasn't done you any harm, Stella—not really. Come—you have so much—and I have so little. Don't you think it's unethical to object to being of service?"

"It is a very disagreeable way to help one's friends, I must say," said her reluctant hostess. "Have you another such benefaction to propose for your further advancement?"

"Now it's no use trying to freeze me out, Stella. You don't do it well; you're too kind by nature, and too much of a lady. Besides I haven't come on my own interest this time—but to do you a service, really. I want to protect you—I do, honestly. I don't think you realize how people are beginning to talk."

"Let them," said her unwilling friend. "I can't help people talking about me if they choose."

"Ah, but it's not about you now—not you only, that is."

With every startled nerve held in perfect calmness Stella only replied, "Let them talk about me and whomever they please then."

"But it is your husband they are talking about now, you poor dear—and Alicia Cushing."

Malina's keen spying eyes were on her, but they saw no change of expression, no nervous movement.

"Well——" Stella rejoined meditatively. "I should think they would."

Malina sat back with an explosive ejaculation. "Oh, you see at last, do you?"

"I see Mrs. Cushing often, and so does my husband, of course. He is her cousin, you know. She is a widow, still young and very pretty. I can see how people—some kinds of people—would talk—and of course the newspapers."

She fanned herself quietly, looking at Malina with steady eyes. But that person was by no means discouraged. Animadversions upon her chosen profession did not disturb her.

"And your name being so much before the public now, that helps, of course. You see it makes a good story—everyone wondering why the society woman has plunged into literature. Now they think they know. Say, Stella—if they do write this up it makes a bully story— she being in the same house and all."

"So I begin to see." The fan moved quietly, steadily; her color was unchanged, her eyes cool.

"And you are still pretending there is nothing in it?"

"I am still attending strictly to my own affairs, Malina. I wish I could say as much for you."

Malina grinned. "It is my business to attend to other people's affairs. Mostly I don't mind, but I have a great admiration for you, Stella. You've always been kind to me—even when you hated it. And I feel horribly about this. Look here. . . ." She leaned forward, her elbows on her out-slanting knees, hands loosely clasped. "Why don't you leave him?"

Now whatever secret purpose of this sort Mrs. Widfield may have entertained, or however she may have heroically suggested it to Mrs. MacAvelly, she had no mind to receive such suggestion from Malina.

She rose, with finality.

"Will you have the kindness to go away, Miss Peckham? If I distinctly tell you that I never wish to see you again, if I distinctly ask you to leave my house and never come back—never, will you do it?"

Malina was quite unmoved, emotionally or mechanically. "Oh, I'll go away—presently. I won't promise never to come back though. It's fun, getting in in spite of you. But see here, Stella—I'm in earnest about this. I really want to stave off a flare-up in the papers. I've never said one word about this thing, though I've felt pretty sure of it for ever so long. You can always be suspicious when there's another pretty woman around. Men *are* such brutes, the best of 'em!"

Stella turned away conclusively.

"If you won't go, I will. Good evening, Miss Peckham." She rang for the maid, and promptly departed into her own room, locking the door after her.

Malina flushed darkly and stood irresolute for a moment. But when grim Hedda held the door open, she went out.

13

Morgan sat for some time moodily alone among the packed shelves of his library, smoking, and looking at the books as one looks at a well-kept lawn. He had been reared in the unquestioned conviction that every gentleman must have a library, with various classics, standard authors, and solid works of revered authority, with a certain amount of "light reading." His library furnished these, and more, with a veiled iridescence of new and individual work gradually added by his wife. He was always pleased to have her buy books, though he might not look at them.

He was bitterly lonely.

This new wife of his, so serene and quiet, so brilliant and able in her unexpected development as a writer, had grown dearer even as she grew remote. He missed her. She failed in nothing of her wifely care of him; she was in no way neglectful or unkind, but she was not *there*, somehow.

As for Alicia, whose sweet quiet had once been a pleasant contrast to Stella's too visible demand, he had found too much Alicia like too many bananas, and had lost his liking for the diet.

What had Stella come home for? Was it a headache? Of course it was; he had never known her to lie. He was sorry for the headache, wanted to go and comfort her—then heard Mrs. MacAvelly come in and voices in continuing murmur.

Presently he determined to go and finish his cigar in the open air; he would be better for a walk perhaps.

Colonel Cushing, hat and overcoat on, met him in the hall. "Whither away, my boy? Whither away?"

"Just going out for a bit of air," Morgan answered.

"It's wet," the old gentleman demurred. "I came in just now myself. Very chilly—and snowing a bit—unseasonable weather."

Morgan stood irresolute. He had forgotten the weather.

"I was just coming down to see if you were disengaged. Alicia's gone to bed, I think. I hate being alone."

"Come in, come in." Morgan opened the door for him. Let's sit in my room. We shall be more out of the way. Unless you'd like to see Stella and Mrs. MacAvelly?"

"Not just now. I only want to smoke and grumble. You've got the best wife in the world, I don't doubt. I had once, and Mrs. MacAvelly is a very nice woman, very nice indeed. But after all, my boy, do the best they can they can't help making trouble."

Morgan laughed dryly as he gave his guest a comfortable chair. "You are incorrigible, Colonel Cushing. I don't doubt the amiability of your wife, and anyone can see Alicia's, yet you continue to carp. It's pure prejudice."

The Colonel looked shrewdly at him, pulling at his cigar, and settling luxuriously back in his chair. "I have the whole world's opinion back of me. No doubt there are occasional exceptions; we all know of some, but take 'em by and large they're all alike, my boy, they're all alike. 'There's no mischief in the world done, but a woman she is one.'"

They were silent, Morgan's gloom but faintly lightened by this familiar tone of condemnation. The older man watched him with real tenderness. He was fond of Morgan, admired his business ability, and had long appreciated his friendly kindness. For some time he had felt that all was not right with the Widfields, and wished that he might be of some service, but there had been no opportunity.

"Those fellows knew what they were talking about," he continued. "Popular sayings like those old saws represent a large bulk of public opinion. And what is the opinion? 'Weal and women cannot pan; woe and women can.'" He chuckled. "They were a bit severe now and then. How's this? 'An ugly woman is a disease of the stomach; a handsome woman a disease of the head.'"

Morgan laughed outright at this, though he had heard it often enough before. "To listen to you one would think that men were angels—and women the opposite," he commented.

"Well, it approximates that at times. 'A man of straw's worth a woman of gold.'"

"Nonsense—rank nonsense! I wonder how you can quote the stuff. Just a mass of ancient foolishness."

His visitor rather bristled at this.

"Nothing foolish about it, my boy! Not in the least. Condensed public opinion, that's what proverbs are. And one of 'em says: 'Man, woman and the devil are the three degrees of comparison.'"

"Oh, tut, tut, Colonel! That's too much. It reminds me of the statue of the hunter and the dead lion—and what the lion said. Wait till they make proverbs about us!"

"You are mighty generous, Morgan. I like to see you stand up for them. But in your secret heart, my boy—come—I don't believe you *enjoy* being called 'the husband of the clever Mrs. Widfield.'"

"They say I object to that?" Morgan inquired calmly. "Well, please correct the impression as far as you can. I am extremely proud of the clever Mrs. Widfield, and of being her husband."

"Well played!" said the Colonel admiringly. "Well played, indeed! I'd like to see the woman who could do as well. If they have a trouble they confide it to all comers—light-minded babblers!"

Morgan looked at him. What did he mean by "a trouble"? Had he shown any signs of his distress—to anyone? It could not be possible that Stella had "babbled" to anyone—of anything.

"I'm very fond of you, Morgan," said his friend. "I am really. And I am a much older man than you. I have seen all manner of troubles in the world, and, frankly, there was always a woman in the case. Even theft, burglary, murder, what they call men's crimes—who drives them to it? I tell you those old fellows were not far off the mark—what is it? 'A wicked woman and an evil is three halfpence worse than the devil.' . . . Morgan, my boy, I haven't asked you a question and I don't intend to, but I can see that you are not easy in your mind. If there's anything under the heavens you'd like to tell me, I'm a perfect grave for confidences."

"And I'm a believer in cremation," Morgan answered lightly, offering him a matchbox.

When the Colonel finally took his departure he followed upon the heels of Miss Peckham, who had gone out softly and was standing meditatively by the elevator.

He thought he had seen her at the Widfields before, but not in such elaborate costume, and was now uncertain whether he knew her or not.

She greeted him sweetly.

"Ah! Colonel Cushing, I believe. I should know you anywhere. I've seen you in the parades, you know."

He was much flattered. "Have you indeed, and remembered my face, Miss—Mrs.——"

"Peckham," she interpolated. "Miss Malina Peckham. We have

met at Mrs. Widfield's—she is a very old friend of mine. . . . Yes, it is not the face only, but the figure. I do think that a fine man in uniform, a man who carries himself well, is simply unforgettable."

The Colonel shook his head. "I fear it was the uniform—not the man. A weakness of your sex, my dear young lady."

She took him up lightly. "Oh, we admire the uniform, if it is a handsome one, naturally. But not when it's empty! And I've seen you in plain clothes, too—the same back—the same shoulders!"

He straightened himself up at this, expanded his chest, threw back those same shoulders. "You flatter me, I am sure." He wondered at so impressive a lady being alone there at that hour, and suggested: "We have both been at the Widfields, I fancy—a kind of Quaker-meeting visit." To offer to press the button for the elevator seemed like a wish to shorten her stay, so he did not make it.

"Yes, I was there," she agreed, adding a little sadly: "But not visiting. I came on business. You see, I have to work, Colonel Cushing—I'm on a newspaper."

Malina's features were greatly softened by the figured veil, the large, soft curving hat. She had also, if the truth must be told, made up a little for the present part as well as dressed for it. He could hardly believe that a lady of such attractions was a newspaper-woman, which only showed how primitive were his notions.

"Do you—er—enjoy it?" he asked.

"Indeed I do not!" she murmured. "No real woman could. The long hours—the exposure to the weather—meeting all kinds of people—and worse than all——" She gave a little shiver. "Going alone through the streets at night. Dear me," she broke off, looking at her watch and down the elevator shaft. "How late it is! I must be off this minute. Where is that boy!"

That boy was dozing peacefully on the bench below. No jarring bell had stirred his slumbers yet.

"My dear young lady, do allow me—let me go with you."

"Oh I couldn't think of it, Colonel Cushing. It's wet and chilly—and so late."

"All the more reason you should have someone with you. It will be a pleasure to me, I assure you. And we will stop somewhere and have a little something warm to eat and drink. You must grant me the privileges of age, my dear."

"You are by no means old enough to claim them," she protested, though without violence.

"The privilege of our common friendship then—possibly of a new one between ourselves, Miss Peckham."

"Any friend of the Widfields is to be trusted, I am sure. Thank you," she said after a moment's hesitation. "It will be very nice."

And without one condemnatory proverb the worthy gentleman accompanied her.

14

"It's no use, Mrs. MacAvelly," Alicia explained in her unemphatic way. "I am interested, of course, but I haven't the brains. I wish I had."

"You underrate yourself, as usual. You not only have the brain, but you have the culture, the habit of life, the special kind of experience. I wish you would let me bring him up."

"I'm perfectly willing you should bring Mr. Smith—and I'm sure I shall be delighted to listen to him, and glad enough to be of any assistance if I can, but really and truly, Mrs. MacAvelly, what can I do that you cannot?"

"That ought to be plain to everyone," her visitor replied, and Alicia felt that she must be very dull in not seeing it. "It is fortunate that he came tonight, the Colonel being out, and you for a wonder alone. He's parading up and down my rug this minute, smoking as usual, and wondering why he should be wasting his time on me. Especially when I'm not there! I'll run down and get him."

Alicia was really pleased at the prospect. Mr. Tillotson was a "writer," but Mr. Smith was a "genius," and a genius in that unacknowledged state where one can still claim credit for discovery. Why Stella had so patently lost interest in him she did not know, but at any rate she was now to have a chance to feed the young lion's vanity a little, and was glad.

"Nonsense!" said Mr. Smith brusquely when his hostess proposed that he go with her to read some of his work to Mrs. Cushing. "What do I want of your fine friends?"

"But you surely remember Mrs. Cushing? She's that sweet woman who sat opposite you at our little dinner last October. She was tremendously impressed with your work then, and has often spoken of you."

He did remember and was somewhat mollified.

"But why do we go anywhere?" he persisted. "I came to see you— that is, I came first to see Mrs. Widfield. But she is always either out or 'engaged' now. I do not believe it!"

It had dawned upon Mr. Smith's consciousness after many fruit-less attempts that he was being made the victim of that paltry sub-terfuge of the bourgeoisie—"not at home."

"You mustn't think that," she reassured him. "Mrs. Widfield is so busy now with her own work that I doubt if she has as much sympa-thy for anyone else's, that's all. But Mrs. Cushing is sincerely inter-ested. You know it is not always the most brilliant women who are most appreciative."

He allowed himself to be persuaded.

He was working on a novel now, a novel he considered to outrival the Russians', a novel which should at last—at last—force a gross world to feel. This novel required even more definite knowledge of the habits and prejudices of "the master class" than had his play, and he bore in mind Mrs. Widfield's suggestion that he must not exhibit ignorance of this species if he was to portray them at all.

His pockets bulged with manuscript, his mind teemed with the matter and method of this latest work. And the mind of Mr. Smith was nothing if not ruthless in its preoccupation.

So charged, he was brought into Mrs. Cushing's pretty parlor, and his intensity partially assuaged by a particularly soft large-featured chair.

"I am so delighted," murmured Alicia warmly. "I have never for-gotten that splendid play you began to read to us that night."

"Play? Oh, yes—that! It is finished. I am now engaged upon a far larger work—far more important." His hand sought his pocket.

"Oh, but how could it be more important? I'm sure that play was tremendously impressive."

"I have forgotten it." He waved the play out of existence and pulled out his manuscript.

"Ah, but I have not, you see." Alicia beamed upon him. "Why, I shall never forget it. There was that wonderful young Russian, Panin—Oscar Panin—such a splendid strong creature! And that hor-rid man from Chicago or Omaha or somewhere—a pork packer, I think he was. And the wife, Elaine. I knew a girl called Elaine and she was really just that sort of woman. She looked cold, that haughty, indifferent kind, but just think, she ran away with her father's chauffeur."

He paused as he shuffled the loose papers. "Was she an American woman?" he asked sharply.

"Of course she was," Alicia answered him. "But American women have hearts, don't they?"

"You see," Mrs. MacAvelly suggested, "not all of us share Mrs. Widfield's strong views on the temperament of your Elaine."

He crushed the paper in his hand. "I knew it!" he cried. "I was right! An artist should trust his own instincts—always."

"Why, of course!" Alicia gazed on him, round-eyed. "I thought they did. You don't mean to say that you let Stella influence your work, Mr. Smith?"

Mr. Smith started to his feet and walked up and down. "She certainly did not!" he asserted with some violence. "No one has influenced my work. No one can. But we did have an argument upon that very point."

"It was the scene when he shows he loves her," Mrs. MacAvelly put in. "Panin, I mean."

Alicia's face lit up. "Oh, I knew it! I knew it! I felt sure that he would—that he did—it showed already, Mr. Smith, in that wonderful first act. Oh, do tell me how it came out, Mr. Smith—do!"

He stuffed his manuscript back into his sagging pocket, and stood irresolute, the vivid interest in that piece of work reviving fast. "But I have it not with me," he said.

"I have," Mrs. MacAvelly told him. "You know you let me have a copy of that act to read over—after that time we were at Mrs. Widfield's—and you never asked for it. I'll bring it this minute."

She was not long, and the flame of his new interest had not waned under Alicia's gentle fanning when the act was put into his hands.

"You see," Mrs. MacAvelly explained a little breathlessly, "Mrs. Cushing cannot discuss technic with you as Mrs. Widfield could——" (He tossed his head, as if Mrs. Widfield's ideas on technic were of no faintest consequence.) "But she can give you her point of view. I think she would respond to the note you touch unerringly."

"If Mr. Smith will only be good enough to read me the scene, I can tell him what I think—or rather, how I feel about it."

"Good!" said Mr. Smith. "That is what I wanted."

He looked a little disgusted, as if, in spite of his denial of all influence, he had not got what he wanted before.

"This is not a situation for thinking, for theories; it is a situation that calls for feeling. Now see——"

In spite of her eagerly protested remembrance he went over the first act in some detail from memory, carefully explaining how long Panin had been there, how much he had been with Elaine, often the two alone, and what her attitude had been toward him so far.

"Here we have them," he explained, rising and placing chairs to indicate his setting. "Here is the desk, the typewriter—Panin at work. The husband has gone—she comes in."

He read rather hastily the first part of his scene. "There—they are alone together. Her brutal owner is away—how she has learned to hate him! They have two hours—or think they have! From nine till eleven. Now she comes in. Remember that she loves him. He has made her love him in spite of herself—in spite of all her conventions and principles and fishlike ancestors. She was one of your cold American women, but he has melted the snow. He says:

"'It is only nine now. We have two beautiful hours.'

"She answers—she is trying to resist, you understand, but weakening. She says:

"'You will have your two beautiful hours all to yourself—I am going away.' He stops her——

"'No, Elaine. You are not going away. You are going to stay here—with me.'

"*Elaine*: 'You seem very sure.'

"*Panin*: 'I am sure. I know you are strong and proud, but love is stronger than your strength—stronger even than your pride!' He seizes her hands."

Mrs. MacAvelly broke in at this point: "And Stella says he would not—that is, that she would not let him."

"Oh, but she would!" cried Alicia. "Of course she would! How could she help it!"

"Do not interrupt!" Smith was visibly annoyed. "People are always interrupting me in this scene. Perhaps—" he interrupted himself, with a critical pause, "perhaps there is some error in the construction which allows it!"

"I am certain there is not," Alicia assured him, with heartfelt admiration. "It's perfectly splendid—do go on."

He resumed:

"*Elaine*: 'But my husband trusts me. He has never dreamed that I could care for anyone else.'

"*Panin*: 'Let him dream on. You are awake at last. You know that you love me.'

"*Elaine*: 'I will admit it. I love you!' And she throws herself into his arms."

"And Stella said she would not do it," said Mrs. MacAvelly. "She offered to show him how she would have answered."

"Why, Mrs. MacAvelly, how could she say so! Why, of course she throws herself in his arms. But I think she'd have done it before."

"Before?" Mr. Smith looked from one to the other. "Before what?"

"Look here!" said Alicia eagerly. "I used to be good at theatricals myself when I was young." A dimpled smile seemed to suggest some comment here, but got none. "Do let's try it——" she continued with unchecked enthusiasm. "Here, let me look at it a moment."

"I'm going to see if Stella is there," said Mrs. MacAvelly, and she slipped out.

They did not heed her. With pretty eagerness Alicia ran over the few lines and said she was ready.

"There—now you be sitting here—this little table will do for a desk—and I'll come in——" She drew her visitor to the chair, retired to the dining room door and entered as Stella had done; their flats were similar.

"'Is not my husband here?'" she began in a sweet, hesitating voice.

Mrs. MacAvelly told Stella that she had not come to see her, but wanted to run off with her husband for a moment. "Do come with me," she said to him. "I want to show you something very amusing—very. No, I won't tell you a word. You've got to come—quick! Softly, now!"

With finger on lip she led him across the hall, and into Alicia's dining room.

As he caught the first words in the room beyond he started as if struck, but she held him fast, and parted the curtains a little. There was Alicia, delicately confiding to Mr. Smith that her husband trusted her, and there was Mr. Smith, violently assuring Alicia that she knew she loved him.

Mr. Widfield stood staring, and Mrs. MacAvelly left him so and darted back across the hall.

Alicia, coy yet melting, with laughing glance and outstretched hands cheerfully replied: "'I admit it. I love you. I cannot resist longer—Edmond—' or whatever his name is. I think she'd answer like that, don't you, Mrs. MacAvelly?"

She saw that her suggestion did not wholly please the author, and then caught sight of the new spectator. "Why, Morgan—how you startled me! You've spoiled Mr. Smith's best scene."

Mr. Smith presented no urbane assurances. He looked from one to the other with divided disapproval, and rolled up his manuscript with nervous hands.

"It is not the first time," he snapped. "But it is the last. I was a fool to come here—here where I am always interrupted." And he brusquely departed.

Morgan came in slowly, with the expression of a sleepwalker rudely aroused. "So that's what you were doing!" His mind was so swiftly illuminated that the very glare confused him. He did not hear Mrs. MacAvelly give Stella a warm kiss and leave her, nor her soft steps behind him.

"Yes," said his cousin, eager for his approval. "Don't you think I did it well?"

"Did what well?"

"Why, the play—the woman's part—the surrender."

"If you want my honest opinion, Alicia, I think you surrendered far too easily."

"Oh Morgan! I wouldn't speak to you like that."

"No, my dear cousin, I hope you wouldn't. Nor should I ask you to."

"You know I didn't mean that, Morgan. I think you're very unkind tonight. I'm going to say good night." Which she did with great dignity, and retired.

"Of course you didn't mean that, sis," he called after her. "Good night," and added sadly to himself: "*You* don't know how many kinds of a fool I've been. . . . Why, Stella!"

She turned without a word and fled back to their own home. He was with her; he stood, hesitating, at a loss for words. She began to smile, a bright sweet smile that brought light to her eyes and girlish curves to the cheeks that flushed softly as he came nearer.

"Then you don't—really—any longer——"

"I don't really deserve the wife I've got—nor ever did," he replied tensely, coming nearer. "My dear girl—can you forgive me for—for what I'm ashamed to insult you by mentioning?"

"If you'll forgive me for the same thing, dear—precisely the same thing. Only it was no insult. I didn't blame you a bit—she is so attractive."

"She's an exceedingly tiresome, foolish, kindhearted little woman. I'm fond of Alicia, of course—but surely Stella, you couldn't think that I——"

She faced him mischievously. "But don't you really think she did the love scene better than I did?"

Morgan met her glance with an air of great seriousness. "I'm not quite certain. I think I'll try your version again—and I hope we shall not be interrupted. I ought to know the lines by this time—'You are awake now—you know you love me'——"

Whereat Stella abandoned her version altogether, and threw herself into her husband's arms.

BIBLIOGRAPHY

"The Yellow Wall-Paper" (1892; 1899)[1] – short story
In This Our World (1893; 1895; 1898)[2] – poems
*Women and Economics: A Study of the Economic Relation Between Men
    and Women as a Factor in Social Evolution* (1898) – nonfiction
Concerning Children (1900) – nonfiction
The Home: Its Work and Influence (1903) – nonfiction
Human Work (1904) – nonfiction
The Forerunner (1909–16) – magazine
What Diantha Did (1910) – novel
The Crux (1911) – novel
The Man-Made World; Or, Our Androcentric Culture (1911) – nonfiction
Moving the Mountain (1911) – novel
Our Brains and What Ails Them (1911) – nonfiction
Suffrage Songs and Verses (1911) – poems
With Her in Our Land (1911) – novel
Mag—Marjorie (1912) – novel
Won Over (1913) – novel
Benigna Machiavelli (1914) – novel
Social Ethics (1914) – nonfiction
Herland (1915) – novel
With Her in Ourland: The Sequel to Herland (1916) – novel
*His Religion and Hers: A Study of the Faith of Our Fathers and the Work
    of Our Mothers* (1923) – nonfiction
The Living of Charlotte Perkins Gilman: An Autobiography (1935) –
    autobiography
Charlotte Perkins Gilman Reader (1980) – collected fiction
Charlotte Perkins Gilman: A Nonfiction Reader (1992) – essays
The Diaries of Charlotte Perkins Gilman (1994) – diaries
The Yellow Wall-Paper and Selected Stories of Charlotte Perkins Gilman
    (1994) – collected short stories
*A Journey From Within: The Love Letters of Charlotte Perkins Gilman
    and Houghton Gilman, 1897–1900* (1995) – selected letters
The Later Poetry of Charlotte Perkins Gilman (1996) – poems
Unpunished (1997) – novel

1. "The Yellow Wall-Paper" was originally published in *New England Magazine*, January 1892. It was published commercially as a chapbook by Small, Maynard and Company in 1899.
2. *In This Our World* was originally published by McCombs and Vaughn in 1893. A second expanded edition was published by James H. Barry in 1895. Small, Maynard and Company published a third expanded edition in 1898.

A NOTE ON THE TEXT

The texts of *Mag—Marjorie* and *Won Over* were drawn from their serialized appearances in *The Forerunner*. Obvious errors in the original texts have been emended. Where appropriate, modern standards in punctuation and spelling have been imposed to enhance readability.